I0561626

Signs of the Zombie Apocalypse

by Debbye Graafsma

©2015 Debbye Graafsma. No portion of this book may be
stored, reproduced, or printed in any manner for any
reason without prior written permission of the author.

ISBN: 978-0-9893214-5-7

DISCLAIMER:
This book is a work of fiction.
All characters appearing in this work are fictitious.
Any resemblance to real persons,
living or dead, is purely coincidental.

For Bill,
Soulmate and best friend

Chapter One

Caleb huddled into the darkest corner of the kitchen he could find. With his back wedged tightly in the corner, he faced the center of the room. From this vantage point, he could see both the outside door, and the door into the living room. He had made sure to lock the back door. In his right hand, he clutched the biggest knife he had been able to find.

He had cut two holes in the blanket pulled over his head so he could see. He wanted to be ready.

He knew they were watching.

Someone was *always* watching.

Reaching down, he felt for his belongings, mentally taking inventory. Next to his Gameboy was his knapsack, in which were candles, a discarded cigarette lighter, his flashlight, a new pack of batteries, and his BB gun. He had refilled his two empty water bottles just an hour ago, and added them to the bag, along with the sub sandwich and candy he had stolen from the grocery store that afternoon.

This morning, he had been sure it would never happen again. But now he wasn't convinced.

He had tried to take his mind off of it, by watching the lions hunting in Africa again. The nature channel had broadcast a show on tigers yesterday. He had watched it for a little while, trying to figure out what they were eating.

But none of it made sense. TV had to be made up.

He had seen. He knew the truth.

It hadn't been so bad in the daylight. He had checked every closet in the house. He had even checked up in the attic. Nothing.

But, it was time. Now, he had to focus. Dark had come.

They always came back when it was dark.

When he heard them, and had enough notice, he could always get into one of the cabinets. He knew from experience they didn't like to go looking. He hoped they would just turn around and leave.

From numerous observations and encounters, the boy had learned it was better to just stay out in the open. That way he could see them coming. That way he could be prepared.

Well ... *sort of* prepared.

It had been four years ago when the first bite happened. After that, he had learned to avoid them, staying invisible when at all possible, praying to God they didn't see him. And then, somehow things had improved. At least they had left him alone.

He had used the time since then to learn. What made someone turn into a zombie? Did it happen the same way to everybody? How did a person prevent becoming one?

And more important: how could a guy protect himself? How could you tell when a zombie was close to you? What was the best course of action to take?

He hadn't had a clue in the beginning.

After all, it took more than one bite for someone to turn into a zombie. He knew that to be a fact. He had seen a lot of people with scars who hadn't been zombified yet. Some of the teenagers in the neighborhood were sure it only took two bites. The movies he had watched said it only took one. But he knew that wasn't true. The drunk guy at the arcade insisted the number it took was ten.

Caleb had believed them; until he saw a man on YouTube who claimed to have been bitten over a hundred times, and said he was fine.

But ... How did he know he was fine?

Caleb figured he had only been bitten three times, and he knew *he* didn't feel fine. He was afraid. He had learned not to trust anyone.

No, it wasn't worth risking your life, he determined. He didn't have to believe any of them. It was smarter not to take any chances.

But, in the learning process, Caleb had learned a lot about zombies. For one thing, they were afraid of light. "Shine a flashlight in their eyes so they can't see," the man at the arcade had said. "They'll run like hell."

Too bad we don't have a basement, he thought to himself. *I wonder how much longer I can stay here.*

It had been awhile since he had seen them in the house. Still, he tried to stay awake in the dark hours. It was the only way to protect himself.

He had decided when he was three to stop waiting for others to take care of him. He would take care of himself. It didn't work to wait anymore.

He would have do what the survivor guy on the computer channel had said. "Eat what you can find. Make sure you have everything you need in your knapsack: a knife, matches, candles. A flashlight for light, food and batteries. And most importantly, make sure you have more than one way to protect yourself."

The boy had watched every episode of that show on Netflix. Twice. He had memorized most of the crucial stuff. He was ready for anything.

It was getting really dark now. Caleb checked at his watch: four minutes after eleven. When had he had fallen asleep?! Still, if they *had* come, apparently they hadn't seen him, or even smelled him. That was good, right? He quietly reached into his knapsack and pulled out the sub-sandwich. Looking through the holes in the blanket, he took a bite. Everything was still the same.

His back and legs were stiff and hurting again. He shifted his position, making sure he was alone. Hopefully, there were no zombies watching in the shadows.

Relax, he told himself. *You're worrying too much.*

Still, he reasoned, it was important to know what to do. Just in case. Even if tonight's setup did turn out to be just a drill.

He just had to stay awake now.

But the boy dozed off once more.

It was two thirty in the morning when Caleb's mother, or step-mother really, returned home. His birth mother had died when he was two or three years old. He didn't really remember her anymore, except that she had been a zombie, he decided. So why did it matter?

He *did* remember his father, though, he decided. Or at least, the man who *said* he was his father. Continually drunk and angry, there had only been one or two kind moments the boy could recall. For the most part, he had left Caleb alone, and the boy had returned the favor.

Loud voices still terrified the boy.

He had thought it was going to get better when Dad married his step-mom. He had brought her home one night, and she had stayed in the house since. She must have been the first woman Dad met after Mom died.

But then the yelling started again. And the hitting. And the throwing things. That was when the boy had cut holes in his blanket.

Six months later, Dad had left, abandoning his new wife; leaving his young son behind.

Caleb had been alone ever since.

The shot causing his mother's death had been the first bite.

His father's abandonment had been the second.

He wasn't sure how many bites it had taken his stepmom to become a zombie. But he was sure she was one.

Come to think of it, his stepmom wasn't really in there anymore. He couldn't really leave, since there was nowhere to go. But he couldn't let her see him, or she would bite again.

He had come to a conclusion. Zombie-Mom had stopped seeing him when his dad left. At first, he had tried to talk to her, but she didn't answer. She acted like she couldn't hear him. Then, when he didn't give up sometimes; she did answer. But those answers always came with a slap or with yelling.

She had broken his leg the day before she started driving away before he woke up, and coming back late at night.

Now, there were many nights she didn't come home at all.

He still remembered the first time she brought a man home with her. He had recently determined she must be a night-hunter. Zombies were all night hunters.

Lately, she had begun to bring men-zombies home with her again. Any man she could find, he decided. Caleb had stopped asking them their names a long time ago. At first, he thought maybe she might bring his dad home again. But that hadn't happened.

For a while, he had hoped for another dad. But that hadn't happened either.

Not even once.

There had been *one* guy who had stayed around for almost a whole year. But the yelling and screaming had eventually started again. When that one left, she had just moved on to another one.

Sometimes the men were zombies. And sometimes they weren't. But they always seemed to be zombies by the time the morning came, if they had stayed with her.

He wondered if his life was normal. Did all kids' dads leave? Did all boys' moms stay out all night?

Caleb had learned how to put food in the microwave at a friend's house at three. But that friend had moved away.

Sometimes, though, his Zombie-Mom remembered him.

He loved the Happy Meals if she brought them home. Even if the fries were cold and floppy, he didn't mind. They were good. And salty. And the fizzy drink that came with them was really good too. It beat the water from the faucet.

He wondered what it would be like to have someone stay at home with him, like some of the other kids in the neighborhood.

When would he be old enough to go to school?

He felt old enough. Would she even let him go there? He knew other kids who went to school. Some of them were his age. They looked happy.

Did they stay awake at night too?

The sandwich was gone now. He licked his fingers, and grabbed a water bottle.

No go. His fingers were too messy to unscrew the lid. He put the bottle down to wipe his hands on the blanket.

Just then, without warning, the kitchen lights came on.

Startled, the boy took an unexpected gasp of air and held it. He peered through the blanket holes. He could feel his heart pounding in his head. Ouch! The pain was still there.

He reached down and felt for his gun.

Frozen, he watched. She *was* there, and there was another new man with her. Even from here, they smelled bad, like zombie juice. They were laughing. She was hugging this one.

She's never hugged *me* like that, he thought.

He hoped they would go down the hall to her room before anything more than hugging happened. Last time, she had stayed with the man in the living room. That had been bad enough. Caleb hadn't seen anything except bare legs, but the sounds they made and the words they said bothered him, even if he didn't fully understand what was happening.

He didn't really *want* to know what zombies did.

He watched Zombie-Mom grab two of the fancy glasses and a big bottle from the cabinet in the corner, and lock it again.

Why do they need more zombie juice, he asked himself? She already couldn't walk straight.

He wouldn't bother her in the morning, he decided. Even though she always tried to be nice when a man was there, he knew she would hit him, or worse, when the man left. So he watched, silent; waiting for her light to go out. The two zombies he could see had to leave the kitchen sometime. He knew she wouldn't drink the zombie juice in the kitchen.

Sometimes, for no reason, more zombies came after the lights were out. He hoped it didn't happen tonight. Those were the nights he couldn't sleep, and couldn't breathe.

Is this how it happened to everybody?

How long will it take before I turn into a zombie, he wondered?

Until today, he had thought all grown-ups were zombies.

The third bite had happened that morning.

Flinching, he shifted his position once more, trying to be as quiet as possible.

Zombie-Mom had been gone for three days before coming home this time. He had tried to find food in the house, but all she left in the pantry was some stale cereal. Getting his courage up, he had finally decided to break a rule again. He made a search, and found some money in Zombie-Mom's dresser drawer. He walked to the store to get something to eat.

He thought he had done a good job.

The survivor man on Netflix would have been proud of him.

But that idea hadn't lasted very long. Apparently, eating wasn't something he was allowed to do.

He had used a shopping cart, and only put good stuff in it: like milk, bread, peanut butter, ice cream, sugar smacks and some frozen meals.

He had noticed a few grown-ups at the store giving him strange looks while he was shopping, though. Halfway through, he realized how dirty he must look to them. So he added a bar of soap, some shampoo, and some laundry soap to the cart. Oh, and toothpaste and a new toothbrush.

He told the checkout lady his mom had been really sick, and had given him a list. He would have to go home and do the laundry and take a bath.

The look in the lady's eyes was weird. Did she look at him like that because he stuttered?

Let her look. He was used to people looking.

Somebody was always watching.

"Oh," she said. "Is your Mom feeling better now?"

When he had nodded, she had said, "I'm sorry, baby."

What was *she* sorry for, he asked himself? *Baby?* Just how old did she think he was? And she kept looking at him – so creepy.

That lady was the first grown-up Caleb had ever seen who wasn't a zombie.

At least... This one didn't *seem* like a zombie. And now, he realized he hadn't had anyone look at him that way before. He knew if he looked at her very long, he would do something stupid, like cry. Angry at himself for talking to the woman at all, he had taken the change and crammed it down into his pocket. He hurriedly left, making sure to look down at the floor.

At home, the boy put his clothes in the washer, and took a bath. He brushed his teeth. Then, wrapped in nothing but a towel, he had microwaved one box of Marie Callender's macaroni and cheese, and then another. While the second box was cooking, he found a good and scary movie called "The Shining" on TV. He was eating the second box, and watching the beginning of the movie, when Zombie-Mom walked back in the door, alone.

Thinking about it now, looking back, he shouldn't have dropped his guard. He should have made sure to put on some clothes. He should have at least drained the tub. He shouldn't have bought the ice cream, either, since that had been what had made her really mad.

And, he winced, shifting once more – Oh, yes, he really should have thrown the broken broom handle away.

Remembering, he realized something. She had seemed to get madder and madder the more she hit him. He had tried to be strong, and not let her see how much she was hurting his back and legs. That had made her mad too.

"You're still not crying?" she had yelled. "I'll teach you to break my rules!"

She had shouted a lot of things. Like she didn't know why his dad had dumped him on her. Like she would teach him she wasn't going to have her life stolen away by a brat. Like why didn't he just grow up? Like how she didn't want him, and wished he would just go away. How she wished she had money to send him away.

That had been around ten this morning. When she got tired of hitting and yelling, she had slumped down in front of the computer. Was she going to be home all day, he had wondered? He hoped it was a matter of just a few minutes' time until she left again. But no such luck.

He had dressed himself in his only other set of clothes, and waited in his Zombie room.

It was early afternoon when Caleb made a decision to go outside. He had to. If he stayed in the house with her, he would get yelled at again for something. Or worse. So, taking a deep breath, he had asked if he could go outside and play. Without looking up from the screen, Zombie-Mom had nodded.

"I don't care what you do," she said. "Come back when you want. I'll leave the house unlocked for you."

Relieved, Caleb had made his way to the store. He decided he would return the empty cart, and then find something else to eat. He still had the change from this morning. He could buy something.

He then knew he couldn't eat while Zombie-Mom was home. He would have to wait for her to leave again before he could eat the rest of his mac and cheese.

If she hadn't thrown it out, that is.

After making his addition to the long line of other carts in the parking lot, Caleb had gone inside to the deli section of the grocery store. Picking up a basket, he put food into it: a submarine sandwich, some chips, and a couple bottles of water. Then, he made sure he got in the line farthest away from the not-Zombie lady who gave the weird looks and called him "baby." At the register, he added a Snickers bar and a small bag of SourPatch Kids to the basket.

When it came time to pay for his items, Caleb burrowed his hands deep into his pockets, looking for the money. Oh no! Where was it? How had he lost it? His heart sank. Had Zombie-Mom taken it?

Then he remembered. The change from that morning's trip to the store was still in the pockets of his other pants in the washer! Panic had risen in his throat. Then nausea. What if Zombie-Mom looked in the washer? What could he possibly tell her?

Sure, he had washed his clothes before. But he hadn't ever taken her money before. Until now, there had always been food, or money left on the table. There had been a time or two when a man with a light on top of his car brought him pizza.

He liked cold pizza.

He had discovered he could live for days on one order.

Without thinking, the frightened and panicky child darted through the grocery store door to the outside, still clutching his basket full of goodies. As he ran, he could hear voices shouting behind him, and footsteps.

Fast footsteps. Were they running?

He would just have to run faster.

He ducked into a neighbor's wooded lot just after rounding the corner. With heart racing, Caleb hid in the bushes, letting the man and lady run past him. For the next hour or so, he waited, making sure he was safe to go home.

He certainly didn't want another zombie bite.

Not today. Not ever.

He decided he would have to hide again. But it wasn't a problem.

Caleb was good at being invisible. He considered it his super-power.

It was close to five when he had arrived home that afternoon. Zombie-Mom had left again. He put his clothes in the dryer, dug all the money out of the washer, and pushed the wet bills into the pockets of the pants he was wearing.

Then, he set up his zombie watch-camp in the kitchen. This time, he made sure he had more than one method of defending himself ready.

But now she was back again, he considered.

How long had it been since the lights went out, he wondered?

The boy looked at his watch. It was three-thirty in the morning now.

Caleb looked at the bag of SourPatch Kids. He was still hungry. Would it be safe to open them now? Or would the crinkly noise from the package make too much noise?

Zombie-Mom would find him if he make too much noise.

No, it wasn't worth the risk.

No more Zombie bites.

His back had begun to hurt even more after he had arrived home from the store. And when he had been hiding in the woods, he had begun to feel the many places on his legs where Zombie-mom's hits with the broken broom handle had connected. They felt tighter now, and it now it hurt when he walked.

Caleb knew from experience what it felt like when bruises on his legs were showing. And at the moment, he could feel the marks more now than before.

For just a moment, the boy under the blanket gave in to the hot tears he had been pushing away all week. He wiped his face with his hands, and felt the unrealized wetness. Angry, he put his head on his knees, exhausted from keeping watch.

How much longer could he live like this, he asked himself?

"S-s-somebody help m-m-me," he whispered. "Is anybody th-th-there...p-p-please...."

It was another half-hour before Caleb drifted off to sleep. His head still throbbed from its contact with the granite counter-top during her beating him earlier in the day.

Eventually, the boy's weariness took over.

He slept until sometime the next morning.

He might have stayed asleep longer, but he was awakened by someone pounding really hard on the front door. Groggy, Caleb opened his eyes, and looked through the blanket holes.

Man. The person at the door was really going to get yelled out. Anyone with any sense knew they shouldn't wake Zombie-Mom, especially when she had a zombie-man with her. Too scared to move, the boy watched, unmoving, to see what would happen next.

Then, riveted, he heard her. "Hey! I'm coming!" she yelled, in her smoker man-voice. "What kind of an idiot wakes a person up at this time of the morning?"

Zombie-Mom was holding a bedsheet around herself. She still wasn't walking too straight either. She stepped behind the door, and opened it, just putting her head out.

"Yeah?" she slurred. "What do you want?"

"Is this 1224 Parrot Circle?" a man's voice asked.

"Yeah," she snapped. "You can see it is by the mailbox. What do you want?"

"Are you Ms. Morrow?" he asked.

"No. This is Landon Morrow's house, and I live here. He's not here right now."

"My name is Peter Lynch. I am a detective with the City of Greenway. These officers and ladies are with Family Services. We have a search warrant. Apparently, some items were stolen from Leonard's Grocery this afternoon."

"What?" Zombie-Mom declared. "I didn't steal anything. I was here all morning. I ran some errands this afternoon, but I didn't go to *that* store. Why did you come *here*? Why *my* house?"

"Well, ma'am," came the answer, "if you will open the door, please, and let us come in...."

"I have a guest," she snapped. "I'm sure you understand. I'm not dressed. What time is it anyway?"

"It's after ten, Ms. Morrow."

"The name is Carnes. You don't call first?"

"Not usually, Ms. Carnes."

17

Oh," she said. "Well then, come in." Shrugging, she opened the front door, and stepped back to allow the entourage inside. "S'cuse me," she said. "I'm going to get dressed."

Zombie-Mom hurried down the hall, muttering to herself, lighting a cigarette. A few minutes later, she returned, dressed in blue jeans and a tee-shirt. She had Zombie-man from the night before with her.

The people had all come in. They were standing in the living room. There were six of them.

"Are you Mr. Morrow?" a man asked.

"Hey, no, dude," the zombie-man told them. "I just met this chick last night. We had a few drinks and came back to her place, for our own party; if you know what I mean."

"About what time was that, sir?"

"I don't know. Close to two-thirty or three, wouldn't you say, Babe?"

Caleb hated it when a zombie-man called Zombie-Mom names like "babe," or "honey." "Sweetie" was the worst. She was none of those things.

"Yeah," she answered, blowing smoke, and reaching for the pack of cigarettes on the coffee table. "Like I said, I left around four yesterday afternoon, and came home late. I was running errands, and then I had a date."

"What is your name, sir?"

"Daniels. Donald Daniels."

"Well, Ms. Carnes and Mr. Daniels," the officer said, "we want you to remain in this room. You can be seated, while we conduct our search. I do have to let you know that if any of the items stolen from the store today are found, the store will be pressing charges, and someone will be going to jail. Please be advised, we will be asking you to come with us down to the station."

Zombie-Mom shrugged. "Go for it," she said. "We didn't steal anything. I'm telling you, you have the wrong house."

Caleb froze in fear. They would find him! And he was the one who had gone to Leonard's Grocery! But it was too late now! They were all zombies. They had to be. And he was going to get bit again for sure.

Oh, no. Now, the six people were splitting up. Two of them had gone down the hall, and two had gone into the garage. The two dressed-up lady zombies were coming into the kitchen. He tried to shrink further into the corner.

Good. Their backs were to him. They were looking in the pantry, and in the cabinets. Then, the refrigerator.

He tried to stay very still. He tried not to breathe.

One of the lady-zombies sat down on the floor next to him. "He's here," she told the other lady-zombie.

Her partner went back into the living room. Caleb could hear her talking to someone.

"There is a child's room down the hall," a man-officer-zombie was saying. "Must be a small child. There's a toddler bed in there. It's decorated in Zombies, so it must be a boy's room."

"Yes, it is a boy," the lady-zombie answered. "He's here; in the kitchen."

Apparently the man said something to Zombie-Mom. "Does your son live with you?"

"Oh, him," she answered. "He's not my son. I'm just taking care of him until his father comes back."

"So, Mr. Morrow is his father?"

Zombie-Mom nodded. "I guess. That's what I said."

"How long has the father been gone?"

"Oh, let's see," she answered. "A little over three years now. He calls every once in a while."

"How old is the boy?"

"Seven and a half, I think."

"And he still sleeps in a toddler bed?"

"Wow. Give a single woman a break, willya? Half the time, the kid's not even here, mister. He's off to god-knows-where. I'm tellin' ya. Y'don't know what I deal with. He's a little brat. More trouble than he's worth. And he's not even mine, after all. His own dad didn't even want 'im."

In the kitchen, the other lady-zombie sat down on the floor in front of Caleb, who was still peering through the blanket holes.

"Hi," she said. "I'm Sarah. What's your name?"

Caleb wasn't sure if he could let himself answer her. It must be safe to talk, he reasoned, because she couldn't really see him under the blanket.

"C-C-C-Caleb," he stammered.

"Are you hiding?" she asked.

"Y-y-yes. This is my z-z-zombie c-c-c-camp," he answered.

"Zombie camp?" she asked.

"For s-s-s-survival, you know. I h-h-have everything I n-n-n-need in here to p-p-p-protect m-m-myself from the z-z-z-zombies."

"Can I see your camp?" she asked. "I've never seen a zombie survivor camp before."

"Sh-sh-sure," the boy answered. He wasn't quite sure why he wanted to let this zombie-lady see his camp and munitions, but he pulled the blanket off his head. Probably wasn't a good idea, he thought, but he was too tired to care right now.

The boy looked around the kitchen as the blanket came away from his face. The two lady-zombies were near to him, and the other man-officer-zombies were now coming into the kitchen. He watched the face of the lady-zombie in front of him. His attention was especially drawn to her eyes.

"Hi there, Caleb," she said. "I'm Louisa."

"Are y-y-*you* a z-z-zombie?" he asked.

She laughed. It was a tinkling, happy sound, like some of the funny TV shows. "Not at all," she answered. "Are *you* a zombie?"

Caleb looked down at his hands. "I — I d-d-don't kn-kn-know," he answered. "I've only b-b-b-been b-b-bit three t-t-times, but I d-d-don't know how in-f-f-fected I am."

"Well," she said, putting her arm around him, "I know a place where we can find out. We can get you some help. Would you like that?"

Caleb nodded. That would be nice.

The other lady-maybe-zombie spoke. "Caleb, can I ask you a question?" she asked.

The boy shrugged. "Sh-sh-Sure."

"Did you take some things from Leonard's Grocery earlier today?"

Swallowing hard, he looked at her. "I l-l-l-left the m-m-m-money in the w-w-washer, and couldn't p-p-pay, and so I r-r-ran. I was h-h-hungry, and Z-z-z-Zombie-Mom d-d-doesn't d-d-do that s-stuff. There was this w-w-weird not-z-z-zombie lady at the ch-ch-checkout, and I was sc-sc-scared. I can p-p-pay for the sandwich, and the w-w-waters."

He looked down at the floor, where he picked up the bag of SourPatch Kids. "H-h-here is the c-c-candy I t-t-took. I th-th-think th-th-there was a c-c-c-candy b-b-bar too.... s-s-Snickers. B-b-but I ate it."

He looked around at them. "D-d-do I still have to g-g-go to j-j-jail?"

The man-officer-zombie spoke to him. "Caleb, do you sleep here? Can you show me your room?"

Caleb nodded, visibly working hard to stand up. As he did, he winced in pain. His sides and back really hurt now, and his legs were stiff.

The lady-maybe-zombies looked at each other, as they observed his struggle. They could see his marks and bruises, he was sure.

By now, they had to know what a bad kid he was.

Would he get in trouble for talking to them?

He hoped not.

Caleb led the man-officer-zombie to his room. He showed him the special box where he kept all of his Zombie survival stuff. "Are *you* a z-z-zombie?" he asked.

The man-officer-zombie chuckled. It was a deep sound, coming from his chest. Caleb hadn't heard a sound like it in a long, long, time; probably since before his Zombie-Dad went away.

"No, Caleb," he answered. "I'm not a zombie. What's a zombie?"

"All the g-g-g-grown-ups I know are z-z-z-zombies," the boy told him. "Z-z-z-zombies d-d-drink z-z-zombie juice, and they g-g-get very an-g-gry. If y-y-you aren't in-v-v-visible, th-th-they will h-h-hurt you."

The man nodded, and rubbed Caleb's head. "I understand," he said. "We are going to try very hard not to let that happen to you again, Caleb. I promise."

"Wh-wh-what is g-g-going t-to h-h-happen n-n-now?" the boy asked.

The man-officer-zombie sat down on Caleb's toddler bed. "We have to make sure you are safe, son. Can you tell me about those marks on your legs and your arms? Are there other marks on you?"

"My b-b-back and s-s-sides hurt," Caleb answered. "I c-c-can't see it th-th-there ...... S-s-sometimes she hits m-m-me there t-t-too. N-n-not all the t-t-time, b-b-but I m-m-made a b-b-big m-m-mistake y-y-yesterday."

"Just let me see, son," came the gentle answer. The man-officer-zombie reached towards the boy and carefully lifted up the youngster's too-thin, too-small shirt. As the fresh bruises came into view, the officer found it difficult to breathe. He had never before seen a body so damaged. In addition to the black and blue lines across the boy's back, Caleb's ribs were out of place. Both of his forearms were curved upward, angled upward at about thirty degrees. The man couldn't tell if the boy had been deformed from birth, or suffered damage since. Additionally, both sides of his little body were covered with fresh bruises.

Broken bones, wrongly fused bones, and internal injuries were not only possible, but probable. How many times had bones been broken, the man wondered, and not healed properly?

How had this boy lived in such a condition? Had it been for his entire life? How had the treatment of such a small child come to such a low point? Why hadn't the neighbors noticed and made a phone call? Where were his teachers?

"D-d-do you kn-kn-know how l-l-long it t-t-takes before you b-b-become a z-z-zombie?" the boy asked. "I've b-b-been b-b-bit three t-t-times now. If it h-h-has t-to h-h-happen, I'd j-j-just as s-s-soon g-g-get it over with."

"I think I understand, Caleb," the man-officer-maybe-zombie told him. "I got bit once too."

"D-d-did you t-t-turn into w-w-one?" the boy questioned, his eyes wide.

"For a while I thought I wanted to," came the answer. "But that was a long time ago."

"C-c-can I p-p-put m-my sh-sh-shirt down n-n-now?" Caleb wanted to know.

"Sure, buddy," the officer replied with a smile.

"Are w-w-we g-going t-to g-g-go t-to the z-z-zoo?"

Chapter Two

Erin took a last look in the mirror before leaving for middle school. She had decided at the last minute to try the new style of eyeliner after all. She had watched the video clip on Facebook about ten times, and still wasn't sure she was really getting it right. She had even purchased two packages of the *good* stuff to practice with. Today was the day to show off her new look!

Looking side to side, she double checked the long lash lines she had painted on the outside of her eyes. Yes, the wider strip of black all around her eyes was evenly done. And oh, the fake lashes looked really good! They had taken a long time to learn to put on.

She had ruined ten lashes figuring it out.

But it was going to be worth it.

Tonight would *make* it all worth it.

She had used the grey and metallic blue colors on her lids and under-eyes this morning.

This is so cool, she told herself, smiling.

"I'm a rock-star!" she murmured out loud. She looked into the mirror. "You should be proud of yourself!"

She made her best pouty duckface at her mirror image one more time. She had to make sure the black lipstick was staying in the right shape. The video had said to use a lip liner first. She was glad she had watched it. The girls on YouTube were so right.

The liner made it way better.

She grabbed her phone and took a selfie.

She couldn't wait to get the second piercing on her upper lip. Dad had promised she could get it when she turned fifteen. Thinking, she ran the underside of her tongue barbell across the top edge of her bottom teeth. Would either of her parents freak when they saw it, she wondered?

Mom would go off. And then, like always, there would be another lecture to sit through. Dad would ask if she was sure about doing it. Erin stifled a snigger.

Like I would do it if I wasn't sure, she reasoned. Why did they over-react so much? After all, it hadn't even hurt to get it done. The clamp had been the worst part. And afterwards? It had felt strange and new at first, but now she was used to it.

Her boyfriend, Garrett, loved it. They had been talking for three months this week, and had become exclusive just last week.

He had told her it would make all the difference.

She was sure he liked the blingy stud in her nose as well.

Erin liked Garrett a lot. He was into the same heavy metal bands she was. Besides, he didn't like his parents either.

"Why would I like either *one* of them, when they don't like each *other?*" he had asked her. "And why should I want to live with either one of them, when *they* can't live with each other?"

He just made so much sense.

She was so glad she was with an older guy.

He had helped her so much to see her life differently.

And Erin agreed with him. He was right. Adults always expected you to do things a certain way; but they didn't even keep their own rules. Her parents didn't fight anymore, like Garrett's did, but then, neither one of her parents even liked to spend time talking at all.

Especially to her, it seemed.

They were all just too busy for each other, her Mom said.

She couldn't remember the last time the family went out to eat together. No one *ever* cooked anymore. Most nights, she ate alone watching her shows. She had worked through all the seasons of "Charmed," and "Buffy," on Netflix. These days, she was watching "The Witches of Eastwick." She had memorized all the vampire movies, and even the more important horror movies. And, even though she knew they were supposed to be kid movies, she still liked to watch the "Harry Potter" series.

Magic was cool. Why couldn't *she* do that kind of stuff and make her life better, she wondered?

The relationships on those shows were what she wished her own life looked like. At least *those* people had friends. *They* had people who cared about them.

This year hadn't been so bad, she considered. She had gained some new friends. And, she had learned to talk with them.

On Snapchat. On Facebook. On Twitter. On Instagram. By email and texts. Her friends had become her family. Who needed adults?

Friends.

At least *they* understood her. Garrett understood her. It didn't really matter, she decided. She was going to move away someday soon and finally be happy.

She and Garrett had been making plans. It was cool. It felt good to have a goal. An escape plan.

She would be going to Dad's after school today. This time it would be for two weeks. Mom was heading out of town again. She was so busy now with her job.

I don't know why it's such a big deal to her where I stay, she thought. *I could so totally stay by myself. It's not like Dad does anything anyway. We eat out, I do my homework, and I ride the bus. When he's not home I order a pizza. He's never there. So what's the freaking big deal?*

"I want you to be safe," Mom had told her. "If something happens, at least you will be with your Dad."

How was her life any different at Dad's, Erin wondered? He was out most of the time too, working at the dealership. Most nights he had a date, or worked late. Yeah, he gave her money, but she was still alone.

She had no idea what he did during the times she wasn't with him.

Her brother and his girlfriend lived over an hour away. Her older sister had moved in with her boyfriend's family in a little town on the outskirts of the city. Dad told Erin they had had an argument. Erin missed her, but gathered her father was telling her the truth, because her sister hadn't returned Erin's phone calls or texts.

Erin sighed, and looked at the mirror once more. "It's just you and me, Bee-ahtch," she said. She looked at the streak of fire-engine red she had added to her hair. "Not too shabby," she said.

Erin looked around her bedroom in her Mom's home. In her mind's eye, she pictured it as it had been when she was nine years old. That had been a good time in her life, she reasoned. Mom and Dad had still been together. They had fought a lot, but at least they had been together. Her brother and sister had still been living at home. They had all *done* things together. They had been a family.

She had felt safe back then. Not like now.

It didn't really matter, though.

She was making her own happiness these days.

They had stopped being a family when it came down to being just her, she reasoned. That should tell her something. She wasn't worth the effort to them.

But now she had Garrett.

He was her boyfriend. He had promised to spend the night at Dad's with her tomorrow night. He was going to climb in the window to her room after she went to bed. Around midnight.

Good thing her room was on the ground floor.

It wouldn't be like the other nights when they sneaked out together. Tomorrow night would be their first time.

Her first time.

She wanted it to be special.

And Garrett was experienced. He had told her he would teach her.

She hoped Dad wouldn't freak when he found out. After all, he had *bragged* to her about *his* first time. He had been her age; fourteen. She hadn't told Mom yet, but she was sure Mom would be cool with it, especially since they had gone together to the doctor to get Erin some birth control pills.

Thinking about it now, though, Erin remembered telling Mom that her best friend, Jeri, had gone to their family doctor because her periods were so difficult. The doctor had prescribed "the pill" to help regulate things, and control her acne.

So, not wanting to be left behind, Erin had begged. Could *she* take "the pill" too? After all, she had horrible cramps every month, and zits were embarrassing.

Finally, worn down, Mom had agreed with her.

First time this century, Erin thought to herself.

Besides, hadn't *Mom* "done it" at fifteen? One year's difference in age really wasn't that much different, she told herself. And anyway, wasn't *she*, the daughter, really so much more mature than either of her parents had been when they were her age?

Neither one of her parents even had a Pinterest account. Or Instagram.

Checking her fingernails, she noticed the black polish had chipped on one of her pinkies. She glanced at the clock. There was no time to fix it now. She would miss the school bus.

Quickly, she grabbed the little bottle of black polish and stuffed it in the front pocket of her overnight backpack. She already had clothes at Dad's. She had just packed a few things from Mom's she wanted to take with her.

She wouldn't be coming back. She had decided.

One last look in the mirror. Her necklace with the skulls and pentagram was in just the right place. She had decided to wear all of her band bracelets today. She checked to make sure the lace-ups in her white shirt and black leather bodice were straight; that the rips in her black jeans were satisfactory.

But her high-heeled boots were getting a little ratty looking, she decided.

Maybe Dad would buy her some new ones. Maybe two pair. He certainly could spare the money.

Yes. That was it.

She definitely would hit Dad up for a mall trip this time, she decided. She had seen some really had-to-haves at Hot Topic when she had been there with Mom last week.

There was one plaid, pleated mini-skirt and some fishnets she just had to have. Oh, and the Keds lace-up boots.

Maybe all of them. And some jewelry too.

Mom always said "no."

Too bad. Dad would do it. She just had to ask at the right time.

He always came through. It was a good thing he made such good money. She was his little girl... Well, step-daughter. And she knew just how to play him.

Would she rather have Dad's money, or his time, she wondered?

At first she had wanted his time. But now, after everything that had happened?

Yes. Definitely had to have his money.

Grabbing her laptop and iPhone, she stuffed her school bag full for the day. Yes, she had the chargers. And, best of all, she had Mom's credit card for lunch and incidentals.

Maybe the band teacher would let her order pizza for him and herself again. He always acted like he wanted to help her not be depressed. He was an idiot.

The way I dress has nothing to do with how I feel, she thought to herself. *Why couldn't the adults in her life just let her be who she wanted to be; let her pierce what she wanted to pierce; and get a tattoo wherever she wanted to? It was her body, after all. Her life, not theirs.*

Why couldn't they just get that?

School was such a waste of time.

Why did they make her learn all of this stuff?

It was useless information, anyway. They tried to cram it into her head so fast, she could never remember....

The world was going to end soon, anyway. It was a matter of time – riots, nuclear blast, war, chemical attack, viral killer, meteor, aliens... Or maybe even a zombie holocaust.

Avoid the zombies. They will kill and eat you alive.

Erin smiled. As if they really existed.

She walked out the door, making sure she set the alarm. Mom had helped her get out of bed that morning with a mug of Starbucks coffee before leaving for the office at six. It was nice she did that every morning, she reasoned. A cup of coffee and a kiss on the top of her head.

Too bad the woman was so busy.

Yeah. Too bad.

Dad didn't do those things. Hadn't ever even touched her.

Silent, Erin waited for the school bus, watching the other kids in her group at the corner.

Why couldn't they all just grow up, she wondered?

The sixth graders weren't so bad. At least *they* weren't pretending yet. They were still little kids. They were *expected* to be stupid; to act like that.

She decided it was the seventh and eighth graders who really got on her nerves. Why were boys that age always talking about body functions? Farts weren't funny. Just gross Burps were nasty. And who wanted to watch someone play a tune with their armpits?

Yeah, boys were disgusting!

At least Garrett was a real guy. A *mature* guy.

He was eighteen. A senior. And built. And smart.

He even had a little bit of scruffy beard. She liked it.

Not like the guys in her classes at school. Even the eighth graders. Or most of the ninth graders she had met.

She smiled to herself. Garrett said he loved her. He had told her he wanted to marry her. He had called her his princess.

It sucked they didn't go to the same school. He was a senior in the high school three miles away from where she went. Maybe she would skip school and go surprise him for lunch one day. It wasn't really that far to walk.

She might even use Mom's card and call a taxi.

She would talk to him about it tonight, she decided.

Chapter Three

Pulling into the parking lot for the Municipal Office of Family Services, Sarah McMillan and Louisa Richards had fallen silent. There were things the two social workers had wanted to say to each other during the forty-five minute drive to the office. But both instinctively knew the words had to be spoken out of earshot of the seven-year-old boy curled up; apparently sleeping in the back seat.

Yesterday, Sarah, the county supervisor, had taken a call from a concerned cashier at Leonard's Grocery in Westwood Village. The female cashier reported a young boy who stuttered as having come to the store, waiting in her line to pay. He had been alone, apparently afraid, very dirty and unkempt; buying practical groceries with a one hundred dollar bill. That had been at ten-thirty yesterday morning.

The same woman had called again that afternoon, connecting the second time to Louisa. Apparently, the same boy had returned to the store, this time without money. He had stolen a sandwich and some bottles of water. Perhaps a few other items. The cashier said the store manager had urged her to call again, since the boy was now walking strangely, and appeared to have fresh marks of a brutal beating on his legs and face.

After comparing notes, both social workers went on high alert to help the boy. They travelled to the store. After interviewing the manager, the cashiers, and other workers, the women searched neighborhoods nearby. The process had taken all afternoon. Then, driving through the neighborhoods within walking distance of Leonard's Grocery, they searched for the boy.

Finally, late in the day, Louisa spotted yet another group of kids playing in the street. Again, they stopped. Again, they asked. Did *they* know a young boy who stuttered? Where did he live?

Bingo.

He snuck out of that house over there sometimes. He talked to them sometimes. They thought he was a little strange.

Did *they* know anything about his family? Had they noticed anything they thought was unusual?

Finding the house, Sarah and Louisa decided they would come back with a patrolmen and a car for support in the morning.

Upon arriving at the Morrow home the next day, they noticed two detectives getting out of a sedan in front of the house. Unknown to Family Services, the inhabitants were about to receive an unexpected, simultaneous visit. And, although it hadn't been planned, it had worked well to complete both visits at the same time.

Donald Daniels had dressed and fled the home on Parrot Circle as soon as he could, after being interrogated by the detectives. Sarah McMillan felt sorry for him. Apparently, he had no idea with whom he had become involved the night before. At least that was his story for now. The more pertinent individual to the case, Ms. Morrow, or Carnes, whatever her name was, had been placed in the back of the patrol car and taken downtown.

Sarah and Louisa had then scoured the Morrow home for records of the boy, Caleb. They found no pictures, no birth certificate; not even an immunization record. Strangely, there was also no mail, no bills, or financial information anywhere in the home. The only clothes in the house were those belonging to Ms. Carnes, and a set of clothing for Caleb in the dryer.

It was as though the people who lived in that house had been planning to move at any moment, Sarah thought. But hadn't someone lived there since before the seven-year-old was born?

In the end, they asked Caleb to bring along the things he considered important. His shoebox, his blanket, and his Zombie Survival Kit were all he asked for. Louisa commented there were no story books, or children's movies, or toys anywhere on the property.

It was quiet in the car. Louisa looked over her shoulder to check the boy's condition. She opened the front passenger door of Sarah's car. "I'll type up the report, call the hospital, and get a therapeutic home set up for him," she said. "Are you taking him to the hospital now?"

Sarah smiled. "I'm headed there, yes. I do think he needs to be seen, and evaluated. Please clear my schedule for the next few days, if you would. And hold off on calling any of our foster families.

34

Let's not place him just yet. Detective Lynch said something about needing to interview him. He needs to be kept as calm and stable as possible. I'd like to help him adjust slowly, if we can."

"Sounds good," Louisa said. "Where should we plan on him sleeping?"

"For the next few days," Sarah told her, "he'll be in the hospital. Officer Summerfield said his back will need to be x-rayed. He might need treatment, so it could be longer. I just don't know." She paused and looked at her colleague. "I was thinking he could just stay with me. My gut tells me to just let him be with us in the office during the day. We have so much work to do, just to help him be ready to speak with other adults, or even think about going into a foster home."

"That's true," came the answer, as Louisa got out of the car. "Keep me posted today?"

"Will do," Sarah promised. "And thanks."

"No sweat, girl."

Louisa pushed the door shut carefully, so as to not awaken the still-sleeping boy. She walked away to enter the Family Services Administrative Center. Her office was on the third floor.

Pulling the car away, Sarah looked into the rearview mirror to check her cargo.

Such a sweet face on this little guy, she thought.

Weaving her way through the downtown maze of lunch-time traffic, she turned into the parking lot for Emergency Medicine for Ginsberg Memorial Hospital. She steered into the designated Family Services parking spot, and waited. A few moments later, an orderly arrived at her car window pushing a wheelchair. Pointing to the back seat, and motioning with her finger to her lips for silence, Sarah opened her car door, and then the back door to her car. Undoing the seatbelt around the boy, she gently rubbed his forehead.

"Caleb? I need you to help me now," she spoke softly.

There was a slight stir. She smiled.

The child had eaten a Quarter-pounder with cheese, most of her large fries, an ice cream cone, and an apple pie before she had told him he had eaten enough for one meal.

"C-c-can I g-g-get more l-l-later?" he had asked.

35

Laughing, Louisa had ruffled his hair. "Absolutely, kiddo," she had told him.

Caleb had looked longingly at the inside play area, and asked if he could come back when it didn't hurt to walk. "C-c-can I c-c-come b-b-back and p-p-play here?"

"Anytime," Sarah told him.

She had given him a dose of Children's Advil.

With his tummy finally full, and a little something to numb his painful limbs, the child had fallen into a deep sleep in the first five minutes of the drive into the City of Greenway.

Sarah looked up at the orderly. "We found him this morning. I brought him in for evaluation and treatment. I don't think he has had a good night's sleep in a long time. Can you lift him if I can't wake him up?"

The oversized, muscular orderly chuckled. His deep, African, bass voice resonated as he answered. "Let me get him, Ms. Sarah. I'll just carry him in."

Sarah stepped aside. The big African reached into the car, to retrieve Caleb. As he slid his huge arms under the boy, the youngster winced in his sleep, letting out a heart-wrenching whimper.

"It's all right, Caleb," Sarah said. "This is Kojo. He's my friend, and he is going to carry you into the hospital."

Still drowsy, Caleb leaned his head against Kojo's chest.

"K-kojo..." repeated the boy.

Kojo looked at Sarah. "He doesn't weigh much at all! How old is he?"

Sarah nodded. "He says he's seven."

"What happened to him?"

"We don't know yet."

Kojo turned around and made his way toward the emergency room. Sarah closed the car door, and followed him into the hospital, pushing the unneeded, empty wheelchair.

Detective Peter Lynch stood with his partner, Evan Davies, in the observation room. Peter looked through the one-way glass, and took a sip of his gas station cappuccino. He tried to assess the attitude of the woman sitting in the Interrogation Room. Ms. Carnes had become a person of interest in the case he was working on. She would be detained here until the Crime Lab was done making a sweep of the house in Westwood Village.

"Pete, you want to go first?" Evan asked him.

"I can," Pete answered, still looking through the glass. "Or you can go first, and I'll be the one to mop up."

"Okay then," Evan moved to the corner, and grabbed two bottles of water from the small fridge. "See you on the other side."

"Yeah," Pete responded, pushing the button on the recording equipment.

A moment later, Evan entered the Interrogation Room, and offered Ms. Carnes a bottle of water.

"Good morning, Ms. Carnes," he said. "I'm Evan Davies. I was one of the detectives who came to your home this morning."

"Yeah, yeah," she answered. "You got any smokes? They took my purse."

Evan patted his pockets. "I don't. But I can get you some. Filtered or unfiltered?"

"Filtered. Marlboro 27's if you got 'em."

"Sure." Evan glanced at the one-way glass. The detectives were under orders to keep this one as happy and willing to talk as possible. The Chief needed answers. There were too many coincidences in this case. There were too many clues leading nowhere.

"They'll bring them to you, Ms. Carnes," Evan told her. The detective pulled out a chair, and sat down across the table from her. He placed his portfolio and the case file folder on top of the table in front of him.

"It's Annabelle," she said. "Don't call me Ms. Carnes."

Evan smiled at her. "All right, Annabelle. That's a pretty name. It's nice to meet you."

He shifted his position. "There are just a few things we need to clear up, and then we can hopefully let you go home."

"Am I in trouble?" she wanted to know.

"I'm not sure about Family Services, or how they will want to proceed. As far as we are concerned, we just need some information."

"I didn't steal nothin'," she declared. "Like I said before, when we wuz back at the house; I was running errands during that time, and had that date. You met him. His name's Donald."

"Yes," Evan replied. "Mr. Daniels is also here in the building. In fact, he is in another room just like this one, answering questions."

"Why pick on him?" she demanded. "He doesn't know nothin'."

"Okay." Evan was observing Annabelle's body language and emotional intensity levels as they talked. He glanced at the video camera before he continued. "Can you tell me about the boy? Is he your son?"

"No, he's not my kid," she sighed. "I told you. He was livin' there when I moved in with Landon. The mom had died. So sad, you know? Landon wanted me to take care of him; the kid I mean, and I tried. I really did. But I wasn't ever cut out to be a mom."

"How did you meet Landon?" Evan asked.

"I was workin' up in Pinegrove back then. Dancing at the Gentleman's Club – Lace, Poker and Leather. I was the headliner. My performance name is 'Candy.' Candy Carnes. So I was making good, y' know? He come in one night t' play the tables. He sent a drink t' my dressing room after. So, like I always do, I's peradventured out to go thank him. He was real nice."

"So you dated him?"

"Nah, I wouldn't say I *dated* him. He isn't that kind. I was between places t' live at the time. My former fiancé, Joey, and I, had a real bruiser of a fight, so I was sleeping at the club, y' know? But only when I didn't have a guy t' go home with. Landon said I should come t' stay at his place. He didn't tell me he had a kid."

"So....Did you and Mr. Morrow have a relationship?"

"Kinda," she shrugged, drumming the table with her open palms, looking around the room. "Hey, my cigs 'ere yet?"

Evan looked toward the one-way glass. No knock. Apparently not.

"Not yet," he told her. "They must have had to go to the store."

"That sucks, man," she told him. "I'm really Jones'n here. Are you tellin' me *nobody* in this building smokes? Can't y' just bum one?"

"Ms. Carnes..."

"Hey! I told you. Don't call me that."

"Okay. Sorry. Annabelle, they will bring them as soon as they can."

"Yeah. Sure. Whatever."

There was a moment of silence in the room, as Evan opened the case file in front of him. He shut it again, and looked at her.

"Let me repeat my question, Annabelle. Did you and Mr. Morrow have a relationship?"

"Yeah. I guess. Yeah, we did."

"What did your relationship involve?"

"You askin' if we slept together?"

"If that was involved; yes, I am."

"Only once in a while," she answered. "He was too busy workin'. I was still datin' guys who came in my club at night. I was workin' too."

"Were there things Mr. Morrow asked you to do for him in exchange for letting you live in his house?" Evan inquired. "Or, was he just a nice guy?"

"No, he's so *not* a nice guy," the woman told him. "He wanted me to be there when packages came. And to make sure the kid had food. I took his messages."

"Did he ask you to keep house?"

"Nah, but I did clean my own bathroom."

"Did you do laundry?"

"Nah, I taught the kid how so he could do his own. I go to the laundromat, and the cleaners. I like having it all done at once."

"So let me sum up," Evan said. "He gave you a place to live and asked you to be there to get the mail, take messages and feed his kid."

"Yeah," she nodded. "That's pretty much it. Coz the boy wuddn't supposed to leave the house. Somebody had got him a

Gameboy before I got there. I got him some games he likes. Kept him quiet that way."

"Which games did you purchase?" Evan asked, making notes.

Annabelle paused, thinking. "Uh, "Teenage Zombies" and "Zombie Hunter....""

"Kind of gruesome for a kid that age, don't you think?"

"My cousin's boy likes those, and he's that age."

"Why didn't Mr. Morrow want the boy to leave the house?"

"I don't know," she said. "Landon said he had to be kept hidden."

"Did you think that was unusual?"

"Sure. I ain't stupid. Hey, Morrow was putting a roof over me. I didn't ask no questions."

"Where is Mr. Morrow now?"

"I don' know," she replied. "The last time he called, he was in Chicago. One time before he was in L.A."

"How long ago was his last call?"

"Uh... prob-ly four months ago."

"What is he doing?"

"Workin'? I dunno."

"Working at what?"

"Hell if I know." She paused. "Hey, where are my smokes?"

"After," Evan told her. He was becoming frustrated at her method of redirecting when he asked a pertinent question. "Annabelle, the only way we will get through this, is if you can answer my questions."

"I could think straight if'n I had a smoke," she snapped. "Why am I even here anyways? I ain't done nothin' wrong! You chargin' me with something? Do I need a lawyer?"

Evan didn't answer her. He opened the case file, and pulled out a stack of 8x10 glossy photographs. One at a time, he laid them in front of her on the table. As each one was produced, Annabelle's eyes appraised the image, and then looked at Evan's face, assessing his motives and purposes. As he placed the pictures, Evan spoke in cool, even tones.

"Do you know any of these individuals, Annabelle?" he asked. "All of them are from Westwood Village. Every one of them has disappeared in the last two months. That's twenty-two missing persons in eight weeks between the ages of twenty-five and thirty-five. Based on the national average for a little suburb like the Village, that's really high. More than twenty-three hundred people go missing in the United States on any given day. But given the fact the Village normally has such a low crime rate, the odds are really high that someone bad is up to no good. The photos in front of you are some of those persons whom we know have been involved in some way with Mr. Morrow and his associates. Since you've lived in his house for more than three years, it would be silly for you to deny you have no knowledge of any of them."

Annabelle peered at the pictures, one at a time. "I might-a met *this* guy," she said, picking up the third picture on the first row. "But he looked different. He had a beard."

She looked at the second row. "I know I met this one," she told him, picking up the fourth one on the second row. "He had a classy, black Benz."

"Do you know what either of these men were doing with Mr. Morrow?" Evan asked.

"Hey," Annabelle answered. "I told you, I didn't know nothin' about Landon's business. He had guys t' the house some, but I'm a workin' gal. I stayed clear of his stuff."

"Were you aware of any drug dealings?"

"Drugs? Maybe. Not sure."

"Not even weed?"

"Landon smoked some, but he did it when I was gone."

"So his son was exposed to drugs when you were absent?"

"I-I don' know."

Just then, someone knocked on the door. It was a female officer with a pack of Marlboro 27's, still wrapped, and a lighter. Evan handed the items to the woman being questioned. Annabelle made sure the sticks were packed well, by thumping the pack's ends on her open palm. When she was finished, she tore into the pack, and lit up. Evan waited while she took a long draw, blew out, and then took another.

"Better?" he asked.

"You got no idea," she said with a sigh. "I've not gone this long without one of these since last year. I was gettin' th' shakes. Tried to quit before then. Even tried a prescription. But I got nightmares of those screaming monkeys. They chased me in my sleep, every night while I was on it. I couldn't do it."

"How many do you smoke a day?" Evan asked sympathetically.

"Almost three packs," she shrugged. "But there's worse things I could be doin'."

"I just have a few more questions, Annabelle," Evan told her, "and then we'll take a break and let you get some lunch."

"Will you just let me go home?" she asked.

"I'm sorry, not yet," came the answer. "The Crime Lab is still working on the items listed on the search warrant. And we still haven't heard from Family Services."

"I'm supposed to go t'work in a few hours, Detective," she told him, becoming a little more assertive. "We be done soon?"

"You might want to call your employer, Annabelle," he told her. "We have a bit more to get through today, and you will still need to speak with Family Services regarding the boy."

"You, son of a bitch!" she shouted. "I've told you everything I know! I know my rights! You can't keep me here against my will! And I don't gotta talk t'you without my lawyer. So I'm done here. You don't scare me. I don't gotta talk t'you."

Evan looked at her evenly. "Are you requesting a lawyer, Ms. Carnes?"

"Yeah, guess so!" she snapped. "I refuse t' say anythin' more 'til he is in this here room with me."

"Okay, then." Evan picked up the photographs, and methodically stacked them. He placed them back in the file folder. Pushing back from the table, he stood to his feet.

"That's fine, Annabelle," he stated. "But you should be aware: we can hold you for questioning for forty-eight hours, without your consent. And, since you are a person of interest in the case involving Mr. Morrow, we can ask a federal judge to prolong that time for as long as we need to. Based on our investigations to

42

this point, you are presently within a breath of being charged with any one of many crimes I could mention, not the least of which is neglect and abuse of a minor child. There are many charges pending, due to our investigation. Additionally, I'm sure Family Services will have a few of their own to add to the list. So go ahead, call your lawyer. I'll have an officer bring you a phone. However, please be aware that any chance you have for making a plea bargain will be swept aside the minute he walks into this room."

Without looking at her, Evan turned and walked to the door, opened it, and exited.

"Way to go," Peter Lynch told him, upon his entering the observation room. "Look at her. You shook her."

Evan glanced through the one way glass. Annabelle was in the process of trying to light another cigarette. Her hands were shaking violently as she held the lighter.

"Yeah," Evan answered. "She knows much more than she's telling. I don't know if she has seen something, or if she has been more involved than she will let on. But she's got real fear in the eyes. She's gridlocked for some reason. I hope we can get her to talk."

Chapter Four

Christine Spada drove her convertible into the parking garage under the Judicial Building in the center of The City of Greenway. She looked up at the blue expanse one last time before entering the building's darkness.

Not a cloud in the sky.

She pressed the switch up to replace the roof of her Mercedes 500SL convertible.

The summer weather was somewhat different here than in Washington, D.C., she considered. The crime rate here was about the same. It was certainly warmer here. Here, in the Deep South? Yes, that was a definite fact; hot, humid, and sunny. Today's heat was making her contemplate getting a haircut.

The City of Greenway was definitely a fresh experience, she reasoned. The entire city had been built around golf courses. The city's founders had loved the pastime so much, they had incorporated the sport's lingo into the town's name. Many of the road names hinted at golf: Fairway Boulevard, Birdie Drive, and Backswing Avenue, to name a few. In fact, in a city approaching a million in population, there were more than fifty country clubs, with *private* courses serving their members, and another forty-two *public* courses: in varying lengths and levels of difficulty. As unbelievable as these numbers were, Christine believed them, because she had counted them online before agreeing to take the job.

In fact, her new townhouse had been built as part of a gated golf community. She couldn't wait to play the course.

But for now, the file-box was calling.

Today promised to be another Southern Scorcher.

Showing her badge to the man in the booth, she waited for the garage ticket to be dispensed. Checking her phone for the time, she realized she still had plenty to spare.

She hoped the judge would be on time today. As with most judges on the bench these days, the docket was full, with court hearings and cases beginning around ten. The morning hours between eight-thirty and ten were usually spent signing warrants and orders, reviewing depositions; additionally, conversing with assistant district attorneys and the county prosecutor.

She was glad she had decided to go into Law Enforcement, instead of litigation. Sure, the paperwork was almost the same, but at least with Law Enforcement, she had had more opportunities to be around people. She had turned thirty-one this year, and now?

She knew she would never have been happy or successful behind a desk.

Remotely arming her vehicle, Christine hoisted her laptop case on her shoulder, and lifted the file box. She walked the fifty or sixty-foot walk to the elevator. After pushing the button for the fifth floor, she made her way to the office and chambers for Judge Anne Ventura.

Arriving in the waiting area, manned by Judge Ventura's clerk, Christine put her file box and computer case on one of the chairs. She approached the desk, and put out her hand.

"Hello," she said. "My name is Christine Spada, and I have an appointment to see Judge Ventura."

The girl looked her up and down. "Congratulations," she answered. "What time is your appointment?"

"Nine."

"She's on the phone with someone, but I'll let her know you're here."

"Thank you," Christine said. "And you are?"

"Judge Ventura's Clerk."

"Yes, I can see that. What is your name?"

"I didn't give it."

"I noticed."

"Look," the girl explained, "when people ask, they usually don't really care or remember, and I have to tell them again. So, just remember me as her clerk. Are you new here?"

Christine laughed. It had a light, gentle quality, and the clerk decided she liked this woman with a file box. "I *am* new here," she answered. "Not only to the courts, but to the city as well."

"Well, I'm sorry for my initial response. My name is Samantha Cruz," the girl told her, finally extending her hand. "I'd be glad to show you around if you like."

"I'd like that." Christine reached into her pocket and pulled out her iPhone. "Give me your number really quick."

Samantha dictated. "602-555-0452."

Christine pressed the digits on her touchpad, and presently, a cell phone began ringing. "Now you have my number as well. How long do you get for lunch?"

"An hour," Samantha told her.

"The case I'm on is going to require I come here on a regular basis. How about some day while I'm here, we do lunch as well?" Christine offered.

"Done!"

Samantha glanced past Christine to the file box on the chair. "Must be a pretty big case..."

Christine looked over her shoulder at the box. "Oh, that," she replied. "Too much stuff. I hope I can get through it all with her this morning. But if we can't, I'll just keep coming back until we finish."

"Sounds good," Samantha said, pushing her chair back from her desk. "Excuse me. I'll just let her know you're here."

As she knocked lightly on the Judge's office door, Samantha pushed it open. "Christine Spada is here, Your Honor."

"Oh, yes. Send her on in, Sam," a woman's voice said. Samantha turned her head towards Christine, and motioned to her.

Judge Ventura finished her phone conversation as Christine entered the room. "Hi," she said. "You must be Christine Spada. That was your boss."

"The Police Commissioner?" Christine asked.

"No," the judge answered. "Deputy Director Edwards."

"The D.C. office? I'm sorry. I've had my cell phone on. Is there something I need to do? Why is Ben calling *you*?"

"Well, my dear girl," came the smiling reply, "Ben is an old friend of mine. He phoned me to call in a favor. Apparently, the case you have been assigned has been moved up in national priority by the Bureau. He wanted me to let you know, since he will be making calls to Law Enforcement here in the city. So, as of today, by federal ruling, *you* are leading the investigation, with their support. He said you would need to get your head around the idea before you arrived in the local precinct later today."

47

Stunned, Christine stopped pulling file folders from her file box. "B-b-but why? How? I'm not ready to lead a case. I don't think I can do it. I just moved here. I mean, I haven't even unpacked. There are so many things..... That means I ..."

She faltered in her words, and glanced up to see Anne Ventura observing her with a smile.

"I'm sorry, Your Honor."

"Call me Anne."

"I'm Christine."

"He told me. He also said you would respond this way. He predicted your first response would be that you weren't ready, and make a huge protest. That's really a healthy response. Means you'll be a good leader and think things through. And congratulations on being the new field office chief."

Christine wasn't sure how to respond. She could feel her neck and cheeks turning pink. "That easy to read, am I?" she asked, embarrassed.

"No, I was forewarned." The judge told her. "Now, what are these files?" Walking to her office door, she spoke into the anteroom. "Samantha, call downstairs to the clerk. Tell them I have had a sudden federal issue arise this morning. I need to push all my cases back to one o'clock. Special Investigator Spada is going to need my help today."

"Yes, ma'am."

"And I will be sending you with her this afternoon, to help her unpack and get settled." The judge turned to Christine. "When did you arrive in town?"

"Well, I closed on a townhouse a couple weeks ago. But then, the Bureau had me travelling, gathering evidence and following leads for this case. I *still* ended up getting here before the moving truck. So, the Bureau let me stay this past week at the Marriott downtown. Tomorrow is my last night at the hotel, because the moving truck arrives this afternoon. Honestly, I was going to fulfill this meeting, and then head over to my new home to make sure the cleaning crew was finished. I wanted to put some shelf liners in. That kind of thing."

Anne Ventura raised her voice to be heard through the door. "Samantha? She's definitely going to need your help."

Samantha's curly hair popped into the open doorway. "What's that, Your Honor?"

"Christine's need for help has become a definite. Make those phone calls required now, while Christine and I work through these files. Make it quick, because I'll need your help in here as well, I think, to complete the number of warrants and orders she needs. When we are finished, we will close the office until one. I will want you to stay with Christine, and help her get moved in. You don't have a date tonight or anything, do you?"

Samantha smiled. "No, no date." She looked at Christine. "I'd love to do that! Is Christine agreeable?"

Anne looked at Christine. "Sound like a plan, Agent?"

"Oh, yes, and please both of you, call me 'Kit.' That's what my friends back home call me." Christine was surprised and thrilled at the turn of events.

"Will do! And call me Sam!" Sam pulled her head out, and shut the door.

"Oh, and Samantha?" Judge Ventura called her back one more time.

The door re-opened. "Yes, ma'am?"

"Call Commissioner Walters, and ask if he is available for lunch at eleven-thirty. If not lunch, we need a morning meeting, and it has to be today. Please let him know it is of the utmost importance."

Sam and Kit exchanged silent glances. What was the Judge up to? Kit smiled. She had decided she liked these women. Talk about Southern Hospitality!

Anne Ventura rubbed her hands together. "Now," she said, "Ben said this looks like a juicy case. What are these files you have?" She pulled a chair up to the side of her desk, and sat down in her executive chair behind the desk.

"You want to put the file box on my desk? It might be easier for us to work with a flat surface."

"How about on the floor?" Christine moved the box as she spoke. "I think we might need the room."

49

"Very well." The judge put on her reading glasses, moving the papers presently on her desk to a tray.

Christine pulled the first three files and placed the stack on the desk. "I have files from all over the country in this box," she said. "More than fifty. But there are fifteen or so which we have put together from this area. Here's the deal, though. Each one of the fifteen has occurred within a forty-five mile radius of Westwood Village. Five have occurred in the Village itself. Our working theory at the moment is that the hub of activity seems to be there somewhere."

"A serial killer?" Judge Ventura asked, looking over her glasses.

"Maybe. Right, now, it's still missing persons," Christine answered. "Actually, the majority of these cases are adolescent females between twelve and sixteen. There are several twenty to thirty-something single men on the list, and one old woman."

"How old is the earliest case?" the judge asked.

"I'm not sure," Christine answered. "The more I dig, the more I discover. We might even discover more as we continue. Unless another one turns up, I think the earliest one might have occurred a little over eight years ago."

"What do you need from me?"

"For some I need search warrants. For some I need permission to exhume a body. For most, I need bank records, and phone records. It's somewhat different with each case."

She opened a newer file, and pulled out a stack of papers stapled together. Flipping to the third page, she showed the judge the results of a Forensic Sweep done in a house in Chicago.

"There is a house in Westwood Village," she began, "which seems to fit the profile of what are calling a 'hub-house' discovered in Chicago. We still are not sure whether all of this is connected, but if it is, we don't have much time to act. If they know we are on to them, they will submerge and start up in another area."

"What did the raid of the Chicago house find?" the judge asked.

"Hidden remote cameras were set up in every room, with recording equipment attached somewhere. But, there was also a wireless transmitter, good for five miles away. Additionally, the entire house was bugged. Strangely, when we went through, there were no personal items, no records, no photographs. Yet, two of the bedrooms had been apportioned quite luxuriously for guests. In a third bedroom, we found processing equipment for identity theft activity, such as duplicating credit cards and the like. There were supplies for printing passports as well. We also found a gross of handcuffs."

"Police handcuffs?"

"Yes. One hundred and forty-four sets. There was a well-used tattoo machine, complete with needles, grips, ink, gloves, and such. There was evidence of drug use as well, but no processing equipment remained."

"Strange they would leave all that behind. Were they surprised?"

"I believe it was a shock. You think we weren't supposed to find everything?"

"It seems too easy, doesn't it? I always wonder in cases like this if the things in the house were designed to create false leads... but it is always possible the finds are legitimately connected to the case. Can I see the report?"

"Hmmm," Christine answered, thinking. "Here it is."

The agent waited silently while the judge read through the pages she had described. When she was finished, Anne Ventura put the paper down, and looked at the young woman.

"And you think something like this is going on in Westwood Village?" she asked.

"Yes ma'am," came the answer. "I need to show you the files of the missing persons from this area."

So saying, she leaned over and rifled through the file-box. "There is a house on Macaw Drive, with suspicious traffic, including semis, coming and going at all times of the night. A family supposedly lives there, and the husband works at a car dealership here in town."

"Okay," the judge said.

"Yesterday, the Forensic Team here made a sweep of a home two streets over from the one on Macaw Drive. Parrot Circle, I think.

Some of the older cases named that address as a sort of hub. The preliminary showed evidence of blood spatter all over the walls and ceiling in one of the rooms. We believe the owner, Landon Morrow, disappeared about three years ago. His girlfriend is still living in the house, and is now a person of interest in the case."

"Have you questioned her yet?"

"No, not sure I'll need to. City Detectives on my team spoke with her yesterday, and she is speaking with Family Services today."

"Why Family Services?"

"Mr. Morrow's seven-year-old son was also found on the premises, badly traumatized, with signs of brutality and symptoms of Generalized Anxiety Disorder. He is now in their care."

"And you now have leverage to gain information."

"Right." Christine paused. "The thing is, Mr. Morrow worked at the same car dealership."

"You think there's a connection between the houses and whoever is behind the disappearances?"

"That is our suspicion. We have both houses under surveillance at the moment, to see where those inside might lead us."

"Christine," the judge began, "I assume you have evidentiary cause for each of these needed warrants and orders?"

"Yes ma'am, right here," she answered.

As Christine pulled the rest of the files out of the box, the judge pressed a button on the intercom. "Sam, are you done with the phone calls?"

"Yes ma'am."

"I need you to bring your laptop in here. We need to create and print forms for Agent Spada."

A few moments later, Samantha was sitting at a work-table in the corner of Judge Ventura's office. Working through the files with Christine, each case was provided with the federal form needed to allow the investigation to continue.

By 11:00am, all pertinent forms were printed and signed; copied and ready for filing and distribution. As they were finishing, Anne Ventura looked at Samantha.

"By the way, Sam," what did the Police Commissioner say about lunch?"

"He will meet us at Spinner's at eleven-thirty," came the answer. "His secretary set us up with a reservation."

"Oh, great!" exclaimed the judge. "Kit, you are in for a real treat. At the top of the tower down the street, there is a rotating restaurant. In an hour's time, it provides the diner with a full-circle view of the City of Greenway."

"Expensive?" Christine asked.

"Oh, they've got a great Caesar salad, and I love their house wine," Samantha replied.

"This is my treat, girls," Anne told them. "You can order anything you want. So make it good!"

It was midnight. Erin's Dad had gone to bed an hour earlier. She was watching Netflix in her room, while she prepared herself for her date with Garrett. He would be coming to her window any moment now. She lit a few candles.

She grabbed her phone and texted a message.

"I'm ready. Can't wait to see you."

Then, ten minutes later, she sent, "Are you lost? Can you find my house?"

She waited another thirty minutes. He hadn't replied.

It was now twelve-forty. He had told her to expect him at midnight.

Had something happened?

Maybe his parents had grounded him. She set her phone to vibrate and set it on her chest. If he called, the pulsating would wake her up.

Disappointed, she dozed off to sleep.

An hour, or perhaps even three hours later, Erin woke up, startled. Her room was completely dark. Her TV had been turned off. Even the bathroom nightlight wasn't working. The only light in her room was filtering through her bedroom window. And, since it was cloudy tonight, there wasn't much light to speak of.

Had there been a power outage?

As her eyes grew accustomed to the shadows, she became aware of two bulky forms standing next to her bed. Suddenly, a third shadow pounced on top of her from somewhere in her peripheral vision. Then, she felt something heavy on her stomach. She reached up to push it off. But she was too weak. Someone was sitting on top of her!

She began to scream; to shout out.

Without warning, a hand came down hard, clamping across her mouth, hurting her. She could taste salty blood from her bottom lip in her mouth.

"Shut up!" the man hissed, holding a knife to her throat. "If you make any noise; *any* noise at all, I will freakin' *kill* you. My knife is really sharp, and with one move I can slit your throat wide open. We'll let you just bleed out right here in your bed. So you just do whatever I say. Do you understand?"

Feeling the sharp point of the knife pressing into her neck, Erin nodded. Her eyes were wide. She was trying very hard not to give in to tears. She was finding it difficult to breathe. Finally, the man decided she had agreed to fully comply. He removed his hand from her mouth, but remained on top of her, holding her arms down with his knees. He continued to maintain a constant pressure with the knife.

The man nodded to the other two figures, who went into action. One pulled Erin's feet together and tied them. The other put tape over her mouth; then a fabric bag over her head. She felt herself being turned over, her hands then being secured together behind her. When her arms were pulled too tightly, she whimpered.

"I said not a sound!" the leader repeated. "I should cut you right here! Do what I tell you, or you die!"

With that, he pulled a syringe out of his jacket pocket, and jabbed it into her neck. Within seconds, she was out cold, in a deep sleep.

Without a sound, the leader moved to the open window. Following his signals, one intruder climbed through and made ready to receive the girl. After she was passed through the window by the remaining abductors, he threw her over his shoulder like a large sack of wheat, and ran to a running van, waiting in the cul-de-sac. The driver had turned off its lights to avoid drawing attention from the neighbors. His cohorts climbed through the window as well, and ran to enter the van.

As they pulled the doors shut, the gang sped from the scene. Undetected, they headed down the street, and out of the neighborhood.

The entire abduction had taken less than ten minutes.

Chapter Five

The next day was bright and sunny. Christine was awakened by her phone alarm. It had been late when she and Samantha had decided to stop unpacking for the day. They had stopped for salads at a Wendy's on the way to Samantha's apartment, when Christine had driven her home. Kit had then headed back to the hotel.

"Sam" was nice, she decided. They could become good friends if things continued this way. They had spent much of the time together in laughter.

Although their backgrounds were similar, the roads taken to arrive at the present moment were different. Samantha had moved to the city from a small town, adjacent to a city, and so had Christine. Sam had finished law school, and was clerking for Judge Ventura until she could afford to take the Bar Exam. Ostensibly, a struggle was presenting itself, she said. Now that she had the degree, she wasn't sure it was what she really wanted to do with her life. But there wasn't money to learn something else. So, for now, she was clerking.

"I know I'm putting it off," she told Kit. "I just want to get a little more court experience under my belt before I try to 'do' a case in front of a judge and jury. All those people focusing their attention on you just makes me nervous."

Christine had likewise shared her own education experience. She had finished her Master's degree in criminal justice, with minors in forensic science and psychology. Additionally, she had received special field training during several cases cooperating with Interpol. She was fluent in English, Spanish, French, Russian and Arabic.

It was good to have something in common with another single woman her own age, Kit determined. Neither liked to shop, unless it was for shoes. Both young women had experienced painful relationships with men, and had decided to become career focused for the time being. Both just wanted to get out of debt.

As she showered, Christine remembered tonight would be her last night to stay at the hotel. She decided to pack as much as would fit in the car, and make a quick trip to the townhouse before going into the office.

The last item to go into her car was the box of files she had carried from Judge Ventura's office the day before. For now, she was keeping it in her possession at all times. Stopping at the townhouse, she unloaded the back seat and trunk of her car, before heading to the Police Precinct in Westwood Village.

While she was there, Christine did a quick walk-through of her new home. The utilities had been turned on a few days ago. Her refrigerator, stove, dishwasher, washer and dryer would be delivered tomorrow; on Saturday morning. Yesterday, the movers had placed her furniture, and set up bedframes with the appropriate mattresses. She and Samantha had unpacked almost everything, and made the beds.

It would be good to settle in.

Looking around, she nodded in approval.

This place was a little larger than her place in D.C. She loved the big windows facing the golf course. She had a fireplace, and jets in the garden tub. Each of the bedrooms had its own bath, which would be nice when her mother came to visit. There was also a half-bath for guests who remained on the main floor. The third bedroom, soon to become her office, was almost set up. The bookcases were in place, as was her desk, the computer, and the daybed. For the most part, her new home was ready to move into.

The phone/internet and satellite TV companies were coming tomorrow as well.

Might need to purchase a kitchen rug, a few pictures, and a mirror, she mused. *Definitely need a wastebasket or two. And smoke alarms. And food.*

Maybe Samantha would go with her tomorrow, after the appliances arrived.

On the way back to her car, she pulled out her cell phone, and called the toll-free number for ADT once more. It took just a minute or two to set up an appointment for the technicians to install a monitoring system the next day.

She realized she was looking forward to unpacking her books, and connecting her computer to the D.C. office network.

She knew she would sleep better with a security system installed.

Good. That's done. Now to get to work.

Christine was intently focused on her relocation tasks. Her intuitive, highly-developed instinct to observe and perceive danger in situations around her was benumbed. Recording a final mental list of moving chores on her iPhone, she was unaware of the silver sedan pulling out of an adjacent parking space. Inside, two men were somewhat discernable through the darkly tinted windshield. Not discernable, however, was an eavesdropping cone, attached to a recording device.

As she entered the expressway, settling in for the fifteen minute ride to the Westwood Village police precinct, her cell phone rang. She pressed the answer button on her steering wheel.

"Hello, Spada here."

"Christine, its Pete Lynch. Are you on your way in?"

"Affirmative. Running late this morning. Be there in twenty."

"Are you going by Starbucks?"

"What do you guys want?" she asked, suppressing a laugh.

"I'll text you. You don't mind?"

"No, I'm going anyway. Gotta get my go-juice. But you'll owe me."

"No problem. Got it. We already had two calls this morning. One is a missing girl. Could be a runaway. She fits the profile, but I think you're going to want to check it out anyway. Her home is in Westwood Village, and her father works for Rutger Asami's dealership. He's the manager of Asami's Pre-Owned Luxury car lot."

"Wow. *Another* link to the dealership? And his daughter is missing? What's the other call?"

"We've got a body over in Eastgate."

"Isn't that on the other side of the city? Why did *we* get the call?"

"The detective in charge found something that made him think it was part of our case. From what they said it's a real mess."

"Why the sudden cooperation? Weren't they guarding territory just last week, arguing with Westwood for jurisdiction? I wonder what happened since then?"

"Oh, and that's another thing. Commissioner Walters sent out a city-wide email this morning. Who do you know?"

Christine was baffled. "I'm not sure what you mean."

"He said the entire police department was to, and I'm reading it to you now, 'Provide Special Investigator, Christine Spada, now among us in the field, with your full and complete cooperation. She is an officer from the Federal Bureau of Investigation Office in Washington D.C., with your full and complete cooperation. She has been assigned to the Westwood Village Police Precinct for the next few months. Should she or any of her associates contact you for help or information, you are under direct orders from this office to respond speedily and with full disclosure.' Then, he wrote; get this, 'Treat Agent Spada with the same regard you would provide to myself, or anyone on my staff. This request will be fully enforced.' It's signed, 'Commissioner John Walters, blah, blah, and so on.'" Pete paused. "What d'ya think?"

"Wow."

Lynch paused. "Who do you know?"

"I don't know who I know. I wasn't even sure he would remember me."

"What do you mean? You know him?"

"Well, I went to see Judge Ventura yesterday, to get the federal warrants and orders we need for what we have so far. She and her clerk took me to lunch at Spinners. She also invited the Commissioner, and he came. I'm surprised he remembered me."

"Oh, I see how you are."

"What's that supposed to mean?"

"Nothing."

"Well, I'm at Starbucks now. Text me your order. See you in a few. Spada out."

Christine touched the "end" button on her steering wheel. This was a new turn of events. What had Deputy Director Ben Edwards, her D.C. supervisor, discovered? What had prompted him to make such a call to Anne Ventura?

While she waited in line at the Starbucks drive through to order, she pushed the call button on her steering wheel. "Call Ben Edwards."

"Calling Ben Edwards," her phone responded.

"Can I take your order?" The barista asked over the speaker.

Grabbing her cell phone, she read the text from Pete and Evan. She then gave her own order, adding a breakfast sandwich.

"Hello. Director Edwards, DC."

"Hi Ben. It's Kit. How's your day?"

"Good. What's up, Kiddo?"

"I went to see Anne Ventura yesterday, per your orders. She is just like you said she is. I can see why you told me I should speak with her before trying to work with any other judge."

"Yeah. She's great. She's an old friend."

"She was on the phone with you when I arrived in her office. Is there anything new I need to know?"

There was a pause.

"Ben?"

"Yes."

"What happened in the case? Are you concerned about something?"

"I don't want to scare you, Kit."

"Forewarned is fore-armed you have always told me."

"Just be alert. Watch your back. Try not to be alone."

Kit felt a sudden chill.

"Why?" she said. "Ben, you have to tell me."

"Okay. Okay. We found three more offshore accounts tied to the network. We have frozen two of them. We left one open for our future purposes in this case. Then, yesterday, one of our agents in Chicago was found strangled."

"Williams or Young?"

"Sherry Young."

Kit was silent. Sherry had been a good friend. They had gone through training at the same time. And, no matter how long it had been between their encounters, Sherry had always made her feel as though no time had passed at all. She felt tears rising. Sherry? Strangled?

"And Kit?" Ben was speaking.

"Yes, sir?"

"She was tortured."

61

His words hung in the air, reverberating in her ears, swirling around her, gaining strength. Suddenly, the case had taken on an entirely new dimension.

"But why? Is there more?"

Ben was quiet. His voice dropped to a lower register.

"Kit, we discovered two more channels out of the country. One connects cargo shipments from Los Angeles to Indonesia. The other one.... led us to Iran. And you already know about the India connection."

"Oh," she said, suddenly somber. "So, it's bigger than we thought."

"Yeah," Ben answered. "I want you safe. I've sent you some help. They'll be working for me, until you need them."

"Really? I don't even have office space carved out yet. But then. Well, maybe. But not yet. If I need them, I'll let you know," she told him. "Thanks for asking."

"You know you're like my own daughter."

"I know. You're important to me too. I'll send you the reports. I should have my computer hooked up by tomorrow afternoon. I'm at the precinct now."

"Looking forward to hearing from you. See you soon."

"Yes sir. Thanks. I'm out."

Christine hit the end button on her steering wheel. She grabbed the coffee carrier. A young, uniformed officer was coming out of the precinct as she stepped from her car. She beckoned him over.

"Excuse me," she said. "Are you in a hurry?"

"Not, really, Ms. Spada," came the answer.

Surprised, Christine assessed him. "How do you know my name? Have we met?"

"I don't think so, ma'am," the young man replied shyly. "But one of the guys described your car, and you're the only officer here in a Mercedes."

"I got a really good deal on it," she told him. "Don't go thinking things that aren't so, now. You know where that gets you."

The young man laughed. "Just trying to express a cooperative attitude. After all, Commissioner Walters sent everyone on the Force an email this morning."

"Oh great," she said. "Pete didn't tell me it had gone to everyone." She opened the back door of her car, and leaned in for the file-box.

"I can get that for you, ma'am," he offered.

"No," she groaned, lugging the box out of the back seat. "I can't let this thing out of my sight. But if you would, you could grab my briefcase there, and the bag on the floor ... And the coffee?"

"Sure thing," he answered.

"Thank you," she said. "What's your name?"

"Chase," he said.

"Last or first?"

"Last or first what?"

"Chase. Your name. Is that your first or last name?"

"Oh, first. Chase Stanford is my name."

"Well, Chase Stanford," she said, "Can you help me get these upstairs?"

"Sure thing."

Christine continued, making conversation. "Are you a patrolman in here Westwood Village?"

"Yes, ma'am," he smiled. "But we cover the outskirts of the Village as well. My partner and I are on bike patrol. And I do some of the smaller jobs around the precinct. I also fly helicopter surveillance when I'm needed."

"Bike patrol?" she queried.

"Motorcycles." He stepped behind her into the elevator.

"My Dad was a motorcycle cop," she offered, "before his promotion."

"Wow. What's he doing now?" Chase asked.

"Oh, he's gone now," she answered evasively. "He was the Chief of Detectives in Washington, D.C. for sixteen years."

"Why sixteen?" Chase asked. "I thought the terms were five years long."

Christine looked down. "They are. He was murdered when I was a teenager."

"I'm sorry," he said. "I didn't mean to bring up a sad subject."

"It's all right," she answered.

"Can I asked how it happened?"

"He was shot execution style. It was never solved."

"Man, that's a great reason to go into Law Enforcement," Chase told her. "Have you been able to solve the case of his murder?"

Christine looked at him, assessing.

They exited the elevator on the fourth floor.

"Wow," she said. "That went really deep really fast, didn't it?

"Sorry," Chase replied. "I tend to say things before I think sometimes."

"Well," she answered. "I actually became a crime fighter and investigator because I want to continue his legacy. He was a really great man."

She put the file-box on her desk, next to the adjoining desks of Detectives Lynch and Davies.

"Sorry again, Agent Spada," Chase said. "I'll put these things here on the floor." He put the bags on the floor by Christine's desk. "By the way, Ms. Spada, you wouldn't want to go out with me sometime would you? You know, get a pizza, or take in a movie?"

"Hey Chase," Detective Lynch interjected. "Are you hitting on our resident celebrity?"

"No, not really," he said, somewhat shyly. "I don't mean to. But a guy has to keep trying. You know?"

"Thanks for asking," Christine answered. "But I think I might be a little old for you."

The young man straightened. "I'm twenty-two."

Christine took his hand, and smiled. "I'm thirty-one, Chase," she told him. "But a friendship isn't out of the question."

"I understand," he answered, visibly disappointed. "But hey, can I get your digits?"

"My digits?" she asked puzzled.

"You know, your phone number. As a friend."

Christine smiled at him. "You don't give up, do you?"

"Not hardly," he answered with a twinkle in his eye.

"Okay, but strictly as a friend." Christine gave him her cell phone number. "Don't abuse it."

"I would never do that to you, Agent Spada," he told her. "But... if you're ever bored, and you need a little brother to talk to....." He turned and walked to the elevator, where he pushed the button. Waiting for the doors to open, he looked back over his shoulder.

"Way to go, Spada," Evan said with a chuckle. "He just met you, and you've broken his heart."

"It's what blonde bombshells do," Pete offered, looking her up and down. "And FBI Special Investigator Christine Spada is definitely a blonde bombshell."

"You think so?" Evan asked, amused. "I wasn't sure how to tell."

"Well, look at her," Pete continued, his voice rising, his view focused on Christine. "Tall, but still wears those three and four-inch stripper heels. That makes her eleven feet tall! No wonder she's still single. What man would want to be towered over? Sounds like a defense mechanism to me. She also always wears a suit. Usually a skirt. A tight, straight skirt. Which brings me to her beautiful legs. Attached to a nice, round, firm .... Well. And then there's the two round, firm .... Let's call these her great, round, firm appendages. Top *and* Bottom."

He looked at Evan. "She been here over a week, and they drive me to distraction. Bright blue eyes that look right through you. Drives a killer car. Yeah, this one's definitely a bombshell."

Pete looked expectantly at Christine, hoping for a kidding reaction of some kind. It was then he noticed ear-buds hanging from her ears. Had she even heard what he said?

Of course she had heard, he considered. Hadn't she just been speaking with Chase moments before? But had the ear-buds been there then? Couldn't have been. He had to admit he hadn't noticed. The ear-buds and cords were black, after all.

This would never do.

"Kit!" he shouted. "Can you hear me?"

Christine looked up, faking surprise. "What? Oh, did you call *me?*"

"Yeah," Pete told her. "We just were telling you how you broke poor Chase's heart."

Christine pulled the ear-buds from her ears. "My *friends* call me Kit, Detective," she said.

"Yes, Agent," he replied, with attitude. "Kit is what I called you."

"Oh, nay, nay, nay, Detective. My friends don't talk about my legs, or my ass, or my chest. So, that friend list? You can't be on it now."

"I don't understand."

"My friend list. You are now shunned."

He looked down at his hands. "Apparently you heard me. Can't you take what I said as a compliment? I thought we had an understanding."

"I thought we did too, but apparently you have a bit to learn about integrity when it comes to having a friendship. When I am someone's friend, I don't make cynical observations like that. It's called having professional ethics."

Pete was incredulous. "Are you serious right now? You must have an awfully high opinion of yourself!"

Christine looked at him evenly, never taking her eyes from his face. "Wow. What do you say about me when I'm not here?"

Pete opened his mouth to answer. Christine's hand raised with an open palm in front of her. "Just a second. When I was assigned this post, I specifically asked for support personnel who had no issue with the gender of their person-in-charge."

"Christine," said Evan. "Come on! He was kidding!"

"Seriously?" she asked. "You are defending him? I think I just decided not to join your Men's Club. I ain't now, nor will I ever be, 'one of the boys.' So please, for your own sake, get over yourself. My tight, round 'appendages' are not here for you to drool over."

Evan wanted to push the point. "Agent Spada, where's your sense of humor? Aren't you a people person?"

She smiled faintly. "Well, now that you ask, I *am* a people person. I'm just not a *stupid* people person, Detective. Hey, we haven't even really started this case yet. How about if I just make a call and request a new team? I'm sure you guys would much rather go back to your prior assignments than finish this case with little-ol'-me."

She pulled the ear-buds from her ears and placed them back in her purse. "May I have the address for the Eastgate body, please, gentlemen?"

Stunned, Pete drew in a breath. Silently, watching her, he picked up a file from his desk, and offered it.

"Thank you," she said, taking it. "Now, what about we put this behind us and get some work done on this case today? And if the two of you still want to be part of the Bureau Taskforce, let me suggest you go to the Asami car dealership, and interview the Dad of the missing teen."

She looked at both of them with a kind smile. "And oh, enjoy your coffee."

Taking her own coffee from the carrier, she moved to her desk. Coolly, she pulled three of the most pertinent missing person's files, and handed them to Evan. "Detective Davies, I would appreciate it if you would organize the search teams for these three localities. I believe they are three distinctly different warrants, but are the most pressing at the moment. We need to conduct all three of these searches early Monday morning."

Evan looked at her blankly. "Yes, Ma'am," was all he found himself able to say. "Sorry ma'am. I'll get right on that." He paused. "Do you still want me to go with Pete to the dealership?"

Christine did not look up. "Yes, that would be fine, Davies. You can organize the search parties when you return. We will be working on the rest of these searches and interviews for some time."

Dumbfounded, Pete watched her sit down at her desk, and begin reviewing the file on Erin's disappearance.

Crap, he thought to himself. *I did it again. I am definitely not good with women. Especially this one.*

Opening a drawer, he grabbed his revolver, made sure it was loaded, and put it in his shoulder holster. He checked his supply of ammunition, just in case. Then, he stood and put on his jacket.

Then, for just a moment, standing at his desk, he watched Christine quietly. He had met a lot of women in his time, but he was realizing this one was different. All of the women he had ever known, his mother and grandmother included, would have retorted to his sexual comments with a few of their own, continuing a sort of brash and bawdy banter. Most would have at least laughed and encouraged more conversation along the same lines.

But not Agent Spada.

Not Christine.

She was puzzling. A moment ago she had been speaking fiery words, pushing back against perceived prejudice and harassment. Her challenge regarding his ethics and integrity had stung him. Had he really been unethical? Wasn't it normal for all men to tease women the way he had, using sexual humor?

But, he concluded, for him it hadn't really been about ethics at all.

For some reason, the idea of having hurt this woman bothered him. Apparently, Christine Spada was a woman he could respect. Even though, so far, there was a gentle vulnerability about her.

Was it a good idea to respect someone without his anger or ego being part of it? He didn't know. It was a new idea to him that someone could have no hidden agenda. Was this the authentic girl – or would a mask come off some time in the future?

Standing there, Pete considered. The conflict had stirred something inside of him he had never felt before. It was inexplicable. For some reason, he wanted to protect her. To keep her safe.

Was he developing a weakness, he wondered?

Evan nudged him. "You ready partner?"

"Sure. Let's go."

Evan handed him his coffee, and then moved to the elevator.

"Thanks," said Pete. Still watching Christine, he walked to her desk, and stopped when he was standing next to her.

"I'm sorry," he offered.

"Okay," she answered, continuing to write, not looking up.

"No, Christine; I mean, Agent," he said, looking down at the floor. "I wasn't aware of the effect of my words. No woman I have ever known has responded the way you just did. And what you said was right. So I'm sorry. After hearing your responses, I realize I don't know how to tell someone they interest me. I was wrong to say those things."

Christine decided to look up, still feeling somewhat defensive. She had started to interrupt him, to correct him for using her first name; but seeing his face, she realized he was sincere. Putting down her pen, she waited for him to finish speaking.

"Thank you, Detective Lynch," she said. "I appreciate that."

"You're welcome," he answered. "And if it's alright, I'd like to remain on the team you're building."

"I was hoping you still felt that way. Captain Edwards said you are one of his best."

Pete was surprised. "Really. That's surprising." He stepped away from the desk. "Are you working here all day?"

"No," she answered. "I'm headed to Eastgate after I've read the file. And then, I have an appointment with the medical examiner. "

"You want company?"

"Sure, if you guys are done by then," she told him. "See how good a read you can get on the Asami dealership while you're there. There has to be something about someone over there that's connected to this whole thing...."

"Will do. See you later."

"Thanks. Spada out."

Chapter Six

Christine arrived at the Eastgate precinct an hour later. After connecting with the patrol officers who were first to the scene, she made a second stop. After the initial responders, one of the Eastgate detectives had called the Westwood Village precinct to connect the body to the federal case.

Senior Detective Eric Janzen had been a city detective for nineteen years. At his temples, his hair was graying. Cropped on top, his hair provided a hint of his prior career as a Special Investigator for the Navy. He'd lost count of the cases he had helped solve, and the number of international miles he had travelled.

He greeted Christine with a bright smile.

"Agent Spada!" he exclaimed. "I've heard so many good things about you! It's so good to finally put a face with the name. Ben has talked about you for years!"

Christine was surprised. "You know Ben, my boss? Ben Edwards?"

"Oh, he didn't prep you, did he? The old goat." Detective Janzen laughed. "We were in the Navy together. In fact, when he left to join the Bureau, I joined the JAG Corps as a Special Investigator. We've been friends for years."

"And now you work for the City of Greenway?" she asked.

He nodded. "You know, after a while police work is all the same. You get a lead and run it down. You solve the puzzle and move to the next case. Hopefully, you don't get shot or sliced along the way. Doesn't really matter who you work for. As long as they're on the right side of the law."

Christine smiled. "My Dad used to say something like that."

Eric looked at her kindly. "Is he in police work too?"

For the second time that day, she uttered the words. "He was Chief of Detectives in Washington, D.C. for sixteen years; most of my childhood. He was murdered when I was fifteen. The case was never solved."

The older man patted her arm. "I'm sorry, dear girl. I remember when my own father died. No matter when it happens, it is a hard day."

He paused, thinking. Poor kid. It was time to re-direct. "You want a cup of coffee?"

"Thank you, no," she replied. "I just finished some."

"Something cold then?"

"That would be lovely. Thank you for the offer."

Eric Janzen ushered her into his office and shut the door. He opened a small refrigerator. "Now, let's see," he said. "I have Coca-Cola, Dr. Pepper, Sprite and Arizona Green Tea. Oh, and Diet Coke."

"I'll take the Diet Coke, please," she answered.

The detective took a tea for himself, and handed the Diet Coke to the now seated Christine.

"Before we move on to the case, can I ask you one more question?"

"Sure," she told him, opening her drink.

"What was your Dad's name?"

"Spada. Antonio Spada."

Detective Janzen face showed visible surprise and wonder.

"Tony?" he exclaimed. "You're Tony Spada's kid? Which one are you?"

"I'm Kit. The second girl. I have one sister older and one sister younger, and then my two brothers came much later. How did you know my Dad?"

"We worked on a few cases together when I was in DC. We had one involving a Congressman and an outlaw biker club. Now, that one's a story, baby."

He stopped and looked at her, shaking his head. "Tony Spada's little Kit?! Can't believe how small the world is. I came to your house for dinner several times when you were little. Your hair was the same color then that it is right now. Wow, how you've grown up!"

"How old was I then?" she wanted to know.

"Oh, I remember you the first time I came to the house. You were six or seven I would say. But I think the last time I saw Tony, or you, was on your fifteenth birthday, or at his funeral."

Without warning, Christine's mind was flooded with a mental image of her fifteen-year birthday cake. The candles were lit. Her Mom was standing behind her, and her father was seated just across the family dining room table. Leaning up against the wall was his closest friend, a Navy man; "Uncle" Jannie. She closed her eyes, watching the memory unfold until the candles went out and everyone was clapping. Tearing, she opened her eyes. Too much loss.

She looked at the detective. "Are you Uncle Jannie?"

Eric laughed. "I haven't been called that since the last time I saw *you!*"

"Did you ever get married?"

"Well, this job tended to treat my wives like they were the other woman!" he answered. "After three times with a woman, I decided it's too much to ask a lady to share her husband with the job. So it's just me and Lady Justice."

"I don't know how my Mom did it," Christine mused. "Any kids?"

"One son," Eric told her. "He's from my third marriage. He's eleven, going on twenty-five. His name is Edward..... So, how old are you now?"

"Thirty-one and single," she told him.

"Sometime, Kit, when you're ready, I'd like to hear about how you've been doing; catch up on our lives. For some reason, I've been thinking about Tony, your Dad, a lot lately. Seems like a sign our paths crossed."

Her interest piqued, Christine nodded. "Okay, Jannie. Maybe you could come for dinner when I'm settled into my townhouse."

"You're moving here? To Greenway?" he asked.

"I'm the present face of the Bureau here – at least for the time being."

"Oh," he said. "*You're the one* spear-heading the training for a new field office."

"What makes you say that?" she asked.

He shrugged. "I hear things. And I've just been around awhile," he told her. "That's why Commissioner John Walters sent out the email this morning. He's paving the way for the FBI."

"Oh, I see," Christine said. "That makes sense."

Eric laughed easily. "Can you tell me what this case is about?"

"I really don't have all the details yet. We are still in the learning stages. I'm not sure any of us know how big it is. Even the guys in DC. What I do know to tell would take too long today," she answered carefully. "But if we could talk about the body your people found, that would help me. There's so much I need to know. I'm sure you can identify with me, with all the experience you've had. The work load on this thing is becoming unbelievable."

A little subdued, the detective responded quickly. "Oh, sure thing. I get it. Let me get my keys. I'll take you to see the woman who found the body, and then we can go to the crime scene. Did you bring the file I sent over with you?"

"I have it right here."

"Okay. Good."

For the following three hours, Christine rode with Eric Janzen in his Crown Victoria, unmarked sedan. She met a series of individuals, none of whom were directly related to the case, but each of whom had been tragically connected with the dead body.

There was Rosa; the hotel maid. She had unlocked a double-door suite at the Best Western Hotel, expecting to do a routine cleaning. When she walked into the bathroom, she first screamed, and then experienced a panic attack. Another maid had come running to find her huddled in a fetal position, unable to breathe.

Had she seen anyone else around the room? No.

Observed anything suspicious? No.

Had she seen the occupant of the room the day or night before? She didn't think so, but who could have possibly known? The face on the body had been unrecognizable.

They had gone from Rosa's home to the Best Western. The crime scene had been taped off, to prevent evidence tampering. The Crime Lab had already done a thorough sweep of the room. The body had been taken to the Medical Examiner for an autopsy.

Janzen told Christine he thought it looked like the person had been strangled, but he wasn't sure.

"Was the person male or female?" Christine asked.

Janzen shrugged. "We couldn't tell."

"What do you mean? Why couldn't…"

"The body was mutilated. You know."

"I know there was dismemberment," she answered. "I saw the pictures. But I would think the genitals would still have been visible for identification."

Eric looked at her. "Kit, listen. I know you saw the pictures. They don't show the inhumanity of this massacre. It was grisly. I've been doing this job for almost forty years now. I've never seen a human body so… well, destroyed. There was blood everywhere. And look at this carpet!"

Christine appraised the scene. Apparently, the murder had taken place on the bed. Somehow, the body had been transported to the bathroom. Piece by piece?

"What do *you* think happened, Jannie?" she asked.

"The victim was checked in as Masters. No first name, just a surname. The address is international; somewhere in India. The number given was non-existent.

"In my opinion, whoever did this made it personal. Or the person is a sociopath who kills just to feel something. There is such rage here. Some profilers might say it was an act of passion, but I don't know. It feels cold to me.

"The killer piled the body parts in the bathtub. It feels macabre to me; almost like whoever did it is warning others in the circle. But then again, how could someone do something like this and *not* be cold? I'm not sure the killer didn't hold on to a body part or two; like for a trophy, or even to use as a warning. It looked like there were pieces missing to me."

Christine shuddered. She agreed with Jannie. The scene did feel cold. Like steel. Like ice. She hoped she would be able to sleep tonight. He waited while she inspected the room, looking for any evidence the Crime Lab might have left behind.

"What are these large puddles around the bed in splatter positions, Jannie? What caused them?"

"I noticed those. It's possible they were the product of blood spurting when the legs were removed," he told her.

75

"But the person would have to still be alive when they were cut apart for the spray to get this far," she reasoned. "And the killer would have been *covered* in blood if that were true. Wouldn't that mean there would be more blood on the bed? It's just such an unusual spray pattern."

She took her iPhone out of her pocket, and took pictures of the blood splatter.

"You have a pocket knife, Jannie?" she asked.

"Sure," he answered, pulling it out of his pocket, and handing it to her.

"Thanks." Christine took it. She got down on her knees and cut out a square of the carpet where the blood splatters had stained.

"What's that for?" Jannie asked.

"I just want to know how much blood made these stains," she answered. "If the stains are all the way through, then your theory is most probably correct. If not, they must have happened another way. By the way, what made you think this was related to our case in Westwood?"

"Oh, yeah!" Detective Janzen exclaimed. "I forgot! I'm getting too old for this stuff, Kit!" He pulled two small evidence bags from his jacket pocket. "I pulled these from the evidence log for you, and I sent the rest of it over to Westwood."

Christine looked up from what she was doing. "What did you bring me?"

Janzen held the bags where she could see them. "One is a car key; one of those pushbutton things. We dusted it for prints, but found nothing. It's from Asami Motors. The other is a smart phone, with a case that looks like it belonged to a teenage girl. The two items just seemed to tie the body to your case."

"Wow. Thanks, Jannie. Give me a minute to finish here."

Christine worked for another fifteen minutes, before she spotted something on the carpet. "Jannie!" she cried. "Look at this!"

The detective came next to where she stood. He squatted down. "Whatcha got?"

Christine reached into her pocket and pulled out a small metal box. Opening it, she pulled out a pair of tweezers and a two-inch Ziploc bag. Very slowly, very carefully, she picked up a chunk of something from the middle of a blood puddle stain on the carpet. Meticulously, she dropped the chunk in the bag.

"I don't know," she answered. "It could be a leftover from a meal. But my guess is the body was shredded when it was cut apart. I bet the DNA of this chunk of meat matches the victim."

Her cell phone rang.

"Hello. Spada here."

"Hi Agent Spada. It's Detective Lynch. We finished the interview, and made a sweep of the missing girl's home. Found out some really interesting information. Can't wait to share it."

"That's great," she said.

"You can't talk, can you?"

"That's a great observation, Lynch."

"Do you want me to meet you at the Medical Examiner's office?" Pete asked. "Or, I can come where you are right now, if you aren't sure it's safe."

"I'll meet you there in twenty minutes. Text me the address."

"Yes ma'am!" came the reply. "You sure you're okay? See you in a few."

"Thanks, Lynch. Spada out."

Sarah McMillan had had a very busy couple of days. In addition to her normal case load, which was considerable in anyone's frame of reference, she was voluntarily keeping watch over a traumatized seven-year-old boy.

It had been the right thing to do. Her instincts had proven true once more.

Especially now that the FBI was involved. They had "suggested" protective custody for the boy. Sarah had given some pushback, simply because she sensed it would drive Caleb deeper into his psychosis. She wanted to be the one to take the time to help him unravel reality from his hallucinations. But, after a long conversation with a Ben Edwards, Deputy Director of the FBI, she agreed the boy needed someone to stand guard outside his hospital room twenty-four hours a day. For now, it would be a uniformed police officer.

The boy was now a material witness in an issue of national importance. He needed to be protected.

"But, if we create too much stimulation in his life," Sarah told Edwards, "especially since all he has known is isolation, we could lose the opportunity to glean the information you need."

Deputy Edwards had listened to her. He had also recommended that when Caleb left the hospital, he stay with her until the case was closed. He was sending an additional protection detail, he told her. He didn't want her to be afraid, however. And then, he had explained to her the FBI's reasons for raising the national priority level of the case.

Caleb had seen things and could identify individuals who might not be captured without his testimony. His memories were vital to the solving of the puzzle.

As a result, Sarah had made some decisions of her own. Ben Edwards had helped her to gain a better understanding of the dangers surrounding the case. She had ended the call, sensing a hyper-vigilant awareness having been stirred within her. She wanted to protect the boy from the criminals, but also, she decided from exploitation. It would be easy for someone in Law Enforcement to see Caleb simply as a tool to be used and exploited just to solve the crime. Such an approach could destroy his hope of a normal future.

She was not an "at any cost" advocate. The seven year old's life was too precious for that.

Even after the case was closed, Sarah knew Caleb would need years of therapy. He would also need a semi-permanent, therapeutic, foster home where he could develop into a healthy adult, without the typical emotional distancing and hardening which happened to most foster kids.

Adoption would be a better option. With people who knew how to help traumatized kids like this.

Why weren't more homes for kids like Caleb available, she wondered in frustration? He would need constant one-on-one for a long time if they were to steer him clear of a difficult adult life.

She would certainly need to make sure whatever foster parents he was placed with received a more intense, personal screening than usual. A lot would have to fall into place before she let this child leave her side.

Sarah glanced over at the boy. Still asleep.

He had experienced night terrors the night before. The medical staff had sedated him around two in the morning. As a result, Caleb had slept longer than she had expected.

Staying in the hospital room with him, she had been able to rest for a few hours since then. She had made careful notes of his dreamtime mumblings.

Interestingly enough, the boy had not stuttered in his sleep.

Her colleague, Louisa, had been kind enough to retrieve some of Sarah's clothing and toiletries from the supervisor's apartment. Her laptop, briefcase, and current case files had already been in the trunk of her car when they had rescued Caleb that morning.

After Caleb was settled into his room, Sarah had set up a temporary office of sorts, in the room next to his bed. She planned to camp out at the hospital for a long time. She had already delegated several of her more urgent cases to other social workers on her team.

For now, Caleb would need consistent comfort, care and kindness. He would need lots of her time. He had never learned what it meant to trust anyone. So, it would be a gradual process, taking dedicated effort. She knew from experience that if any shreds of his emotional quotient were to survive the strong imprinting that neglect and abuse had inflicted, the work would be long and intensive.

Sarah had become a social worker to do this very thing, she reflected. To rescue the "at-risks"... the physically and emotionally endangered.

The cast-offs. The innocents.

Her mind reviewed the number of children her team had saved from abuse just over the past twelve months. For their small office, the number was over nine hundred. However, she knew those few represented a small part of a burgeoning need on the national and international levels.

She had read the current national report just last week. What had the statistic been? Some eight hundred and ninety-nine thousand children had been rescued during the prior year from various kinds of abuse in the United States alone.

It still weighed greatly on her mind that eighty-five percent of saved children had been under the age of four.

"Every time we rescue a child, we are preventing the development of a criminal," the state director had told her.

Sarah agreed. If just one rescue could prevent the development of another serial killer or sexual deviant, she was happy to have made a difference.

Thinking back over the past two days, she realized just how tired she really was. But then, she sensed her awareness of Caleb's needs overriding her weariness.

What exactly had this boy experienced in just seven short years? Whatever it was, it had been outside any realm she'd ever heard of.

Thinking ahead of the day, she knew the hours would be filled with exams, tests, and interviews. Per Ben Edwards' instructions, she was to keep written records of all of Caleb's interactions.

She made a mental note to ask permission to take him to the Greenway Children's Zoo. Officer Summerfield had said he had asked to go.

She doubted he had ever even seen such a place.

Chapter Seven

Erin dozed in and out of sleepiness.

Still groggy, she couldn't remember what day it was. What time was it? Had she slept through her alarm? Had Dad left early for work, and not stirred her?

She already missed her Mom. She could feel it. Coffee would have been nice right now.

She shifted her position. Her wrist hurt. How long had she been holding it above her head in this position?

She pulled on her arm, still not quite awake.

Ouch. Something was caught. Opening her eyes, her awareness rising, she turned her head in exploration. Why would her hand would not obey her?

Then she remembered her abduction.

She no longer had a bag over her head.

Erin touched her mouth, feeling for the remnants of adhesive. None were found.

She looked down. Someone had undressed her, and re-clothed her in a nightgown. A fancy, satin nightgown. She hoped it hadn't been the man who had held a knife to her throat.

Just the thought made her feel violated.

She looked around the room. It was dimly lit, and there were blackout curtains on the windows. She tried to sit up, her final goal being to get off the bed. Something made a clinking sound.

Handcuffs?

Someone had handcuffed her left arm to the vertical side rails of the brass twin headboard.

"Sh—shh! Please," groaned a female voice from the other side of the room.

Erin started. Another girl was in the room with her!

"Sorry," she answered. "What's your name?"

"My *real* name, or my new name?" the unseen girl wanted to know.

"Your new name?" Erin echoed, not sure what was meant by such a phrase.

"Angelica," her roommate answered.

Realizing she had received the girl's new name, Erin asked, "What is your real name?"

"I'm Sandy Zarduc. Did they let you keep your phone? Can you help me call my parents?"

"No such luck," Erin replied. "I was about to ask you if I could call mine. I'm Erin Kasabian, by the way."

"You're making that up," Angelica groaned in return. "That's too fancy a name."

"No, honest to God, that's my name. How long have you been here?"

"I've been here almost five weeks. And I think I've taken all the classes. When did you get here?" Angelica asked.

"I don't know," Erin said. "Last thing I remember was a man holding a knife to my throat, and then a bag over my head."

"Did they come in the middle of the night?"

"Yes, did they with you?"

"No, but they did with the girl who was here when I came," Angelica told her. "Apparently, they have a lot of different ways to take girls our age. For me, it started with an email. I was posting sexy pictures of myself on my Facebook page, and Pinterest, and this guy messaged me. We started talking."

Erin thought about what she was hearing. She swallowed hard. "Have they taken a lot of girls?" she asked hoarsely.

"I think so," came the answer. "Katie, the girl before me, said they steal us to sell us, and they are good at it. They've been doing it a long time."

Erin felt a lump rise in her throat. "To sell us?" she whispered. "To who? For what?"

"To rich men, or anybody with the money, really. For sex, or whatever they want," Angelica told her. "Compared to the groups who steal girls in Asia and Africa, we are treated pretty well. But that was just what Katie told me. I think they told her that. I have no idea if that's true. Every time I come back to this room, they handcuff me to the bedframe."

"Who are they?" Erin asked.

"I've never seen the faces on any of them," Angelica answered. "Except for my handler, and Ms. Anastasia; but I'm sure that's not *her* real name. You'll see. Now, if you don't mind, they kept me up for hours in a class last night. And I know they will be coming for me soon. I need to get some sleep."

"Okay," Erin answered. "Sorry."

She paused. "Oh, Angelica?"

"What is it?"

"You said 'classes.' What kind of classes?"

"Oh," groaned Angelica. "The give us classes on *everything*. Now go to sleep. You'll see. But when they come for you, you're going to wish you had slept."

"Okay. Thanks."

Angelica fluffed her pillow, and tried to become comfortable once more. She closed her eyes, and tried to make herself go back to sleep.

Erin sat in the shadows, listening to Angelica's breathing as it evened out and finally became rhythmic. She squinted in the dimness, trying to assess the prison she was sitting in. From what she could tell, it was a bedroom. In what felt like a house. The room appeared to be well apportioned, just like a bedroom in one of the wealthier homes in her own neighborhood. The floors were carpeted. A bathroom was attached. No clocks were visible. The glow from the bathroom nightlight bulb provided dim illumination to where she was sitting.

She couldn't see her belongings anywhere.

She was naked under the nightgown.

Just exactly who had *seen* her naked, she wondered?

Erin had tried to sleep naked only one time before in her lifetime. She hated it. She liked her t-shirts and Old Navy pajama pants.

"They steal us to sell us and they're good at it," Angelica had said.

Erin shuddered. *"For sex or whatever they want."* The phrases haunted her.

She put her hand to her lips once more. Wow. What nerve! They had removed her lip piercings! And her tongue bar was gone as well! She put her hand to her stomach. At least they had left her navel piercing. And her nose stud was still in place.

83

Who *were* these people?

She felt dishonored. They hadn't respected her rights!

Didn't they realize who her *Dad* was? And how many guns he owned? And oh.........! There would be hell to pay when Mom found out what these idiots had done! If Dad didn't kill somebody first.

Come to think of it, if her parents didn't do anything, her boyfriend would! He *loved* her! They had made plans together. He would be concerned the minute he didn't get a text from her to say "good morning."

The minute she didn't answer his call, he would call the cops.

She wished she had her cell phone.

Garrett would save her.

What kind of people would break into a house and steal a *person?* What could they possibly hope to gain?

Unexpectedly, Erin heard noises outside the bedroom door. For a moment, she froze. Then, thinking better of it, she scooted down under the covers, and closed her eyes. If someone came in, she would pretend to be asleep.

Was someone knocking? Really?

Who had ever heard of a *polite* kidnapper?

Then the door opened.

Erin tensed, and tried to lay still.

Someone came into the room, and approached her. Then they moved away. Probably to check on Angelica.

Erin had seen a lot of cop shows. She decided to listen for clues, and then try to get away as soon as she could.

"Angelica?" a man's voice spoke softly. "Angelica."

Erin listened as the man apparently sat down on the other girl's bed. She listened carefully to the man's voice. Perhaps she could identify him later if she could memorize his voice.

"Angelica?" he repeated. "It's time to wake up. Today is your big day. You fly out tonight. You need to get up now."

The girl across the room stirred. "What time is it?" she asked.

"It's a little after six," he answered. "Sweetheart, you have to get ready. You get your final makeover today. And tomorrow? You will be with your Prince Charming."

"Really?" Angelica asked.

"Yes, really," the man answered. "I told you. You're going to have a good life now. Just help us to help you."

"I can't believe it!" Angelica declared. From the rustle of fabric, Erin assumed she had reached out and hugged him. "You have been so good to me, Garrett."

Stunned with realization, Erin gasped.

"You're so beautiful, Angelica," he was saying. "You deserve someone so much better off than me. You're going to live like a queen."

"I'm so glad I met you, Garrett," the girl replied.

In the shock of her discovery, Erin experienced an emotional stab of real fear. The dire peril of her situation was beginning to sink in.

Her hopes for rescue sank.

Garrett?

Garrett was one of *them*.

How long would it take for someone... *anyone*... to discover she was missing?

Saturday morning began early for Christine Spada. After packing the rest of her belongings from the hotel in the back seat and trunk of her car, she checked out of the hotel. On her way to her new townhouse, she went through the drive-through at Starbucks for breakfast. Samantha would be meeting her at the townhouse at eight. Getting to the house early would give her a little time to enjoy the place, and think things through.

In actuality, there were only a few boxes left. Her forensic textbooks and field manuals were research supplies she was discovering she desperately needed. She could feel some of her silent suspicions melding together, forming semi-concrete conclusions in the present case.

Her priority today would center on making her home workplace usable. Monday morning would arrive before she knew it. And Monday morning would mark the true beginnings of the investigation.

It was during her wait outside the Starbucks window, Kit's attention was drawn to a black SUV with tinted windows waiting in line two cars behind her.

Typical surveillance. Who had tailed her?

Couldn't the Commissioner just let her do her job?

She smiled slyly. She knew from experience whoever was inside the vehicle couldn't back up, and certainly wouldn't try to leave it. So, she decided to have a little fun. She checked the safety on her service pistol, and tucked it into the back waistband of her belted shorts, just in case. She jumped out of her car. Moving towards the SUV, her back against the building, she kept her eyes on the black vehicle's windshield.

Who had been assigned to follow her, and why?

As she reached the window over the back seat of the sedan immediately behind her in the line, the SUV driver's, tinted window lowered. Momentarily, Kit stopped, not sure whether she would see the barrel of a gun or a uniform.

But it was a familiar face that smiled back at her.

"Hey Kit! What's a nice girl like you doing in a place like this?"

"Josh!? Is that you?" Kit relaxed her posture, recognizing her former partner, Joshua Morgan, from the D.C. office. "You jerk! Who's with you?"

She made her way to his open window.

"Ramirez," he told her, laughing.

Christine had reached the SUV. She leaned on the open driver window. "Hey Felipe!" she exclaimed. "What are you guys doing here?"

They laughed. "We're waiting for you to get your coffee, for one thing."

"And?" she probed.

Josh smiled. "We arrived last week. Ben sent us."

"To help with the investigation?" she asked.

"Sure. And to protect. You, the boy, the team." Josh looked at her evenly. "To use the boss's words; 'there's too much at stake here.' And, Ben wanted us to inform you of some changes in person, and help."

"Sounds like a plan," Kit answered. "Say..."

A voice surprised her. "Hey, Lady!" the woman in the sedan behind hers was yelling. "Do you plan to talk to your boyfriend all day, or could you see your way to get your coffee? I've got to get to work!"

"Oh," Christine answered, face turning red, suddenly flustered. "Sorry." To her co-workers, she said, "I'm headed to my new townhouse. Follow me?"

She turned to return to her car.

"That's what we've been doing!" Felipe remarked out of his own window.

"I'm really sorry," Christine told the angry woman in the car as she hurried by.

"I get it. And it's fine," the lady snapped. "I'm just really late for work. The cashier has put her head out to look for you twice now."

Christine got into her car, apologetically paid the barista for her breakfast, and pulled forward into the parking lot, where she waited for Josh and Felipe to receive their own coffees.

Twenty minutes later, she pulled in to her assigned parking space at the townhouse, with the two agent-friends following. A few minutes after that, she unlocked the front door of her new home.

Josh and Felipe helped her in unloading her car, and then immediately went out to their SUV to "grab" a few things. While they were busy, Kit began arranging her computer, monitors, speakers, and the other electronics needed in her home office. They had been pulled from the boxes earlier in the week, when she and Samantha had worked together. She had postponed arranging things until now.

"Hey, Kit?" Josh's voice was heard upon entering once again. "Where are you?"

"In here; the office," Kit answered. She looked up to see Josh and Felipe with a box marked, "Fernando's Stuff."

"What's that?" she asked.

Josh put his finger to his lips, and signaled to her. "A gift from Ben."

Kit's eyes widened in surprise. Not understanding completely, she asked, "What is it?"

"Oh, this is just the first one. There's more in the car. You want to help?" Felipe asked.

They motioned for her to follow them outside.

"Sure," she answered. "What did he send me?"

"You'll see," Josh answered mysteriously. "It's a surprise."

"Then lead the way," she told them.

Silently, the threesome made their way out to the walkway, then to the black SUV, parked across the parking lot.

"Get in," Josh told her quietly, looking furtively around.

As soon as they were all in the car, Felipe reached into a second box, and pulled out a small black box. Extending its antenna, he pushed a series of numbers into its keypad. He waited for three beeps.

"Okay," he sighed, looking at Josh. "We can talk now." He looked at Kit. "It scrambles sound frequencies, so if we are being bugged, our conversation's signal is broken, and can't be traced."

Kit looked at them incredulously. "What is going on?"

Josh looked at her squarely. "Ben wants us to keep you safe. After Sherry went down, he doesn't want us taking any chances, or making any assumptions.

"Felipe and I have been here in Greenway since you left for London; what; six weeks ago? We've been tailing you for three days. We have been watching your movements, looking for anything out of the ordinary."

He pointed through the darkly tinted side window of his vehicle. "You see that silver sedan?"

"Yes," she answered. "I think the guys who drive it live in my unit. I've been really careful. Honest."

Josh put his hands up in front of him, so as to prevent a conflict. "I'm sure you have. And you've noticed, it is driven by two guys. We've been watching them too. They *don't* live here in your neighborhood. We followed them back to the Village yesterday. It's a new address. Looks like a private residence on Biarritz. That particular house is not under surveillance yet. They apparently are part of the network in the case you're working on.

"What's more, they have been following you. I don't know exactly how they do it, but they change cars every day."

"Okay," she said. "What do they want?"

"We don't know yet," Josh answered. "But after you left two night ago, they jimmied your locks, and were inside your townhouse. They came back for several hours yesterday, while you were in Eastgate. Ben thinks they planted listening devices, and perhaps cameras. We think it might be part of their standard practice, and an explanation for how they stayed one step ahead of us in Chicago. It would also explain how Sherry was compromised."

"I still can't believe she's gone," Kit told them.

"I know," Felipe told her. "I missed her killers by just minutes. She was still alive when I got there." He looked at Kit with pain in his eyes. "She was a real mess. They had really gone after information. She told me she hadn't told them anything, and to tell her little boy she loved him. And then she was gone." His eyes misted.

Josh lowered his voice. "It's okay. You did your best, partner."

Still focused and aware, Josh resumed the conversation. "This morning, I'm going to conduct a full sweep of your house for bugs and bombs, and Felipe is going to set up your computer system." He pointed to the boxes in the back of the SUV. "We brought some extra goodies for you, since Ben also wants us to make sure no tracking or transmitting hardware has been somehow added to your computer tower. He wants that accomplished before we network your system with theD.C.servers."

"Also," Felipe added, "someone needs to stay with you for protection. Ben said it should be one of us."

"I have to check on the Morrow boy, and report back to Ben," Josh told her, "and I know in my gut that little guy will need our protection. So, since Felipe is the geek between the two of us, he will be camping out in your office for the remainder of the case. He will be working on setting you up with a full blown field office, small as it might be."

Kit looked from one of her colleagues to the other. She was flooded with gratitude. They were such good partners and friends.

"Absolutely," she said. "Felipe, I have a daybed in the office, and we'll make it up for you. I haven't gone to the grocery yet, so you'll have to tell me what you like to eat."

Josh smiled and winked at Felipe. "She's a great cook, too," he told his partner. "And Ben said we would need a cover story."

Kit eyed Felipe, then Josh. "Oh really? And just what did Ben have in mind?"

"It's all set," Josh told her. "Felipe is your IT repair/video gaming fiancé who doesn't like to go out of the house. We have his alternate ID all set up. Oh, and there is an arsenal of firearms in the last box in the back here. We have marked everything with the words "Fernando's Stuff," so it looks like he is just now arriving, to move in with you.

"Ben came up with your new fiancé's name. It is Fernando Rafaello. Since Felipe has monograms on many of his belongings, we decided to let him keep his initials. He works from home. You are very much in love, so you will have to put on an act in any public setting. We posted pictures of him on your Facebook account, and fabricated a story about how you met. For those who have been watching you, I'm his best friend who is dropping him off. He will need to use your car."

For the next few minutes, Josh and Felipe briefed Christine on her new "fiance's" cover story.

"After we get rid of the bugs in your townhouse, we will be able to talk more freely," Josh told her. "We can also use the scrambler when needed. I think we should go back in now, and get some real work done."

"Sounds like a plan," Kit answered. "I have a friend arriving to help me unpack, at any moment. Her name is Samantha. She is a clerk for the federal judge Ben sent me to get warrants and orders from."

An hour later, Samantha arrived. She had brought bagels and cream cheese, and a half-gallon of apple juice.

"Just thought you might need the carbs," she told Christine when the door opened.

"Oh, you're a lifesaver!" Kit told her. "Come on in. My fiancé arrived last night, with his best friend, Josh. I'd love to introduce you!"

Sam was surprised. "You didn't tell me you were engaged," she replied. "In fact, if I remember, you said you weren't dating anyone."

Kit shrugged. "Sorry about that. We're a pretty private couple. I guess it's hard for me to trust new people."

Sam passed it off. "I get it. I don't think I'd want my life 'out there' if I was a federal agent."

They were standing in Kit's office. "Hey, Sweetheart," Kit said to "Fernando." "This is my new friend, Samantha. She's the one I was telling you about."

Felipe looked up, nonchalant. "Hey, good to meet you," he said. "Thanks for helping my girl! Just setting up my video gaming system."

Kit laughed. "He is so into computers. He writes games, and tests games, and does IT repair. I'm not sure I even remember how we got together sometimes."

Samantha smiled. She extended her hand as she looked at Josh. "And you are?"

"Oh, I'm Josh," he replied. "I used to work with Kit in DC. I'm just helping her get set up here for a few weeks. Fernando needed a ride, so here we are. He just couldn't seem to live without her."

Kit looked at Sam. "So, you want to help me set up my resource books today? And I thought we could unpack the DVD's and get rid of all the boxes."

"I'm in," Samantha told her. "And next Saturday, it's my turn. You have to come to the gym with me. Have you ever done Zumba?"

"I've done dance cardio," Kit answered. "But I've always wanted to try Zumba."

"Yeah," Sam said. "I love it. All the stress of the week just melts away. It's like everything disappears for one hour. I can't think about anything but the steps. It's the best hour of my week."

"Let's do it, girl!" Kit told her. "What time's the class?"

"Eight."

"On a Saturday?"

"You can always take a nap in the afternoon."

Kit laughed. "And then eat a pizza." She paused. "You play Golf?"

"No, never have," Sam told her.

"Tell you what," Kit replied. "I'll do Zumba if you do Golf."

"Deal."

At that point, Felipe spoke several sentences in Spanish to his "fiancé," and Kit responded in kind.

"What did he say?" Sam wanted to know.

"You don't speak Spanish?" Josh asked.

"I'm not sure I get it," the clerk replied. "I'm an American. I've never been out of the country, so I'm learning. I tried to learn Swahili once. But it didn't take. I must not be destined to speak more than just one language. Must not be my gift."

It was an hour later when Josh informed Kit her townhouse was free of bugging devices and remote wireless cameras. He had discovered more than a dozen such spyware items sprinkled throughout her home. He let her know he would make another search later in the day.

When Josh finished the first sweep, Felipe plugged in a detecting device. In Spanish, he told her it would expose any signals from hidden cameras, bugs, cell phone devices, GPS devices, and much more. Later, he would show her how to check her car for unwanted surveillance.

Sam and Kit did away with all boxes, and placed Kit's décor for Christmas and other holidays in her storage compartment. All of her books and forensic research resources were put in place on the office shelves. Watching Josh's intelligence work, then Felipe's work on her computer system, Kit had to admit she was grateful to Ben for sending them.

In spite of her unhappy dating history with Josh.

After the unpacking was completed, Kit suggested she and Sam make a trip to the grocery store, subsequently stocking the pantry and fridge. That way, they could bring back lunch.

Arriving back at her home two hours later, Kit was relieved to discover all the various servicemen had arrived to set up internet, cable, landline telephone, and the alarm system. To each installer,

Felipe had introduced himself as Christine's fiancé, and asked for personal and professional identification before allowing the person to do their job. Josh had followed each one around, making conversation, asking questions, and silently assessing their methods in installing the services required.

Additionally, the appliances were now delivered and installed. Kit was thrilled.

Josh and Felipe were more than willing to take a break when they saw the Subway sandwiches the girls had brought home for lunch. The four of them sat in the living room, around the coffee table.

As the day wore on, the four found they got along well, and laughed at the same things. Samantha regaled them with stories of her urban, African-American grandmother. Felipe shared accounts of his six brothers, and his large family in the Dominican Republic. Josh and Kit told of funny experiences they had shared during prior field assignments.

That night, they all went out for Chinese to celebrate the completion of a full-day's tasks. It was good to finally be settling into her own home, Christine decided.

Sunday afternoon, a somewhat disheveled woman walked into the lobby of Ginsberg Memorial Hospital. She introduced herself to the volunteer staffing the Information Desk as Annabelle Carnes.

"Caleb Morrow is my stepson," she announced. And I really want to see him this afternoon. Can you tell me what room he is in, please?"

"I'm sorry, Ms. Carnes," the volunteer answered, after checking the file. "He is in protective custody with Family Services, and is not allowed visitors."

Ms. Carnes was not about to be trifled with. She raised her voice. "I want to see my stepson! I know my rights! I demand to speak with the hospital administrator on duty!"

Appearing slightly flustered, the volunteer looked around for someone on the hospital staff who would be able to help her soothe this irate woman. She was under orders to never leave the Information Desk without delegating to another volunteer or staff member in her place. And, since today was Sunday, there were less volunteers on duty than usual.

No surgeries were taking place today. Few procedures were scheduled. Most of the medical offices on site would remain closed until the next morning. In all honesty, the volunteer serving at the desk had no idea whether an administrator was even on the hospital grounds. She looked at Ms. Carnes.

"I will make a call upstairs, and see if anyone is here who can help you," she said. Picking up the telephone, she pressed a set of numbers for an extension. And waited.

"Yes, hello," she said. "This is Karen Stewart. I am the volunteer on duty at the Information Desk downstairs. A woman is here, who says she is a stepmother to a patient who is in protective custody upstairs. I have communicated with her that her stepson has been posted as receiving no visitors, but she wants to speak with a hospital administrator. Who is here she can speak with?"

The voice on the other end of the phone spoke for several minutes. The volunteer put her hand over the receiver's mouthpiece, and looked up at Ms. Carnes.

"I'm sorry to make you wait," she said. "She's checking on his location."

Ms. Carnes drummed her fingers on the desk. "This is ridiculous!" she stormed. "You cannot keep me from seeing my child!"

"Please be patient, ma'am," the volunteer told her. "We are doing the best we can."

"Can't *you* just tell me what room he is in?"

Karen Stewart smiled her kindest smile. "I understand, Ms. Carnes. I am a stepmom myself. I love my husband's kids like my own. It's so painful when something like this happens. I've had to push to be recognized as a Mom too. Believe me. The hospital staff will do everything they can to help you. Please just be patient. There just isn't a whole lot I can do."

"I'm sorry," Ms. Carnes offered. "I'll just sit down here, and wait, if you don't mind."

"That would be great," Karen told her. "I'm sure someone will be down to help you as soon as possible. It just gets busy around here. Especially on a Sunday. I'm sure you understand."

Still appearing a bit nervous, Caleb's stepmom sat in a chair close to the Information Desk. About ten minutes later, the desk phone rang.

"Hello, Information. How may I help you?" Karen spoke into the receiver. "Yes..... No..... Yes.... All right. I will send her right up."

Hanging up the telephone, she looked at the waiting woman, and smiled once more. "That was the Hospital Administrator's office, Ms. Carnes. You may go on up to room 427. Just take the north elevators, and follow signs for the pediatric wing."

"Thank you so much," the woman replied. "Is the Gift Store open?"

"Yes, ma'am," Karen replied. "Are you going to get him a gift?"

"Some balloons, I think," came the answer.

"That's a great idea! I hope your visit goes well," the volunteer told her, as she walked away.

Five minutes later, the hospital lobby was filled with local Law Enforcement, uniformed and in plain clothes. Detective Peter Lynch stepped into the hospital Gift Shop, where the would-be visitor, Ms. Carnes, was waiting as six balloons were being inflated with helium.

"Excuse me," he said to the clerk. "Karen wanted me to let you know you have a phone call."

"I do?" the man asked. "Has my wife gone into labor?"

"I don't know," the detective shrugged. "It must be important, though."

The young man smiled at him. "Thank you!" He looked at the waiting Ms. Carnes. "I'll be right back. Thank you for your patience."

"Not a problem," she said.

As soon as the clerk was out of the store, Lynch quietly pulled his service firearm, and inched up behind the Ms. Carnes. Placing the barrel at the back of her head, he spoke in soft tones.

"Put your hands where I can see them, and get down on your knees."

"Excuse me?" she said.

"You heard me." He raised his voice. "Put your hands where I can see them, and get down on your knees."

Caleb's stepmom raised her hands, and looked up through the shop's ceiling to floor glass window. Standing just outside the shop, with guns drawn and aimed at her head, were five more uniformed city policemen.

"Down on your knees, NOW!" Lynch repeated, raising his voice slightly.

His gun's barrel followed her head down as she dropped; first to her knees, and then on to her belly.

As she went down, an officer brought her arms behind her, preparing to handcuff her. The detective looked in the large purse she had been carrying. Inside, he found an envelope with a banded stack of one hundred dollar bills, a revolver, and a photograph of Caleb. On the back of the picture was written, "Alias: Annabelle Carnes, stepmother. Cadaver: Caleb Jacobs, seven year-old."

"Oh, isn't this tidy? We won't have any problems with your conviction. Cuff her and take her downtown," the detective told his counterparts. "Read her rights to her before you make another move."

"What gave me away?" Ms. Carnes wanted to know.

"Well," he smiled. "Seeing that we know exactly where the real Annabelle is, means we know you *aren't her*. And then there's the fact we didn't tell anyone where Caleb would be receiving treatment…… so you figure it out."

"This isn't over," she snarled in retort. "You have no idea who you are dealing with."

"I'd love it if you'd tell me who your bosses are. And oh, we're just getting started," Pete replied. "How much did they pay you? Hope it's all in your purse. They won't be very happy with you, when they discover the boy is still alive."

"I want my lawyer," she demanded.

"Oh, that," Pete answered. "I'll have to check on that. This is a federal case now, and since it involves the lives of American citizens and unidentified persons from other nations..... That means the Patriot Act is now in play. You might even have to be held as a terrorist. I'm sure we'll figure it out before the end of the week."

He looked at one of the undercover officers nearby.

"Read her rights and take her downtown. Put her in a room by herself. And post a watch on her."

With that, Detective Peter Lynch went to room 301 in the Pediatric Wing to check on the boy Caleb. He had received a cell phone call from an FBI agent named Joshua Morgan from Washington, D.C., just an hour ago. Would Pete be willing to meet him at the hospital, and help him interview the social worker, and the boy?

Pete smiled. He could tell the case was ramping up. Things were about to get busy.

Chapter Eight

Monday morning dawned bright and early. Christine's daily routine began at five. While coffee brewed, she completed a twenty-minute weights workout in her room, followed by another thirty-minute strength/cardio regimen on her elliptical.

At six-thirty, she heard Felipe's alarm through the closed door to the office down the hall.

Felipe had worked hard yesterday, she considered. In setting up her computer system, he had discovered not just one, but three sets of tracking malware and spyware, designed to give "someone" the ability to not only see everything she was *doing* on her machine, but to clone it as well.

"This is *one* of the things they did when they broke into your house, Kit. Had we not removed it, this software could have infiltrated the Bureau's network, and become knowledgeable regarding anything the Bureau is involved in," Felipe told her. "CIA, Interpol, everything. We are the first ones they've tried this with. Which makes me wonder; just how far reaching are these people?"

"Is this the same program they tried to use in Chicago?" Kit had asked. "I know you were the one who found that system."

"Yeah," he said, "but more involved. They've added a few modifications to make it harder to detect. It's amazing we've managed to stay ahead of them so far."

The night before, Christine had watched him work for a while after returning home from the group's celebratory Chinese dinner. Pete had left from the restaurant to check on the rescued boy at the hospital. Samantha had gone back to her apartment in Southern Pines.

Thinking things through, she spoke out loud to herself. "I have to interview that little guy today. And the psychiatrist."

In the shower, Kit reviewed the facts they had gathered on the case so far. She had never guessed this case would have become so extensive and diversified when it had been assigned to her, when she first joined the Bureau. Since then, hub houses had been discovered and shut down in Los Angeles, in Chicago, in New York, and now here. She knew instinctively many of the situations her team would be encountering would be catalysts to the rewriting of Bureau and Intelligence Agency policies for years to come.

As she dressed and prepared her breakfast, she mapped out her schedule for the day. First, she would be meeting with Pete, to review their interview with the medical examiner about the body found at the Best Western. Then, she they both would go with Evan for a sweep of the house on Mackaw. Then, she probably would arrive at the hospital around the same time as Josh.

She was looking forward to meeting the little guy named Caleb. After reading the paperwork, she was also curious to understand his statements about seeing zombies.

Were the zombies real, or had he lost himself inside a world of his own making? What had the boy seen? The social worker had mentioned Caleb having developed a psychosis of some kind. She was curious to hear what the psychologist who had done the boy's intake evaluation at the hospital had to say. She knew it would be a while until the psychological assessment was completed.

Just before leaving, Kit knocked on Felipe's door.

"Fernando?" she called, for the benefit of any planted surveillance. "Are you awake?"

A low chuckle was heard inside the office. "I'm up," he said.

Kit opened the door, and was greeted by a view of Felipe still in his boxers, lying on his back under the computer table, making further adjustments and connections.

"Did you sleep at all?" she asked.

"I did," he answered with a wink. "You know I can't rest unless I have my video games ready to go."

"You want coffee?" she asked.

"I'll get some in a bit," he told her, not looking away from the task at hand.

He stood up and reached for the scrambler. Then he looked at her. "I want to get us networked with the Bureau today. My goal is to get all of this up and running today. Then I can help get you some shortcuts for quicker connect when you're working on the case."

"Thanks," she said. "Oh, Samantha and I got some microwave meals for you to tide you over when you get hungry. I put them in the freezer. Help yourself. And no, they're not all pizza."

"I appreciate that, Kit. Thanks."

"No problem. I really appreciate all you are doing to help us carve out a field office," she told him.

"Just doing my job, Amiga," he said. "I'm also going to install some micro cameras around here for security. You will have a third monitor in this room dedicated to personal security. Since, for all practical purposes this will be our field office for a short season."

"That will be great!" she answered. "Hey, will you be here tonight around seven?"

"Yeah, why?"

"I'm calling a team meeting to review everything we have so far. I want to build the case long-board here. I know we can trust Lynch and Davies, but I'm not sure about the rest of Greenway's City police force yet. I keep finding new situations this group network has reached its tentacles into. It's going to be safer to play our cards close to our chest on this one. I keep wishing I had known all of this when we started in Los Angeles. I have a sneaking suspicion we haven't reached the bottom of the barrel yet."

Felipe met her gaze. "I'm with you on that one," he said. "The technology they installed here was pretty high-end. When I get the network up and running, I'll be making a full sweep of the exterior of your townhouse unit and the complex for more cameras this afternoon."

He nodded to her, and reached over to turn off the scrambler once more.

"Thanks, Fernando," Kit said with a giggle. "I'm on my cell if you need me for anything."

"Oh," he said, suddenly remembering. "That reminds me. Give me your cell, *mi amor*. I have a surprise for you. If you can wait ten minutes, I'll give it back to you."

"Sure," Kit answered, surprised. "I'll get it."

When she returned with her phone, Felipe opened it, and motioned for her to be quiet. As the battery cover was removed, a black computer chip fell out. Quietly, Felipe picked up tweezers,

101

removed it, and dropped it into a half-full glass of water sitting on the desk from the night before.

He turned on the signal scrambler once more. Then he spoke.

"I should have checked for it earlier, but I got involved in the setting up your office. It was a tracking chip, which also sent signals of your conversations and wireless communications to whoever was watching the cameras."

Kit was stunned. "How long has it been in there?"

"It's hard to tell," he answered. "While you're working today, try to remember the last few times you left your cell phone unattended. Maybe in your purse at the precinct while you were in interrogation; on the table in the cafeteria when you went to the restroom, even during a date....."

"Okay," she said. "I thought I had kept it with me continually. I'll try to give that some thought today."

"By the way, I also found a GPS attached to your car. They've been keeping an eye on where you go in the city. That's probably how they had an opportunity to get in and place the cameras and computer clone software."

Felipe suddenly turned serious. He stopped what he was doing, to look into her eyes. "Seriously, Kit, Ben's right. These people don't mess around. Remember what they did to Sherry. They don't need much of a reason to kill. From what I can see, whoever calls the shots in this group enjoys messing with Death way too much. Promise me you'll be careful."

Christine smiled. "Absolutely. And that's why Ben sent you to bring me up to date in person," Christine answered, putting pieces together slowly. "Yes, I will watch it. Thanks."

Felipe reached and turned the scrambler off once more.

"*Te amo, mi Corazon,*" he told her.

"I love you, too, Fernando. Have a great day here. I invited some friends over to meet you tonight."

"That will be fun. Maybe I can bake something today," he said with a chuckle.

Evan and two teams from the Crime Lab fulfilled the warrants and orders for three of the many files Kit continually carried with her. One order was for the exhumation of a twenty-three year old male's body; David Fletcher. Evan's team was to assist and protect the delivery of the body to the county medical examiner.

The second order was a Search and Seizure of the house on Mackaw. This appeared to be an ongoing hub house for the network. Arrests and the gathering of evidence would be of paramount importance. The family on Mackaw had no idea they were coming, so the element of surprise was on their side. Processing information provided by this warrant would take several days of dedicated work. Evan wanted an eyes-on account to add to the meeting that night.

The third order would allow them access to the family home of a missing girl; Katie Curtin. It had been a little over three months since the girl had disappeared. There had been no trace or word of her. Evan's team was to return to the girl's room to find any potentially missing evidence they might have missed the first time around.

How did these people cause young women to completely disappear like this? Why hadn't they been able to discover the method these people used? Four cities.... really? Now they were operating in Greenway. How had they evaded discovery for so long? How did they communicate without being detected?

Detective Evan Davies was driving away from the cemetery. He had fulfilled the first warrant, and his mind was filled with thoughts. He was running through the facts he knew the case so far. Considering his past experience in law enforcement, he tought back over past cases. In all of his experience so far, images from surveillance cameras had to be stored in some form, whether on videotape, DVD, CD-rom or USB drive. He made a mental note to check the house on Mackaw for some sort of storage. Thinking now, he realized he had not checked the house on Parrot Circle for himself. He had expected one of his colleagues had taken care of it. He decided to return to the Parrot Circle house after the search on Mackaw was completed.

He thought back over the interviews he had completed in the past few days. Erin, the newest missing girl, had been taken from a house not too far from the house they were headed to. Was it possible she might have been taken by the same people? Could *she* be hidden in the house on Mackaw?

Erin's father had been an attention-grabbing interview. A naturalized citizen from Armenia, Omar Kasabian worked as one of Asami Motors' managers. The fact he was the third person to surface as being attached to the dealership owner, Benjamin Asami, was reason enough in Evan's mind to pull Asami himself in for questioning. But Agent Spada wanted to see where Kasabian's connections to Mr. Asami might lead them. If they pulled Asami this early in the game, the network would be alerted and leave Greenway altogether. There were too many questions still presenting themselves.

Was there a "higher-up" who was calling the shots?

Evan's gut told him there was still much more to be uncovered.

His mind drifted to the girl; Erin. How did a fourteen year old become involved with people like these? Come to think of it, Omar Kaabian had seemed tense; afraid during his interview. The detective was certain Kasabian was lying when he denied knowing where his daughter's cell phone was.

Strange, Evan reasoned. They hadn't been able to find even one of the missing girls' cell phones. Subpoenaed phone records they had obtained, however. He hoped he would have time to go back by Erin's home, and check other rooms for the girl's phone while her father was at work.

Was Landon Morrow one of the masterminds? Or was he on the run, and hiding? Or worse, was he dead? Was he a victim, or one of the criminals? And what about the young *men* who had disappeared?

His mind went to another girl who had vanished two weeks after Katie Curtin. Her name was..... Sandy Zarduc. Katie had been sixteen. Sandy fifteen. Where were they? Were they truly runaways; lost, and on drugs somewhere?

Had they been violated, then murdered; their bodies waiting to be discovered somewhere?

Or worse. Had they been trafficked; sold to a wealthy buyer and spirited out of the country; now forced to do the unthinkable?

And did the missing twenty-five to thirty-five year olds really belong with the same case? He knew the FBI thought so, since monies were all deposited digitally, converging into the same accounts. So far, the maze of shell companies hiding the true identities of the masterminds had not been fully deciphered.

How did the two cases fit together? Or did they?

Evan was beginning to have doubts.

"It's gotta be a serial killer," he said out loud. But in his heart, he knew that answer didn't fit. That would be too easy.

"We need to wait until we have a full picture," Kit had told them one day. "If we move too soon, the guys in charge will slip through our fingers like they did in New York and Chicago. The best plans will land the guys in charge in jail."

It was late afternoon. Dr. James Ainsworth, Pediatric Forensic Psychologist stepped into the hall from Room 301 on the Pediatric Wing of Ginsberg Memorial Hospital. Accompanying him were social worker, Sarah McMillan, and Agent Christine Spada.

Following Caleb's medical tests and x-rays, Dr. Ainsworth had come to visit the boy, hoping to get to begin the process of getting to know him. He knew it would take more time than usual to gain this lad's trust. He had decided not to try to make any assessments until a relationship had been established with the boy. Relationship was the only healthy method of beginning the journey of providing actual help.

As was his mother, Mary, before him, he was a firm believer in Attachment Theory.

Medically speaking, it had been a hard day for any seven year old. Without immunization records, or birth records, the pediatrician and orthopedic residents had resolved that morning to begin Caleb's immunizations. The reading of Friday's MRI had revealed the boy had experienced many greenstick fractures, none of which had healed properly. Only one of his ribs had survived the past seven years without cracking or breaking. His vision was impaired in his left eye, which appeared to relate to a crack in the skull just above his left ear.

Saturday's EKG, endoscopy, colonoscopy, MRI and allergy testing had taken place in the afternoon. Surprisingly, Caleb's only food allergies were to shellfish and strawberries. Environmentally, he showed adverse reactions to ragweed, a few pollens, and cat dander.

For size, the boy was on the low end of the normal percentile for his age group. He was forty-four inches tall, weighing in at fifty-five pounds. Sarah still had difficulty believing the boy was seven years old. His intelligence far surpassed the age of a second-grader.

Caleb did not seem to be able to read or write very well. He was right-handed, but had experienced a breakage on his right thumb, middle and fourth fingers. He did know the basic sounds the letters made, and he did recognize numbers. He could sound out words phonetically, but seemed to have trouble processing the consonant blends, like "pl" and "st."

"S-s-sesame S-s-street," the boy explained. His vision and hearing tests had been completed on the toddler level for this reason. "And I l-learned s-s-some th-things on P-P-PBS."

In the meeting this morning, Dr. Jim Ainsworth, was meeting with Sarah and Christine to set up a series of appointments for Caleb. A full evaluation would need to be completed before he would be able to even try to adjust to a new pattern of living outside of the house on Parrot Circle. From experience, the psychologist knew that only small window existed for now. Caleb's ability to remember the details of his trauma would only float about on the surface for a short time, before becoming willfully submerged.

After repression, reemergence could take years, if the boy could access the trauma at all. However, if they ignored the issues, and just waited for them to resurface on their own, the boy would suffer from unexplained anger and depression for years.

In addition to his full time job with Ginsberg Memorial, Ainsworth took on additional clients in specialized circumstances, working for The City of Greenway. In a case like Caleb's, the psychologist realized it was important to work within the system in order to see the most fruitful outcome in the long run.

However, he was unsure as to exactly whose jurisdiction the boy's care would fall into, since the Bureau was involved. He wasn't taking any chances with this little boy's future. He told Christine he would be calling a pediatric psychiatrist to confer on the boy's condition.

After setting the scheduled appointments, Ainsworth returned to his office on the hospital's Behavioral Health floor.

According to the orthopedic exam, Caleb needed to undergo corrective surgery in the near future. Both forearms were badly misshapen, and needed to be re-broken, strengthened with titanium, and casted until they healed properly. He had minimal usability of his right hand. The same procedures needed to take place to correct the femur on his right leg, and the tibia on his left. When the boy walked, the surgeon noted a habitual rolling of both ankles to the outside. Caleb walked on the outside edges of his feet only. He had communicated he did so to avoid the pain of walking with flat feet. He limped continually

Being at least seven years of age, the boy had walked that way without shoes for so long, he would not be able to change it with physical therapy alone. The deformity demanded correction as soon as possible if it were not to become permanent.

Then, there were the visible issues with his teeth and gums. That would have to wait for now. But a dental exam would take place in the near future.

In addition to his need for surgery, Caleb showed signs of malnourishment. Apparently, Sarah noted, the boy was used to eating in what she called an "Installment Method." He was almost like a bulimic, binging but without purging. She had kept track of his eating. He told her he never really knew when the next meal would happen. So he always ate all he could, and took extra for later.

Thursday, he had eaten two full boxes of macaroni and cheese, a submarine sandwich, chips, and a candy bar.

Yesterday, on Friday, he had eaten a quarter pounder with cheese, half of Sarah's French Fries, an ice cream cone, and an apple pie.

Since then, she observed, he had eaten only a small amount of hospital food. She had the feeling he had learned to go on a hunt for food when his stomach was empty.

"It's wh-what th-the l-l-lions d-d-do," he told her. Then he had asked, "Wh-when d-do we g-go t-t-to the z-z-zoo?"

"Soon, little guy," she told him. She would make a note to plan a field trip for him. Sarah looked at her watch. Agent Spada would be on her way about now.

Christine wanted to make instant friends with Caleb. So, on her way to the hospital, she called Sarah, and asked a few questions. Then, she stopped and did a little shopping.

An hour later, when she walked into the hospital, she carried a large gift bag for Caleb, and a bouquet of red, black and blue Zombie balloons from the Dollar Tree.

"Hi, Caleb!" she said, coming into the room. "I'm Christine! I'm a friend of Miss Sarah's, and I wanted to bring you a birthday present!"

Caleb had looked at her blankly. "I d-d-don't have a b-b-birth-d-day," he told her.

"Oh, that's silly! Everyone has a birthday! So I know you do too!" Kit declared. "Even if you don't know when it is, you know you were born, right? So can today be your birthday?"

"O-k-k-kay!" Caleb said, brightening. "D-d-do I g-g-get a c-c-cake?"

"You sure do!" Kit declared. "And a pizza will be here in about ten minutes."

Caleb stared at her, disbelieving. "R-really? Wh-wh-what k-k-kind?"

"I wasn't sure, so I got a large one we all could share. Extra cheese on all of it, and extra pepperoni on half. Does that sound good?" she asked.

Caleb clapped his hands. "Oh, g-g-good!" he exclaimed.

"And, while we're waiting," Kit told him, "I brought you some presents to open."

Caleb's eyes were shining. "H-how d-d-did y-you kn-n-ow wh-what I l-like?"

Kit giggled at him, and smiled a bright smile. "I think a little birdie told me," she said, "named Miss Sarah."

The boy looked at both of them. "Th-th-is is the b-b-best d-d-day of m-my whole l-life!"

Sarah ruffled his hair. "Today is the tenth of August. We're going to make today your birthday!" She looked at Kit. "Your life is getting a new beginning right now, Caleb! We are happy you were born, and today we are celebrating your life!"

Kit put the gift bag on top of Caleb's legs. "Open your presents, Buddy," she said.

Glowing, the boy reached into the bag, and pulled out a package of underwear.

"Z-z-zombie Hunter?" he cried. "I w-wanna b-be one! H-how d-did you kn-know?"

He reached in again, and found two pair of Zombie Hunter pajamas. He looked at Sarah. "C-c-can I w-wear th-these?" he asked.

"Sure!" the social worker answered. "You want to change from that hospital gown right now?"

When Caleb nodded his assent, she began helping him to change into them. As she pulled his tiny arm into the sleeves, she noticed tears in his eyes.

"What's wrong?" she asked, concerned. "Are you okay? Do you hurt somewhere?"

"N-no," the boy shook his head. "I'm j-just s-so ha-hap-py!"

"When you're done changing," Kit said, "there are two more items in the birthday bag."

Caleb was surprised. He looked up at Sarah. "C-c-can I?"

Sarah nodded, tears now filling her own eyes.

"Y-you ok-kay?" the boy asked.

The social worker looked at Kit, and then back at him. "I'm happy too, Caleb. That's all."

Caleb reached once more into the bag, and pulled out a DVD. He looked at it carefully, sounding out the letters. "World War Z," he said. "Is th-this a Z-Zom-b-bie m-mmovie? D-Do th-the Z-Zombies d-d-die?"

"Yes, it is, and yes they do," Kit told him, laughing. "Have you seen it already?"

"I d-d-don't kn-kn-know," he answered, "t-til it s-s-starts."

"Okay," Kit told him. "Maybe you can watch it while we eat our pizza." She paused. "There's one more thing in there."

Dutifully, the boy reached once more into his birthday bag. He had felt the softness before, but had not pulled out the stuffed animal, because he wasn't sure he would like it. But, as the stuffed lion came into full view, he giggled, and hugged the soft, eighteen-inch, plush toy close.

"I love him!" Caleb said, without stuttering.

Sarah and Kit glanced at each other, aware, but pretending not to notice.

"Lions are very strong animals," Kit told him. "Male lions are protectors. They fight for the right."

"And they don't quit until they win," Sarah added.

"Are th-they s-s-stronger th-than z-z-zombies?" Caleb asked.

Both the Agent and the social worker nodded. "Much stronger," Sarah answered.

"I'm a l-l-lion!" he declared. "C-can I be a l-lion?

"Okay then!" Sarah offered. "You're our lion-in-training!"

Kit looked at the boy, assessing him, as she folded the gift bag. "Caleb, can I ask you a couple of questions?"

"Sh-sure," came the reply, as he clutched the lion in a tight grip.

"These are hard questions, and you can nod up and down for yes, and shake your head side to side for no."

"O-k-kay," he answered. "C-c-can I talk t-too?"

"Absolutely," Kit told him, with a smile. She noticed he wasn't stuttering as much when he gripped the stuffed lion.

"You talked with Miss Sarah and Miss Louisa about zombies. Have you ever seen a real zombie?" she asked.

Caleb nodded, his eyes wide.

"Are they in the movies?"

He pointed to the DVD he had just received. "Yes."

"Okay, sorry," she replied, laughing. "Are they *only* in the movies?"

He shook his head back and forth.

"Are they on your GameBoy?"

"Y-yes, b-but n-not j-just p-p-pretend. I t-touched th-them. Th-they are r-real t-too." He hugged the lion tighter. "Th-they were in m-my h-house," he told her.

"You're sure? A *real* zombie?"

Caleb nodded again. "M-My M-M-om w-was a z-zombie."

"Oh," Kit said. "Do you mean the lady who has been living in your Dad's house; Ms. Annabelle?"

"N-N-no! N-Not Z-zombie-M-Mom!" he declared, somewhat frustrated. "Sh-she's mean. M-My r-real M-mom."

"Do you remember your mom?" Kit asked, surprised.

Caleb nodded. "A l-l-little. Sh-she d-died wh-when I w-was a l-l-little k-kid."

"Do you remember how she died?" Kit asked softly, her hand stroking his hair.

The child's reaction was immediate. Caleb's eyes widened suddenly. He pushed himself up against the headboard of the hospital bed. Beginning to whimper, he pulled his knees up against his chest, in a fetal position, and began to suck his thumb.

Sarah reached both arms around the boy, and lifted him up. She maneuvered herself onto the hospital bed, and put Caleb in her lap.

"It's okay, Caleb," she whispered. "You're safe with me. See my arms around you? I've got you now. Nothing will get through me to hurt you." She waited a few moments, for the boy to calm somewhat. She continued to soothe him with her words. "I am so proud of how brave you are." She looked at Kit, who responded with a smile and a nod.

"We are almost done for today," she told the Agent. "I think we are right at the line of limitations; this is about all he can handle for today."

Sarah spoke once more to Caleb. "Can you answer Miss Kit's question?"

Slowly and gently, Kit repeated her question. "Caleb, honey, do you remember how your mother died?" she asked carefully.

Caleb began to shake, as though a volcanic eruption was beginning in his core, and emerging upwards. In an anguished cry, he began to wail.

"Sh-she w-was a z-z-zombie! And I sh-sh-sh-shot her!" he blurted out. "I-In th-the head!"

The exertion of the disclosure had exhausted the small boy. He buried his face in Sarah's blouse, and began to wretch with sobs. His weeping gained in volume and momentum, coming and receding in waves. Gradually, he calmed. All the while, Kit stroked his hair, and Sarah hugged him, gently rubbing his back. They spoke kind, encouraging words.

What atrocities had this boy witnessed, they both wondered? What other actions had he been forced to take?

Sarah glanced up at Kit. "This is one for the record books," she muttered.

"Mm-hmm," came the reply.

They remained in silence for the next few moments, contemplating the pain contained in the boy's words. How had it taken place? And why?

It was into this atmosphere Peter Lynch arrived some six or seven minutes later.

"Hey all!" he greeted, walking through the door. "Guess what I have?"

Still somewhat subdued, Kit responded. "Hey Pete."

Disinterested, Caleb turned his head to see who had come into the room. At the sight of the pizza box, he looked up at Sarah. "M-My b-b-birthday p-p-pizza?"

"That it is, my boy," Detective Lynch answered. "And...." From behind his back, he pulled out an ice cream cake, "we have a birthday cake as well!!!"

Caleb's traumatic revelation was momentarily forgotten. He smiled, sitting up. He brushed his tears aside. Once more, he was the small child, excited to celebrate. Pete put the food boxes down, and, from a bag carried in on top of the pizza box, he produced party hats, napkins, cups and plates.

Kit had brought in a small cooler when she arrived some time before. Providing each cup with ice, she poured Coke into each person's cup.

"Y-you g-got the f-f-fizzy d-d-drink!" Caleb exclaimed. "Th-th-this is the b-b-best!"

Kit wondered how he would respond when it came time to make a wish and blow out his birthday candles.

Chapter Nine

The meeting at Kit's townhouse that evening was upbeat. She had stopped on the way home for subway sandwiches and a few salads. She had also purchased a variety of chips, a raw veggie tray, fruit dips and drinks.

Preparing to get into the checkout line, she called Felipe. Was her "fiancé" hungry? She knew he had been at the townhouse all day. Did he need her to pick up anything? No, didn't need anything for himself, he told her, except some cereal. "Fernando" was doing fine, but could she bring home chocolate icing? He had taken a break and made brownies that afternoon for the friends who were coming over.

Yes, she told him. She would get the icing and cereal. Could he set up her work-boards (evidence longboards) in the office? They would need to be structured during the meeting, with everyone's discoveries addressed on them and readily seen for problem solving.

At the last minute, she made a call to Samantha. She was in dire need of someone to take minutes of the meeting, and help her organize the field office. At the moment, she knew of no one else trustworthy enough to help her as an administrative assistant.

She could hear the phone ringing in her ear.

"Hello, this is Samantha."

"Hi, Sam. It's Kit."

"Oh, hey there! How was your day?"

"It's ramping up," Kit answered. "Tonight I have a meeting with the rest of the Taskforce."

"That's right," Sam replied. "You told me. You need help with anything?"

"Really?" Kit asked. "I don't want to overwork you."

"If I offer, I mean it."

"All right then. I need a part time admin for a few weeks, or longer. You could help us in the evenings, and if you can't come on an evening, I understand. I will pay you as a part time employee of the Bureau."

Sam was silent on the other end of the line.

Kit checked to see if the phone had become disconnected. "Sam? You still there?"

"Oh, sorry," Samantha replied. "I was thinking. Yes, I'm here. I can do it. What do I need to bring?"

"You can use my laptop," Kit replied.

"No, I mean, do you need my background check, or anything?"

Kit laughed. "Oh, yeah," she said. "And we can do that stuff tonight as well. I assume the city had you complete a background check and a physical in order to work for Judge Ventura."

"That would be an affirmative," Sam told her. "So I will need to provide all that information again?"

"Eventually," Kit told her. "But I'll get the wheels in motion for you tonight."

"I'll bring the copy of that file I have here at home. And, thanks! I'd be glad to help you."

"Okay," Kit told her. "Can you come to my townhouse at seven this evening? We are having a light supper while we work. Fernando, my fiancé, even made brownies. He asked me to pick up icing for him."

"Sweet," Sam said. "Sure, see you in a few."

"Thanks, girl."

Two hours later, after everyone had eaten, Kit cleared the dishes away. She looked around the room, deciding she was glad to have chosen the largest bedroom as the temporary field office. The two evidence boards took up the majority of the doorway wall. Felipe had installed two 2'x4' tables under the boards. Each one had the appearance of an old fashioned blackboard, but was surfaced like a white board, with cork squares interspersed between. This way, notes pertinent to the case could be written on the white surfaces, and pictures could be tacked onto the cork. Lead-threads could be stretched between pictures of suspects and persons-of-interest.

It was old school, but Christine liked it better than using a Smart Board or computer.

She had instructed each member of the team to bring their notes, pictures and files of their discoveries so far in the case. There were so many connections happening at this point, Kit felt their main need at the moment was to organize the variety of information.

After considering the evidence, it was her hope that the case would become divided into at least two segments by the end of the evening.

After calling everyone in to the "field office," where they each sat on folding chairs, she began the meeting.

"Okay," she said, pulling several files from the file-box, and opening them. "Let's start with the houses."

She pinned a picture of the houses used as hubs in New York to the first long board. Under it, she pinned a picture of the houses in Van Nuys (Los Angeles) and Chicago. Lastly, she pinned pictures of the houses on Parrot Circle and Mackaw Avenue. What have we discovered in common in each of these houses?"

She looked around the circle. Next to her empty chair, sat Samantha. Then Felipe and Josh. Then Pete and Evan. She wasn't quite sure how they were all going to develop into a team yet. She was thankful for Josh and Felipe's help in setting up the field office, and for their protection.

She knew Ben had sent them because of her prior working relationship with Josh. But, she was realizing, she would have to remain professional with him at all times. At the moment, she could sense the uneasiness which still existed between the two of them.

After all, she had broken off the engagement only six months ago. She had requested a new assignment, and Ben had sent her here; to oversee the setting up of a new field office.

She paused. *Why* had he decided to send Josh? Ben knew the situation. Surely, he knew how difficult having Josh around would make things for her.

She decided she would call her boss the next day, and try to talk things through. Had he misunderstood?

It was Felipe who answered her question. "We found hidden remote cameras, with wires clipped and pulled. There were no evidences of recording equipment attached outside. In every location so far, wireless transmitters were good for five miles' radius around the house. Additionally, each house was bugged."

Kit wrote the observations on the white board next to the posted pictures.

Josh spoke up. "There were no personal items in any location. No photographs, family records, birth certificates. However, in Chicago, and in Van Nuys, equipment *was* left behind. It was like we surprised them before they could completely sweep the hub house completely clean."

"Can you remember *what* equipment was left behind in those locations?" Kit asked. "Were they the same in each location? I know you two were directly involved in those raids."

Felipe responded. He closed his eyes in order to visualize his experience, since he had an Eidetic, or photographic memory. "A credit card embossing machine for credit and debit card production. A camera for stills. A digital video camera. A green screen. A case of one hundred and forty-four sets of handcuffs. Oh, there was drug paraphernalia for marijuana as well. We didn't find any drug production equipment however.

"We found sheets of bonded leather in various colors. Heavy bonded paper of various shades. We assume these are used to produce passports. Small sheets of gold and silver foil; I think for foiling on passport covers. There was a tattoo pen, complete with ink, and a short stack of paper stencils of Chinese figures. The figure most repeated was the word *"huanle,"* which translates into English as "joy," "delight," or "great pleasure." Two bedrooms were furnished in antique furniture, decorated quite luxuriously, in burgundies and gold. Each furnished bedroom had two twin beds. The dressers were filled with satin nightgowns in a variety of sizes.

"Each house had a third bedroom, in which we found all of these pieces of equipment. The kitchens in each house were supplied with a full sets of china and linens. There were creams and lotions and candles. There were bunks in the fourth bedroom. Between twelve and twenty beds."

"How about the house the team swept today?" Kit asked. "The one on Mackaw Drive?"

Evan spoke up. "It sounds a lot like the Chicago house. As far as we can tell, they cleared out less than a day ago, and left everything behind. But again, there were no pictures, no documents. No evidence of people being there, except the furniture. The place was empty. "

"So far, what do we believe these houses are used for?" Kit asked. "Even if it's just a nagging thought, speak up."

"They sound like trafficking houses," Pete offered, "but more high class than what we have encountered before in sex rings."

"But what would they do with the other equipment?" Samantha asked. "Don't the girls who usually go missing leave everything behind?"

Kit looked at her. "Yes," she answered. "But we are finding indicators that this group is different somehow. And, they seem more highly organized than the typical sex ring."

She looked at the board. "Okay, before we move forward, let's stop here for a moment.... *If* this is a trafficking ring, what would they possibly use these pieces of equipment for?"

"Why would they have full sets of china in the kitchens?" Evan asked. "And furnished bedrooms? I mean, those bedrooms look like they belong in a mansion!"

"And the silk nightgowns!" Pete added.

Everyone was thinking for a moment.

Kit spoke. "What if the girls aren't shipped out right away? What if they are held there for a time and taught table manners, and things like that?"

"If that's true, then the market for these girls would be much different than the street-slave trade," Josh offered. "That might explain why they don't resurface with other trafficked victims."

"Sam, make a note, please," Kit ordered. "We need to look for advertisements that would fit the kind of girls being prepared for this kind of sale; publications and online sites catering to wealthy men. It's worth a shot, anyway."

Samantha began making notes.

"Agent Spada," Pete said, slowly. "What if all of the girls are being sold to overseas buyers? But let's say they aren't sent in shipping containers... What if these guys are using commercial or private planes?"

Felipe caught Pete's idea, and it sparked another. "They would need passports for the country they are headed to, as well as paperwork with new names and birth certificates, and the like."

"And what if the Chinese word is tattooed somewhere on their body, like a label in the back of a shirt?" Samantha offered.

The room fell silent, as everyone stared at Samantha. The truth began to sink in. Until now, the scope of this investigation had been underestimated.

"Okay," Evan said, looking at Samantha. "You might be on to something. But how do you get a girl who has been taken from her home and family not to *say* something, even *secretly* to a flight attendant, or a crew member? Seems like we would have had something leak out if an operation were this big; if that's what they were doing."

Kit pondered. "Unless...." She paused, thinking her idea through. "Unless, they did something *to* the victims to convince them to agree to cooperate..... Like promise them money.... Or even brainwash them."

"But reprogramming takes months," Felipe argued. "And I'm not sure that makes sense, since we haven't found any evidences of torture left behind. Most networks like this get rid of their people within a few days. I wouldn't think any of these girls could be held onto for more than a month before they are shipped out."

It was Samantha who broke the silence this time. "I wouldn't *want* to be a *slave*, anytime, anywhere, for any reason. But, if I was between twelve and sixteen, and my home life wasn't good, or if my folks were divorced, I would be online all the time. Judge Ventura sees girls like this in her courtroom. They post naked pictures; and videos; looking much older than their true ages. They all are looking for love.

"If it were me, I would want someone to rescue me. And, not only that, *maybe the guys lie.*"

Everyone laughed at the starkness of her observation.

"Of course they lie!" Evan exclaimed. "They can get someone naïve and full of dreams to believe anything. A little charm, a little candy, throw around a lot of money and a lot of promises."

"So what are the cameras for?" Sam asked.

"Passport photos, photoshoots for buyers? Videos for buyers? Maybe a sort of catalog, anything like that," Kit answered. She paused.

"Okay, I think we have an idea towards grabbing a better handle on things. Let's move on to the girls. I want to focus on the last three victims: Katie Curtin, Sandy Zarduc, and Erin Kasabian."

As she spoke, Kit put the pictures of the three missing girls on the second row of corkboard. She wrote each girl's name on the whiteboard next to the corresponding photograph.

"Now," she said. "What do we know about each of these young women? And I'd prefer not to speak about any of them in the past tense, please."

Everyone in the room nodded their agreement.

Evan looked down at his portfolio, checking his notes from the day's interviews. "Katie is sixteen, Sandy is fifteen, and Erin is fourteen," he read. "Katie and Erin each have a parent who lives in Westwood. Sandy lives in Southern Pines with her father. All three have experienced divorce between their parents, are the only child at home, and have issues with anger and detachment. All three have posted to Facebook, Instagram, Kik and/or Snapchat with a fascination for sexual fantasy and death. Erin seems more Goth in her style than the other two. Sandy and Erin have body piercings. None of them have tattoos, however, as far as their friends, parents and teachers know. All three have, or did had, smart phones."

He paused. "Let's see...."

"Do any of them have older siblings who have moved away?" Pete asked.

"Yes," Evan answered, checking his notes once more. "Erin has a sister who lives with her boyfriend in Denniston, and a brother who lives up in Musketville, about ninety minutes up Route twenty-one. Sandy's older sister lives in France. Katie is an only child."

"Anything else?" Kit asked, smiling.

"I have my notes from today's warrants and searches if this is a good time," he said.

"Sure. Go ahead."

Evan looked around the room. "Well, the first court order we fulfilled this morning was to exhume the body of a twenty-three year old male; David Fletcher."

"How did it go?" Kit asked.

"The coffin was empty," he told her. "We are calling in the family and funeral home for interviews tomorrow morning. Who is he, and how is he connected to this case?"

"He was personal limousine driver for Benjamin Asami. He showed up missing three years ago. His mother insisted he had been *murdered* by Asami, but the interviewing detective didn't put much weight in her story, because she had been declared mentally incompetent the week before. When he asked Asami about it, he was told the guy had contracted a flu virus, and had a reaction to his medicine. He had died of natural causes. The detective saw the death certificate, so he wrote it off as a solved case. It was a closed casket funeral." She paused.

"But then, two months ago, Interpol faxed the D.C. office a picture of a man brokering medical supplies in Germany without a permit. The man was David Fletcher. He was using an alias. So, yes, because Mr. Asami is somehow involved, it is by *some means* connected to the case. We just don't know how it relates."

"I already told you about the Search and Seizure of the house on Mackaw," Evan continued. "That was our second order. Our third was another Search and Seizure at the home of Katie Curtin. We were looking for anything pertinent to our case."

"Did you find anything worthwhile?" Kit asked in anticipation.

Evan smiled. "Well, I went through her room myself. Her mother's house is in Westwood, but she was abducted from her father's home in Applegate Plaza. She lives with her mother full-time, and her father has visitation every other weekend. When she was abducted, we only searched the bedroom in her father's house. Today, I searched her room at her mother's in Westwood."

"What did you find?"

"Well…." Evan waited for effect. "I found her cell phone."

"What?" Kit was thrilled. "How?"

"Apparently, Katie was not allowed to take her cell phone with her to her father's house, because he did not reinforce any restrictions or set hours for her usage. Her mother Katie she has a bad habit of surfing the internet when she was supposed to be asleep."

"What's wrong with that?" Felipe asked, kidding.

"Apparently that's when she was communicating with the perpetrators."

"Did you get a chance to read through her texts?" Kit asked.

"No, I didn't," Evan answered. "Because, additionally, I revisited the house on Parrot this afternoon. Something occurred to me. We have seen a consistent thread of video and audio surveillance in each of the hub homes. Is it possible we might have missed something simple?"

"Like what?" Pete asked.

"A storage of video images on site somewhere. Something that would have to be delivered to whoever the masterminds are – wherever they are. The house on Parrot Circle was a no-go. But then I went back to the Mackaw house."

He paused and looked around. "I thought since it appeared to be like the house in Chicago; they must've left in a hurry. Perhaps they had left behind a security DVR somewhere we hadn't looked."

"You find something?" Kit asked.

Evan nodded. "It's a twenty-four channel system. It was under loose floorboards, in a corner of the equipment room. Someone must have pulled the wires when they vacated. They ran wires from the cameras through the walls and under the floor. From what I can tell, they would dump images onto a portable USB drive and then just continue recording. The storage on this one is one terabyte. I don't know how long ago they dumped the images. I brought it with me. It's now in plastic in your living room. I was going to take it to the Crime Lab in the morning."

"Wow. Great work, Evan!" Kit exclaimed. "Samantha, please make a note for me to call the Chicago office to let them know about the DVR we found. There might still be one in the house up there.

We also need to get in contact with Erin Kasabian's siblings. It's possible she might have contacted either one of them with information about her contact with this group before her abduction. Anything we might be able to use."

She looked at the group. "We need to meet here again tomorrow night. Will the same time work for all of you? We'll be reviewing those images, along with some other files." She looked at Evan. "Do you have more?"

"I do have one more thing," he responded. "I called Pete when he was on his way over here. I thought I would get time to go back to Omar Kasabian's home before tonight's meeting. I know he told us he didn't have any idea what Erin was doing; that if anyone knew, her mother would know. I just don't believe him. He works as a manager for Asami Motors. So, I figure he probably knows *something*. And, since we had permission to search the house in relationship to the kidnapping, I wanted to check in places the *Dad* might have hidden her cell phone, or maybe even disposed of it."

He looked at Pete, who picked up the story from here.

"So I went there just before coming here. When I arrived at the house, no one was there. So, I pulled into the driveway, and went around to the back. The window to Erin's bedroom was still unlocked, so I climbed in, and began the search. The Crime Lab had done a thorough sweep of her bedroom, and of her bathroom. I walked through the house, looking for hiding places. I checked thoroughly in all rooms of the house, and then found her cell in a drawer in the kitchen. Apparently, her Dad knew about her abduction. Either he was threatened and afraid, or he was complicit. Whatever the reason, he did not surrender the phone, and denied knowing where it was when we asked. In fact, was defensive about it. I haven't checked the phone yet. But here it is."

He lifted a sealed plastic bag, which held an iPhone six in a bright blue case, with a bleeding black skull printed on it.

The group burst into applause.

"Way to go, guys!" Kit told them. "Is there more?"

"Just one more thing," Pete told them. "Several days ago, when I interviewed Erin's band teacher at the middle school, he told me she ate lunch with him most days."

"Doesn't she have friends she eats with?" Sam asked.

"No," he answered. "She fits the profile perfectly of a candidate for this group to kidnap. But he said she had been happier the past few days than he had ever seen her. She told him she had a new boyfriend, and she was in love. He was going to meet her at her dad's house at midnight. He was going to teach her how to make love, because she had never had sex before."

"So, at the time of the abduction, she was a virgin," Kit noted.

She looked at Samantha. "Sam, take another note, please. We need to discover if the other girls, Katie and Sandy, were also virgins. That could become a clue in anticipating this group's next move." She looked at Pete. "Did she happen to tell the band teacher her internet boyfriend's name?"

"Garrett," Pete answered. "She said his name is Garrett, and he attends the high school in the same district. He is a senior."

Kit looked at Samantha.

"Got it," Sam answered, anticipating.

"Okay," Kit said. "Now, I want to introduce the second board before we stop for the evening."

"Kit, before we move on, I need to ask a question," Evan said.

"Sure, what is it?"

"It bothers me that the house on Mackaw was empty. It was in use just a day ago. All the surveillance shows activity. So, how did they know we were coming? The only people who knew about the raid are in this room."

"And Captain Edwards," Kit reminded him.

Josh spoke up. "Someone told me he was new to the force here. That the old guy before him was too young to retire. You think there's a possibility he could be a dirty cop?"

"I honestly don't know the man," Kit told them. "He does know we are opening a field office here. He knows I'm the frontrunner. I have been communicating with him on each step, so we have his cooperation, and availability to extra manpower."

"You want me to look into it?" Evan offered.

"Please," she replied. "And I'll modify my communication methods with him, and we'll see what happens. Fernando, my love, would you do a background check for me, on the federal level?"

"Sure thing, babe," Felipe answered.

She moved to the still empty evidence board to the right of the board they had been working on. She began putting up pictures of the missing persons aged twenty-five to thirty-five from the files she had been carrying around with her for several weeks now.

"I am not putting all of these up here right now," she said. "And I will add names and abduction points to each of these before we meet together again. Tonight, I want to at least get the Eastgate body discovery on this board. Detective Eric Janzen, from Eastgate Precinct, felt it was connected to our case in Westwood Village, so I want to include it in our discussions."

She put a picture of the Best Western hotel bathtub, filled with body parts, on the evidence board. "This is our victim. The Crime Lab is reconstructing the body, and we should know something more by tomorrow night."

She put a picture of the carpet blood spatter, and the chunk of tissue she had collected as a specimen from the scene. "This is the blood spatter pattern around the bed. The bed apparently was the scene of the murder. As far as we can tell at the moment, the body was then cut apart on the bed. I believe the dismemberment took place postmortem, and the parts were then transported to the bathtub. It was a real mess. The face was unrecognizable. And we aren't even sure all the parts of the body were there. It will take them awhile. The Crime Lab has a lot of DNA to sort through."

"Agent Spada?" Pete interrupted. "Why did Detective Janzen feel it was connected to our case?"

Kit stopped and thought. "He gave me what he called "most pertinent connections:" a car key from Asami Motors, and what appears to be a teenage girl's cell phone. Westwood should be receiving the remaining logged evidence on the case from that precinct tomorrow morning, if it isn't already there."

"Do you trust him?" Pete asked.

"I don't know, actually," Kit answered. "He is a good cop; been around a long time, in several different fields of Law Enforcement. So I trust his judgment. He knew my father."

"So you *know* him," Pete offered.

"Well, not really," she replied. "He was in the JAG Corps as an investigator, and he was a friend of my Dad's when Dad was Chief of Detectives in D.C. I haven't seen him since my fifteenth birthday party. I had no idea he worked in Greenway."

"Oh. I just wondered," Pete replied. "I've heard his name associated with several cases in my career. You're right. He's been around a long time. Do you mind if I do follow up on this with him?"

"Go for it," Christine told him.

"I have a question," Evan said. "Do we have DNA on any of these missing persons?"

Kit smiled. "We do, and each one has been entered into CODIS." She was referring to the FBI's program of support for criminal justice DNA databases nationwide, known as the Combined DNA Index System.

"Have we gained any information from Annabelle Carnes?" Josh asked. "Or from Caleb?"

"Good question," Kit replied. "Nothing from Annabelle we didn't already know, so far anyway. But, while she has been in custody, a woman claiming to be Annabelle presented herself at Ginsberg Memorial, demanding to see Caleb. She called the boy her stepson. When we apprehended her, she admitted to being a hired assassin. She had a photograph in her possession of Caleb. The words on the back of the photograph read: 'Alias – Annabelle Carnes. Cadaver – Caleb Jacobs, seven years old.'"

"So the boy's name is *Jacobs,* not *Morrow?*" Samantha asked.

"Apparently, that's an affirmative," Kit replied. "But, Annabelle Carnes *and* the boy himself believe Landon Morrow to be his father. And, because Caleb is mentally fragile, we are moving very slowly with him in retrieving information. He has been greatly traumatized. So far, in the process, we have discovered he doesn't remember ever having celebrated a birthday, or a birthday party. We had the privilege of giving him a birthdate today. Caleb Jacobs' new life began this morning, and his birthday is August tenth, and we gave him his first birthday party in his hospital room."

In response to the smiles and murmured comments, Kit laughed. "Being able to help people like Caleb is one of the reasons why we do what we do!" she said. "Thank you everyone! Go home and get some rest. I'll see you downtown in the morning."

Chapter Ten

Very early Tuesday morning, Christine Spada left her home and headed for the Westwood Village precinct. On the way, she decided to stop by Ginsberg Memorial hospital. She wanted to check on Caleb and perhaps get a chance to speak with Sarah.

Exiting the elevator on the third floor, Kit noted how quiet the hospital was this early in the morning. Lights had been dimmed in the hallways.

She made her down the dim hallway, looking for Caleb's room.

"Good morning," she said to the uniformed officer on duty sitting just outside the boy's door. She observed his badge number. When he realized she had stopped outside room 301, he stood up, and assessed her.

"ID please," he replied.

Christine showed her Bureau ID.

"Good morning, Agent Spada." He checked her face with the photograph on her ID. "How can I help you?"

"I need to speak with Ms. McMillan and the boy," she answered.

"Go right in."

Christine opened the door slowly, in case Sarah was sleeping. As she entered, she noticed the social worker curled up in the recliner next to the bed. Sitting up in the bed, wide awake, was Caleb. He was playing with his Gameboy.

"Hi, Caleb!" Kit said in greeting. "What are you playing?"

"Z-Z-Zombies," he answered.

The agent came to stand just behind his shoulder. "Is it hard to play?" she asked.

"N-Not really," he answered, his fingers still working furiously. "I j-j-just k-kill 'em."

He stopped playing and put the Gameboy down. "Hi, B-B-Birth-d-day L-Lady," he said with a smile.

"Hi there, Caleb!" she responded. "You can call me Miss Kit. How long has Miss Sarah been asleep?" She sat down beside him, on his bed.

"Sh-she went t-t-to s-sleep after I d-did," he answered. "Sh-she works a l-lot."

Kit nodded and whispered conspiratorially. "I think she does too. You're right."

There was silence.

"Hey," Caleb whispered. "Y-you want t-to see m-my g-gun?"

Surprised, Kit responded. "Absolutely!"

Caleb leaned over the side of his bed, trying to reach his backpack on the floor. Kit reached down to pick it up, then placed it on the bed in front of him. The boy unzipped it and rummaged in it until he found what he was looking for. He glanced up at Kit.

"Here it-t-is!" The boy pulled out a large black pistol.

Intrigued, Kit looked at it. "That looks like a real gun!" she whispered.

"It-t-is real! M-my M-mommy g-gave it-t-to me."

"Really?" she asked. "When did she do that?"

"Wh-when sh-she t-t-told me to sh-shoot her," he answered, his eyes filling with tears. "Sh-she s-s-said sh-she was s-s-sick. Th-they k-k-kept hurt-t-ing her. Sh-she was t-tired of b-being a z-z-zombie."

"*How* did you shoot her? Can you *show* me?"

Caleb picked up the pistol. He put both hands around the grip, and his finger on the trigger. Kit moved to the side as he pointed the gun in her direction. With her finger, she moved the barrel aside.

"Whoa, Buddy!" she whispered. "Is the safety on?"

"Wh-what's th-that?" the boy asked, lowering the gun.

Cautiously, Kit put out her hand. "Can I hold your gun for a minute, please?" she asked.

Caleb nodded, and handed her the gun. Kit took the gun, and checked it. The safety was off. After resetting it, she released and slid out the magazine off to check whether it was loaded. She counted twelve BBs in the magazine.

Holding the BBs, she looked at Caleb. "Have you shot this gun a lot?" she asked.

"I sh-sh-shot it only one t-t-time," he informed her. "Wh-when I sh-shot my M-mom."

"Where did you shoot your Mom, Caleb? What part of her body did you aim for?" she wanted to know.

Caleb shook his head. "Sh-she s-said the oth-th-er z-z-zombies were g-going to m-make her g-go away. Sh-she p-p-put that p-p-p-part of it h-h-here on her h-h-h-head."

The boy touched the end of the gun barrel, and then his left temple.

Kit inspected the gun. "How did you shoot it?"

"Sh-she s-s-said t-to p-pull really h-hard, s-so I d-did. It m-made a l-lot of b-b-bb's c-come out."

"Caleb," Kit queried. "Can I borrow this gun for a little while? I promise I will give it back really soon."

"T-take it," he said. "Y-you're g-going t-t-to l-look for D-DNA, aren't y-you?"

"How old are you, kid?" she asked.

"S-seven, I th-think. I d-don't really kn-know."

"My friend, Dr. Ainsworth, can help us find out."

"I kn-know h-him. He c-came t-to s-see m-me."

"Yes, he did. He was here when I came for your birthday yesterday, remember?"

Caleb nodded.

Kit continued. "He can play some games with you, called Ages and Stages. I had a friend who played them a long time ago. They can help us to discover your real age."

"Is h-he c-coming t-t-day?"

"Would you like me to call him for you?"

The boy nodded once more. "Is h-he g-going t-t-to t-take me t-to the z-z-zoo?"

She put her hand on top of his. "I'm going to work on doing that," she promised, "just as soon as the doctors tell us it's okay."

Kit stood up. She pulled a Ziploc bag from her purse, and placed the BB pistol in it. "Caleb," she said, "can I borrow your backpack? I know it's a lot to ask, but I need it for a few days."

"C-can I g-get m-my g-games and c-candy out f-first?"

"Whatever you need, Buddy."

Caleb searched through his backpack, pulling out his package of SourPatch kids, two additional zombie games, the Gameboy charger, and a pack of batteries. When he was done, he handed the bag to Christine.

"Wh-what are y-you g-going t-to d-do?" he asked.

"More DNA," she said, smiling. "Can I ask you something else?"

Caleb nodded.

"What do zombies look like?"

The boy picked up his Gameboy and pointed to the image of a zombie on the small screen. "J-Just l-like th-this."

"Can I ask you one more thing?"

"Wh-what?" Caleb asked, focusing on opening his bag of candy.

"Why did you say your Mom was a zombie?"

The boy was silent. For a moment, the only sound in the room was Sarah's deep breathing, and the crinkling of a stubborn candy wrapper.

Christine thought for a moment she had pushed too hard. "Caleb, are you okay?"

Thoughtfully, he spoke. "Sh-she w-was s-s-supposed t-to b-be one of th-them. Sh-she t-told m-me. B-But th-the z-z-zombie m-men d-didn't kn-know sh-she was p-p-pregnant."

The agent was stunned with this revelation. "Oh, Caleb," she offered.

"Th-They k-kept t-telling h-her sh-she w-was g-going to d-die. He h-hit m-me a l-lot. B-but sh-she d-didn't d-die. W-we s-stayed q-quiet, a-and th-they l-left us al-lone. Sh-she g-got us f-food wh-when th-the m-mean oth-ther l-lady and th-the o-th-thers w-were g-gone. Sh-she m-made m-me sh-shoot h-her. Af-fter th-that, th-they all w-w-went aw-way, ex-xcept th-the b-big one. H-he t-told m-me t-to s-stay out-t of s-sight. Th-then h-he was th-the onl-ly one w-with Z-Z-Zombie-Mom. H-he t-told m-me h-he w-was m-my D-dad."

Kit wasn't sure she could maintain her composure. Her hand went to her cheek. Feeling the wetness, she brushed the tears away.

"Are y-you c-crying, K-Kit B-Birth-d-day L-Lady?" Caleb asked.

She reached up and hugged him. "Yes, I guess I am," she answered. "I'm so glad we're friends."

"I'm y-your *f-friend?*" the boy looked at her in surprise.

"Absolutely," she told him. "Can I bring you anything when I come back?"

"Y-you h-have t-to l-leave?"

"I'm sorry. I have to get to work. And the sooner I get my work done, the sooner I can come back to see you. Can you tell Miss Sarah I was here, and ask her to call me, please?"

"Y-yes m-ma'am," he answered. "Th-thank y-you f-for c-c-coming t-to s-see m-me."

"You're welcome, buddy! I'll see you soon."

After leaving the hospital, Christine made her way to the Westwood precinct. Considering the flow of traffic, she realized that even with a longer visit to the hospital than she had planned for, she was on the road much earlier than early morning rush hour.

As she pulled through the Starbucks' drive-through, her mind was swirling with questions. Was the boy crazy, and mixing his games with his real life? She had heard of such things happening. Sarah had called it a psychosis; a break in sane thought.

But Caleb seemed sane; just filled with anxiety. She wondered what he had witnessed that had caused him to stutter. Had it been being forced to shoot his own mother?

Who had Caleb's mother been? And, what role did Landon Morrow play, since the boy's name wasn't really Morrow, but Jacobs?

And how were zombies involved? Were they real? The boy had told her they looked like the zombies in his game... but he also said he had *touched* them.

There are no such things as zombies.

Christine shook her head. This case was starting to mess with her head.

The boy has a psychosis.

Gazing at Starbucks' black-screened speaker to order her morning coffee, she was reminded of Caleb's pistol. Who in their right mind had purchased a CO2, BB pistol for a three or four year old? Why hadn't the boy's mother just purchased a .22?

She didn't have money? She couldn't go out? Caleb said they had to be quiet and had to hide.

Where did they hide in a house full of cameras? How did they hide?

No, there would have to be a record of a .22 sale, wouldn't there? And, if the girl was ordering a weapon by mail, she would have planned it well. Christine hadn't seen a BB pistol like this one before; it had a magazine like some of the old-school handguns guns she had seen when her Dad was alive.

She had noticed a dried substance sticking to the end of the pistol barrel. Granted, it could be French fries, or old ketchup. Or even both. But, if Caleb had held the barrel to his mother's temple and he had pulled hard on the trigger, the gun would have fired in semi-automatic mode. There were twelve left in the magazine. His mother had loaded it for him.

Christine decided she would get it to the Crime Lab right away.

And where had Landon Morrow gone? What was his real name? And, if he wasn't Caleb's father, what was his purpose in the network? Was he even still alive?

Erin Kasabian awakened early Tuesday morning, long before Garrett came in to wake her. He had been so nice, and had apologized for lying to her. He wasn't really eighteen, he told her. He was twenty-nine. She had just been so beautiful he had fallen in love, he said. He had watched her for days before they met on Facebook.

She could feel the struggle happening inside her head. She felt confused, but she didn't want to think about it. Had she really been so angry with her family?

She was feeling better since the Relaxation Classes started on Sunday.

This place wasn't at all like the nasty storage areas she had heard about. In those places, the girls slept on mattresses on the floor and begged for food. Garrett said those ideas came from the shows she had seen on television.

Apparently, what he had said was true. Angelica had told her these people were different than most groups like this as well.

If she was honest about it, she considered, she had been treated very well. Sure, they had handcuffed her, but Garrett said it was to keep her from getting lost. The house was in the middle of nowhere, and they were concerned someone might shoot her if she went outside the house. It wasn't safe for her.

She felt so protected.

Thinking about it, she hadn't been outside of her room since Angelica left. It *had* been a little lonely. But she was used to that, she considered.

Garrett said she would be thankful for the quiet once the classes really started. They had given her copies of her favorite magazines to read. No one had hit her; no one had hurt her. In fact, they had been kind to her. She had been fed all of her favorite foods. All she had to do was ask.

So far, she had been given a massage every day, and a foot treatment. The body waxing hadn't been fun. She had watched DVDs and Netflix for hours. Tomorrow she was going to get a complete makeover, and extensions.

They were making her take vitamins.

And the nurse had given her shots that made her sick for a day or so. The woman had explained they were keeping her healthy. She would be going to a country where the immunizations she was receiving were necessary.

The stories her mother had told her about groups who stole girls just weren't true, she decided. Her mom only knew what she saw on television too, Erin determined.

Mom was *so* out of touch.

Angelica, the girl sent away just before her, had warned Erin's beginning would be difficult, but if she held out, and went through all the classes, she would be a rich man's wife, with servants and a pool. She would be able to do anything she wanted.

Wow. Erin was amazed.

How did *she* get so lucky, she wondered?

There was one caveat, however. She wouldn't *ever* be able to go back home again.

Who cared, she reasoned? She felt disconnected from her parents anyway..... Did it really matter if she didn't see them? After all, *they* had caused the distance she felt.

Did she *really* want to pass up the idea of living the dream?

Garrett told her his job was to get her ready for her Prince Charming. Then he had kissed her. It had been a real kiss. She had felt it down to her toes.

"Will *he* kiss me like that?" she wanted to know.

"Better," he told her.

"Are you still going to teach me?" she asked.

He had just smiled, and touched her cheek. "Don't worry about it, baby," he told her. "You will have all the sex you want sooner than you think."

Other than that kiss, he hadn't been intimate with her. But he was taking her through the Relaxation Classes.

She hadn't taken classes like these before. A Relaxation Class? First, a Yoga instructor had come to her room, to teach her how to stretch and relax. The lady had given her brand new designer exercise clothes. Then, at the end of the session, Garrett had come in and asked her to sit in the recliner in the corner where she usually watched her shows.

The first Relaxation Class had taken place Sunday night. She didn't recall what had happened completely. She did remember the spa music. She sat in the recliner, and Garrett came behind the chair, rubbing her temples, speaking softly.

She had never felt that way before, she realized. Garrett had told her to close her eyes and think about her favorite place. Then, he instructed her to visualize a stairway leading downwards. She remembered beginning to count the stairs.

Then she woke up.

It was becoming increasingly difficult to remember anything before she had come to this place. Except her name. "My name is Erin Kasabian," she murmured to herself. "I have need to *remember.*"

She did still remember the GPS/identity chip being inserted into her shoulder. It still was a little uncomfortable. That had been the first day. She couldn't reach the wound, and hadn't been able to check it out in a mirror yet. On the other hand, the bandage had been removed a couple of days before. And this morning, the stitches were being removed.

Garrett said they had inserted the chip because she was so important to the man who was buying her. She could never get lost or be forgotten in a country she didn't know. He told her not to worry. It would heal quickly. Besides, he promised, she would forget all about it before long.

He told her she would be getting a tattoo soon. Right on top of the incision line, so the scar would be well hidden.

This was really cool, she thought.

All she knew was she finally felt excitement about her future.

Today, she would get to begin Deportment Classes with Miss Anastasia. Miss Anastasia had lived all over the world, and could speak many languages. She had worked for the government. She was going to teach her how to please her Prince Charming. That would ensure she would live the dream for her whole life.

She had asked, but Miss Anastasia hadn't revealed what happened to girls who didn't make their buyer happy.

On another note, Garrett told her they would give her a new name. She would always be Erin Kasabian, but her new name would make her able to travel with a passport. Now, part of her training would include developing a habit of answering to that name. Her Prince would always call her by her new name.

Erin hoped her new home would be Paris. She had always wanted to see the Eiffel Tower...

It was late that night when Christine's phone rang.

"Hello. Spada speaking."

"Hey, Kitten."

"Hi Mom. How was your day?"

"About the same as it usually is," her mother replied. "You?"

"We're working on a new case. Director Edwards has me opening a new field office in Greenway."

"He told me."

"Just a minute, Mom. I'll be right back."

Christine put her phone on mute, and walked into the office area of her townhouse. She ensured the wireless scrambler was working. There were things she wanted to say, that she didn't want to be overheard.

"Okay," she said. "Sorry. I just had to make sure of something."

"Surveillance scrambler?"

"How'd you know?"

"I was a cop's wife for over twenty years, Honey," came the reply.

Christine laughed. "Oh, yeah, I forgot," she teased. She paused. "What's up?"

"You've been on my heart this morning."

Kit's guard went up immediately.

"Oh, Mom. Can't you just say you miss me? Why does it have to be about impending doom all the time?"

"I do miss you. But it's not like that."

"Yes, it is. Ever since Dad's death, you see disaster everywhere."

There was silence on the other end of the line. Although she regretted her words, Kit said nothing. Finally, her mother answered.

"I mean it. I woke up with this feeling this morning. And I haven't been able to shake it all day. Are you all right?"

"I'm fine, Mom. But think about it. You know I'm not somebody's secretary. I have to carry a gun."

"I think the Lord wants you to be aware and be careful."

Christine rolled her eyes and sighed. "Okay," she said. "Now you're using God to get through to me. I get it. You love me. I gotta go."

Her mother paused. "Hey! Don't be like that!" she said.

"Like what?" Kit protested. "I know you found religion after Dad died. But I didn't. That's great for you. Let's just leave God out of it. Okay?"

"He cares about you, Kitten."

"Yeah, yeah, I know. Jesus loves me," Christine said. Again, she was sorry almost as soon as the words left her mouth.

Her mother sniffed. "Sorry I bothered you."

"I'm sorry, Mom."

"It's okay. I forgive you."

"I'm just stressed."

"I'm still going to pray for you."

Christine took a deep breath. She had hoped for a long time her mother would come back to normal. But that wasn't happening today.

"Thank you, Mom. I love you too," she replied.

"Call me."

"Yes ma'am. Talk to you soon."

Annabelle Carnes was tired of being held in the WPCC, or the Westwood Village Police Precinct and County Correctional Center. She had spent the past five days being shuffled to various areas of the Corrections Buildings: Interrogation Room Five in the precinct building, a 6'x8' jail cell, the prisoners' mess, and the exercise yard.

Under the Patriot Act, Annabelle was classified as an alleged terrorist. As such, she had not been allowed a phone call, nor had she been allowed to contact an attorney.

She resented both of these. After all, she was an American citizen. It wasn't her fault if she had relationships with people who had been involved in trafficking.

She hadn't killed anyone – at least personally.

In her own opinion, she hadn't done anything wrong.

But these do-gooders thought they had the right to get into her business. Landon would be pissed.

She wished she knew where he was.

She wished she knew where the kid was.

More than anything, she wished she knew what Donald Daniels had told these jerks over the past few days. The detectives had appeared to believe his cover story the day they found the kid in the house on Parrot Circle. It was a thin lie, and she knew it. Just a little digging past the veneer could cause huge trouble for the big bosses.

She shuddered. She hoped she wouldn't be on the bad end of that stick.

At the moment, Annabelle was once again in Interrogation Room Five, sitting across a table from yet another party wanting information about the house on Parrot Circle. This woman, however, was not a police detective. She was just a social worker. Louisa, or whatever she had said her name was, had no idea about the operation. Apparently, she just wanted to know the seven year old boy's story.

Annabelle had considered the problem of Caleb's existence for most of the past few afternoons. The detectives had taken the boy, and there was no telling how much he had spilled, or not spilled. If shw told the truth, she wasn't really sure he how much he even understood about the things he had seen and heard.

Smart kid. Too smart for his own good.

Annabelle had to admit she was worried about him.

But not enough to want to protect him.

It was a matter of time before someone took him out.

"Ms. Carnes, did you hear me?" Louisa asked.

Shaking her head, Annabelle looked at the social worker in anger. She flicked her cigarette ashes into the ashtray, and then took another draw. After blowing out, she answered.

"No," she retorted. "I'm kinda tired of being abused. I'm not a terrorist. I'm just a stripper. You know, a workin' girl. When my lawyer hears about this, you guys will have a king-sized lawsuit on your hands. I want to go home, and I want to go home now."

Louisa smiled kindly. "I'm sorry, Ms. Carnes, that is out of my hands. There are some charges pending against you, but I'm not the one you need to speak with about that, I need to get my questions answered. When I have satisfactory answers from you regarding the care and living conditions of Caleb Jacobs, you will be closer to being able to go home. I will repeat the question. Who is Caleb's father?"

"Are you kidding me?" Annabelle exploded. "I have answered this question ten times already."

"But not for Family Services," Louisa replied. "You said in your first interview that a Landon Morrow is Caleb's father. You stated that he is the owner of the house at 1224 Parrot Circle. Do you remember making those statements?"

"Yeah," Annabelle sneered. "That's what I said."

"Okay," replied Louisa. "We have new information from various sources which indicate you have lied to us. I personally find it difficult to believe your initial answers have merit."

"Oh, yeah?" the stripper answered. "I don't know anything. I can't tell you what I don't know."

"Tell me about the games you bought for Caleb."

"The Zombie games? So, I bought the kid some games."

"Did you know he has a BB pistol?"

"Yeah, but he just waves it around, and looks at it sometimes."

"Where did he get it?"

"He had it when I came to the house."

"Landon Morrow is not the boy's father, if his last name is Jacobs."

"Who told you his last name was Jacobs?"

"Never mind."

"What can you tell me about the boy's mental state? Are you aware he thinks he sees zombies?"

"I know. He says he sees them all the t me. The kid is crazy, and he's a killer. Did they tell you he killed his own mother?"

Louisa made a note. "Tell me about that."

Annabelle sighed. "Okay, but I need protection. These people are dangerous, and you have no idea who they are connected with. I don't want to end up dead because I talked to you."

"Ms. Carnes, you've been here for five days. They already believe you have given us information. You might as well cooperate with us. Help me to help Caleb. If you remain quiet, believe me, I will see to it you are charged with abuse of a minor, attempted murder of a minor, negligence and emotional cruelty. I promise you I will add as many charges as I can to the list, to make sure you never see the light of day again."

Annabelle was surprised. This lady was no slouch. It was true, though. By now, the bosses knew the house on Parrot was compromised. They knew she had been arrested. In reality, she was surprised they hadn't sent someone to get rid of her.

Yeah, the chick was right. She was as good as dead.

"Fine," she said. "What do you want to know? I don't know much about their operations, but I know they's big."

Louisa observed Annabelle's body language.

Yes, the woman was willing to talk. Annabelle appeared to understand just how precarious her situation really was, and she was scared. If anyone knew about Caleb, it would be this woman. But Louisa's curiosity was aroused. Who were "they's," and what were their "operations?" She paused to consider her next question.

"Annabelle," she began, "tell me about Caleb. Tell me how he thinks. How old is he? What kind of stuff has he seen and heard? You said he killed his mother. Do you know how he did it? How has he been abused? Did you abuse him? And if so, how? When did he begin to stutter, or has he always stuttered? We need to help him have a bright future, and become a contributing citizen."

"Well," Annabelle began, "Caleb is very smart, much smarter than his years. When she was at the house, Miss Anastasia taught him to read some, but he doesn't want anyone to know. I think he's older than seven, but I don't know. He just knows too much, and makes too many connections in his head, you know?"

Louisa nodded. She was taking notes. "What has he seen and heard?" she prodded.

"Apparently, his mom was one of the abducted girls. Morrow was on the kidnap team then. His guys didn't do their homework. The girl was four months pregnant. He got scared and lied to the bosses. Then he found out the girl's boyfriend had been involved somehow. So, he ripped a camera outta one of the back rooms, and set her up in there. After she 'ad the baby, he told the bosses the house had been compromised, and they set up the house on

142

Mackaw Drive. I wasn't in the house on Parrot then, but a chick who works with me at the strip club was sleeping with Morrow then, and sometimes slept over there."

"What is her name?" Louisa asked.

"Doesn't matter," Annabelle told her, lighting up once more. "They killed her."

"What kind of things has Caleb seen?"

"A lot I would think," Annabelle answered with a shrug. "Every month or so, they steal a girl. They put them through some sort of finishing school, and then sell them. They make them customized for the buyer, you know?"

"But what did Caleb *see*?"

"He probably saw people die. He saw lots of blood. He saw lots of violence. Yes, he killed his mama. They was going to sell her and then kill him. When she died, Landon decided to let the kid live. He tol' him he wanted t'be 'is father. That's why I thought he was."

"Did he see any zombies? Besides the ones on the games you bought him?" Louisa asked.

"All the time!" Annabelle was incredulous. "You didn't know that?"

Louisa was writing furiously now.

"And, yes," she said sneering, "I did abuse the boy, but he deserved it. I also kept him alive. I could have let him starve. I didn't have to keep my mouth shut when he went sneakin' out into the neighborhood. I left him alone."

"Did you buy him clothes and shoes, or underwear?"

"I did my best. I'm no mother, and I never had one. So don't go thinkin' I knew what to do and just didn't do it."

"It didn't occur to you to feed him regularly? Or to purchase new clothing that fit him? What about shoes — don't you wear shoes? Why wouldn't he?"

Annabelle was irate. "Are you for real?" she shouted. "I told you; I never 'ad a mother! I 'ad to raise meself! All I know how to do is take my clothes off, and work on my back. I never even had a dog. I didn' have no Dad neither. I fed the kid when I remembered. And I did buy him his clothes. He wasn't supposed t'go outside, so I didn't

143

think he needed shoes. Morrow wouldn't let me take him to a doctor, or nothing, so don't blame me. He's not even my kid!"

Louisa stopped writing. She looked at Annabelle. "If you want to avoid prosecution, let me suggest you make a deal with the detectives. Offer to tell them everything you know in exchange for immunity. Their response might surprise you."

Chapter Eleven

When seven o'clock came that evening, the taskforce met once more in Christine Spada's townhouse. Each team member attended, after working independently most of the day.

Felipe worked more than nine hours to complete networking the FBI's new field office with servers in Washington, D.C. He was eager to surprise the team with a video conference with Deputy Director Edwards during dinner.

For his part, Josh spent the day following the silver sedan as they tailed Christine. During her time in the hospital early that morning, the two men assigned to follow her had placed another GPS tracker under the left rear wheel well of her car. While watching them, Josh ran their license plates through the Department of Motor Vehicles. He discovered the car belonged to a John D. Daniels. With the man's address in hand, he headed to the taskforce meeting.

That day, Pete began an investigation sparked by the taskforce's meeting the night before. There were several persons of interest he wanted to look into with a more intense light. Christine had told him to go for it. Halfway through the day, Louisa had sought him out in the precinct to let him know that Annabelle Carnes wanted to make a deal: immunity for information. That interview had gone very well. In fact, he felt they would make great steps forward because of her testimony.

Evan had spent the day setting up a second set of team for several Search and Seizures, along with other warrants provided in files in Christine's file-box.

Samantha had driven to Christine's immediately after leaving Anne Ventura's office in the Judicial Building. She and Christine met in the club house weight-room provided by Kit's Homeowner's Association.

Christine was used to doing her cardio exercise at home in the mornings before heading out. Her new friendship with Samantha was teaching her new way to improve on her muscle strength. She decided she was thankful for Sam, and the communication they were developing. Sam was turning into a real friend. Not only that, the young woman was a natural at personal training. The afternoon exercises really pushed her limits.

After the work-out, Samantha came back to Kit's until time for the meeting. She talked with Felipe while Christine made sure all was ready for the meeting. There were several discoveries which Christine wanted to share with the team that night, in addition to items already on the agenda.

As they came together, Christine opened communication with a question. "Pete," she said, "Louisa said Annabelle Carnes wanted to see you. How did your meeting go?"

Pete winked at her. "She starts working with a sketch artist in the morning."

"Oh?" Christine's eyebrows went up.

"Yeah," he said. "She's going to help us get a picture of Landon Morrow. His name keeps surfacing, and he's not in any database, and there are no records of any kind we can find with that name. The sketch artist is Allen Peel from the SouthPark precinct."

"Oh, good choice," Christine told him. "I remember seeing one of his sketches when he first joined the force. Sometimes I can't tell if his sketches are photographs or drawings. Can I ask you a question?"

"Sure," he answered. "What's up?"

Christine laughed. "How hard would it be to kill someone with a CO2, BB pistol?"

Peter sobered. "You're serious?"

"As a heart attack."

"What kind is it?" the detective asked.

Christine opened the file and read the description. "Crosman, semi-automatic air pistol, CO2 tank. Eighteen BBs fill the magazine. It shoots a BB at four hundred and fifty feet per second."

Pete walked over to where she stood. "Where was it aimed, and by whom?"

Christine lowered her voice. "Our little seven year old had it in his backpack. He said he was forced to shoot his mother when he was little, because she was a zombie, and she asked him to. From what he told me, she loaded it, put the gun to her temple, and told him to pull the trigger as hard as he could."

"That would kick the gun into semi-auto mode," Pete told her. "How many went into her?"

"I counted twelve left in the magazine, so it looks like six went into her," she answered. "There was matter on the end of the barrel, and what looked like dried ketchup. I'm sure her fingerprints are on the gun somewhere; At least on the magazine. The boy says he hasn't fired it since. Although, he says he has held it. I sent it to the Crime Lab for processing."

Pete let out a slow whistle. "That's a new one," he told her. "Yeah, that would definitely kill someone."

"I thought so, too," she said. "Thanks.

Raising her voice, Christine called out, "Okay, everyone. Let's get started, since there is much more to cover tonight than I thought there would be. And, I'd like us all to have time for all of us to get a chance to view some of the video on the USB from Mackaw Drive."

Everyone began making their way into the townhouse office space from various rooms on the ground floor.

As the taskforce was taking their chairs, she said, "Let me begin by saying 'thank you' to all of you for the hard work you are doing on this case. Right now, I feel like we all are playing 'catch up' in order to find ourselves on the same page. That being said, does anyone have anything new to add regarding the evidence boards we created last night?"

"I do," Evan spoke up. "Per your request, I called the offices in Van Nuys, New York, and Chicago this morning, and asked each of them to check for DVRs in the hub houses used in each city. I also called NamUs (National Missing and Unidentified Persons System) for a listing of young women who might have been pregnant when they disappeared between the ages of twelve and sixteen. Each of these groups will send their information in the next few days."

"Awesome," Kit told him. Anything else?"

"I thought tomorrow I would interview David Fletcher's family members about the empty casket, and see if I can get a read of what they know and don't know," Evan offered.

"Go for it," Kit answered. "Pete?"

Pete took a deep breath. "After I left you at the hospital, I took a drive up Route twenty-one to Musketville to interview Erin Kasabian's brother. He had not seen her. He hasn't even talked to her for over ninety days. I checked his phone records, and he was telling me the truth. From Musketville, I drove to Denniston to see Erin Kasabian's sister, Cody. Cody Kasabian told me that as far as he knew, the sister had stopped all contact with the family over a year ago. She had moved in with her boyfriend at that time. But, when I got to the address we were given, the boyfriend was there, working on his car. He hasn't seen the girlfriend since a year ago last fall. She just disappeared."

Kit paused, surprised. "Are you telling me the other Kasabian girl is missing as well?"

Pete nodded. "That's what I'm saying. No one has heard from her, parents included, for over a year."

Samantha was incredulous. "If I don't call my mom for two days, she goes into super-stalker-parent mode. How could a parent not talk to their grown child for over a year?"

"You'd be surprised," Josh told her offhandedly.

"Did the boyfriend know what happened?" Kit asked.

Pete nodded. "I took his statement. She had sent him with some of her belongings, to move into the house. She was going to follow in a few days. He said he had called the police when she didn't arrive. He was concerned she had gotten lost on her way. The police found no sign of her between Greenway and Denniston. So, he gathered she had changed her mind about moving in. It never occurred to him she might have been abducted. He figured she was mad. They had been fighting a lot the week before.

"Did you ask for DNA, Detective?" Kit asked.

"I sure did, Agent," Pete smiled at her. "I have her toothbrush, a hairbrush, and a pair of underwear he had not been able to wash or get rid of. In fact, her clothes and belongings were still in the box she sent with him when he moved. He told me he was waiting for her to return to him."

"Eww," Samantha interjected. "He didn't wash her underwear?" She looked at Felipe. "Do guys do that? Really?"

Felipe looked at her. "Some guys. That guy. Not this guy," he said.

Kit laughed, and then coughed into her hand. *Don't blow your cover with her as my fiancé,* she thought.

"Fernando, Sweetheart?" she directed the title towards Felipe. "What discoveries did you make today?"

"Los sientos, *mi amor*," Felipe told her. "We are now networked with the D.C. office. While I was working, I also did some research with the main database. It seems the medical supplies being distributed by David Fletcher overseas are being shipped from Gallagher Medical in Denniston, just outside the city. We will need to do some undercover work, I think, to get the 'who' and 'what.'"

"Probably," Kit answered.

Josh spoke up. "Something interesting came to light today as well. The silver sedan that's been tailing Kit for the past couple of week has plates in this state. When I ran them, I expected them to take me back to Asami motors, but no such luck. The car's plates are registered to a John D. Daniels, address 1224 Parrot Circle. Seems too coincidental to me. Anyone else?"

"Doesn't that little detail give us a reason to tie Asami to this whole thing *in person*? I know we have been collecting evidence to build a solid case against the guy, but this is definitely a bigger chip in the game. Do we want to pick him up yet?" Felipe was asking.

"Not yet. I'm almost sure we need to get more. I still have questions unanswered. We probably should wait to speak with Director Edwards," Kit replied.

Felipe looked at his watch. "We have a video conference call set up with him at eight this evening. I set it up to surprise you all."

Kit looked at her watch. "It's three minutes til!" she said. "Let's pick this back up after the conference call."

The phone began to ring. Felipe clicked the computer mouse and Ben Edwards appeared on the screen. Seeing his face, Kit was reminded how much she appreciated and respected this man, who had stepped in as a second father when her own father had died.

"What a great group of agents!" he greeted them. "Hi, Kit, Fernando, Joshua, and the rest of you! I'm Deputy Director Edwards. Who are the other three investigators I don't know yet?"

Kit laughed. "Ben, this is Peter Lynch, Detective first-class, and Evan Davies, also Detective first-class. Both of these are now on our taskforce, and I hope to send them for field training at some time in the near future." Both detectives stood as their names were spoken, and nodded towards the large computer screen.

"And who is the beauty queen?" Ben asked, looking at Samantha who was smiling shyly.

"This is Samantha Cruz. She is presently working full-time, clerking for Judge Ventura. By night, however, she is helping me as an admin and support person."

"How do you like things so far, Samantha?" Ben asked.

"Fabulous, sir," Sam replied, with a bright white smile.

"It's good to have all of you on the team," Ben told them. "Kit, in the next few days, several agents are going to be pulling off of the investigations on this case, in cities where the trail on this group has gone cold. Call me in the morning, and let's talk about increasing your taskforce."

"Yes sir," Kit answered.

"It's good to meet all of you," he said once again. "Have a great evening."

"Thank you, sir," Kit told him.

"No, thank *you*, Agent Spada," came the reply.

The computer screen went to the FBI Shield, and then Felipe clicked the mouse once more to close the call.

It was Pete who spoke as soon as the screen went black. "Agent Spada?"

"Yes, Detective?"

"Thank you for the opportunity to serve on this team."

"You're welcome. Thanks for the hard work you are doing."

Pete paused. "I have something to add to our conversation. The Crime Lab printed out phone records for the two cell phones belonging to Erin Kasabian and Katie Curtin that Evan and I retrieved yesterday afternoon. Both girls were texting a young man named Garrett who claimed to be a senior at Hunter Ridge High School in Westwood. He used the same phrases and persuasive words with both girls. He seems to be very skilled in parental alienation."

Kit looked at him with interest. "Do you think this Garrett really *is* a student?"

Pete shook his head. "No. He's probably a sexual predator. Although he's most likely much older than eighteen; maybe even in his thirties or forties. I doubt any of the girls met him in person before they were abducted. Now, Erin makes it clear in her texts to him that she has never had sex before. Katie doesn't say it *clearly,* but her answers are very naïve and inexperienced. And, even though she is sixteen, and most girls that age have become sexually active, that kind of communication indicates she probably is a virgin as well."

Kit gave the matter some thought. "Let's go with that supposition for now. This group is targeting young women who have experienced a divorce between their parents. All of these girls show themselves to be angry and unhappy with their lives.

At some point, they become alienated from both parents. Most are loners. This makes them vulnerable to any young man with charm. Over time the girls begin to send illicit texts, and photos of themselves to draw attention. They use FaceBook, Snapchat, Kik and Instagram.

A majority of young women who fall into this category participate in sexting with their future abductors. This can occur over several days, weeks, or even months. When we are dealing with a sex ring, one member will emerge at some point, as the primary contact person. This is the person who will suggest meeting the girl in person; usually promising to have sex with her.

"Now, we have recovered a third teenage girl's cell from the hotel room murder site in Eastgate. The texts on that phone were almost identical to the other two. This girl's name was not clear from the phone, because her Facebook page was not linked to her phone like the other two, and she used code names for Instagram and Snapchat. I'm not sure why, unless a parent had put controls on her emails and texts. She would have needed to get around those controls with the two Applications.

"In all three of these cases, the girls made an appointment to meet Garrett; which is, incidentally, the same name these kidnappers used in Chicago. Also, the night of each appointment coincides with the time of each girl's disappearance."

"Hey," Felipe interjected. "I have a question. In which cultures overseas are girls married as soon as they start menstruation? I mean, it seems like those countries would be where we should begin to search for potential buyers, and lost girls."

"That's true," Kit replied.

"Oh, and Kit?" Samantha spoke up. "I had some spare time in the Judge's office today. I got to thinking about the meeting we had last night. I went online, and looked for publications that specifically target rich men, here in the States, and abroad. I found a pretty good list. Isn't it also possible that classified ads have been placed in newspapers in the same nations like Fernando suggested?"

"Those are great leads, Sam," Kit replied. "Can you keep working on that, and give Fernando any websites you might find?"

"Will do," Sam answered.

"Okay," Kit said. "Let's look at the murder case in Eastgate, and the Crime Lab's report."

She pointed to the picture of the bathtub full of body parts. Then she added the square of carpet she had taken from the Best Western's suite room floor. The pictures of the bloody sheets, the mattress and the bed were posted under that. Then she attached the Crime Lab report received earlier in the day.

She glanced around at the taskforce, assessing her team members. Samantha and Josh were looking like they were about to be sick.

"The Crime Lab had difficulty on this one. At the moment, they can't put even one body back together. Not only were body parts missing, but the parts belonged to more than four different persons."

"What do you mean, missing?" Josh asked. "And more than four?"

Kit looked around, focusing on Samantha and Josh. "I was physically ill when I first read this report," she told them. "So, if you begin to get nauseous, I'll stop, and let you leave the room to take care of any problems before we continue."

152

She posted pictures of the Crime Lab's examination tables, showing dismembered limbs of four mutilated bodies, on separate tables, with parts missing. Each one was loosely pieced together according to DNA matches. The process had taken all day.

Christine continued. "The Medical Examiner's team has done a great job of cleaning these body parts up. They have done a lot to help us. Apparently, a chainsaw, or something like a chainsaw, was used post mortem, to separate the legs from the trunk and the arms from the trunk. We found only one head in the bathtub, which explains the confusion of the parts all belonging to one person. However, in regard to this one head; the eyes, cheeks, ears and lips had been removed. The trunk of one body was present, but internal organs were missing. However, there were four full spines present.

Now, there was a mixture of DNA and blood types found, soaking into the sheets and the mattress. The Lab was unsure as to whether they could separate those well enough to draw reasonable conclusions."

She paused. "We did run the DNA matches through CODIS and found some connections."

She put the pictures of the victims on the board. "These are the victims, when their faces were intact. Each of these four were already in the file-box I have been building for the past few months.

However, not *everyone* in the bathtub was from the Greenway area. In fact, one gentleman was from Ontario, Canada. Also, not all of the DNA from body segments in the bathtub have been assigned to persons. Some pieces they are still working on.

"I'll give you a few minutes to absorb this part of the case."

Silently, she moved back to the first board. After a few moments, she spoke once more.

"Before we watch the video from the house on Mackaw, I have one more thing to share. I spoke with Caleb Jacobs this morning, the seven year old boy rescued from the house on Parrot Circle. We mistakenly thought his name was Morrow, since Annabelle Carnes told us Landon Morrow was his father."

She posted Caleb's picture on the first evidence board. "But.... Caleb told me this morning that his mother was a zombie, and that he killed her with his BB pistol."

Josh and Evan involuntarily laughed.

"Seriously?" Josh asked. "You've got to be kidding!"

"Yes, seriously," Kit answered. "Apparently, the mother was an abducted girl who was pregnant when kidnapped. To quote the boy: Caleb said the 'big one' made her hide in a back room on Parrot Circle. The other zombies would hurt her. It's unclear how old Caleb really is. It's my personal opinion that Caleb is older than seven. He will undergo psychiatric and psychological assessments within the next week, to see if he has experienced a psychological break.

"What he told me is pretty interesting, however. He said the zombies were going to send his mother away, so she bought him his CO2 BB semi-automatic pistol. Apparently, *she* loaded it, and placed the barrel on her temple. She then asked her small son to pull the trigger as hard as he could. He obeyed her, and it killed her. From what we can tell, the gun released six BBs into her brain, killing her."

"Excuse me, Kit," Josh asked. "Did you say *zombies?*"

Kit nodded. "I know, it sounds crazy. But it's weird. This kid *isn't* crazy. He just really *believes* he's seen zombies. He says his *mother* was a zombie. This morning, he showed me his gun. The Crime Lab analyzed some matter I found on the end of the barrel today. They dusted the inside cartridge for fingerprints. The matter is human flesh, probably brain matter, and the dried substance I at first thought might be ketchup is human blood, Type A. The DNA and fingerprints belong to a Melissa Anderson, a young woman reported missing from a New York City family back when the hub houses were operating there."

"How is it we have the DNA of a teenager?" Samantha wanted to know.

Kit looked at her. "Oh, her parents ordered the identification kit we recommend from the National Child Identification website when she was small. It helps parents have a complete record of their kid's identity; DNA, picture, fingerprints, that kind of thing. Melissa's Mom is a nurse with CPS in New York and did one for each of her children. When Melissa disappeared, she handed it to us, hoping it would help us rescue her."

154

She posted the picture of Caleb's mother next to the boy's photograph. On the white board, she wrote their names: Caleb Jacobs, and Melissa Anderson.

"Apparently, Caleb's father has no idea he has a son, since Melissa was in hiding from her pregnancy forward. It's my guess she named the boy and used the father's name. It would probably be a great service to him to add 'finding Caleb's father' to our list of tasks. I don't know about you. I'm a little overwhelmed at the moment, and I think we all need a little time to think these pieces of evidence through."

"Christine, you want to watch the video from Mackaw Drive now?" Felipe offered.

"That would be great, Fernando," she answered.

Felipe moved to the computer once again, and accessed the USB drive. He clicked on the file he wanted to pull up, and pushed the arrow for play. He was the only one who had seen the file so far, and there had been no time to brief Christine on what he had discovered. As a result, an atmosphere of shocked surprise filled the room.

No one was prepared for what they were watching.

All of the perpetrators on the video, with the exception of one old woman, and a tall, modelling-worthy young man...*looked like characters from a zombie movie!*

The taskforce members looked at each other in shock. It was evident the perpetrators appearing on the video were wearing masks, but realization was hitting each one on the team. The people involved in this crime ring were much more organized and technologically savvy than anyone had anticipated.

Samantha was the only one to speak. "Wow!" she murmured quietly.

At three in the morning, a call came through the Greenway Police Dispatch non-emergency line.

"Good morning, Police Dispatch. Officer Collins speaking. How can I serve you?"

"Yeah. There's a truck up here, disturbing our sleep in the middle of the night."

"I'm sorry, madam. Is this an emergency?"

"No, it's not. Isn't this the non-emergency line?"

"Yes, ma'am, it is." Officer Collins could think of ten things he would rather be doing than answering a complaint call about a trucker returning home from a run. He could just see this woman, probably nosy, with nothing else to do, peering through her window blinds, spying on her neighbors. Why the woman on the phone taken a sleeping pill?

"Well?"

"Is the trucker a resident of your neighborhood?"

"I doubt it," she replied. "I've never even *seen* a semi in our neighborhood before."

"Was the house in question recently purchased?"

"No, unless they did it without a sign in the yard."

"Is it possible the house was inherited, and the new owners are moving in?"

"No. I'm not sure."

"Okay." There was a moment or two of awkward silence.

"Listen, Mister, something weird is happening. The house has been sitting empty for more than a year. But the people never moved out. Somebody came to take care of the yard and the mail. We thought they must have moved away, but every once in a while since then, I seen the man come back. For a while, I thought we would see renters move in. But now…. Well, it's just weird."

Collins was beginning to listen. "What do you mean?"

"Well, my husband works at the freight yard up by the railway station. He said stuff has been going on for a month now, but he just mentioned it to me at breakfast this morning. I been watching all day, and I'm seeing what he sees. I followed one of the cars this afternoon, and they went to Asami Motors, and traded a car in the parking lot, and came right back."

"Maybe it's a loaner while they get their own car fixed," Collins offered. "And what is your name?"

"Mary. Mary Marshall. My husband and me; we live on Ennis Lake," the lady said with a sigh. "And, no. It wasn't a loaner. They

156

had the keys. They just parked next to the second car and transferred their stuff, then got in and took off. It was like they owned that one too. And just parked it there."

"Mrs. Marshall, how much television do you watch in a day?" Collins asked the question before he thought.

"Excuse me?"

"Nothing. Go on, please. I apologize."

"Listen, I know I sound crazy, but someone needs to know. Jim, that's my husband. He works down at the freight yard by the railway station. Well, Jim's job is to record the numbers of the shipping containers when they come off the barges, you know. He writes a report on every train that comes through from the barges. He keeps the records of where those containers go, too. You know, the shipping docks and Port Authority from all over."

"Yes, I'm aware."

"Well, the semi-truck that's unloading in front out here into that empty house came off a barge in Georgia two days ago."

"It might just be the new owner's furniture. Maybe they are from another country and had their stuff shipped."

"I wondered about that, until I started watching them an hour ago."

"Okay." Officer Collins took a deep breath. This lady was creepy; watching her neighbors in the middle of the night. "What is your concern, Mrs. Marshall?"

"Well, the guys unloading started about forty minutes ago. They are all wearing hoodies, pulled up over their faces, like. And baseball caps. Think about that. It's still eighty degrees outside. So, I get the feeling they are trying to not be recognized. When I first saw that, in this kind of weather, and remembered Jim said that container had been part of his daily report, I went and got our binoculars."

"Okay," replied the officer slowly.

Collins rolled his eyes. Protocol required him to allow the woman to tell her entire story, and then let her know they would check it out first thing in the morning. Why couldn't this woman just let her neighbors be? He tried to imagine what one of her neighbor's expression if this woman showed up wanting to borrow a cup of sugar.

"Did you *see* the furniture? Is it oriental, or modern?" he asked.

"No," she snapped, finally frustrated with this man who just wasn't getting it. "I'm telling you. Something criminal is happening over there!"

"Like what, for instance?"

"Well, can you tell me of any *normal* shipping activity where several young women have to be carried from a shipping container into a house?"

"Oh." What the woman was saying took a moment to register with Officer Collins.

"I'm sorry, ma'am," he said. "I'm a rookie cop, and this is my first week on the job. I didn't understand. Hold on a minute."

After several minutes, another officer was on the line.

"Hi, Mrs. Marshall?"

"Yes."

"This is Lieutenant Boyd. Can we send some detectives out to interview you in a couple hours?"

"Uh. Sure, I guess," Mary replied. "What you *need* to do is help those girls. Those people are up to no good, I'm tellin' ya."

"Yes, ma'am. What is your address?"

"2205 Hydrangea Court Drive, Ennis Lake."

"And a phone where I can reach you?"

"602-555-0908."

The lieutenant repeated both sets of information back to her, confirming what he had written down. "We will send someone out first thing, Mary. Thank you for letting us know."

Hanging up, the lieutenant looked at Collins. "That will be a big break in somebody's case, you watch. Good job, Collins."

"Really? At first I thought it was a prank call."

"No, you did good kid."

As he walked away, Lieutenant Boyd pulled his own cell phone from his pocket. Looking around, he found a quiet place to have a private conversation. There, he decided. Next to the vending machines. After touching numbers for a call, he put the phone to his ear.

"Yeah. It's Boyd."

"I know, but this is important."

"Today's shipment delivery was observed."

"Marshall. 2205 Hydrangea Court Drive, Ennis Lake."

"Marshall. 2205. Yeah."

"Seriously? You know I can't do that."

"Oh, yeah? How 'bout I blow *yours?*"

"No, I can't. Every incoming call is recorded."

"Okay. Yeah.

"I'll do that, but I have to hand in the report with the log."

"You too. Tell your guys to be more careful. One more of these, and ..."

"Right. I get it. I'll take care of it. Boyd out."

In the shadows behind the precinct's vending machines, Officer Chase Stanford stood, dumb-founded. He had tried to find an undisturbed place where he could review and double-check traffic and parking tickets he had written that evening. He was tired of sitting. He had been leaning against the hidden side of the snack vendor.

Motorcycle duty was not his favorite, and he knew it wasn't any other cop's goal either.

As the lieutenant returned his call to his pocket, and walked away, Chase quietly stepped into the light. He made his way to Dispatch.

"Hey, Hunter," he said to the officer on duty of the non-emergency line. "How's it going?"

"Not bad," Collins replied.

"You need some coffee?" Chase asked.

"That would be great man," the rookie replied. "But I can't leave my post."

"Oh, I'll get it for you. How do you like it?"

"Just black."

"Got it. Be right back."

Chase headed to the break area, when he grabbed a couple of mugs, and poured coffee for Hunter and himself. He sat down next to the man at the Dispatch non-emergency desk.

"You get any live ones tonight?" he asked lightly.

Taking sip of his coffee, Hunter answered. "Thanks for this, and yeah, my last call was a real corker. The lieutenant had to finish it for me."

"Really?" Chase asked. "Don't get those very often. Can I see the dialogue?"

"Sure." Hunter pushed the cursor arrow up to review the last call.

As he read, Chase glanced at the rookie. "Wow. This is good stuff."

"I know, right?" Hunter responded.

"Can I get a copy of the printout?"

"Am I allowed to do that before handing in the report?"

"I don't know. I don't think there's a regulation on that," Chase told him with a smile.

"Sure, if I can't get in trouble for it, go ahead."

Having worked the desk as a rookie also, Chase copied the text in question, and pasted it to a new document. Then he pushed print, and sent the document to the main printer.

"Thanks, Hunter. I owe you one," he said. "I'm out of here."

"Whatever, Dude," Hunter answered. "Thanks for the coffee. See you tomorrow."

"Yep. Tomorrow." Chase was halfway to the copy room.

Before leaving the precinct, the young officer sent a text.

"Agent. This number. Call your 'little brother' ASAP."

Chapter Twelve

Two hours later, Christine Spada woke up to the sound of her phone alarm. The night before, she had placed it across the room, after turning the volume completely up. She had been so tired, she had decided it would be the only way she would be able to get up in the morning.

"I'm going to need a nap this afternoon," she muttered, making her way into the bathroom. She brushed the remnants of sleep from the corners of her eyes, and tapped her cheeks as she looked into the mirror.

"You need an extra early espresso, Kit," she said to her reflection. "And it's only Wednesday." She threw on her robe.

On her way down the hall towards the kitchen, she knocked on Felipe's door. "Time to rise and shine, Fernando, my love!" she called.

"Up and at'em!" she heard his answer. "You making something strong *before* you get your Starbucks this morning?"

"You betcha'!" she laughed. "I'm so tired right now, I could sleep all day."

"Sorry, Baby," he said, for the benefit of those they knew were listening. "I know you've had a long coup e of days."

Kit measured the coffee and water, set the coffeemaker brew meter to "extra strong," and then made her way back to her bedroom for a little cardio.

"Get your blood pumping, girl," she murmured. But weariness overtook her efforts. Her workout was half the normal time. Her mind was filled with thoughts of the case.

How did medical supplies tie in with the rest of this group's operation?

How did the body parts get into the hotel? And had the crooks *intend* to get caught? Surely, if the traffickers were so well networked and organized, *and* this was part of their operation…. It seemed like they would have had a plan to continue their activities undetected.

She was beginning to understand the scope of the trafficking side of the case, but she still had some questions. They kidnapped the girls to sell them, but *why* were *men* taken as well? And what about the old woman and the young man in the video? What did they know about the network?

After showering, she set a couple of plates on the kitchen table, and poured herself an extra-large mug of coffee. She then set to preparing herself some protein for breakfast.

"Coffee's done, Fernando!" she called. "And I'm making some eggs!"

She heard his door open. "Thanks, *mi amor!*" he said, coming into the kitchen. He began pouring himself some coffee, as she dished equal parts of scrambled eggs with cheese on each plate. "You want toast?"

"I'll make it," Felipe offered, nodding to the table. "Have a seat. I noticed someone sent you a text overnight."

"Really?" Kit asked. She sat down and picked up her phone, checking out his observation.

"Oh," she told him, after reading. "It's just a note from my brother." Silently, she showed Felipe the text from Chase. *(Agent. This number. Call your "little brother" ASAP.)*

"What's he say?" Felipe asked, nodding to her he understood.

"Not much. Probably needs money again," she answered with a light laugh. "I'll call him when I can. No biggie."

She sat down to eat once more, and began to text.

"I thought I would work on stabilizing my communications for the software development side of things today, Babe," Felipe told her. As he spoke, he wrote a message on a napkin.

Who?

Cop named Chase, she wrote in reply.

"So when will I see you?" he asked.

"I'm knocking off early tonight," she replied. "Probably need a nap before our date tonight."

"Did I tell you where I'm taking you?" he asked her in a teasing tone.

"No," she answered. "I trust you. Just surprise me."

"I will miss you today, *mi Corazon*," he told her.

"Fernando," she replied. "You are entirely too romantic. Love that Latin blood in you."

He opened the front door for her, allowing her to exit with her briefcase. He followed her to the car, keeping watch for the two idiots in the silver sedan. Yup. There they were, complete with their amateurish eavesdropping cone pointed towards the kitchen window. The conversation had been for their benefit. He used the signal jammer in the evenings, knowing by that time of day both of them were ready to quit for the day, and return to their base camp. He smiled to himself. These guys were way too predictable to be very high up in the organization they were dealing with.

He opened Kit's car door for her, and checked it for bugs. Then, placing a finger under her chin, he tilted her face upwards, and lightly kissed her. "Be safe today, Kit," he whispered.

Hugging him, she gave a light answer. "That's the plan!"

Pulling the driver's door shut, Kit pulled out of her parking spot, and waved goodbye. "Fernando" watched her drive out of sight, sighed for the benefit of the idiots, and went back into the townhouse.

On the way to the office, she made the call.

"Hello?" a sleepy voice answered.

"Chase? This is Christine Spada."

"Oh, hi, Agent," he replied. "Sorry, I was sleeping."

"No, I get it, you were on second yesterday, weren't you?"

"Yes ma'am," he replied.

"You want to call me later?" she asked.

"No ma'am. Are you heading into the precinct?"

"Yes."

"I don't want to tell you over the phone. I'll be there in fifteen minutes."

Christine was surprised. "Why? Wha.."

Chase interrupted her. "No worries, ma'am. I just need to tell you something I observed in person."

"Okay, Chase," she told him. "Meet me at my desk."

"See you in a few. Chase out."

Christine pushed the "end" button on the steering wheel. Frowning, she spoke out loud. "Call Ben Edwards."

The phone began to ring.

"Hello. Edwards here."

"Good morning, Ben. It's Kit Spada."

"Morning, Kitten! Enjoyed meeting your team last night."

"Yeah, about that. Can I ask you a question? And I'm not asking it because I'm upset. I just need some clarification."

"You want to know why I sent Joshua as protection detail, when you had asked me to help you get away from him."

She sighed. "You know me! That's it exactly!"

"I would hope I know you. Your Dad asked me to take care of you. He was the brother I never had."

"So why *Josh*, Pops?"

"Well, he still has feelings for you, and he begged me for the case."

"But I told you. We aren't a fit. He's all about himself."

"I understand, Kit," Edwards answered. "But here's the thing: He wanted to protect you, and he is already invested. So, he'll do a better job than another agent. Besides that, he was your partner for three years, and he knows how you think."

Kit laughed. "You would think so, wouldn't you? But I don't believe that's true."

"You want me to call him back to D.C.?"

"No, I can handle it. I just wanted to be sure you weren't matchmaking. I don't think I can handle that kind of pressure, especially if it's coming from you."

Ben paused. "I want you kept safe. He was the best candidate for the job. When this case is done, he's back on my team here."

Kit breathed a sigh of relief. "Thank you, sir. I will do my best to not create drama for the Bureau during this case."

"Okay, Christine. I believe you," he answered. "I appreciate that. Is there anything else?"

"One more thing," she told him. "There is a detective here in Greenway, who got called in on this case. He is the "someone" in the City of Greenway who called Westwood precinct. He

164

determined that a bathtub full of mutilated body parts was tied to our trafficking case. He found a keychain from Asami Motors, and a teenage girl's cell phone in the same hotel room. He called us. Should I involve him on the taskforce? He says he was a friend of my Dad's, and I do remember him being at my fifteenth birthday party."

"I'd like to check him out first, Kiddo," Ben answered.

"He says he was in the Navy with you, and when you went into Police work, he went into the JAG Corps."

"Name?"

"Eric Janzen. I used to call him 'Uncle Jannie,' or just 'Jannie.'"

"Hm-mm.... Don't remember him. Let me get back to you."

"Yes, sir," she answered. "No problem. Talk to you soon."

"Be safe, Kit. You're an angel. Edwards out."

As she hit the "end" button on the steering wheel, Christine pulled into the Starbucks drive through. She placed an order for herself, for Pete, and for Evan. As she was paying, the phone rang once more.

"Spada here."

"Agent," it was Pete's voice. "Are you on your way in?"

"Sure am, and I'm bringing you guys coffee," she answered.

"That's good, because your little brother, Chase, is bugging the crap out of me," he told her. "He says he has pertinent information and will only speak with you."

"Yeah, I know," she replied. "He texted me at three something this morning, but I didn't get it 'til after I woke up at five. Keep him there. I'll be there in a few. Spada out."

Stepping off the elevator onto the fourth floor of the Westwood Precinct, Kit immediately surveyed her surroundings. Evan was working at his computer, apparently researching something to do with the case. She made a mental note to catch up with his progress. Josh was gathering printouts from the printer. Chase was sitting at Pete's desk, where he and Pete were in the midst of what appeared to be an intense conversation.

"Good morning, all!" she greeted, walking to her desk.

Chase stood up immediately and moved towards her. "Ms. Spada, did you get my message?"

"I did, Chase," she told him. "But I got it late, because I didn't look at my phone until I was eating my breakfast at 5:30. Sorry. What's going on?"

The young officer lowered his voice, and moved closer to her. In his hand, he held the printout of the three-thirty in the morning non-emergency call. "Please read this, ma'am, and tell me what you think."

Christine put down her briefcase and handbag, and handed the coffee carrier to Pete. She took the printout and sat down to read it. When she was finished, she looked up at him.

"How did you get this?" she asked.

"I asked Collins to print it out for me. I was behind the vending machines in the corner downstairs. I was trying to find a quiet place to organize my traffic citations before turning them in. I can't really do that on the bike, and there isn't a desk open where I can do that that. While I was there, I overheard Lieutenant Boyd from Homicide made a phone call to someone. He didn't know I was there. It was concerning."

"Why?"

"He said that yesterday's shipment had been observed by someone named Marshall at 2205 Hydrangea Court Drive in Ennis Lake. Whoever he was talking to was upset about the call. He said he couldn't do something they asked him to do, because he had to turn in the Non-Emergency Dispatch Report. Then he said all calls were recorded. They said something, and he said he would take care of it."

As he finished, Chase took a deep breath, and watched Christine for a reaction.

Christine looked at him, and took his handwritten notes. She stapled the transcript of the recorded call to the notepad, and placed it in her open briefcase. She looked at Evan.

"Detective Davies," she said, "We need to head to Ennis Lake immediately for a Search and Seizure. I will make the necessary phone call while you collect a SWAT team."

"Yes, ma'am," Evan responded.

"Detective Lynch," she said, "please arrange for Officer Chase Stanford to join our search team this morning."

"Wha--?" Chase exclaimed.

Christine smiled at him. "Your information. You should be part of the collar."

"Thank you, Agent Spada! You won't regret this!"

"I better not, officer," she teased. "I think you need to go home and put on some jeans and a T-shirt. You have a leg holster?"

"Yes."

"Put it on, and wear a jeans jacket and a baseball cap if you have them."

"I can do that," he smiled.

"Attach your badge to your belt, and get back here as quick as you can. And wear your Kevlar. I need you here, ready to go in forty-five minutes."

"I'll be here. It's just ten to my apartment, less if I take my patrol bike."

"Do it," she told him. "Use your siren if you have to."

Chase turned on his heels and headed for the elevator. Christine then looked at Josh. "Agent Morgan, can you put a tail on Lieutenant Boyd, please, until we know how this turns out? If he tries to leave town, we need to find a reason to detain him."

Josh looked up from his computer. "Will do, Kit," he answered. "Oh, and Allen Peel from the SouthPark Precinct dropped off his sketch of Landon Morrow, from Annabelle Carnes' description. I asked him to sketch the fake Annabelle for us, so we can get an identification."

"Great idea!" she replied. "Thank you!"

"I scanned it into the computer. It's searching through the database to find a facial match, or something close. It'll probably take a while."

"Let's let Fernando do that, Josh," Christine told him. "The field office database is much larger, and we have access to Interpol as well."

"I keep forgetting we our own, bigger system, now."

Christine smiled. "You'll get this. It's not as hard as it looks."

Pete motioned to draw Christine's attention. "We had a message on the machine this morning. A woman named Rosa called."

"The maid from the Best Western?"

"The very same," Pete replied. "She said she kept having something go through her mind about the body in the bathtub at the hotel. She said she has been thinking it's something you needed to know."

"What's going on?"

"She said to tell you that some parts of the body were very, very cold, like it had been in a freezer. But there were other parts that looked soft, like they were warm."

Christine gave the message some thought, and gave Pete a quizzical look. "That's weird. That would confirm all the body parts not being from the same person. But why would there be frozen parts in with fresh parts?"

She jotted down a note to herself. "Thanks," she said.

Pete continued. "I sent an email to the New York City school system, asking for Melissa Anderson's school transcripts. I'm also double-checking her parents' present home address and contact information. Hopefully, that will give us a head start in finding Caleb's father.

"Also, when I got here this morning, I did a driver's license search for the John D. Daniels listed as the owner of at the Parrot Circle address. Interestingly enough, his name came up as John *Donald* Daniels at that address."

"Hey, isn't that Annabelle's 'date' who said he slept over when we swept the house on Parrot?!" Evan queried.

"Yes sir, it is," Pete said. "Apparently, both he and Annabelle lied to us about his involvement."

She smiled at him. "Good work, Detective! Can you have the guys downstairs pick him up and hold him for questioning? He lied to us, and that never goes very well."

"Sure. Oh, and I made a call to the Best Western to request the house surveillance video for the hallway near the hotel room where the body parts were found."

"What did they say?" she asked.

Pete sighed. "They are going to check on it with the manager. The clerk said there *is* a camera in that part of the hotel, but when he checked the security feed, there was no signal from that camera.

He didn't know if it had stopped working, or if it had been disabled. He said he would have the manager call me back."

Her phone began to ring mid-sentence.

"Oh, great. Well, we're back to square one," Christine said to Pete. "Gotta go. Got another call. Spada Out."

"Hello, Agent Spada speaking."

"That's a great way to answer the phone, Kid," a familiar man's voice spoke.

"Well, thank you. It's habit," she replied, still not sure who she was speaking to.

"Kit Angel," the man said. "You still don't know who this is, do you?"

"Jannie?" she asked, recognition kicking in. "It's good to talk to you. What's up?"

"Oh, I don't know," he answered. "I guess I just wanted to talk to someone this morning, and I thought of you."

"Well that's kind of you," Christine said. "Can I call you back in a little bit, Jannie? I'm kind of in the middle of something here, and..."

"Oh, no, Kit," he hastened to reply. "Nothing's going on here. Just wanted to see if we had a date for dinner yet."

"I'm still working on it," she told him. "I do want to get together. And I won't forget about you."

"Okay then," he replied. "I'll let you go. Is there anything with you case I can help with?"

Christine smiled. There it was. He was missing the danger and excitement of his younger days. "I'll tell you all about it when there's time. But I really have to go now. Sorry. Spada out."

Pressing the close call button, and then opening the numbered keyboard, she called Samantha Cruz's cell phone.

"Hey Sam, its Kit."

"Yes, we need a Search and Seizure. Yes."

"For evidence and victims of human trafficking."

"No, I don't have the exact address, or a name."

"I would think it would be either 2202 or 2204 Hydrangea Court Drive, Ennis Lake."

"Can you get her to sign it, and scan it in and send it to me?"

169

"Oh, sorry. You're right."

"Sure. Okay."

"See you in a minute. Spada out."

In the City Crime Lab, two members of the Forensic Team were assessing the condition of the bodies still displayed on tables in the morgue.

"Look at this!" Jennifer, the Assistant Coroner declared. "Someone stripped the arteries and veins from both of these legs!"

"Which victim was it?"

"Um, I can't remember the name," Jennifer replied, "but it was the twenty-five year old guy who ran marathons."

"Those would be pretty healthy legs, then," her co-worker replied. "Did you see the arm on Number Three?"

"No," Jennifer answered. "I haven't made it that far yet."

"The entire skin surface was removed in what appeared to be three and four-inch flaps."

"Like someone would use for a graft?" Jennifer asked.

"Exactly like that, but they've done it like a donor situation. The body was female."

Jennifer stopped and looked at her colleague. "So, where are the rest of the body parts for these people?" she asked. "All I have are the DNA records from CODIS and NamUs. So far, we've had matches that appear to be family matches, but nothing exact."

"I have no clue. This is just weird," came the reply. "And worse, why were these people dismembered like this?"

Jennifer stopped to think. "Cannibalism?" she suggested with a shudder.

Somewhere in the small nation of Paraguay, South America, a billionaire financier was preparing to walk down the aisle in the largest Roman Catholic cathedral in the country. Surrounded by his bodyguards, he looked at the priest in concern.

"Is my lovely bride here yet?" he asked.

"Si, Don Paredes," the priest answered, smiling. "Her maids are helping her prepare to come down the aisle in just a few minutes."

Forty-two year old Juan Paredes, three-time widowed father of eight, and drug cartel, clapped his hands in excitement. "I am so blessed of the Virgin Mother, to be marrying today! Finally, the love of my life has descended from Heaven, just for me!"

"You have experienced so much tragedy, my son," the priest told him, placing his hand on the younger parishioner's shoulder. "More than your share. Perhaps, today is a day of new beginnings for you!"

An altar boy stepped into the anteroom where the groom and his party were waiting. He whispered something to the priest, who nodded in response.

"Are you ready, my sons?" the priest asked.

"More than ready, Father," Juan replied.

A few moments later, the cathedral's great pipe organ began to play. The priest motioned to the groom, and his bodyguards, who were serving as groomsmen. The entourage followed the priest out, into the sanctuary of the cathedral.

Taking their places in front of the altar, the men turned to face the main entrance doors to the church. The church was filled with people. It seemed the entire city had crowded into the cathedral, to witness and honor the union of the two people about to be married. Candles in glass globes stood on cast iron stands at the end of each row of pews. Flowers covered the altar, the platform, and each candle stand.

As the music played, the first bridesmaid walked down the aisle. Everyone knew the bridesmaids were the daughters of Juan Paredes, reported to each be of legendary beauty. His smallest children were appearing as ring-bearer and flower-girls.

Juan's fourth bride was said to be an American woman of incredible beauty. She was younger than he, it was reported, by perhaps as much as twenty years. Those who had seen her said she was somewhere around twenty-six or twenty-seven years of age.

According to the housekeeper at the Don Paredes Estate, the lonely widower had courted his bride for almost a year by long distance.

The servants' gossip mill had buzzed furiously six weeks ago, when Paredes' private jet had landed on his private airstrip, carrying Victoria and her bodyguard. Since then, the woman had spent time on his estate, preparing for the wedding.

As the bride walked down the aisle, she did so without a veil. She was smiling nervously, wearing a head-dress of orchids and traditional mantilla lace. Well-rehearsed, she stepped slowly, in time to the music. Her eyes were only for her new husband. On her hand, she wore a three-carat diamond ring. Her trailing bouquet was made of expensive white orchids and roses. Behind her, two armed bodyguards followed at a reasonable distance. As she cleared the sanctuary entrance, they remained behind to secure the door.

A professional photographer flitted to and fro throughout the room, preserving family memories for days to come.

In the second row of the cathedral, sat a hulk of a man calling himself Landon Morrow. Muscles rippled under his suit jacket. Having accompanied the girl on her journey from Westwood Village, he acted as her jailer, body-guard, and guardian, complete with a well-travelled Irish passport.

Sixteen year old Katie Curtin had all but forgotten her true identity. Today, and for the rest of her life, she was Victoria Mendoza, descended from Spanish aristocracy, raised in the United States. Her life history, birth records, passport, and pedigree had been furnished to her buyer, her new husband, for the sum of two and a half million dollars.

At Ginsberg Memorial Hospital, Dr. James Ainsworth was sitting on Caleb's bed. He and the seven year old were playing a series of games together. In the process, Dr. Ainsworth would stop momentarily to make notes, or check a box on an assessment form. He explained his pauses to Caleb before they began.

"My job is to try to find out how old you really are and where you might need to begin classes for school, and behavioral therapy."

"Wh-what's b-b-behav-vioral th-therap-p-py? Caleb had asked.

Dr. Ainsworth smiled at the boy, and winked. "It's not scary, son, so you don't have to worry. There are people, probably one or two, and I will make sure I get to be one of them, who will help you. We will help you learn how to feel comfortable when you are around other people. We will help you begin to feel safe when you have to speak with someone you don't know. We might even be able to do something about your stuttering. We will show you have to make friends. That kind of thing."

"C-c-can w-we d-d-do th-that t-t-today?"

"You are a smart boy, Caleb! That's exactly what we are beginning to work on today!"

Caleb smiled, his eyes bright. "G-g-good."

The first game involved a series of pictures. Caleb's job was to describe what he saw, and tell where he thought the situation pictured was taking place. What might the people in the picture be doing? The objective was to determine the boy's ability to integrate logic and relational, or emotional, information.

The second game was actually a reading and imagination assessment. How well did Caleb read? Could the boy tell Dr. Jim his favorite story?

After the second game, Dr. Jim suggested they go to the cafeteria together, to eat some lunch. After Jim and Sarah helped the boy into a wheelchair, Dr. Jim placed a cowboy hat on the boy's head, and told Caleb to try to touch his chin to his chest.

"We want to keep you safe from the zombies," he told the boy, with a chuckle.

Caleb smiled. Dr. Jim was the first person to understand his fears. He decided he liked this man. *He* wasn't a zombie. Maybe he hadn't even been bitten.

Wheeling the boy to the elevators, Dr. Ainsworth checked the hallways for video surveillance. The risk of harm coming to the boy with all the undercover cops stationed in the lobby downstairs was minimal.

Caleb had been admitted under the name "Bobby Jones." Sarah McMillan had requested the hospital adjust his condition, listing it as "Evaluation for Bone Growth Issues." An undercover policeman met the psychologist and the boy in the elevator.

As soon as the hospital room she shared with Caleb was empty, Sarah pressed the call button to request a changing of Caleb's linens. When the room had been serviced, she closed her laptop, put her supplies away, locked her briefcase away, and took up her duffle bag.

"I'm going to get a shower," she told Rick, the uniformed cop at the door. "There is a lot of confidential stuff in there, because the room has become my temporary office. Don't let anyone in or out, please, until I get back. I shouldn't be more than twenty minutes or so."

As she had done only once before in the past few days, Sarah felt she had a window of time in which to take a shower. Feeling self-conscious about her appearance, she opened the room door, and looked furtively down the hall in both directions.

"Taking the surgery elevator?" Officer Rick asked, watching her, amused.

Smiling, Sarah nodded. "Sure am," she answered. "Hair's greasy. I'd rather not see anyone I know, thank you."

Officer Rick chuckled in response. Smiling, he watched Sarah walk away. Entering the surgery elevator, she pushed the button for the ground floor of the hospital. She was heading for the doctor's showers, next to the Emergency Room and Trauma Surgery Center. As the elevator made its way downward, Sarah watched the numbers above the keypad, waiting for them to change. When the doors opened on the ground floor, she took a deep breath, and looked carefully both ways before exiting.

Christine's cell phone rang.

"Hello. Spada speaking."

"Hey, Kitten. It's your mother."

"Hi, Mom," she answered. "We're heading into a raid."

"Okay. I'll make it fast."

"What's up?"

"Someone in our prayer circle had a dream about you."

Christine rolled her eyes. Not now. Why now?

"Okay," she replied carefully. "Who was it? Do I know them?"

"You might, but she's new. Her name is Joanna."

"It doesn't matter," Kit answered. "What was the dream?"

"Well, she said she saw a house by a lake. There was a dark cloud over the house. There was a semi-truck in the driveway of the house."

A little shaken, Christine said nothing. She was staring at the scene her mother was describing.

"Then," her mother continued, "two black trees grew out of the cloud, and there were shadows under them. When Jo looked more closely at the shadows, she saw a map of Eastern Europe under one tree, and a graveyard under the other one."

"Is that it? How did she know it was about me?" Christine asked, skeptically.

"She said she saw you in a big window in the front of the house. A man had a gun, and he tried to shoot you. Then she woke up."

"Wow," Christine told her. "That's some dream. I'll let you know if someone tries to kill me."

"Christine Angelina!" her mother exclaimed. "I know you don't put any stock in my beliefs. But please don't mock me like this!"

"Sorry. I wasn't, Mom," Kit answered. "It's freaky. That's all. I mean I'm sitting in front of a house by a lake, and it has a semi in the driveway."

Her mother was surprised. "Really? You're kidding!"

"No, I'm not kidding," her daughter told her. "Listen, I can't do any more of this spooky stuff. I have to go to work."

"Just be careful. Please," her mother insisted.

"I will be."

"Oh, there was one more thing."

"Yes?"

"Jo said she saw a big metal box in the dream, like the size of a small freezer. It had blood splattered all over it. She didn't know what it meant."

"Mom, you're scaring me. I have to go."

"Okay, Honey."

"Yeah."

"I'm praying for you."

"Stop it, Mom. I mean it. Spada out."

Chapter Thirteen

As the SWAT Team van, a second police van, and three cars turned off the highway, Christine double-checked the GPS on her phone. Two more turns: Left on Wisteria Lane, then right on Hydrangea Court Drive. She kept her car close to the bumper of the SWAT Team van in front of her. Pete Lynch, the driver, braked to turn left onto Wisteria. She hoped this house would still be in operation; not abandoned once more.

They so badly needed a break in this case. There were too many loose ends. Too many clues. So many faces.

"God, help us," she whispered.

Were they even on the right track, she wondered? What clues had they missed?

Just before the right turn on Hydrangea Court presented itself, the entire taskforce was forced to pull to a stop. A County Sheriff's patrol-car blocked the road, with lights flashing. The officer directing traffic approached Pete's driver's side window. Christine reached for the necessary paperwork she was carrying, and opened her car door.

As she approached the van, she overheard snatches of the conversation taking place between Pete Lynch and the deputy.

"We have a Search and Seizure on this street," Pete was telling him.

"Ain't gonna happen, man," the deputy replied. "Sorry, but this is county jurisdiction. I have my orders."

"Excuse me, deputy," Kit said. "I have my orders too."

Flashing her FBI badge to the deputy, and pointing to the letters on her windbreaker, she held up the paperwork.

"Who is this, Pete?" the deputy asked.

"She's my new boss," the detective told him with a smile. Watching Spada deal with Henry would be amusing, he considered.

Christine interjected, extending her hand in greeting. "Agent Christine Spada, Special Investigator, FBI. Our Search and Seizure on this street is for a national priority case. Why is the road blocked?"

"Agent, there's been a multiple homicide on this street," the deputy told her. "What address are you heading for?"

Christine was not volunteering information. "Where did the murders take place?"

"2205. Family named Marshall," the deputy replied, looking at Christine, and then at Pete. "The guy works at the Freight Transfer."

"It's okay, Henry," Pete told him. "That's not who we need. We got a totally different house."

"More than one big case in the same neighborhood? That's a real problem. Homicides involved in the federal case too?"

"We think so," answered Pete.

"Well then, go on through. I'll radio ahead and let the officer in charge know you're coming. We are pretty much just waiting on the Crime Lab to get here at this point, anyway."

"Thank you," Christine replied. "Oh, and Henry? Please *don't* let them know we're coming."

Surprised, Henry responded. "You sure?"

"Absolutely."

"Yes ma'am."

Christine went back to her car, making ready to head in for the search. As she did, Pete looked at Henry.

"By the way, Henry," Pete asked. "Who's the lead on the multi-murder case?"

"Well," Henry told him. "So far, it's a puzzle. Sheriff Jackson is in there himself. Said he's been on orders to process any multiple situations like this himself, when they happen in the county. But, now, there's a guy from your precinct in there as well. Aren't you from Westwood Village?"

Pete tried to hide his surprise. "Yeah."

"Well, he says it's his case; his jurisdiction."

"Huh. That's strange. Who is it?"

"Not too strange, I guess," Henry offered. "He has a brother who lives up this way, and he told me he had been visiting him. He was just leaving for work, when he said he heard a woman scream from inside the house at 2205. Apparently, it was one of the Marshalls."

"Oh," Pete answered. "I probably know him then. Who is it?"

Henry pulled a business card out of his shirt pocket. "He said his name was …. Lieutenant Alexander Boyd, from Homicide?"

"Oh, we'll get with him then," Pete replied nonchalantly. "I'll look for him. Thanks. And Henry, can you call my cell? Just in case I need to talk to you later."

"Sure, Pete." Henry pulled his cell out of his back pocket, and Pete gave him the number. The two men exchanged a wave as the SWAT Team van led the way around Henry's red and blue lights, heading up Hydrangea Court Drive.

In the temporary local field office in Christine's new townhouse, FBI Special Agent Felipe Ramirez was searching for answers to some very elusive evidence.

After watching the two idiots in the silver sedan follow Kit out of the parking lot, he had gone to work in the townhouse field office. Specifically, he had begun several searches on the Bureau's and Interpol's servers for information regarding key individuals in the case.

He liked calling them that. Idiots.

That was before Kit had called him on her way to Ennis Lake.

"Ramirez here."

"Hi, my love. It's Kit. I'm so secure with you."

Recognizing the code phrase, he turned on the scrambler before answering.

"Line's secure. What's up?"

"We have reason to believe a shipment container having something to do with our case made its way here by train from the Georgia Port Authority. It was delivered to a home by semi, 2205 Hydrangea Court Drive in Ennis Lake this morning. Can you track down the container's owner, and the list of contents? Also, I need the true identity of the woman this group hired to take out Caleb Jacobs. I'd like to get that interrogation done today, if possible. And I need more information than we've have in hand at present."

"Sure thing, Kit," Felipe answered. "Edwards has me looking for a face behind the Medical Supply Company who hired David Fletcher. He thinks that that will give us some major pieces we need to get this thing solved."

"Thanks, Felipe. It's good to have you on the team."

"No sweat," he answered. "Hey, off the subject.... are you and Josh....well, you know?"

Kit smiled. "Did he put you up to this?"

"No," Felipe responded. "I'm just asking."

"The answer is a definite no. There is no chance for things to work out with him," Kit answered. "We broke up for religious differences."

"I didn't know you were religious."

"I'm not." She smiled. "It's just... well, he thought he was a god and I disagreed."

Felipe laughed. "Got it."

"Okay," she said. "Gotta go now. Spada out."

After ending the call, Felipe temporarily minimized the screen on the investigative work he had been working on for Edwards. He began pulling up information on the Georgia Port Authority; specifically information regarding shipping containers unloaded in the past week or two, headed for Hydrangea Court Drive in Ennis Lake.

"Let's see what we can learn here," he murmured. He searched for the daily shipping manifests. While they were printing out, he went back to the director's assignment. Utilizing the photograph Kit had posted of David Fletcher, Asami's former limo driver. Since the photo had been taken in Germany, Felipe looked for German-based medical supply companies. He also searched for companies dealing in medical supplies who were based in other parts of the globe, but did business in the European nation.

Additionally, he initiated a facial recognition search on the server for any photographs of Fletcher taken in the past couple of months, no matter the name used.

Finally, he called the Westwood Precinct, and asked to speak with Police Captain Allen Edwards. Requesting a photograph of the hired female assassin, he gave his Bureau email as a place where it could be received.

"Okay," he said to the computer, "what's next?"

Within ten minutes, his cell phone notified him of a received email. Then, after opening the Captain's photograph on the networked computer, he initiated a second server facial recognition search, this time on the female would-be assassin.

As Bureau network servers were searching, he returned to his initial investigative work that day. Director Edwards wanted the names of the Medical Supply Company's umbrella corporation, and its board officers as soon as possible. He had already called Felipe once this morning.

This was going to be a busy day.

Heading out of the elevator on the third floor of the hospital, Dr. Jim Ainsworth pushed Caleb in his wheelchair. Looking down the hall, he noticed the usually occupied policeman's chair outside the boy's hospital room was empty. Making a quick decision, he headed to the nurse's station.

"Excuse me," he said to the nurse at the desk. "Can you help me?"

"Yes, sir," David, the male nurse, looked at him closely. "You're Dr. Ainsworth, aren't you?"

Dr. Jim smiled. "That's right, and this is my friend."

David stood up and looked over the counter. "I know Caleb," he said. "Hi, Caleb! How's my buddy?"

"F-f-fine!" the boy replied with a smile. "Y-You're D-D-David!"

"That's right! You're looking good!" David looked back at the psychologist. "What's up?"

"There is no policeman on duty at Caleb's room. Did something happen?"

"Not that I know of,"' David replied. "I'll go with you to check it out. We were given strict orders to take extra good care of Caleb. Let me call house security before we go."

In less than two minutes, three hospital security guards arrived at the third floor pediatric nurses' station. Since the attempt on Caleb's life had taken place less than a week prior, all security staff had been provided firearms, and instructed to be ready to use them in the event of suspicious activity. After all, the event had prompted the hospital's builder and owner, Isaac Ginsberg, to call a meeting of the hospital's administrative staff.

In response to his urging, the hospital had issued a statement to the press:

> "The priority of Ginsberg Memorial Hospital is and always has been the safety and security of all patients, staff and their families. For this reason, all of our security personnel will from this point forward be armed when on duty."

"We will wait here," Dr. Jim told them. "Would you please check the room, and make sure there is no threat to the boy?"

"Yes, sir," David replied. Nodding to the security guards, the four men made their way down the hall.

Ainsworth quietly watched their movements from a distance. He was concerned about the effect experiencing this situation could have on Caleb. Would the boy suffer a negative reaction? Would it deepen his psychosis?

After checking all entrances, exits and neighboring rooms, the four men returned to the nurses' station. The lead security guard spoke with Dr. Ainsworth.

"There's nothing down there at all, Professor," he said, using the staff's pet name for the psychologist. "In fact, it looks like somebody got the room ready for a new patient."

Ainsworth assessed what he was saying. "Did you see Ms. McMillan, Caleb's social worker?"

"No, not at all."

"In fact, it doesn't look like anyone has been in the room at all," David interjected. "Not for a while."

"Was my briefcase in the room, or my books?"

The male nurse shook his head.

"We need to find Sarah," Jim told him. "It doesn't feel right to me. No. This isn't good at all. Listen, I am going to take Caleb with me to my home. I'm not convinced he is safe here. I will take care of getting him back here for surgery. Do you have an extra set of scrubs I can borrow?"

David looked at him. "For you, sir?"

Jim shook his head and silently pointed to Caleb.

"I may have just the thing," the nurse responded. He ducked into the file room, and returned in a few moments. In his hands, he had a child-sized Miracle Network T-shirt, and a pair of stretchy gym shorts. He handed them to Dr. Ainsworth.

"Will these work?" he asked. "The shorts are really stretchy, so they'll be comfortable."

Dr. Jim crouched in front of Caleb. Before he had a chance to speak, the boy asked a question.

"Th-the z-z-zom-b-bies c-c-came wh-while w-w-we w-were d-d-down-s-stairs, r-r-right? Y-y-you w-w-want m-me t-t-to l-l-leave w-with y-y-you, in th-th- those c-c-clothes."

"You are a smart boy!" the psychologist told him, beaming. "Do you think you can walk?" As he spoke, he wheeled the boy back behind the nurses' station desk. In the back room, he and David helped Caleb change into the shorts and T-shirt from his hospital gown.

"Y-y-you p-p-promised t-to k-keep m-me s-s-safe," Caleb said. "Th-they w-watch ev-v-ery-wh-where."

"Yes, I did make that promise," Dr. Jim told him. "So, you are going to be with me; 24/7 until we have the answers we need."

Caleb stood up from the wheelchair. He looked at David. "C-can I h-have a h-hat, t-t-too?"

The nurse smiled at him. "Sure! He rummaged in the lost and found drawer, and came up with a pair children's sunglasses, and a boy's baseball cap. He also produced a pair of sneakers. The smallest ones in the drawer, they were a little big for the boy, but would have to do.

"Caleb," the doctor told him, "I am going to carry you out to my car. We will have to hurry. I want you to close your eyes and put your head down against my shoulder. Put your nose as close to my neck as you can. Put your arms around my neck. Even if I have to run, I want you to hold on tight and keep your eyes closed. Okay?"

Caleb nodded. "Y-y-yes."

"Ready?"

The boy nodded once more.

Ainsworth looked at David as he began the journey out of the hospital. "Something's happened. I have to get this boy to a safe place. You've got to find Sarah McMillan."

That being said, the psychologist quickened his steps, and moved to the stairwell.

David looked to the security guards. "We need to search the entire hospital for Ms. Millan. My guess is she went down to the surgical showers to clean up while Caleb was with Dr. Ainsworth and out of the room. Housekeeping probably cleaned the room while she was out as well. Did you guys check the closets in the room, and the cabinets?"

"No, we were looking for a gunman," one of the security guards answered.

"I'll check those areas and then I'll join you in the search," David told them.

"And where did the cop on duty go?" the lead security guard asked.

"Good question," David replied. "I was in special forces years ago, so I'd be glad to check the showers. In fact, I'll check the stairwells on my way down."

"Great. We'll be sure to check all the areas of every room and conference area," the guard replied.

On his way down the hall, David responded. "All the bathrooms and the chapel as well. Anything unlocked."

A few moments later, Dr. James Ainsworth remotely unlocked and started his sedan, standing in the hospital lobby. Having parked in his designated space in the physicians' parking lot, Jim estimated he would need to carry the boy a little less than one hundred feet from the front doors to reach his car. As he walked through the doors, leaving, the elderly woman stationed as a greeter smiled brightly.

"Have a great afternoon," she told him.

"You too," Dr. Jim responded. As he stepped off the curb into the parking lot, he whispered encouragement in Caleb's ear.

"You're doing really well, Buddy. Keep your eyes closed. I'm going to run now."

Breaking into a slow run, Dr. Jim's long legs set a rhythm. He was so focused on getting to his car, he completely missed the first bullet until it whizzed by him.

"Ainsworth!" a man's voice behind him shouted. "Get down! Get down now!"

As the words registered, the psychologist felt a searing pain go through his right shoulder. Then, he felt a line of fire rage through his left thigh. With adrenaline surging, the man sped up. He made it to his car. Opening the back door, Jim tossed Caleb inside, and slammed the door. Ducking behind the driver door, he jumped inside.

"Duck!" he commanded the boy, as he did so himself. "Keep your head down!"

Somewhere, he could hear bullets hitting his sedan. He reached for the door, pressing the automatic locks.

"Lay down, Caleb," he said, as he took his own advice. "I'm going to try to get us out of here."

Pulling the gearshift into "Drive," Ainsworth drove forward, through the empty parking space in front. As they increased distance from the shooter, Caleb sat up and looked out the back window.

"D-D-David g-g-got him!" he shouted. "L-l-look!"

Jim sat up, and turned the car around, heading back to the hospital entrance. As the car approached, a subdued gunman could be seen, his face down on the pavement. A jubilant David was sitting on top of him, holding the man's arm behind his back. He had one knee in the man's lower back and the other on his buttocks. Kicked some six feet away, was a Smith and Wesson MK-22 with a silencer attached.

Jim rolled down his window. "You okay, man?"

"I'm good," David answered. "You got any rope?"

"I might," Jim answered. "My wife and I were at Home Depot yesterday, and I can't remember if I unloaded the trunk or not."

185

Stopping the car, Jim got out and rummaged in his car's trunk. Finding a roll of duct tape, he tossed it to David, and then closed the trunk. As he did so, he commented.

"No rope, but I have duct tape."

"That's even better!" the male nurse exclaimed. With Jim's help, the gunman's hands were secured together, as were his feet. Tape was put over his mouth. For an extra measure, the men secured his arms to his sides across his chest, and taped his legs together around his calves and his thighs.

"That will have to do until the police arrive," David said.

"Did you find Sarah?" Dr. Ainsworth wanted to know. "You said she had gone to take a shower."

"This guy came from there. I was headed there, but then I saw him follow you out the door. When he drew his gun, I decided to tackle him. But it's okay. Kojo is checking the showers," David told him. "If you've got this, I'm going to help him."

"No sweat, Dave. I've got this," Jim answered.

As David bounced up and headed back into the hospital, Jim pulled out his cell phone. Pulling up Kit's cell phone number, he made a call.

Inside, Kojo, was calling Sarah's name. He was walking through the physicians' showers.

"Miss Sarah! You here?" his deep bass voice resonated through the area, bouncing off the walls. The huge man stopped to listen for an answer. He could hear heavy breathing nearby. Where was it coming from? He began to pull shower curtains aside, searching for the source.

In the fifth shower, he saw a shadow through the fabric. He spoke softly. "Miss Sarah, is that you?"

He pulled the curtain aside, unprepared for what he encountered. A uniformed police officer was stretched from the inside of the shower into its adjacent dressing area. He was lying in a pool of blood.

"Oh, no!" Kojo declared. He ran to the officer, and tried to assess the man's condition. "You gonna be okay, man. Stay with me, now. Stay with me."

The officer gasped for air. "He. Shot. Her... Oth.er... side."

"He shot Miss Sarah?" Kojo repeated numbly. "We gonna get you help. I be right back."

Kojo ran through, checking each shower stall. In the last shower on the opposite side, a wide blood trail was spread across the floor. "She must've dragged herself," he muttered.

Searching, he followed the trail to a bathroom stall. He knocked on the stall door. Checking underneath, he saw no feet, but he did see blood dripping from above, into a small puddle near the stall.

"Miss Sarah, it's Kojo," he said. "We gonna get you to the ER."

He reached into his pocket, and grabbed a quarter. He placed the coin in the outside indentation in the center of the door lock, and turned it. Carefully pushing the door open, he was greeted by the sight of Sarah McMilllan sitting naked on the toilet stool, her knees pulled up to her chin, in a fetal position. Her face was cut, her eyes were dazed, and blood was dripping from her body. He couldn't tell where her injuries were just yet. She held her head in her hands.

Grabbing a sheet from a nearby linen closet, Kojo ran back to Sarah. He wrapped her with the sheet. Then, he picked her up in his herculean arms. The giant African held her like an oversized beach ball, and made his way into the Emergency Room.

Standing near the Reception Desk, Kojo looked at the nurses. His voice startled the entire waiting area. "Hey! I need some help here! This woman's been shot! Miss Sarah's been hurt."

Seeing the now bloody sheet wrapped around Sarah, the admitting clerk passed out. But others around the big man went into overdrive.

Back in the showers, David had discovered Officer Rick. "You've lost a lot of blood, Officer."

"Help. Sarah. First," Rick wheezed.

"She's taken care of," Dave told him. "She's going to be fine. And so are you."

"Can't. Breathe."

David yelled as loudly as he could. "I need help here! Can anybody hear me?"

On the other side of the showers, a man's voice was heard. "This is Doctor Erickson. I'm a surgeon. Where are you?"

"Here," David yelled once more. "On the other side."

Erickson appeared some moments later, with a towel around his waist. "What's wrong?" he asked. And then he saw Officer Rick.

"He's lost a lot of blood," David looked at the surgeon. "What can we do?"

"Has he spoken?"

David nodded.

"Slide your arms under on that side," the surgeon told him. "I'll do the same here. We need to get him into surgery."

Working together, the two men lifted Rick and carried him, one step at a time out of the showers, across the hall, into the scrub room, through the door, into an empty surgery. As soon as the officer was on the table, Erickson tightened the shower towel around his waist.

"I need scrubs. And an OR team."

"I'm on it," David replied. "I'm a pediatric nurse. Can I assist?"

Erickson laughed. "I wouldn't know what to do without you."

David applied pressure to Rick's wounds, and called for a team for the operating room. At the same time, Dr. Erickson dressed in disposable scrubs, and readied himself for surgery.

At the same time, in the connecting surgery next door, another emergency surgery was taking place. Sarah McMillan had been shot four times in the abdomen. Amazingly, somehow, the bullets had missed her spine. She would be in reconstructive surgery for several hours, the nurses explained. It was unclear at the moment as to whether either of the two victims found would make it through the rest of the day.

Waiting was hard, Kojo decided.

It was less than thirty minutes later when the Crime Lab arrived. They taped off the crime scene, and gathered evidence. Both David and Kojo were checked for wounds, and asked to give a statement. The gunman was taken back to the Westwood Precinct for booking, and interrogation.

When it was all over, it was Caleb who turned off Dr. Ainsworth's car, and handed him the keys just outside the doors to the Emergency Room. The boy had taken Jim's arm, and tugged on him, pulling the man into the Emergency Room. By that time, Jim had lost a sizeable amount of blood. He had fainted on the floor. The psychologist became the third gunshot survivor in one day for Ginsberg Memorial.

It was close to one in the afternoon when David finally found Caleb, curled up and sleeping, still wearing his sunglasses and baseball cap, on the pillows in the children's video area of the Emergency Room.

In the same moments the gunman was stalking Sarah McMillan and Caleb that morning, the Westwood based FBI Taskforce was arriving stealthily at the location of the day's surprise raid. They were within walking distance of the newly discovered hub house at 2205 Hydrangea Court Drive in Ennis Lake. As the SWAT Team was disembarking their van, Christine briefed them quickly.

"This is the first hub house to be discovered in mid-stride of its usage. In every other city, in every other location, the Bureau has been just one step behind the network. The houses Parrot and Mackaw in the Village were just two examples of more than twenty suspected hubs over the past five years."

She looked at Matt Williams, the SWAT Team Commander, who picked up the briefing at that point.

"Men, based on what Agent Spada has told me of this case, the perpetrators do not appear to hold any value in human life, so using tear gas is not an option. They would simply kill the hostages. We are certain the perpetrators as well as the hostages are still in the house, simply because they haven't had time to evacuate. Additionally, they have not been provided opportunity to leave the area, due to the presence of our vehicles involved in the murder investigation taking place across the street. The element of surprise is our only fail-safe at the moment, so we need to enter utilizing all entrances at the same moment. So, let's synchronize our watches."

"Agent Spada," Williams continued, now speaking to Christine, "you are our *Incident* Commander. When all of our team is in place, helmet cameras are up, and such, I will give you a verbal signal. Then, when *your* team is ready for the raid to begin, you will give us the 'go,' and we'll take it from there. We are on our own frequency, so I will ask you to utilize this radio." He handed her a small radio that looked like small tiny walkie-talkie. He showed her a button on its side.

"Push here and speak into it. Standard issue. We have designated the 'Go' word as 'Pizza.' So, when you want us to storm in, just give us the 'Go' word."

"Uh, Commander?" Christine interrupted.

"Yes, Agent?" he replied.

"Can we just say 'go' or 'okay?' I'm not sure I won't forget in the middle, and mess it up."

Commander Williams chuckled. He winked at her. "No problem, Agent. We've got this."

He nodded to his men in groups of five. He spoke to the first group. "Find your position in the upper floor. Go." He looked at the remaining fifteen. "We will take positions on each side, and surround the building. Go."

As the last group peeled off to take their position, the Commander joined them. Christine could hear the Commander's communication to his team over the tiny radio she had been given.

The mission of any SWAT Team was to take out armed resistance and secure a site, rescuing hostages. At this point, Christine realized, they had no idea how many people were actually inside the house. Mrs. Marshall's call had been made to inform the authorities of the multiple kidnappings of young women. How many, she had not said. Now, there would not be an opportunity to interview her. She was dead, along with her entire family.

Christine glanced at the bay window in the front of the Marshall home. Some lights were on, and visibility was limited. However, she could see shadows and forms of individuals moving about inside. She made a mental note to investigate the murder site in person when the present operation was completed.

"What's going on over there?" Startled, she looked to her left to see who had spoken. Peter Lynch had spoken. He also was watching Marshall's the bay window.

"I don't know, Pete," she said, "but it's somehow tied to everything happening on this side of the street. The wife in that house paid a huge price for informing us about the girls we're about to rescue."

"I have a concern," he whispered. "Henry, the deputy sheriff at the traffic stop, is a good friend of mine. He said the County Sheriff, Aaron Jackson, told his men that he'd been given orders by someone higher up the chain of command to handle any multiple killings himself in order to protect security. He's in that house right now."

"Those orders would have had to have come down from someone in the D.C. office," Christine told him. "What's your concern?"

"Well, Henry said one of the detectives from Westwood Village Precinct was the first officer on site. Guy works Homicide. I'm not close to him, but he's been on the force for about four years now. Name is Alexander Boyd. He told the sheriff's deputies he was ordered to take jurisdiction of the case, because it is tied to a much larger case his precinct has been working on."

"What case?" Christine asked. "And *who* would have given *him* jurisdiction of an FBI case, and not notified the field office? Or me?"

"Exactly," Pete replied. "Something's screwy. I want to go over there, and check things out. It just doesn't smell right to me."

"Okay. Go for it. But be careful."

Pete smiled. "No sweat, Agent."

Christine watched him as he walked away.

Checking around himself, Pete broke away from the taskforce, and moved down the street, staying on the same side, so as to not arouse the attention of anyone who might be watching. When he reached the van, he got inside. He checked his service weapon, and pulled another from a bag between the seats. This one, he tucked into the back of his khakis.

Then, he made a cell phone call.

A few moments later, Pete walked up the sidewalk on the other side of the street. After he arrived at the Marshall home, he stepped through the open front door, and greeted the working members of the Crime Lab.

"Sheriff Jackson?" he inquired in a loud voice.

"In here!" A man's voice resonated from a back bedroom.

"Pete?" another man's voice spoke. "Pete Lynch? What are you doing here?"

Pete looked in the direction of the voice speaking. "Boyd? Hey, I didn't know you were working today. How are you, man?" Not stopping to talk, the detective continued walking down the hallway from the Marshall's living room. Boyd followed him.

Across the street, the SWAT Team's preparations were finished. The Commander's voice crackled on the small radio in Christine's hand. "We are in place, Agent."

"Good job, Commander. That's a 'Go!'"

In synchronized unison, the SWAT team stormed the house.

Before notifying Christine, small packages of explosives had been meticulously attached to the locked doors on each entrance into the home; the front door, the back door, a root cellar (which apparently led to a basement), a walk-in door attached to the three-car garage, and the French doors on the second floor, giving entrance from a balcony.

When the explosion took place, Christine realized that even though she had been watching the house intently, she had not noticed SWAT members who had taken their places on the house's second floor balcony.

The explosions were followed by shouts of "Stop where you are!" "Freeze! FBI!" and "Hands on your head!"

Into every entrance to the home the rescuers made quick entrances. Christine held her breath, hearing several gunshots from inside.

The radio in her hand crackled. "We have an officer down. We need a bus and transport for prisoners." She recognized the voice as the Commander's, and responded.

"Copy that." She nodded to Evan Davies, who stood beside her. "Make the call."

"Dispatch," Evan repeated, "this is Detective Evan Davies. We have an officer down at 2202 Hydrangea Court Drive, Ennis Lake. We are mid-raid. We need an ambulance and transport for prisoners."

"How many prisoners you need to transport?" the operator asked.

Evan looked at Christine. "Around twenty or more," he replied.

"It's gonna be a busy day, Detective," she commented.

He smiled. "They're on their way."

It was many minutes before Christine knew with certainty the SWAT Team's raid had been victorious. In single file, an exodus of inhabitants streamed from the house, each one at gunpoint, marching forward in detainee posture, open palms resting on the top of the head. They were gathered into a group in the side yard of the house, and surrounded by SWAT team members.

As the detainees emerged, Agent Spada counted them.

From the wrap-around balcony, eight persons were led to the back of the home, where stairs took them to the ground.

From the root-cellar door, four men were led up steps to the ground level.

From the back, front, and garage entrances, twenty-eight persons were gathered.

Officers moved among the suspects, handcuffing each one, requiring them to sit down on the ground, separating men from women. Once divided into pertinent groups, they would await transport. As soon as this segment of the raid was completed, Commander Williams radioed Christine.

"All yours, Agent," he said. "I still have team members inside, making a final sweep for any further suspects, who might still be undiscovered."

"Thank you, Commander," she radioed back. "We will take it from here."

Christine, Evan and the rest of the team moved into action. They moved among the prisoners, working to separate victims from perpetrators. Each member of the taskforce had viewed video images from Chicago and from the house on Mackaw. That being said, each taskforce member carried wallet photos of recently abducted young women.

Each one also carried an awareness there could be just one victim. There could be many more waiting to be sold and shipped to buyers. The team had also anticipated an unknown number of armed guards, whose job descriptions might vary; depending upon the destination of the abductee.

For her part, Christine hoped they would discover an older woman, a "Miss Anastasia," based on something Annabelle Carnes had said in interrogation.

She and Evan moved among the seated suspects to learn identities. As usual, Christine found her multi-lingual abilities extremely helpful. And, although she had fulfilled this same assignment in the past, she realized this was her first time to do this type of interviewing as Agent-in-Charge.

She began working her way through the women sitting on the ground. As expected, the first of her secondary languages to be used was Spanish. She discovered two women from Mexico, three from Nicaragua, and one from Columbia. Then, she spoke with two French-speaking, dark-skinned twin-sisters from Haiti. Neither woman spoke English. One more was of Asian descent, and could speak only Mandarin Chinese, and broken English.

"I'm sorry," Christine told her. "I don't know Chinese yet. What is your name?"

"Sung Li," the girl answered. "They say I get passport and job."

"Who told you that?" Christine asked.

"I show," Sung Li offered, her eyes wide.

"Yes. Absolutely. Let me come back to you in a moment," Christine replied. "Please wait for me."

Christine moved on to the next girl; a dark brunette. It was hard to tell much more about her since she had pulled her knees to her chest, and was bending her head forward. Her long hair fell in curly tresses, hiding her face. She was dressed in a satin nightgown.

"Hello?" Christine said to her. "What is your name?"

"I'm Caressa," the girl answered.

"That's an unusual name," Christine told her. "Did your mother give you that name?"

"No," came the response, "but it's my new name."

"What was your name before?"

"Allison," she said. "Allison Williams, but I'm not supposed to say it anymore."

"Can you look at me, Allison?" Christine sat down next to her. "Please, I need to see your face."

The girl raised her head, and gazed into the Agent's eyes. Christine assessed her. "How old are you, Honey?" she asked.

"I'm twelve."

"Allison, how long have you been here?"

The girl began to cry. "I don't know. They don't use clocks."

"What's the last thing you remember?"

Allison closed her eyes, the tears coming more freely now. "I've been in Garrett's Relaxation Classes. I never remember much after those. But I think I'm from... *Miami?*"

"Do you know if anyone has reported you missing?"

The girl shook her head. "Maybe. I don't know. I ran away. I remember my parents were fighting. Dad left. I don't remember much after that."

She recounted the events slowly, as if they were being retrieved from deep fog.

"But I do remember my Mom put me on a plane to go live with my Grandma."

"Where does she live?"

"I --- I... I'm sorry," Allison put her head on her knees once more. "I don't know."

"Did you have a flight attendant accompany you when you flew? What airline was it?"

"I – I can't remember. I don't know." The girl began to cry.

Christine put her arm around her. "Don't worry. We'll work hard to find your family. It will be all right."

"I'm not sure I want to go back there anyway," Allison told her. "These people told me I was going to be like Cinderella. My Prince Charming can't wait to meet me."

195

Christine took a moment to write down her notes regarding Allison, and then moved on.

Another girl in a satin nightgown sat near Allison. She also had her head resting on her knees, and it was difficult to see her face. She also was a brunette, with long, curly hair.

"Hello," the agent greeted her upon approach. "My name is Christine, and I'm with the FBI. Do you mind if I ask you a few questions?"

The girl looked up. Her eyes were dazed, and looked somewhat hollow. She had bruising around her nose. She didn't speak.

Christine assessed her. "What is your name?"

"I don't know. I can't remember anything."

"What is the last thing you remember?"

"I was in my grandmother's car. We were going somewhere. I have a picture that keeps coming back when I dream. It's a big building filled with light, but then someone hits me on the back of my head. I don't remember hitting the floor. Maybe I hit a wall with my forehead. I can't remember anything."

Christine raised her voice, and called for an EMS officer. She gave the girl the name, "Jane Doe," and gave orders for the girl to be sent to the hospital immediately for evaluation.

"Oh, they said I'm not sick," the girl informed Christine.

"I'm sure they did, and you are probably just dealing with some temporary amnesia, but let's make sure. Okay?" she said with a smile.

"Okay. Thank you," the girl replied.

As she turned to introduce herself to the next young woman, she realized not one, but two girls, leaning against each other, were immediately in front of her.

"Hello," she said. "What are your names?"

The girls stared blankly at her. "Hablas Ingles?" she offered.

Still blank. "Parlez-vous Francais?"

Still nothing.

Then, remembering something which happened during a case in Morocco, she smiled. It was worth a try. She patted the ground and said, "America."

Both girls nodded. Smiling, they repeated, "America!"

Christine smiled back. She put her hand over her heart and said, "I am American."

Both girls nodded, indicating they understood.

Christine pointed to them, and asked, "What is your country?"

The girls looked at each other, as though to confer, wide-eyed.

"Mali?" They gazed at the Agent expectantly. "Somali."

Was it Mali or Somalia? How and why had they travelled so far, she wondered?

She decided to try Arabic. "Hal tatakallam al-lughah al-'Arabīyah?"

The girls nodded vigorously. "Nahma!! Nahma!!" they answered. Hearing a tongue from their own country stirred deep emotion in these two young women. Suddenly excited, they immediately began to speak simultaneously, with tears flowing at the same time. After a few minutes, the agent asked a few questions, assuring them everything was going to be all right. In the process, the girls told her they were cousins, and had been sold by their families in Mali, because the need for food was great. Their fathers were brothers, and had agreed that neither man could provide a dowry. In that culture, that realization caused the daughters to be perceived as burdens to their families. Each man had been afraid his daughter would die, slaving at gunpoint in the mines; digging by hand for mercury and artisanal gold.

Additionally, the girls informed Christine that their older brothers were friends; members of the Jihadist group Al-Shabaab. The first purchaser had been Mauritanian. He had paid about two hundred US dollars for each of them. Those funds would provide food for at least six months for their families.

Both girls felt fortunate they wouldn't starve, or be made to work in the mines. This meant they would live. Their families would be fed. The purchaser had taken them, by camel, to the west coast of Africa. To travel, they had been provided food for two weeks; water canteens, dried meat and fruit, and a little flat bread. Then, in a desert wadi, they were sold again; this time to a man with a freight barge coming to the United States. They been on the barge for a month. They were both sick when they had arrived at the house on Ennis Lake. But traffickers or not, the girls were thankful that the people had provided a doctor. They both were sure they would feel better soon.

Stalled, and intrigued with their stories, Christine suddenly realized there were still several women from which to get statements. These had been watching her progress with interest.

Looking up, she noticed Evan was also working his way through the circle of men suspects. She noticed there were three men whom he had separated from the others. She would have to go over and give him a hand in a little while, she realized.

The next woman was older. Christine greeted her.

"Hello. What is your name?"

"I want to see my lawyer. Until I see him, I will say nothing!" The feminine voice was smooth and silky. The trace accent was …. Italian, Greek?

Christine smiled at her. "I'm sorry. Under the Patriot Act of 2001, persons connect with this case are not entitled to a lawyer."

"What do you mean? I am not a terrorist."

"Tell that to the people you work for," Christine replied. "They started this. If they didn't want to be classified as terrorists, they shouldn't have blown up the house in Los Angeles. That explosion killed over fifty people, in a neighborhood just like this one."

"That was a fool's accident."

"So you say," Christine replied. "Do you intend to give me your name?"

The woman shrugged. "I was promised I could retire and live in my villa in peace if I became a teacher for these girls. I am not a terrorist."

"I'm sure we will be able to better sort this out when we get back to the precinct. If what you say is true, I'm sure someone will listen. Right now, I just need your name."

The woman sighed. "I am Lady Bereniece Fraire, widow of the Italian Ambassador. But the girls call me 'Miss Anastasia.' I believe I have diplomatic immunity. Can you take these handcuffs off, please?"

Christine didn't flinch, nor did she acknowledge the request. She smiled. "Why Anastasia?"

"Oh, you know. The lost Russian princess? It's just something they do to create mystery, and a sense of romance for the girls. They used the same name with the woman who taught before me. I'm not sure you understand these people, Agent. They really are quite nice. They are not doing this with the usual methods. They are.... No *we* are preparing these girls. We are providing each one with a better life."

"Oh, I'm sure it must be totally humanitarian in nature," Christine replied. "That's why your people steal children while they are sleeping."

Lady Fraire made no reply.

Wow, she's good, Christine thought silently. She moved on, making notes. *These people must really believe the crap they sell.*

Abruptly, Christine was startled by her cell phone. Without checking to see who it was, she answered.

"Hello. Spada here."

"Hi Kit. It's Eric Janzen."

"Oh, hi, Jannie."

"That's not much of a greeting. You busy?"

"Uh-yeah. Kind of in the middle of something here. Can I call you back?"

"I thought you were going to, but you didn't."

"I haven't had much of a break."

"It's okay. I heard about the raid, and I was worried about you."

Christine looked around. "How did you hear about the raid?"

"Oh, I have my sources," he answered with a laugh. Then he added, "Pete and I have been comparing notes on things. He said you wanted him to follow up with me on the case, so we've been talking some. Call me when you get a few."

"Thanks, Jannie. I'll call you soon. Spada out."

Detective Evan Davies was experiencing some confusing encounters of his own. So far, he and Chase Stanford had taken statements from eight of the ten men arrested in the raid.

The first three they had separated from the group were medical personnel. Christine would want to hear those statements. Evan asked Chase to complete taking those statements. What were they doing here?

Of the remaining five: one was a computer geek of sorts. He claimed to have no connection with the rest of the detainees. He had just been in the house to adjust the security system. The two others were well-dressed, telling the detective they were couriers for a medical supply company. Another claimed to be a chef, who came each morning and left each evening, cooking meals for whoever was in the house.

The eighth interview he had just finished had been a little puzzling… The only thing the guy would say was, "I'm just here for the girls." The statement was followed by a quizzical smile, bordering on a sneer, Evan decided.

Not that the entire case wasn't beginning to feel a little insane, Evan considered.

When Evan asked for a name, each of the five detainees had responded in the same manner.

"My name is Landon Morrow."

"My name is Landon Morrow."

"My name is Landon Morrow."

"My name is Landon Morrow."

"My name is Landon Morrow."

He moved on. Perhaps the next guy would yield a little more information. He approached a somewhat bulky man, apparently part of another group of five, whom the SWAT Team had placed a little distance away from the others.

"Hello. What is your name?" He spoke to the largest man of the five, assuming him to be their leader.

"Nicholas," he answered. His accent was thick and difficult to understand. "I am Nicholas Urikov. I am emergency medical transport only."

Evan assessed him. "Where are you from?"

"I am Ukraine. I speak Russian. You speak Russian?"

"Dah." Evan answered. "Ya govoryu Rooskiy!"

"Dah! Korosho!" Nicholas repositioned himself, as though to communicate. The conversation became quickly animated, as the Ukrainian was enabled to communicate in a language he understood. As the two men began to talk, the four other men seated with Nicholas joined in.

"What are you doing in this house?" Evan asked them.

A younger man, seated behind the others, answered. "We are not part of whatever this business is. We were paid to come to do emergency medical transport. We have refrigeration units and we have to hurry. You must let us do our job, please. Lives are at stake here."

"What is your name?" Evan asked.

"Gregor Budnikov. I am the supervisor of this team."

"Oh." He glanced at Nicholas, who chuckled, and then spoke.

"Yes, Agent. I am bigger than he is. But I am only the muscle. He is the thinker."

The other three men with Gregor and Nicholas laughed in agreement.

"I'm sorry," Evan told them in Russian. "I don't have the authority to release you. You will have to wait."

He looked at the third man. "What is your name?"

"Vitali Durov. I am working my way through medical school. This job pays my bills."

Evan looked at the fourth man.

"Yuri Gusarov. I am trying to get my green card."

The agent's view went to the fifth and final man on Gregor's team.

The man returned his gaze, and did not speak.

Evan fixed his eyes on him. Evan spoke once more. "Can I have your name please, and the reason you are here?"

The man's gaze did not waver. He spoke in German. "Du sprichst Deutsch?"

The other men looked at him blankly. It was obvious none of them spoke German.

Evan motioned to him to stand and walk away from the group. The two men stood together some feet's distance from the four Ukrainians, and continued to speak in German.

Evan was curious. German wasn't wasn't his *best* language, but he would give it a go. He nodded and replied carefully and slowly in German. "Ja, Ich spreche Deutsch."

Still in German, he asked, "What is your name?"

"I am Patrick MacNaulty. I am from London; with MI6. We have been investigating a kidnapping ring. Thought it was based in Russia. That's how I ended up with this crew. And now you know the rest."

Evan pointed to the group of three men he had formerly separated from the others. "Go over and join those guys," he said. "I'll retain your cover. You still have to go through the system. Oh, you got a passport on you?"

"Yes," MacNaulty replied. "It's in my back pocket."

As Evan removed the passport, the man said, "Thanks."

Evan helped the MI6 agent to his feet, and repositioned him in his new position. Upon returning to the Ukrainians, he explained his actions, speaking once more in Russian.

"Do you guys have any idea what a bad guy you have on your team? It's amazing none of you haven't been killed. He's on the FBI's most wanted list. We've been looking for him a long time."

Wide-eyed, the Ukrainians stared at Evan, and then looked at Patrick in unison. It was like watching something in slow motion. Had it happened in a different setting, it might have made a great video clip.

Even Evan found himself smiling, as he moved on to the remaining detainees seated on the side yard.

Chapter Fourteen

Christine Spada sat in the Marshall family home on Hydrangea Court Drive, surveying the damage. Whomever had committed the massacre in this home had left behind a grisly scene.

The Crime Lab had arrived not long ago. They had begun gathering evidence from the hub-house across the street almost an hour prior. They had finished gathering shooter's evidence from Ginsberg Memorial. The second team would be arriving at the Marshall family crime scene in a few hours.

It had been five hours since she spoke with Jim Ainsworth. At that point, Sarah had disappeared, and he was going to take Caleb to his own home for safety.

Christine knew she needed to check on Sarah McMillan, and Caleb. When she arrived at the Marshall's, Pete had informed her of Sarah's shooting, and told her the social worker was undergoing surgery. In the midst of conversation he confided he had heard two additional rumors. Jim Ainsworth had also been shot and was in surgery. Rick Anderson, the protective officer, had also been injured. The policeman had suffered massive blood loss and damage to his lungs. It was anticipated all would survive. But all three would be in Intensive Care for some time.

She sighed.

Who would try to kill a seven year old boy? And why?

Who would shoot a social worker?

Or a housewife because she made a call to the police?

Christine tried to think about the case objectively. It felt like someone was trying to kill a mosquito with a sledgehammer. It was definitely an over-compensation for anyone to kill an entire family just because one person had seen something.

Which took her thoughts to the call she had made to the Non-Emergency Dispatch that morning. She had asked for an email of the transcripts of calls between midnight and five a.m.

When Christine received the email, it contained no record of Mrs. Marshall's three in the morning call. So, Christine called Officer Collins at the precinct. Yes, he remembered the call. Would he come to the field office this evening to make a statement? Sure, he told her. He would be happy to.

How had Chase known to request a printout before the report was illegally edited and handed in? Who in the precinct's chain-of-command had been responsible for processing the report? How had Mrs. Marshall's call vanished?

Pete was working with Sheriff Jackson when Christine arrived at the murder scene.

At the moment, she was in the midst of a conversation with Alexander Boyd from the Westwood Village Precinct. The Lieutenant had pursued her, seeking information, it seemed.

"I didn't expect to see you here, Agent Spada," he told her. "I thought you were working on a federal case."

She nodded. "We are," she answered. "Our first reason for coming this morning, as you know, was the SWAT team raid across the street. But I saw the lights, over here, and I heard there was a murder in this house. Do you know what happened?"

"Actually, I do," Lieutenant Boyd answered with a sigh. "I was the first officer on the scene this morning. It's been a long day."

"I agree with you," Christine told him. She walked over to the fireplace hearth. She sat down, and took her left shoe off. Looking down, she began to rub her foot. "It's been a very long day."

"I was in here at five this morning," Boyd told her. "I came up here, to the lake, after my shift yesterday. My brother lives on the lake on this same street; Hydrangea. See? It's the grey house on the cul-de-sac."

He pointed out the window, indicating a house several doors away. "My brother's family was hosting our family reunion this weekend. His house is so big, over time it's just become the center for our family get-togethers."

"Oh, that's so cool," Christine told him. "That would be impossible with my family. We're spread all over the place."

"Mine too," came the reply. "But they've been planning this thing for months. Some of us come from as far away as California and Texas just for these three days."

"That sounds so great," she told him. "Did you get to take the weekend off to enjoy it?"

The lieutenant shrugged. "Not really. I did trade all my shifts except yesterday. But you better believe; I high-tailed it back here as soon as I could, to be with everyone one more time last night. They all headed out today."

"I've never had the opportunity to stay in a lake house," Christine offered. "I bet the view is nice to wake up to."

"Oh, it's great," he replied. "I stay with Cameron and his family whenever I can."

"That's awesome." She paused. "Which home is theirs?"

The lieutenant pointed to a large home, three doors down from the hub house, on the same side of the street.

Christine made note of its location. "So, did you forgot to tell me what happened this morning?"

"Oh, that," he replied, nonchalantly. "Well, it was before 5 this morning. I went to bed a little after eleven thirty last night. I got up early, and wanted to beat the rush back to the precinct. I was heading out to my car, when I heard a woman screaming. So, I broke down the door and ran in. I was the one who radioed in the call."

"Wow. That would wake you up, I would think," she said.

"Yeah, really did," Boyd answered.

"Do you mind me asking what you saw?"

"No, Agent, not at all." The lieutenant adjusted his the waistline of his dress pants with an air of self-importance, and put his hands on his hips. He looked around, pointing to each location as he spoke.

"Well, like I told you, I broke in the door. The screaming was coming from one of the back bedrooms. When I got back there, I saw the master bedroom door was open, and there was blood everywhere. Another bedroom door across the hall was open, and there was blood in there too. The room at the end of the hall, was open, and there was a guy standing behind a teenage girl. I guess she must have been the Marshall's daughter. As I walked through the door, he slit her throat, and blood went all over. He saw me, and bolted through the open window in her room."

"Didn't you go after him?" Christine queried.

"I was in shock, Agent. I don't think I've ever seen that much blood in once place before. So no, I didn't."

"Can you describe the guy? The killer?"

"Sure. I'll be making a full report later. But he was stocky, and had on a navy baseball cap. He had a trimmed beard. I think his hair was reddish brown. I remember he had carpenter blue jeans on. You know, the ones with the loops on the leg and the extra pockets? He had Skechers lace-ups; they were brown and tan. I know because I've had a pair just like them on my Amazon wish list."

"Did you get a good look at his face?"

Boyd shook his head.

"Maybe you should be looking in the mirror, Alex." Peter Lynch spoke as he walked into the room from the hallway.

The lieutenant turned around to face Pete. "What are you talking about, Lynch? You don't have to be jealous, just because I was given jurisdiction here."

Christine spoke up. "By whom, Lieutenant?"

"What?"

"Who gave you jurisdiction?" she asked.

He stammered. "Well, by the Captain, and yes, the Commissioner himself."

Pete exchanged glances with Sheriff Jackson, and then Christine.

"That's funny, Alex," the detective drawled. "Because I spoke with the Captain *and* the Commissioner today, and neither of those men remember giving *you* jurisdiction of *anything.*"

Boyd put his hands up in front of himself, as though in surrender. "Okay, so I might have misunderstood something, guys."

"I think you must have," Christine told him, "since this case falls under FBI jurisdiction, and that would mean me. I've had no such communication. So, I'm booking you on suspicion of a multiple homicide."

Alexander Boyd appeared to be stunned. "I told you what happened!" he cried. "I was just the first officer on the scene! I have an alibi. I was at my brother's house all night long. Ask him. He'll tell you! I couldn't sleep, and I kept him awake."

"Probably woke him up when you came in at four-thirty," Pete commented.

"This is a frame up!" The lieutenant protested.

"I thought you might say that," Christine told him. She looked at Pete. "Collins?"

Pete smiled at her. "He's safe."

She continued, standing once more. "Okay, Lieutenant. Let's cut to the chase. We know you are lying. But, because you are a fellow officer, I will give you one chance. One chance only, to rescind your story, and make a deal. If not, I will need your gun and your badge," she told him.

He pulled his service pistol from his shoulder holster, and removed his badge from his belt. "You don't have anything on me," he sneered at her, handing her both items. "Nothing you can *prove* anyway."

"Okay, Alexander," she began, disparagingly. "How about I show you a printout of the Non-Emergency Dispatch Log, showing *you* on the telephone with Mrs. Marshall at three-forty this morning? How about an eyewitness who places *you* in front of the precinct vending machines at three-fifty this morning, discussing the problem of a shipment being observed; and you telling that party you would take care the problem? How about we add to those things, the doctored Dispatch Log, which conveniently omits Mrs. Marshall's call, *and* your part in that call? How about my digital recorder, right here in my pocket, that is recording this entire conversation?"

Lieutenant Alexander Boyd wasn't giving up just yet. "Hey, this is entrapment! It's still just your word against mine. I want a lawyer, and I'm entitled to a phone call!"

"He doesn't get it," Christine said to Pete.

"Doesn't get it at all," Pete responded, making a soft, clucking noise with his tongue.

"Get what?" snapped Boyd. "Don't talk about me like I'm not here!"

Pete smiled at him. "This case comes under the Patriot Act. You're not entitled to a lawyer. You're a detainee in a Federal Homeland Security Investigation. Sorry."

"Oh." Boyd slumped. He was caught and he knew it.

"Okay, I'll make a deal," he told them. "But you have got to protect me. These people; you don't know how dangerous they are. If they even get a hint I'm blown, I'll be dead in an hour."

"Protect you? Like you protected the Marshalls, you mean?" Sheriff Jackson said to him, incensed. "Listen, if these two weren't federal officers, I'd skin you alive right here. You make me sick. We don't take kindly in this county to honest, hard-working people like Jim and Mary Marshall, *and their children,* being murdered in their sleep. The Marshalls happen to have been *friends* of mine. My wife is going to take this one hard."

He looked at Christine and then at Pete. "Agents, I'm sure you guys have things to finish up here. Let me get him out of here for you. I'll deliver him anywhere you say."

"Can you take him to our mutually discussed isolation cell? Eventually he will be held in the Correctional Facility in the Village.... But for now.... Well, you know."

"Yes sir. I'll do it myself. And I'll take a deputy along with me for good measure."

As Sheriff Jackson was speaking, Boyd suddenly leaned over, and pulled a second pistol from a leg holster under his suit pants. In one quick movement, he turned and fired his weapon at Sheriff Jackson. Surprised, the sheriff ducked to the ground, while pulling his own weapon. He fired a shot, hitting Boyd in the hand. His weapon fell to the ground.

Well-experienced, however, Agent Christine Spada had fully expected Boyd to try "suicide by cop" once his cover was blown. So, while Boyd was aiming for the sheriff, Christine fired two shots: one into Boyd's right shoulder, and one into his rear end.

Boyd fell to the floor, holding his right hand, he screamed in pain. Christine stood up, placed her gun in its holster, and looked at Pete and the Sheriff.

"Sheriff Jackson," she said. "Are you okay?"

He stood up, shaking his head. "I'm fine, Missy. The Good Lord was protecting me again."

"Sure was," Christine answered. "Pete? You okay?"

Pete nodded, placing his gun in his shoulder holster.

"Hey!" Boyd shouted, lying on the floor "I'm bleeding here! Don't you care how *I'm* doing?"

"Not really," Pete told him, stepping over his body. He looked at the Sheriff. "What do you say we just let him bleed out right here?"

"Sounds good to me," Jackson replied.

"Naw… we can't do that, can we? We're the *good* guys," Pete chuckled.

"I got this, Pete," the Sheriff informed him. "I'll have a doctor come stitch him up." He pulled on the arrested man's injured arm. "Get up, Boyd, and come on. Let's get you locked up where you belong. Frisk him, Pete."

Alexander winced in pain as he came to his feet. Pete checked the man's frame for additional weapons. He found a sheath of throwing knives strapped around the man's other leg, and a third pistol in his jacket pocket.

"A little woman's Ladyfinger? A baby .22? Really?" Christine asked. "Where were you planning to use that?"

"I don't have to answer that, do I?" Boyd wanted to know.

"You can plead the Fifth Amendment if you want to go back on that promise of making a deal to turn state's evidence," she told him, while the Sheriff was handcuffing him.

"Oh yeah, that. I was holding it for somebody."

"Right." Christine radioed for another ambulance.

It took a little time for Christine to begin to feel secure about Lieutenant Boyd's arrest. After speaking at length with Sheriff Jackson, she felt herself instinctively relax. She could sense he was a trustworthy man.

Come to think of it, there was something about him that reminded her of her father, she realized.

She stayed on watch until she was certain Boyd had been secured in an ambulance. The Lieutenant would be medically treated in isolation in a padded cell, under suicide watch for the night.

"We probably will need to return here again tomorrow," she told Pete quietly. "And we need to conduct an interview before we do anything else."

"Now?" Pete asked.

"Now," she replied, "before the Lab gets here."

After telling Evan they would return in a moment, Pete and Christine made their way to the home of the lieutenant's brother, Cameron Boyd.

As they approached the house, they noticed several cars outside, typical for a family reunion. Pete pushed the doorbell. The two agents waited for someone come to the door. When no one answered after three rings, Christine checked the front door.

It was locked.

Glancing at each other, both agents pulled their service weapons. Holding the handguns with both hands, just in front of the chest, both officers moved warily forward. They furtively checked backwards, forwards, and under bushes. Approaching the back yard, Christine quietly opened the gate, allowing them to slip through.

As they entered the backyard area of the home, Pete tapped her on the shoulder, and pointed up to the soffit above them. A security camera. Christine's awareness was now piqued. Someone could jump out of the bushes any moment.

Coming around the back corner of the house, they realized the atmosphere seemed unusually still; especially considering the number of cars out front, and Boyd's story about a family reunion taking place.

Where was everyone?

There was no one in the pool.

Or the hot-tub... Or the cabana.

Quietly sliding open the glass doors, Christine edged her way into the living room. Pete entered behind her and made his way to the kitchen. As they edged through different areas of the house, the investigators shouted to each other, "Garage clear!" "Kitchen clear!" "Laundry room clear!"

However, upon entering the hallway leading to the sleeping quarters, Pete noticed lines of blood on the door of the guest bathroom. It looked as though someone had fingerpainted two palms in blood, and then slid down the surface of the door face first.

In fact, there was lots of blood.

But there was no dead body.

There was no blood trail leading out of the bathroom.

"Is anyone here?" Pete yelled. "We are FBI. We are here to help you."

He stopped and listened. Nothing.

Christine moved by him and entered the first bedroom, which apparently belonged to the adolescent son. There was no blood; no body.

Pete checked the second bedroom, decorated in pinks and creams. Definitely belonged to the daughter. Again, no blood; no body.

But the master bedroom was a different story. It was almost a perfect repetition of the Marshall's master bedroom scene. The husband and wife had both been murdered as they slept.

The bodies were still in the king-sized bed.

Pete pushed the button on his radio "Dispatch, this is Detective Lynch. We have double homicide, and a possible double kidnapping at 2011 Hydrangea Court Lane, Ennis Lake. We need a bus, and Forensics team immediately."

Christine nodded to him. She began opening closets in the master bedroom. Unexpectedly, from the top shelf of the closet, a black cat growled and then, hissing, leaped into her face.

Instinctively, she screamed.

Pete came running. "Kit," he asked, "you okay?"

Touching her forearm to her face, she answered with an awkward smile. "Just a cat," she muttered.

"Oh," he answered. "Sorry."

Unconsciously, they both began to laugh.

"He just pounced on me when I opened the closet!" she said, laughing and crying at the same time.

"I think we're both going to need therapy when this case is done," Pete told her. "You need a hug?"

Christine nodded her head, wiping tears from her cheeks.

Pete put his arms around her. "Just a brotherly hug. No strings attached," he said.

"Okay," she answered. "But watch yourself."

She buried her face into his chest, enjoying the momentary sense of protection.

For a few moments, it was quiet, as they both considered the enormity of the case.

"And don't call me Kit," she complained weakly.

"Yeah, I know," he whispered. Silently, he sniffed her hair, and kissed the top of her head.

That night, Felipe and Christine kept their "date." The strain of maintaining their cover as an engaged couple was beginning to get to Christine. She wasn't sure why Ben had ordered the cover. She found herself wondering whether the case was becoming too much for her to handle.

Felipe must have sensed she was experiencing stress.

True to "Fernando" form, he greeted her upon her arrival home with a dozen pink roses, and a bottle of her favorite perfume.

"Oh, Sweetheart!" she gushed, hugging him. "I am so glad to be home. I couldn't wait to see you. I missed you so today. We had three really dangerous situations happen today. All of them on the same street. And, I had to fire my weapon at a suspect. Several people I have been working with in this case got shot, and are now in the hospital."

Felipe read her face, and showed instant and genuine concern. However, true to form, he utilized his accent.

"*Mi Amor*! Are you okay? Who was shot? Were *you* injured?"

"No, I'm okay. My feet hurt, is all. They sent a shooter after the boy, and the psychologist, and the social worker in the hospital."

"*Mia Cara*! You want to go to see them before we eat together?"

"Fernando! Really? I know how you planned for this evening."

"It's no problem at all. Yes, let's go to the hospital."

She hugged him.

"But there is more, si?" he asked, winking at her.

She nodded. "Si. I mean, yes. There were two multiple murders today, and an unexpected raid. I was involved in all of them in some way. All three houses were on the same street. I don't think I've ever seen so much blood."

"Oh, my," he responded. "Would you rather stay in? We could put on soft music, and drink a little wine? We can go out another night."

"Oh, Fernando," she replied. "You are so good to me."

She thought for just a moment. "You know what I would really like?"

"Just say it, *Chiquita*."

"A pizza. From Tony's."

Felipe grinned at her. "You mean the big pizza pie that you fold over to eat it; the slice?"

"That's it. With extra pepperoni and extra cheese."

"Si, *Mia Cara*. That's the best. Magnifico."

"And a beer."

"A beer?" he asked. "You are eating like your father tonight."

She smiled. "How well you know me. That is exactly what I need to do."

"You want it delivered, or shall we eat out?"

"Give me an hour, and we can go out. Is that good?" she asked.

"*Mui bueno*. Is a better solution than to dress up tonight. We can go whenever you are ready. You still want to go to the hospital?"

"No, Sweetheart," she answered. "Let me soak in the tub for a few minutes. I'll go to the hospital tomorrow."

"No problema, *mi amor*," Felipe answered.

While Kit was soaking in the bathtub, her cell phone rang. Looking at the caller ID, she saw it was Samantha, and decided to decline it. She had set her phone to a Pandora station, and just wasn't ready to talk. She ducked her head under the water.

Its quiet under water, she thought. *And its weightless here. What would it be like if you could breathe under water. Why can't I just stay here for awhile?*

213

She resurfaced for a breath, and went back down for another moment or two. How could so much happen in one day? Was it going to be like this every day as a Bureau Field Chief? She hoped not.

Giving herself a good scrub, she washed her hair, and then got ready to go out.

Tonight's "date" was important to the case, or at least it had been until now. The plan was to leave false evidence in the townhouse, in order to set a trap for the traffickers. Ben Edwards, her boss, had not told her what the evidence would be, or what leaving it to be found would provide in helping to solve the case.

But now that they had found the hub house, Christine wondered if there was still a necessity for tonight's sting to take place. Felipe had assured her that yes, it was still necessary.

So, the "date"' was on.

Thirty-five minutes later, "Fernando" and Kit left to go out to Tony's Chicago Pizza. They anticipated being tailed, and Ben Edwards had ordered kevlar vests be worn. Felipe opened the passenger door for Kit, kissing her lightly as she passed by him to sit in the Mercedes. He shut the door and went around to the other side, getting into the driver's side.

In his hand, he held a portable wireless scrambler. As they pulled away, he pressed the button. Looking in the rear view mirror, he smiled.

"They're back there, same silver sedan," he told her. "Idiots."

"Abbot and Costello?" she asked.

"You know it. I just put the scrambler on. Catch me up on the day, if you will, and then I'll tell you what's happened in the office."

"Okay," she said. "Thanks for giving me the time I needed to regather my brain cells. I'm really looking forward to a junk food meal tonight. Comfort food!"

"Like with pizza and beer?" he laughed.

"Exactly like pizza and beer!" She paused. "How about we talk over ice cream afterwards?"

"I think just my side will take more time than that," he told her, with a wink and a smile.

"Then why don't you start? *During* pizza and beer?" she suggested. "I don't mind taking the end game."

"You got it, partner," he said.

Pulling into the parking lot at Tony's Chicago Pizza, Felipe noticed the silver sedan was parking on the street, still holding a listening cone in their direction. Felipe had run the pictures of the two men inside through the network that day, and discovered their identities. Both had arrests and priors going back at least ten years.

"Excuse me, *Mia Cara*," he said. "I have to make a phone call." With the portable scrambler in his pocket, he opened his cell and called Central Police Dispatch.

"Yes, my name is Fernando Rafaello. I live in a townhouse in Alpine Circle, near Westwood Village. Over the past couple of weeks, two men have been parked outside my home all day every day. They don't live in my housing complex, and they use an eavesdropping cone to hear what my fiancee and I say to each other. Tonight, we decided to go out on a date together, and they followed us. Could someone have a patrol officer go to their car and take them in for parking next to a fire hydrant? They are just outside Tony's Chicago Pizza near Alpine Circle, on Jefferson."

He paused.

"Yes, I'd like to press charges."

"No, it's in my fiancee's name."

"Christine Spada."

"Yes, she is working at Westwood Village. That's correct."

"Yes, she has had a long day. Thank you for noticing."

"Would you?"

"Thank you. I really appreciate that."

"Okay. We will wait right here."

Hanging up, he went back to the car, where Kit was waiting. After getting back into the care on the driver's side, he grabbed her hand and kissed it. "Gracias, *Mi Corazon*," he whispered. "We need to wait here for a moment or two. Do you mind?"

"Not a bit, Fernando." She put her head back on the headrest, and closed her eyes. She dozed off for a few moments. When she opened her eyes, Felipe was standing in front of her car, speaking with a Sheriff's Deputy. Abbott and Costello were apparently cuffed, and seated in the back seat of the Sheriff's vehicle.

She looked again. Wasn't the man he was talking to one of Sheriff Jackson's deputies?

When the conversation was finished, Felipe returned to the car. "Those guys won't bother us again," he told her, as he closed the car door.

"How do you know?" she asked, surprised.

"Well, let's just say we found a friend to help us when we need it, at least until we are reasonably certain the City of Greenway's Law Enforcement is reliable and trustworthy again."

"So what's happening here?"

"Ben Edwards called me this afternoon, just before you got home. He wanted these guys off your tail. Said you have enough to worry about, and it was time you had a break. He was really impressed with the way the taskforce led the raid this morning."

"I haven't even filed the report yet," she told him. "Did he say how he knew?"

"You know Ben," Felipe shrugged. "Somehow he got word."

"That's true," she noted. "Ben's got connections everywhere."

"And we just gained another one," he told her. "It seems Sheriff Jackson from Ennis County wants to make sure he contributes his part to help in this case. He was very impressed with both you and Detective Lynch. He called the Deputy Director himself. It was probably his contact Ben was referring to."

"He called Edwards?" she asked.

"Yes, ma'am, he did," Felipe answered. "Looks like we are making a dent in the case."

"Yeah."

Just then, a tow truck pulled up, hooking up the silver sedan for transport to the impound yard.

"Okay, Kit," Felipe said. "Time for pizza and beer. I have so much to tell you."

Upon their arrival home, as anticipated, "someone" had broken into Kit's townhouse. Two new cameras had been installed,

216

and four audio surveillance bugs were discovered. There had also been a second set of gadgets added to the main computer in the office. As they destroyed each added element, Christine took note. The criminals were intent on cloning the field office's setup.

The two Agents smiled as they did a sweep of their living environment. The sting had been successful.

Earlier that day, Felipe had built a false website for the FBI, complete with online links filled with false information. In short, the plant was designed to cause the criminals to believe they had nothing to worry about; that the investigators had no idea what was actually taking place. Like the actual FBI servers, the false website was encrypted and password coded. A computer genius, Felipe had layered the site in such a way that those hacking the software would not discover the nature of his programming for a long, long time.

Hopefully, they wouldn't discover the truth until the case was closed.

When he had installed the false server sites, Felipe had also temporarily disconnected the field office from the actual FBI main servers. The software he had created would lead the traffickers in the wrong directions, and send them looking for fabricated persons and locations.

Chapter Fifteen

Samantha Cruz was on a morning coffee break from her clerking job. Her mind was filled with the case files she had been researching for her boss, Federal Judge Anne Ventura.

However, at the moment, she was browsing Facebook on her smartphone. As she pressed the pad to exit the application, and go to Pinterest, her phone vibrated in her hand. She was so startled, she dropped it, and then caught it again.

"Gets me every time," she complained. Then she answered.

"Hey Kit! I thought you might have dropped off the planet. How's it going?"

"So crazy. Sam, you won't believe all the stuff. You and I have a bunch of office work to do."

"No, you mean *I'm* going to have office work to do."

"Yes, there is that...." Kit paused. "You called me yesterday. I'm sorry. I was kind of in the weeds all day."

"In the weeds?"

"Sorry. It's a term we used when I was working as a server. It's supposed to describe having all your tables full, with a long wait, and no end in sight."

"Got it. Sounds crazy."

"Let's just say I had to fire my weapon yesterday," Kit offered.

"Oh no, you didn't," Sam replied. She was surprised. Despite television, she knew from her research that real Law Enforcement officers only fired their weapons three percent of the time.

"Oh, yes, I did," Kit giggled.

"Violence?" Sam asked.

"Three situations. All on the same street."

"That's just nasty."

Kit smiled. "Did you have a reason for calling me yesterday?"

"Oh, yeah," Sam told her. "I have been browsing through websites and magazines, looking for the ads we talked about in our meeting the other night. You know higher end stuff?"

"Yeah," Kit answered. "I'm listening."

"There's two things. First, the same classified ad has been posted in several men's fitness magazines, as well as in some of the high-end vacation newspapers they distribute in places like The Hamptons, Napa, the French Riviera, Monaco; places like that. You want to hear it?"

"Sure!" Kit replied. "Can you read it to me?"

"Here goes," Sam told her. "The ad reads: *'American female; certified virgin, cultured and beautiful -- seeks kind, understanding, older man for happy marriage. Must be able to support present lifestyle. No booty calls, please. Only serious inquiries need apply. Pedigree available upon request. Call 1-800-MY-BRIDE for information.'*

"Wow," Kit murmured. "That sounds like our case, for sure."

"I know. Right?" Sam declared. "And I've found the same ad in five different periodicals so far. Then, maybe because I understood what I was seeing, I noticed the toll free number as part of a dating sight ad online this week. It reads: *'Find the wife of your dreams. Call 1-800-MY-BRIDE for information. Serious inquiries only, please. Not a dating service.'*"

There was a pause in the conversation.

"It's really possible, you might have found them, Sam," Kit told her. "Good work!"

"There's more," Samantha told her.

"Really? Go on," Kit said.

"After I saw the ads, I went to one of the Bridal Shops after work yesterday," Samantha continued. "I purchased a copy of every Bridal magazine they carry. There are only a few printed in Spanish from other countries available here in the States. But, I found two. In both of them, there were articles about last week's marriage of billionaire Juan Paredes to his fourth wife."

"Paredes, the Drug Cartel?" Kit asked, suddenly alert to what Samantha was telling her. The girl had definitely discovered some pieces of the puzzle.

"Yes, the same. Anyway, there were pages of pictures in the Spanish magazine. The bride might *not* be the same, but she looks a lot like one of the three girls we have posted on the field office board."

"Which one?"

"The first one on the board. Katie Curtin. But her name in the magazine is Victoria Mendoza. She is supposedly a direct descendant of Castilian aristocracy."

"Bring all of that tonight to the team meeting, will you?"

"Tonight? At seven?"

"Yes, please."

"I'll be there, with my stuff."

"Thanks, girl. Hey, I have to hit it again. Can we talk more later? Sorry. I gotta go."

"Sure. I've got to get back to work anyway."

"You've done well, Sam. Sure you want to be a lawyer?"

Her friend laughed. "Don't forget Zumba on Saturday."

"You got it. You're amazing, Sam. Spada out."

In the penthouse suite of a hotel in Hong Kong, a lonely, young woman looked out the window, taking in the immensity of the view below. From her present perch, she could see the entire city. Today, it was raining, so she had opted to stay in the living room and read.

She glanced at the large clock on the mantel. He would be home soon. She should change.

She had been in her pajamas all morning, then ordered breakfast from the kitchen downstairs. She had gone for a swim in the private pool on the roof just outside. She had tried to watch television, but the only English channels available were CNN and FOX News. The video games attached to the system were children's games. None of them held her interest. She had mastered them all years ago. Besides, she was too old for such things anymore.

She had tried to go out for a walk earlier, but the man posted outside her door had refused to allow her to leave the room. She had invited him to come with her, to show her the city. But he said he couldn't leave his post.

But wasn't he supposed to be her bodyguard?

Finally, it occurred to her to call the hotel concierge.

"Do you have any good mysteries in English I could read?" she asked.

"Oh, yes, Madame Cheung," came the British-accented answer. "We have many titles. Do you have a favorite author?"

"No, not yet."

He laughed lightly. "Then, I will send up a collection for you to choose from."

"Thank you," she sighed with relief. "What is your name?"

"Xiang Lao, Madame," he replied. "If you need anything at all, please call me. I am at your service."

"Hi Lao. You can call me Angelica. Can you help me go shopping? Or see the sights of your beautiful city?"

There was a pause.

"No, I am sorry, Madame. Master Cheung has requested we prevent his precious treasure being lost or mistreated. I know he desires to share these things with you, as his beloved."

The girl rolled her eyes. "I understand," she said sweetly. "Thank you. Do you know whether he is in the building?"

"Yes, Madame," came the reply. "He is in his office."

"If you have a moment, would you let him know I called again?" she asked.

"I will do as you wish, Madame," Xiang answered. "I will call you again with his reply."

"Thank you, Xiang."

A few moments after closing the call, there was a knock on the door. A bellboy delivered a silver tray of brand-new murder mystery paperbacks in English. Also included were two of Barbara Cartland's romances and a book by Danielle Steele.

"Xiang said to give you these, Madame Cheung."

"Thank you," she replied, taking the tray.

Thumbing through the books, she had chosen one by James Peterson, and begun to read.

She had read almost five chapters. The plot was intriguing, but it hadn't stopped the nagging sense of abject isolation in her soul. Now, looking through the large plate glass, she wondered if this day was another representation of the sum total of her life.

She had been married to Cheung Lui-Jing, China's second wealthiest shipping magnate, for a little over a week now. He was supposed to be her Prince Charming.

But ..... He was short and wore glasses. He was very kind to her, and called her his "lotus blossom." He was a good bit older than she. She didn't mind it so much.

But .... There just wasn't a spark between them. In fact, because of the huge difference in their ages, she couldn't shake the feeling she was kissing her father.

It just felt gross. He had told her she would grow to love him, as he loved her. She must learn to make herself respond, he said. She must learn to be self-sufficient. If she would allow him, he promised to help her make her own life. But she would always belong to him.

A new life?

How could she do anything creative if she was kept a prisoner? Would she ever be allowed to go outside somewhere other than the hotel's rooftop?

She looked around the penthouse. It was beautiful; filled with everything she could have ever wanted. She had a hot tub, a daily massage, any spa treatment she requested, any food she desired, any items she had a desire for.

Everything.

Except.

Everything except company.

She remembered being miserable before her abduction, but she remembered a couple of people.... She thought anyway.

Why were things so foggy? She shook her head.

Here, everyone walked in fear of their master. Her husband.

He was a powerful man. Such power scared her.

How she longed for communication. She couldn't remember her life.... Before... had it always been this way?

Was this to be the sum total of her life?

Had he married her to isolate her?

They sell us to rich men for sex, or whatever they want.

Unbidden, the words she had spoken to Erin Kasabian ran across her mind. Where had they come from, she wondered?

"I *am* the trophy wife," she murmured. "He has me on his arm, to dress me up like a Barbie; to be glamorous at parties. He bought me for sex."

She remembered the lessons Miss Anastasia had given her. She remembered asking her instructor what would happen if she *wasn't* happy, or her buyer *didn't* like her. She understood now why the question had not been given an answer.

Master Cheung, her husband, had been known to beat his servants, as well as his former wives. She certainly didn't want to anger him, or forget the things that would keep her from experiencing his dark side.

Nothing had prepared her for the misery she felt. A tear made its way down her cheek, and then another. She stared out the window at the rain.

"I'm a prisoner," she whispered. "And I'm only sixteen years old!"

Back in Greenway, the day was becoming one filled with interviews and taking statements. Christine had come to a conclusion. Officer Chase Stanford was a natural. He had shown investigative instinct in asking for the printout of the Dispatch call. He had instinctively remained hidden by the vending machines, waiting to gather more complete information. He had not confronted Boyd, but had worked through the proper channels.

His evidence would be untainted, and admissible in court.

She had called the Police Captain, requesting permission to utilize the young man on her team, at least for the time being. The Captain was glad to allow it, he said, and would assign Chase to her taskforce temporarily, requiring him to be accountable to Detective Peter Lynch.

Kit had assigned Chase to interview the chef who worked in the house on Hydrangea Court Drive. Specifically, she wanted to know who came to the house regularly. How many girls were in the house at a time? Were there situations the man remembered happening at the house to indicate what had been going on and who was in charge?

"Basically, Chase," she instructed, "I want you to get this man to tell you stories of events happening in that house. I'm sure he will also have stories regarding other houses he has worked in for these people. Keep it conversational. Base your questions on the stories, and on his other answers. Try to keep him disclosing. As an endgame, it's imperative we discover who is at the top of this food chain.

"Usually, domestic servants like this man know a lot more than they get credit for. And, they are easy for the perpetrators to overlook, or talk in front of. If he has worked for them very long, he probably has overheard conversations that could help us a great deal."

"Yes, ma'am, Agent Spada," the young man replied. "Thank you for the opportunity."

"I think you have real potential, Chase," she said. "Let's see how you do."

Detective Evan Davies had arrived early at the precinct that morning, preparing questions for the five Ukrainians, who had checked out to be Medical Transport. All identification checks had come back clean. None of them were hiding crimes, or even what Evan referred to as "mischief predicaments."

The Crime Lab's forensic sweep of the house had provided some evidence to confirm their story. Two mysterious, stainless steel boxes had been discovered in the basement of the house. Both were set on wheels, and were plugged in to 220-volt electric power, like a dryer or electric oven would be.

Evan had not been able to find such an item available for sale on the internet. Further research would show whether it had been custom designed. On the side of each box were printed the words, "MEDICAL SUPPLIES − FRAGILE." Inside each of the boxes were separated and sealed, Styrofoam boxes. Each one was marked with an adhesive label. The labels were marked with combinations of letters, dashes and numbers.

The Crime Lab had confiscated the stainless steel units, taking them back to the Precinct for investigation.

Larry Taylor, MD, the Crime Laboratory Manager, had given orders the boxes were to remain electrically powered until determinations could be made regarding criminal activity. After all, just because part of the house was being used for trafficking activities, did not necessarily indicate *all* activities taking place in the home were criminal. It was Taylor's hunch the stainless boxes were cryogenic storage tanks, but the whole thing would require further investigation. As a detective, he answered directly to the Police Deputy Chief, and wanted to see the case solved. As a physician, however, he had taken an oath to preserve life whenever possible: *Do no harm*.

Evan considered the man's viewpoint. It was conceivable the boxes *were* designed for medical transport. It was possible they contained items the Ukrainians were supposed to deliver somewhere. He wouldn't know until he could interview the four men individually.

Trafficking and Cryogenics. How could two, so completely different endeavors, be tied together, he wondered? What possible connection could a medical transport team have to do with the trafficking case?

He anticipated the four interviews would encompass most of his day. If not, however, Evan planned spending at least part of the afternoon with Patrick MacNaulty, Undercover MI6 Agent. Hopefully by the middle of the day, the man's passport would have been processed. Sadly, he realized, as a lowly detective, he could not release MacNaulty, or even *discuss* the case with him, until he received identity confirmation from the British Embassy, MI6 directly, or CIA at Langley, Virginia.

For his part, Detective Peter Lynch had planned his day around completing the follow-up with Alexander Boyd. The presently "missing" detective, was in a psychiatric solitary lock-up in Sheriff Jackson's jail. Pete had been in the Ennis County Jail since dawn. He was hoping to gain a list of Boyd's confederates within the Greenway's Police Department. He was determined to get the answers he needed.

Agent Christine Spada had been sitting at her desk since four that morning. Exhausted, but unable to sleep, she had finally decided to make her way downtown. For the past three hours, she had been working on a spreadsheet, seeking to define the patterns and profiles of the case.

Before retiring the night before, she had looked through the initial statements taken during the raid. It had been difficult to focus. She had experienced a sense a fogginess, a sort of confusion. It had settled in on her mental faculties. Over the years, she had discovered that when she experienced such a mental barrier, it was helpful to create an organizational chart; developing a reasonable format for all the information.

The present spreadsheet was her fifth attempt to organize the persons involved in the case so far. But she knew the solutions were within grasp, so she contended in her efforts. The raid had provided an immense amount of information. And all of it had come at once.

"I just need some alone time to think," she told herself. And, since Felipe was at the townhouse, sleeping in the temporary field office, she retreated to the only refuge she had; the Westwood Precinct, fifth floor.

So far, she was beginning to grasp the pattern of the trafficking network. A million a girl? Two million? Three? What was their overhead? And who was getting the rest of the money?

Obviously, this Asami Motors character was looking more and more like the kingpin. She would call Ben Edwards, to see if it was time to pick the man up yet.

At least the spreadsheet was giving her a hint of where to begin this morning, she realized. Sitting back, she surveyed the product of her labors.

Things were starting to make sense.

Before interviewing the foreign nationals from among the girls, Christine decided to process the five detainees who claimed to be Landon Morrow. Fingerprints and DNA had been run through CODIS overnight. Now, she felt well-armed to take their stories.

Following those five, she decided to run to Ginsberg Memorial to check on Sarah McMillan and Rick Anderson, the injured protective officer. David Gaines, the pediatric male nurse from the third floor, had assured her he was keeping Caleb Jacobs in a safe, locked-down environment, awaiting his orthopedic surgeries in the next couple of weeks.

Yes, he told her, there was an armed officer on guard at Caleb's door. And yes, the boy was happy, enjoying himself.

That evening, the taskforce came together for their scheduled meeting.

"I thought we'd order in," Christine told the team. "I found an app that will let me order online from almost any restaurant, and then they will deliver it."

"I'm in for Chinese," Pete offered.

"Ooh, that sounds good," Christine exclaimed. "Me too. Anyone else interested in Chinese?"

Everyone agreed except Josh, who wanted a pizza.

"So order yourself a pizza," Chase told him. "Domino's *always* delivers."

"I'll call in the Chinese," Christine offered to the group. "Tell me what you want."

After ordering was completed, the agent began the briefing.

"Thanks for all your hard work this past couple of weeks," she began. "We have seen some significant breaks in this case, and we still need a few more. That being said, let's make sure we are all on the same page."

She looked at Evan. "Can we begin with you please, Detective Davies? What can you share with all of us regarding the case since our last meeting almost a week ago?"

Evan looked around the room. "Well," he began slowly, "yesterday's raid was very successful, as far as we can tell. To bring us up to date regarding Katie Curtin and Erin Kasabian; neither girls was present in the house on Hydrangea. And as far as the two girls being prepped for sale in this house, both are familiar with a young man named Garrett, although he wasn't in the house at the time. But, we are sure he will turn up at some time in the near future. There is no student named Garrett enrolled at Hunter Ridge High

School in Westwood, or in any of the area high schools for that matter."

He shuffled through the portfolio of paperwork he had brought with him, pulling a printout containing the Verizon logo.

"Remember the teenage girl's cell from the Best Western hotel? The number is part of a Verizon contract with Mr. Carl Everest in Northridge. The phone belongs to his daughter, thirteen year old Amanda. She has been missing for about a month, but was not discovered any of our sweeps; not Parrott, Mackaw or Ennis Lake. The presence of her phone in the hotel room, and the texts it contains, indicate she is definitely one of the missing girls involved in this case."

"What does that mean?" Samantha asked.

Evan looked at her. "I think it means she was abducted for a more sinister reason, or that there is yet another hub house here in the area."

"Sam?" Christine called. "Please make a note we need to look for another hub house. Evan, what more sinister reason?"

He shrugged. "I don't know yet. I just have this gut feeling about some of this stuff. I'm trying to make sense of the cryogenics in the case. I'm not sure how they fit."

She nodded at him. "I'm with you," she said. "You have anything else?"

"Oh yes," he answered with a smile. He looked at Felipe. "Fernando?" he said.

"Thank you, my friend," Felipe replied, who looked around the group. "I ran facial recognition software for an identity to the old woman in the Mackaw video, and the young man whom we could see." Always in character, he shrugged. "Unfortunately, there are no *zombie* faces in the database, so ...."

At that point, Josh hit him. Felipe continued.

"Anyway, the old woman came up as Dame Margaret Kearnan, Diplomatic Attaché to the Vice President of the United States, 1970-1982. After her husband died, she disappeared. Everyone assumed she had taken a job with another government overseas. She was known for meticulous cultural instruction, and developing of diplomatic staff."

229

Kit nodded at him. "Wow. That's impressive."

Felipe smiled. "I would have like to have known her, I think. The young man came up as Landon Morrow, citizen of Monaco, and former Director of Staff Operations in the British Embassy in Monaco."

"Another one?" Sam exclaimed. "Just how many guys are there with that name? Was he a real person?"

Christine walked over to the file-box on the table nearby. She ruffled through the files until she found one she was looking for. She pulled a picture from the folder and posted it on the board.

"Dame Margaret Kearnan, reported missing 1984," she told them. "Her daughter lives in Monaco, and asked for help finding her twenty years ago. Are you telling me she was working for these guys all this time?"

"Looks like it," Felipe replied.

"Hold on a minute," Evan spoke up. "Seems like one of the DNA from the Crime Lab had someone by that name. Didn't they?"

"You know, you're right!" Christine replied. She pulled the file folder including the DNA information on the Eastgate murders and thumbed through the pages. "Here's the page. Let me see."

She ran her finger down the list. She looked up at Evan.

"She's the missing old woman, and she was, or part of her was anyway, in the bathtub at Eastgate..."

"Where's the rest of her?" Sam asked.

"Exactly," Felipe answered.

"Is there more?" Christine asked, looking around the room.

"Just one or two things," Evan smiled at her. "I had the privilege of processing the statements from five of the men we picked up during the raid yesterday morning."

"What can you tell us?" Christine asked.

"Well, four of them have genuine Ukrainian identities." He handed Christine the photographs. "They say they are a medical transport team. There seems to be a time constraint attached to their reason for being in the Ennis Lake house."

"What do you mean?" Christine asked.

"Well," Evan replied, "these men have no apparent knowledge of the trafficking operation. They came to pick up what appear to be two, stainless steel, powered, cryogenic containers. Inside each box is a minimum of ten styrofoam boxes of medical supplies for transport."

"What's in the boxes?" Josh asked.

"We don't know, exactly. We assume tissue samples, or blood, or even transplants." Evan looked around the room.

"But here is where it gets tricky. The fifth guy is not Ukrainian. He is MI6. His name is Patrick MacNaulty. He is deep under-cover. And he's the reason we haven't opened the boxes."

"He's MI6. You know this to be fact?" Josh asked.

"All certified today. From the British Embassy, *and* Langley. MacNaulty's a veteran, and he's one of their best."

"Okay," Christine said, leading him to complete his story.

"Yeah," Evan continued. "So, I spent the last part of the afternoon with him today. His mission is to travel with the transport team and find out exactly where the shipment is going. Everything MI6 has discovered on their end, has led them to a much bigger network than what is happening inside their own country. At first they thought it had originated in Russia."

"Benjamin Asami, perhaps?" Pete suggested.

"No, it's even bigger," Evan answered. "Patrick doesn't think Asami has enough resources to fund or oversee something this prolific."

There was silence in the room. This was indeed news.

"I've been telling you guys the same thing since day one," Josh complained. "No one listens to me."

Ignoring Josh, Evan continued. "So, what MI6 has requested, through Deputy Director Edwards, is that we allow the shipment to leave as planned, howbeit one day late. And, that we place our own man on the team with the Ukrainians. That is why the Crime Lab didn't remove the seals on any of the containers. Ben Edwards called them directly."

"Has he a plan?" Christine asked. These events had certainly taken place quickly. Ben had not had a chance to call her to inform her, apparently.

"Yes, ma'am," Evan answered. "I was told he would be calling you this evening."

"It's all good, Evan," she told him. "We all do the best we can. Tell me what's going on here."

Evan sighed. "It all happened so fast. Since Russian is my second language, and I have already made contact with the Ukrainians, Director Edwards asked me to accompany the transport team and support MacNaulty. We also need to know where these alleged medical supplies go. We also need to what they are. All without arousing suspicion. Patrick is briefing me later tonight."

"Okay," Christine said. "We'll miss you."

"Yeah, me too." Evan continued. "Additionally, we are supposed to leave in the refrigeration truck the Ukrainians left in the commuter lot at Ennis Lake. We will be loading it with the stainless steel boxes sometime tomorrow."

Christine smiled at him. "Congratulations, Detective Davies," she said. She was genuinely happy for him. It was his first assignment to work undercover with the FBI.

She wasn't upset with the development, but she did wonder how they would function as team. It would be a skeleton crew for a season. But she did understand. And yes, of all of them, Evan was the best option for the job.

"Go with God, Evan," she said. "We'll be here when you get back."

She continued. "Before I begin my part of this briefing, I do want to commend all of you on the work you are doing regarding the kidnapping end of this case. You are taking the lives of all of these young women seriously. As a result, I think we are getting a picture of what we've been calling "Asami's network," as far as the high end trafficking taking place on that end. I do want to remind us all that we still have upwards of thirty young *men* who have also been kidnapped, from various parts of the globe, who are, as of yet, unaccounted for. While I am aware there might be a market for such young men in the sexual trafficking networks, that request would be rare, I would think. We will need to begin putting some of our efforts into finding these young men as well. Please keep that in mind as we proceed."

She turned her attention to Josh.

"Josh," she asked, "do you have anything to share?"

Josh looked at her with a direct gaze. "Not really," he said. "I've had the job of observing the guys who have been tailing us, and keeping track of their movements. Everything has been about the same as it has been for the past few months. They trade cars, they eavesdrop, but I think we will have to beef up now that we have closed the Hydrangea house. It would be good to get them before they up and leave town and pop up somewhere else again."

He sighed. "All I know is what I see. But I do agree with the guy from MI6. The people I've seen aren't smart enough to run something this big."

"I know, right? What's up with these guys, Dude?" Felipe exclaimed, dropping his accent momentarily. "I started calling the two guys following us 'the two idiots.' They put the eavesdrop cone in plain sight. They won't be bothering us any more, by the way."

Everyone laughed. Except Christine.

"Or," she interjected, with a bit of a reprimanding glance in Felipe's direction, "it could be they are so smart that the two guys we see are just a distraction from what they are really up to."

Josh and Felipe stopped laughing, and looked at her.

"Okay, Killjoy," Josh muttered.

"Give it up, man," Felipe told him. "She could be right."

Christine moved on. "*Fernando,* what do you have for us?"

Startled, Felipe realized he had dropped his character. Quickly, he glanced around, checking the group to see if anyone had noticed his slip. So far, no one had reacted. He looked back at Christine, and silently apologized with eye contact.

"Well, *Mi Amor,*" he said, "I've been working on several things, since I *am* here *alone* all day, *every* day."

The entire group groaned in unison. "Really?" "Aww, you poor thing." "Wow."

"Hey now," Felipe put his hands up in defense, "No one is complaining. At least *I* am getting some work done."

That comment earned him a barrage of small items thrown at him.

"To answer your questions, *Mi Amor,* I reviewed the complete video images from the houses on Mackaw, Ennis Lake, and the ones recently retrieved in Chicago. The images are somewhat

233

the same from each location. There *are* zombies at each location. It appears they are wearing latex masks, each of which are available from costume shops, or can be ordered from Amazon. If you notice, each mask is different. I think this might indicate their method of identifying each other. I am currently working on deciphering the job descriptions, by deciphering the tasks performed by the men wearing each mask."

"Wow, Baby," Christine said, "what masks have you found so far?"

"I can explain it with the video when we are done with the meeting, if you like," he replied.

"Let's do that," she told him. "What else?"

Felipe smiled. "The girls rescued at Ennis Lake were taken from a shipping container. That specific container originated in Greece. It was unloaded in Marseilles, France, and then made its way to Mauretania. From Mauretania, it traveled to Las Terrenas, in the Dominican Republic. From Las Terrenas, it made its way to the Georgia Port Authority. From there it came inland by freight-train."

Josh spoke up. "So, we know some of these girls traveled from Greece, but where they came from before that? How long was the container in each location? Who got in at what stop, and did some get off in some places?"

"Good questions." Felipe looked at Josh. "I was trying to find a port where this particular set of girls might have been put on board. To answer your second question, there was at least a week between each shipment. The only way of knowing if the same girls were in the container for each journey, would be to interview them. People who own containers like this don't typically tell the truth on the shipping manifests."

Felipe looked at Kit. "I'm sorry to say it, but I think it's very possible they lost many young girls in the process, most of whom we will never hear about."

Christine nodded. "I am interviewing each of those women tomorrow, and we should know more by tomorrow night's briefing. But from what I learned in taking initial statements, I would absolutely agree with you."

She smiled at Felipe. "Thanks for all of your hard work. From what I can tell so far, the girls from this shipping container are part of some other piece of this group's trafficking trade. They appear to be coming *into* the country, rather than going *out*. Also, each girl appears to have been sold by someone she knew in the country she originated from. I was unable to speak with only one of these women. She only speaks Chinese, so I have a translator coming tomorrow."

"Their stories are unbelievable," Felipe said quietly. There was a short pause.

"Yes, they are," Christine agreed soberly. After a moment, she continued her briefing.

"Our Jane Doe is in ICU at Ginsberg Memorial," Christine interjected. The neurologist believes she received some sort of blunt force trauma to her head, and she is bruised from a physical beating on her arms and shoulders. Blood has pooled in her brain, and she is now unconscious. They are working on her. I'll keep you posted on her developments."

Felipe interrupted her. "Sorry, Kit," he interjected. "I am running facial recognition software using the photograph of David Fletcher, who is Benjamin Asami's former limo driver. Remember, the photo which helped us discover Fletcher wasn't really dead. He surfaced in Germany, selling medical supplies. So, I ran a search on medical supply companies that deal globally, as well as in Germany. So far, I have found several shell companies claiming to serve the medical field, but I haven't found an actual working group yet. Hopefully, Evan's Ukrainian group will be able to help us with that.

"I also ran a trace on the Asami car key found in the hotel room in Eastgate. Josh returned to the hotel with the key, and found the car. It's a white Jaguar XJ-Supercharged, and it's registered to a Landon Morrow."

"Of course it is," Samantha interjected. "That guy is everywhere."

"At the same time," Pete offered, sarcastically.

Felipe chuckled. "Yeah," he said. "Also, I called the Westwood Precinct, and requested a copy of Allen Peel's sketches of Landon Morrow and the fake Annabelle Carnes. I ran facial recognition software on both of them, and came across some interesting results."

"Can't wait to hear them," Kit offered.

"Well, it appears there are many men in the database using the name 'Landon Morrow.' He is, or was, one of the first traffickers to be photographed. The original man with that name was a diplomat, working in the British Embassy in Monaco. He was the Director of their Staff Operations. As far as I can tell, piecing the story together, he began dealing with trafficking in some form almost thirty years ago. I think his original job was to deliver purchased girls to their buyers. He worked as a bodyguard and courier, I would think. My thought is that as their business grew, they just kept on using that name. Kind of to create the illusion he is everywhere, like Pete said. If the real Morrow is still alive at all."

Christine posted a photo of the real Landon Morrow on the board. The man in the picture was in his late twenties. The picture was black and white, and appeared to have been taken at least thirty years prior. She continued.

"The fake Annabelle is from Croatia. Her name is Katika Knesevic. She was part of the Croatian Secret Service, until she was disavowed in 2005, for use of unnecessary and unreasonable cruelty with prejudice. She has worked as a sharpshooter, an analyst, and as an undercover agent. It appears she works as an independent mercenary these days."

"Thank you, Fernando," she said. "And thanks for being our research team." To the group she said, "Be looking out for anything else pointing us to Croatia. They are one of the few countries who do not have an extradition treaty with the United States. If any of our suspects escape arrest, it is possible they will head to Croatia. We don't know the center of operations yet, however."

The rest of the taskforce verbally agreed.

Christine took the photos Felipe handed her and added them to the board. She looked at Chase Stanford.

"Chase, do you have anything you'd like to add?"

Somewhat nervously, the newest addition to the team spoke. "I spent time with a man named Remi Levesque. He is the French chef paid to feed everyone inside the Ennis Lake house. He told me he has worked with these people for almost five years. They call themselves "The Parent Company." He said in any of the hub houses, at least one girl is being prepped for a buyer in one of the guest rooms at all times. Sometimes there are girls in both guestrooms. They are moved out every four to five weeks, depending on how their "conditioning" progresses.

"Each girl is given a new name, based the information the groomers have gained about the buyer's preferences. The first day a girl is implanted with a GPS chip in her shoulder."

"Like my dog?" Samantha asked. "That's just cold."

"Yeah," Chase answered. "Levesque told me that after the incision heals, they tattoo over the scar to hide it... a Chinese symbol or something. He said the girls are trained by a 'Miss Anastasia.' The person can change, but in all the houses it's an older woman, and that's her name."

"All the houses?" Christine echoed.

"That's what he said. He has worked in four of the hub houses."

"Which ones?" Christine asked.

"He started in a hub house in the Netherlands. There, he says, the laws are completely different. Prostitution is legal with a permit. Drug usage is legal with a permit. He worked in a country house there. From the outside, it was considered a finishing school for young ladies. He was there for almost two years, and had no idea women were being bought and sold.

"One day, someone in the management of the school approached him and offered him a position in girls' school in New York City. He said it had been his dream to come to the United States. But, when he arrived in here, they told him he had been part of a criminal activity in the Netherlands, and they would kill him if he didn't continue to work for them. At the same time, they raised his pay. So, he continued to work in the New York City house for almost three years. He says that house was never discovered or raided by the officials.

"When the company sold the New York house where he worked, they sent him to a house in one of the suburbs in Greenway.

He said he has been stressed since he had been moved here, because they had him working at two houses at the same time."

"Which houses?" Christine asked.

"One is the one on Ennis Lake," Chase answered. "The other one is…… let me get it right, it's in my notes….. 4207 East Biarritz Avenue in Springview."

The taskforce members exchanged glances.

Startled, Chase looked around. "Did you guys know about that house? The one of Springview?"

"Now we do!" Pete declared, slapping Chase's shoulder.

Christine smiled. "Chase, is this guy, this Remi…. Is he complicit with them?"

"No, ma'am," he answered. "He wants us to get him out."

"Let's brief him in the morning, and get him back in that Biarritz house. We can tell him what to look for, and he can help us break this case."

Chase smiled. "Really?"

"Really," she answered. "First thing in the morning."

Her focus shifted once more. "Pete?" she asked. "What do you have for us?"

"Well," he told the group. "I spent the day in the Ennis County lock-up, courtesy of Sheriff Jackson."

"Whadya do, Pete?" Josh asked, prodding him.

"Nothing much. I had the good fortune to arrest Alexander Boyd yesterday," came the answer. "He murdered the Mr. and Mrs. Jim Marshall, who lived across the street from the Ennis Lake House. He claimed to be the first officer on the scene, but in actuality, he committed the murders. Then, he went back to his brother's house to clean up. After cleaning up, he returned to the Marshall home to make the call. He doctored the Dispatch records to give himself an alibi, but that didn't work because our buddy Chase, here, was playing hide and seek in the precinct hallway."

"Way to go Chase," Samantha told him.

"Did he give you anything we didn't know, Pete?" Christine asked.

"Not really," came the answer. "He didn't mention the house on Biarritz either. He did, however, confirm the presence of others on the City of Greenway police force who have been paid off by these people."

"Did he give you names?" Josh asked.

Pete looked him in the eye. "He did."

"Pete, let's talk after the meeting. This sounds like sensitive material," Christine interjected.

Then she looked to Samantha. "Sam, would you share with us the discovery you made this week?"

"Okay. Well, y'all know that I'm not one of y'all, as far as being a law enforcement officer and all that. But I do see a lot of stuff come across Judge Ventura's desk." Samantha's animated style had drawn everyone's attention. "And I'm clerking for her until I get enough money for the Bar Exam.

"Anyway, after our last meeting, I got to thinking about how these traffickers might market these girls. You know, to get them to even think about it.

"The man would have to be wealthy, and busy, and alone. He would have to be old enough he didn't want to go clubbing to find a woman. So, I went through periodicals that catered to rich men. I found the same classified ad posted in several men's fitness magazines, in the back, you know. I also found the same ad in some of the high end vacation newspapers they distribute in places like The Hamptons, Napa, the French Riviera, Morocco; places like that. Here's the ad: *'American female; certified virgin, cultured and beautiful -- seeks kind, understanding, older man for happy marriage. Must be able to support present lifestyle. No booty calls, please. Only serious inquiries need apply. Call 1-800-MY-BRIDE for information.'*

"Then, maybe because I understood what I was seeing, I noticed the toll free number as part of a dating sight ad this week. Here it is: *'Find the wife of your dreams. Call 1-800-MY-BRIDE for information. Serious inquiries only, please. Not a dating service.'*

"After I saw the ads, I went to one of the Bridal Shops and purchased a copy of every Bridal magazine they carry. There are only a few printed in Spanish, and even fewer made overseas. But, in two of them, there were articles about last week's marriage of billionaire Juan Paredes to his fourth wife."

At that point, Christine interjected. "Paredes is a drug cartel, with connections worldwide. He has been widowed three times, each time under mysterious circumstances."

Sam grinned at her, proud of herself for being able to contribute to the meeting. "That's right. Anyway, like I said, there were a ton of pictures in the Spanish magazine. The bride's name is Victoria Mendoza, and the article said she is a direct descendant of Castilian aristocracy. But to me, she looks like Katie Curtin, the first girl up there on the board."

"What did the chef say, Chase?" Pete asked. "They give each girl a new name? We already know they forge and print passports and other legal documents. What if they could manipulate the internet and records to produce a pedigree as well? Fernando, can you see if that pedigree has been published somewhere? And let's do a facial recognition search on the photograph, please?"

"Sure," Felipe answered.

"Oh," Samantha told them. "There's one more thing. The article named her bodyguard as a man named Landon Morrow, and they had a photograph of her with him."

"Of course that was his name," Christine laughed. "Can we do a recon on that as well?"

Felipe nodded.

Christine was writing on the board.

"That brings us to my interview with a woman who told me the girls call her 'Miss Anastasia.' She claimed to have diplomatic immunity. Her name is Lady Bereniece Fraire, and she is the widow of the last Italian ambassador. Apparently, she coaches each girl in deportment and manners, preparing them for the buyer."

"That confirms what we were thinking!" Samantha offered.

"The thing is, they appear to do what she called 'Relaxation Classes.'" Christine told them. "One of the girls mentioned the sessions as well. I think they hypnotize and then re-program the girls to forget, so they become receptive to the idea of being sold. One of the girls referred to her buyer as 'Prince Charming.'"

"You think hypnosis really works?" Josh asked skeptically.

Samantha poked him. "It appears it does," she answered.

"Exactly," Christine added. "One girl wasn't sure she even wanted to go home. She was convinced life with her buyer would be happier than her life at home with her parents."

"Christine, the old woman, Margaret Kearnan, would have had the same kind of knowledge as this Lady Bereniece person," Felipe offered. "Both were well-trained in diplomatic circles, and used to mentoring others in proper etiquette and customs. Maybe this group is using the name 'Anastasia' the way those five guys are using 'Landon Morrow.' If that's true, then she was 'Miss Anastasia' in the Mackaw video."

"That would make sense," she answered. "That way, every girl's story would sound the same, and real identities would be harder to uncover."

She looked around the room. "All of this brings me to the five interrogative interviews I was part of today. All of *them* claimed to be Landon Morrow. We did photo recognition and fingerprint searches on each of them. Based on drivers' licenses, passports, college entrance photographs, or photos available through social media, we were able to find the actual identity of all of them.

"Two of them checked out as emergency medical couriers. They work free-lance, but much of their clientele is in the Red Market."

"What's the Red Market?" Samantha whispered to Felipe, who was sitting next to her.

Felipe looked at her. "The Red Market. It's like the Black Market, except the people deal with much more gruesome wares. Things like body organs, anything really. They charge exorbitant prices. It's an emerging global problem."

Sam was shocked. "Really? You're kidding, right?"

Felipe looked at her, assessing. *She doesn't really know how bad things are,* he thought.

Aloud, he said, "No, it's true. It's why we do what we do."

Stunned into deep thought, Samantha nodded. Christine was speaking. She began listening again. Kit was briefing the taskforce on the initial statements she had taken in the raid. She had placed five photographs on the board. She was printing names under the two couriers.

"Each of these men told me his name was Landon Morrow."

The taskforce involuntarily groaned. "Now, I *know that's* not possible," Pete interjected.

Christine continued. "This one is Jim Phillips, and this one is Austin Caine. Both were supposed to deliver transplant organs to different hospitals yesterday morning. Those organs will now be on the truck with Evan and the Ukrainians. At this point those men will be in custody for some time, until we can gather information about their dealings."

She pointed to the third man's photo. "This is Hiraku Kimura. He is a computer software designer from Tokyo. Apparently, he has designed all of the programs these people use, and oversees their security divisions. It is possible he has designed booby-traps for us to find when we hack into his software."

She moved to the fourth man. "This gentleman is Gerard Albertson. He has a long rap sheet, and is on Scotland Yard's most wanted list. He disappeared in 2005 from a train station in London. Interpol has been looking for him, but no one has had any leads. When he showed up here, London asked us to hold him for extradition. We have some investigation to do, in order to discover his part in the network. Ten years has provided him a lot of time to work up in their chain of command.

"The fifth man," she pointed to the photograph on the board, "would only speak one sentence when I tried to interview him: 'I'm only here for the girls.' However, a little DNA can help immensely. In some ways he told the truth. Apparently, he works as a bodyguard and companion for girls when they are being delivered to their buyer. He stays with them for up to six weeks in their new location, helping them acclimate to their new environment. It appears they have four or five bodybuilders who fulfill this position in the network. This man's real name is Dexter Reeves."

"*The* Dexter Reeves? Like *Mr. Universe* Dexter Reeves?" Josh asked, incredulous. "He's lost weight!"

"He's not on the circuit anymore, Dipwad," Peter told him. "Of course he's lost weight."

"What's he doing with *these* guys?" Josh asked.

"Guess he wasn't smart enough to get a real job," Pete responded dryly.

Christine smiled, observing the banter. She paused. "Any questions or thoughts?" After a second or two, she looked at Felipe.

"Fernando, dear, would you mind pulling up the zombie videos for us? We all need to see what you have learned."

As Felipe opened the video files, he asked for help in labeling the masks seen in the first file, the one from the house in Chicago.

"I need names for these, and then we can identify the same masks in the other two video files," he told them.

But they never got to the other files. For the next two hours, they watched video of zombies, and tried to distinguish differences between the masks. At times, the job was met with laughter and sarcasm.

"That one should be 'NO NOSE GUY.'"

"And that one should be 'BALD WONDER.'"

"Okay. What about UNDEAD BURNED GUY for that one?"

"We could call that one 'SPLIT HEAD.'"

"YELLOW EYED FANG-FACE.'"

"That one's really scary. What about 'OPEN GREEN CHEEKS?'"

"Only one name for that: 'ROTTEN GUMS GUY.' Look kids, this is what happens if you don't brush your teeth!"

"Hey, that looks like a ninja with his hair sticking straight out, except for the blood. 'SPIKE NINJA' would work."

"The eyes on this one creep me out. It's the bloody hair, and the green teeth. How about 'LASER-DEMON EYES?'"

"I think we could remember the second bald one here with a name like 'STAPLE HEAD.'"

Around ten that night, Kit ordered a couple of pizzas. She smiled. This was going to be a long night.

Chapter Sixteen

Since arriving in the city Greenway, almost three months prior, Agent Joshua Morgan had been spending his time shadowing the trafficking ring from a distance. His assignment was to observe the criminals involved, and try to write a schedule of their activities. At the moment, he was outside the Asami Motors Dealership, waiting for two of their "idiots" to change into another vehicle.

He and Felipe had coined the name "Asami Idiot Lurkers" to describe these guys. They weren't good at stalking; no stealth. They weren't good at tailing; too visible. In fact, they weren't good much of anything.

Which made him wonder whether they were just good at being bad. Distractions maybe?

It seemed Asami Idiot Lurkers worked in eight-hour shifts. The teams changed every eight hours, as did their cars. Apparently, each car was outfitted with their "lurking and listening" gear. He could mark the arrival of one of the three cars to certain locations like clockwork.

It was weird. How had these guys been promoted within their organization to do the job they did? They didn't seem to know even the basics about camouflage surveillance. They used the same teams in the same cars in the same locations... every day!

Apparently, no one had taught them to vary their methods to avoid detection.

In contrast, as far as he knew, Joshua had not been detected by anyone in Asami's network to this point. Were they watching the taskforce? Or were they even aware of the Bureau's activities?

He and Felipe had set up their observation systems around Westwood Village during the two months Kit had been travelling all over the world, interviewing victims' families, and organizing evidence, prior to arriving in Greenway. The result of her travels had been distilled into the file-box she carried with her everywhere these days.

That file-box was becoming the key to solving an international crime, Josh realized. Up until now they had thought the case was unsolvable.

Ben was right, Josh decided.

He was beginning to realize he and Kit *had* outgrown each other. It was hard to admit, but the awareness had come upon him slowly; a discovery emerging during the days he had been working on this case. Perhaps that was why Ben had given him the observe and record assignment, rather than expecting him to step back into a cover role as Kit's fiancé.

He hadn't wanted the break-up. That had been Kit's doing. But now...... he had to say he agreed with her, and with Ben.

Kit wasn't for him. Not anymore.

Besides, he didn't really want someone who was as invested in her career as he was in his. But, he really did want a little woman at home; someone who would take care of things....be there waiting at night....and take care of *him.*

He would have to tell Christine at some point, if they were going to continue to work together. He didn't want her to be so guarded with him, he determined. It would help if they could be friends.

Maybe he could just write her a note. Yeah, that would be better. Less stressful.

He had to admit, though, Kit was handling the present case really well. That was sure. He wouldn't ever say so publicly, but he could see why Edwards had given her the field office assignment. She was good with people, and didn't fluster easily. Watching her, he realized Edwards had been grooming her. Her skills were impressive. She did have the makings of a Field Chief.

But he had wanted the job. He had more seniority.

The job wasn't supposed to go to a woman.

And then..... Well.... He considered.

No, she just wasn't marriage material. At least not for him, anyway. He wanted someone who didn't challenge his statements, or bail out on making dinner. Or on having sex. And she definitely needed someone in his life who didn't mind a guy kicking back with a few beers. Sometimes, a guy just needed a good woman, without any expectations attached. A woman who would just tuck under. A woman who knew her place. Who didn't argue about everything like Christine did.

And, who would take care of his children if they both had careers?

Taking a sip of his coffee, he watched as the staff door to the Asami Auto Service Center opened. Team Two of Asami Idiot Lurkers was on duty today, it appeared. The tall, thin one had a weird nose, he noticed. And the shorter, dumpy guy was loping behind. It looked like the big one was driving today.

Josh smiled. Why did this guy think that wearing a thirty-four inch waistband *under* his belly fooled anyone into thinking he was really that thin? He would have been better off with a forty-four inch waistband. The worst part was this particular guy always tried to tuck in his dress shirt, but the shirt-tails just weren't long enough to encompass his entire Buddha-belly and still do what they were supposed to do; make it firmly behind his belt, and cover his hairy navel. The shirt never stayed tucked into the waistband. So the guy's gut just lapped over like a lop-sided inner-tube.

Josh smiled a wry smile. *Too bad the guy didn't own a mirror,* he thought to himself.

The agent wrote down his observations, and added the time in the margin. Apparently, the Asami Lurkers were taking the white two-door sedan today. As he watched, they got into the car, and pulled up to a service door. Big Idiot Lurker honked the car's horn. The service bay door went up.

For a second, Josh was tempted to begin going through his iTunes list; to find some music to listen to while he was waiting; or maybe start an ebook. But for some reason he didn't. His eyes stayed focused on the sedan.

But then, as the service bay door rose, the agent caught sight of a white box-truck inside the garage, on the lift in the next bay over. The truck had a refrigeration unit over the cab roof.

Unexpectedly, a logo on the side of the truck drew his attention; perhaps because it was bright marine blue, with a fire engine red on white background. The center of the logo was a "t," almost a copy of the Red Cross logo, but designed in blue. Attached to the blue cross was a stethoscope, its diaphragm resting on an image of the planet. In an arc over the image, in bold black letters, was the company name: "MedSafe International Supply." Under the company name was a telephone number: 1-800-MED-SAFE. Across the bottom of the truck's side panel was the phrase: *Anything medical.... Anytime... Anywhere!* Below that in smaller print: www.medsafeworld.com.

Pulling out his cell phone, Josh took several pictures of the box truck in the bay and it's logo. Then, he began writing as quickly as he could; seeking to sketch the art, recording the words correctly before the bay door went back down.

It was early morning when Evan and the Ukrainian medical transportation team took off. The men's identities on the team had checked out, and Patrick MacNaulty had been verified as MI6. As a result, the decision had been made to provide the four Ukrainians with just enough information regarding the ongoing investigation that they would be willing to allow Evan to join their team. Also, as far as they knew, MacNaulty was still a wanted fugitive.

"If he is so bad," Gregor asked Evan, "why do you not arrest him?"

"He didn't commit any crimes in America," Evan lied. "But, I am glad I will be there to protect you, if this man turns against any one of you."

"Dah," Gregor told him, slapping him on the back. "You are a smart man. A good man."

A little over an hour ago, they had retrieved the team's windowless delivery van from a commuter lot near Lake Ennis. Then, at three in the morning, Nicholas had arrived at the Crime Lab, where the large, stainless steel, cryogenic boxes were loaded. As the team was loading the truck, Felipe and Josh outfitted it with audio surveillance and a GPS tracking device.

Then, at five in the morning, Evan began his undercover journey. From this point forward, he would only speak in Russian.

He carried no badge and no weapon. He carried nothing to identify him as Law Enforcement.

As they loaded, Nicholas spoke quietly to Evan.

"We are very late now. Vitali is afraid people will be dead because of us."

"Why would people be dead?" Evan asked.

"These boxes contain organs ... tissues for transplant," Nicholas explained. "Our job always has ... how you say, the time pressure. The parts we deliver can go bad if we do not hurry. We never know what parts we carry. There are many, always more than twenty, boxes to deliver inside each steel box. Some of people who need parts are nearby to death. They wait at hospital for transplant to come. Because of police, we are now late. More than twenty-four hours. Some of people waiting can die if parts are not good."

Evan looked at him strangely. "You mean, there are *body parts* in these boxes, and not tissue samples?"

Nicholas nodded. "Tissue samples and veins will be good in cryogenic box for up to five years. Organs are different. Some parts are good for longer than others. But when we wait too long, the person who waits will die. So we hurry. You understand?"

Evan nodded. "Where do the transplants come from?"

Nicholas shrugged. "I do not know. I think, from people who die in accidents. They tell us they have donors here in city. Maybe in other place too? But... They tell us is all legal. All box we deliver has papers. And every box is sealed."

Evan smiled at him. "I'm sure you have done everything you could to make sure you were operating inside the law."

"Is true," Nicholas replied, nodding. "Dah, very true."

The delivery van lurched forward. Gregor and Vitali, apparently the senior members of the team, sat in the captain's chairs up front. The remaining members of the team rode in the back, belted into seats securely installed to the insides of the transport vehicle. The van they were currently travelling in, allowed for a team of six.

"Who else uses vans like this?" Evan asked, looking around the interior. He realized the back of the vehicle had been outfitted with refrigeration units. Between the front of the van and the back, was a wall of chain link mesh, separating the driver from the items being delivered. Electrical outlets had been installed against the van's walls.

"Anyone with the money buys," Nicholas replied. "Many of them are private. I think the company sells to people van like this."

"Ivan," Yuri asked, utilizing the Russian form of Evan's name, "is what we are doing dangerous?"

"I can't believe you all still think what you are doing is *legal*," Patrick told them. "Think this through. People had to *die* for all of these organs to be in the same place at the same time. Some of these people were kidnapped. Some were murdered."

Yuri sneered at Patrick. "You are one to be giving us lecture, aren't you? You are biggest criminal of all. I am glad this man, Ivan, is here to *protect* us from you."

Patrick looked at Evan helplessly. The detective shrugged. They hadn't planned on the Ukrainians giving a negative reaction to Patrick's cover story. At least they were demonstrating their true character.

None of the men were criminals.

Evan lapsed into thought. Faces of the detainees taken in the raid ran through his mind. He had read the statements from the first three men separated from the other detainees he had assigned to Chase the day before. They all claimed to be medical personnel.

Of the second group, two of them, like these men, claimed to be medical transport couriers. Had they also been at the house on Hydrangea for local delivery? Were they also carriers of critically needed organs?

Were the steel boxes beside them filled with human organs?

He wondered if any of the recipients who were desperate for the transplants might still be alive.

He involuntarily shuddered.

It was a certainty the donors were dead.

But how? And why?

Of the first three men Chase had interviewed in the raid; two were EMTs, and one claiming to be a surgeon..... Had *that surgeon* been the one to harvest organs from dead bodies? Or worse; had he taken lives in order to harvest organs from healthy individuals? And why were the EMTs with him? Were they *really* EMTs? If no, who did they work for? And if they worked *with* the surgeon, what were *their* functions in all of this? Was there an ambulance hidden somewhere near the Ennis Lake house, requiring the use of uniforms to complete their disguise?

At an outdoor cafe in Bruges, Belgium, a middle-aged man enjoyed an early afternoon repast between vacation sites with his wife and children.

"I love the architecture here," his wife, Lina commented. "The houses look like they came right out of Robin Hood. Or even the Renaissance. Look at the detail in the restaurant façade."

Her native accent was still very noticeable.

Two curly heads bobbed up and down in excitement. The oldest one spoke. "Papa, can we take a boat ride after this?"

Their father's attention was somewhere else. He continued to stare at his smartphone with a furrowed brow. He didn't answer.

"Sweetheart," Lina said, putting her hand on his arm. "Did you hear Annette?"

Her husband's thumbs were moving furiously, responding to a text he had just received. He looked up. "What did you say, little one?" he asked absently.

Nine year-old Annette looked at him with childish disapproval. "Now Papa! You said we couldn't bring our phones. I asked if we could take a boat ride after we eat."

"Yes, dear. Sorry... Uh, sure, we should do that. Lina, can you find out how we can do that?"

The sound of his cell phone's ring startled him, causing a strong reaction. He checked to see who the caller was, and looked at his wife.

"I'm sorry. I have to take this." He stood up to answer his phone and walked away from the table. His wife observed him as he moved down the sidewalk.

She sighed.

The second child stood up and moved to Lina's side. "I'm tired, Mommy."

"Oh, Adrien!" she replied to her son. "Don't be sad. You want to sit in my lap? We'll wait for Papa to get off the phone, and then we will do something fun again."

"He said he wasn't going to work this time," Annette protested. "He's always so busy. Doesn't he ever want to spend time with us?"

Lina looked at her, as the waiter approached with their food on a tray.

"Annette, don't complain so. You know Papa's job is what pays for us to take nice vacations like this, don't you? Sometimes, he can't get away from his work. He will answer their questions, and come back to us, like always."

She looked at her daughter with eyes of authority. "You must learn to be thankful. Cut up your meat."

"Yes, Mama." Annette picked up her knife and fork, beginning to eat her meal.

"Adrien, sit back down on your chair now. You won't get a boat ride unless you finish your meal."

But Adrien had wandered some six feet away, and could no longer hear her voice. His eyes were fastened on the scene taking place just ten feet away from the café.

While his Papa was speaking on his cell phone, a long black car had pulled up behind him. Four men climbed out and surrounded him. Adrien couldn't see their faces. For a moment, they were talking to his Papa. Then, all of a sudden, his Papa looked at him.

Without a second thought, five year-old Adrien ran to his father. There was no warning. In reaction to the small lad's intrusion, the abductors shoved him aside, knocking him to the ground.

"Stop that! That's my son!" the man cried, reaching for his boy. "What are you doing?"

"Fine then," growled one of the four, aiming a hidden blade into the man's side.

Feeling the point of the knife cut through his golf shirt, the man froze, and looked into the face of the one who held it. Prodded at knifepoint, he moved into the back of the waiting limousine.

Then, just before the last man entered the limo, the fourth member of the team crouched down in front of the boy.

"I'm sorry, Adrien," he said, helping the boy to his feet. "You don't want to be left behind."

He then picked up the boy and threw him into the back of the limo as well.

It all happened so quickly, there was no time to respond. The wife had not seen all of the incident. In fact, the truth of what had happened did not seem to have really registered yet. But then, she had sprung to her feet, knocking over her chair when the assailants had grabbed her son.

Stunned, Lina and Annette Asami watched in horror as the black limousine drove away with their loved ones.

"Where are they taking Papa?" Annette asked her Mama, her eyes wide.

"I don't know," her mother answered numbly. "Who would do such a thing?"

"Why did they take Adrien too?" the little girl asked, starting to cry.

"I don't know, Annie. I really don't know."

Motioning to the manager, Lina paid the bill with a traveler's check. She called for their rented, chauffeured vehicle. She gathered her daughter and their belongings, and climbed into the car.

In perfect French, she instructed the driver. "Henri, take us to the American Embassy, please."

At Ginsberg Memorial Hospital, three uniformed officers stood guard duty on the nineteenth and twentieth floors; one at each stairwell, and two at the elevators. These top two floors were psychiatric floors. Rehabilitation facilities were on the nineteenth floor, and Behavioral Health and Recovery comprised the entire twentieth floor.

Ginsberg's hospital administrators had decided they had experienced enough trauma. There would be no more taking of chances. So, stashing patients who were recovering from gunfire near the psychiatric patients seemed the right thing to do. Especially since the hospital required the use of an elevator key to gain any access those floors.

All visitors to patients on the hospital's top two floors would now be required to accept the accompaniment of a staff key-holder. And, after exiting the elevator, they would be required to pass identity confirmation.

If a person passed identity confirmation, they would then be directed to the Behavioral Health Center, where a hospital staff person would accompany them to their designated area of the Mental Health and Recovery floor. Gone were the days of allowing visitors to walk to see their loved ones unassisted.

On the twentieth floor, rooms 2003 and 2004 had been temporarily designated for the City of Greenway's usage, at least for the time being. These were the rooms closest to the nurse's station. Each room had an additional officer posted outside its door. Each man was from the Westwood Village Precinct, and had been thoroughly questioned and instructed by the Police Captain himself.

In room 2003, Officer Rick Anderson and Dr. James Ainsworth were recovering from the bullet wounds they'd received a few days before. In room 2004, Sarah McMillan and Caleb Jacobs were recovering. That is, Sarah was recovering. Caleb was still in the midst of multiple examinations and assessments.

Dr. Howard Pulmeyer, the hospital administrator, had let all four of them know that the Police Commissioner himself had placed them all in protective custody. They were to remain in those rooms for the duration of the FBI's case.

They would not be allowed to leave the hospital.

Period. No exceptions.

Pediatric Nurse, David Gaines, had received a temporary change of assignment from the third floor to the twentieth. And Nurse Gaines was taking his job seriously. When he was not on duty, an ICU nurse from the seventeenth floor relieved him.

254

Jim Ainsworth's injuries were serious, but less serious than those of his roommate, Officer Rick Anderson. Jim had experienced a shattered right shoulder, and a torn left thigh muscle, along with nerve damage to his leg. After an MRI, trauma surgeons at Ginsberg had performed a complete shoulder and joint replacement on Jim's right side. They had also repaired the man's right hamstring, which the bullet had torn completely away from the femur. They had taken several hours to mend and reattach the psychologist's torn leg muscles.

For Dr. Jim, recovery from both surgeries would include a long stint of physical therapy. Additionally, his recovery was expected to take a little longer, due to the amount of blood loss he had experienced the day of the shooting. Even with a great deal of donor blood given to replenish what he had lost; the man continued to experience great physical weakness.

Officer Rick Anderson was the on-duty police officer who had standing guard when Sarah left to take her shower in the surgical showers. He had gone to find the social worker when she had not returned to the hospital room in the normal amount of time. Rick had encountered the shooter as the man was looming over the young woman; his hands in a choke hold around her neck.

It was apparent the gunman had fired four shots into Sarah's body, and when she did not die immediately, he had lost his patience, trying to choke her to death. Rick had grazed the shooter in the arm with his first shot. The man had broken away to run, but not before he had fired five rounds into the policeman. Two bullets had made their mark: one had lodged in the officer's right lung, causing a partial collapse. The other had entered his right side, ripping through his gall bladder and liver, then exiting through his back.

He also had received a large amount of donor blood through transfusion. Trauma surgeons had worked to repair his body for over five hours.

Sarah McMillan had actually been the target of the shooter. By inspecting the scene, the Crime Lab determined that abducting Sarah had been the primary objective of the killer. But then, when the girl had fought back, his goal had changed to murder. Resorting to a hands-on choking showed the hit-man had become frustrated with her stamina and literally decided to take things into his own hands.

In fact, the entire incident had receded from the young woman's memory. The last thing she remembered clearly was locking up her briefcase and laptop in the third floor hospital room.

So, at FBI request, the trauma surgeons had tried to recreate her attack by assessing her wounds in the operating room.

Sarah's face had received a deep cut.

Because it was vertical, the surgeons determined the assailant had probably tried to stab her at first, or had threatened her. But, she had retaliated. This supposition made the most sense, since the knife had cut into her cheek with a vertical motion, and Sarah had defensive wounds on the palms of her hands.

Then, at some point during the attack, the shooter had pulled his gun and begun to shoot at her. There were four entry wounds into her abdomen and two in her left leg. However, there were only two exit wounds. That meant two bullets were still inside her body when the surgery began.

The bullets had done a lot of damage. Upon entry, they had bounced around like a ping pong ball; perforating soft organ tissue again and again. In addition the setting of her right arm, she had required reconstructive surgery to her right leg. Due to the perforation of her internal organs, Sarah had received an emergency hysterectomy. Two feet of her small intestine had been removed, as had been her gall bladder, and part of her spleen.

"There was just too much damage," the surgeon told her.

Bullets had also nicked her stomach, liver and pancreas. The immense amount of stitches required would cause her recovery to be touch-and-go for several hours following the thirteen-hour surgery.

Every attending physician had asked the same question. *How had the bullets completely missed the woman's spine?*

The day after surgery, her blood sugar had spiked due to a damaged pancreas and liver. Additionally, one of Sarah's gluteus muscles had been shredded by an exiting bullet.

She knew it was temporary, but it was increasingly difficult to sit or lay down. Finally, she found she was able to lay on one side without much difficulty. Her assigned nurse, David Gaines, made sure she was able to face the inside of the hospital room in that position.

And yes. She definitely needed pain meds. She took them, and was thankful someone had thought to invent them.

The fourth victim of the shooting was Caleb.

His body was intact, with no injuries. But the experience had added more shock to an already traumatized young boy's psyche. He hadn't spoken much since the incident. He had refused to leave Sarah's side, and insisted he needed to protect her from the zombies.

In the midst of his trauma, he had begun calling her "Mom."

The day after his surgeries, Jim Ainsworth requested David find him a wheelchair, and roll him into Caleb's room for a visit. With an IV still attached, the determined psychologist ventured into the boy's room.

The first day they took turns playing Zombie Hunter on Caleb's Gameboy, trying to beat each other's scores. Caleb had mastered the game long ago, but Dr. Jim had never played, so the contest was minimal. In fact, Jim asked the boy to teach him how to play.

"What do you like about this game, Caleb?" he asked. "You always beat it. You've got more stored up lives than anyone I know. Why keep playing?"

"C-c-c-coz I c-can k-kill th-the z-z-zombies," Caleb answered, not looking up from his Gameboy.

"That's cool," Jim told him. "Why do you want to keep killing them?"

"C-coz they h-hurt p-people," Caleb replied, his thumbs working furiously. "I h-hate them."

"Wow," the psychologist said. "That's a big emotion."

"Th-they wear th-the masks, b-but not al-w-ways," the boy continued. "The w-watchers, th-they t-tell th-them wh-what t-t-to d-do."

"Are there watchers in your game?" Jim asked.

"No."

"Do you know who the watchers are?"

"I s-saw one of th-them one t-time at m-my h-house. The Big One w-was af-fraid he w-would sh-sh-shoot m-me. He p-pro-t-tected m-me. He put m-me in th-the s-secret s-spot."

"The secret spot?" Ainsworth echoed.

"Y-yeah," Caleb told him. "It's in th-th-the b-back of th-the c-closet. Th-they k-keep th-their g-guns and s-stuff th-there n-now. Here, it's y-your t-turn."

"Oh, okay," Jim replied, taking the Gameboy. Keeping his eyes on the electronic screen, he honestly tried to play, but failed quickly once again. "Caleb, have you noticed your stuttering starts to go away when we talk about the zombies? And when your hands are busy?"

The boy looked at him. "Really?" he asked.

Jim laughed. "Did you stutter just then?"

"No."

"Or then?"

Caleb giggled. "W-we n-need t-to talk more, d-don't we?" he asked. He took the Gameboy back from Dr. Jim.

"I would think so. Why do you think you might be afraid of the zombies?"

"Th-the r-real ones, or th-the ones in th-the g-game?" Caleb asked.

"The real ones."

The boy stopped playing and locked his gaze with Ainsworth. "B-be-c-cause th-they d-don't j-just t-take away p-people's b-bodies. Th-they eat their *souls.*"

"What's a soul, Caleb?"

"It's the ins-side of me. Just m-me. W-without my b-body."

Dr. Jim Ainsworth fell silent.

Surely this child had to be older than seven years.

Chapter Seventeen

Christine was sorting details at her desk at the Westwood Village Precinct when a woman of Asian descent exited the elevator onto the fourth floor.

"Can I help you?" the agent asked the woman.

"I am looking for FBI Special Investigator Christine Spada?" the woman queried.

The Agent stepped forward and extended her right hand. "That would be me. And you are?"

"Jennifer Zheng," came the reply. "I am the Chinese translator you requested."

"Great!" Christine told her. She glanced at the wall clock. "You're right on time!" She swept her arm sideways to indicate chairs lined against the wall. "Let me ask you to have a seat over here. First, I have a few papers you will need to read and fill out, before our interview. The rescued girls should be arriving any moment now."

"Are they being held here?" the interpreter asked.

"Excuse me?" Christine replied, smiling.

"The girls. Are they being held in the jail downstairs?"

"I'm sorry, Jennifer, I'm not at liberty to disclose that information. By the way, did you happen to bring your background check information? The forms we sent?"

For a milli-second, the translator's face registered surprise. Then, a stoic mask of professionalism overtook her once again.

"I did get them," she answered. "But I printed them out, and left them on the kitchen table. Could you give me another set to fill out?"

Christine looked to Pete, who was sitting at his desk, observing the situation unfold. She nodded to him.

Immediately, Pete was on his feet, taking the hands of the Chinese translator and cuffing them behind her back.

"What do you think you're doing?" she cried. "I had an appointment." She looked at Christine. "Really? Because I forgot my background check?"

Christine smiled. Pete answered on her behalf. "The truth is; no one sent you anything, Miss Zheng, if that really is your name. You are under arrest. What did you do with her? Where is the real translator?"

In reaction, the woman's facial expression changed. Christine could read fear in her eyes. Miss Zheng protested. "Hey, I don't know. I really don't. I was just told to show up here at nine this morning, and be ready to translate."

"Who told you?" Christine asked.

"The guy on the phone. I owe some bad people back in China some money. The guy said that if I came here and translated for the girls, I would be in the clear."

Christine nodded to Pete. "Can we put her in an interrogation room for now? I'll see if I can find out what happened to the real Jennifer."

She picked up the phone and called the Police Department's central office.

"Hello, this is FBI Agent Christine Spada. May I speak to Linguistics, please?"

"Yes. Hello, this is FBI Agent Christine Spada. Your Chinese translator, Jennifer Zheng, had an appointment here in our office at Westwood Village this morning."

"They did? When was that?"

"Do you know who called you? Was it a man or a woman?"

She picked up her pen. "What did she say her name was?"

"Mm-mm. Yes. Christine Spada."

"No ma'am, it *wasn't* me."

"Yes, I do still need her. If she is available, could you please send her immediately?"

"Thank you. By the way, how many people in the officer there knew about her appointment?"

"Why would it be available on the scheduling website?"

"Oh, I see. So anyone with the password."

"Thank you."

"No, you've been very helpful."

"You too. Good day."

As she hung up the phone, Christine looked down at the notes on her desk. Her eyes went to the list of young women who were being detained until their exit interviews.

"We'll just start with the two girls from Mali," she murmured. Sung Li will just have to wait for the Chinese translator." She glanced at the clock. "The girls should be here in just a few minutes."

In Christine's townhouse, Felipe had taken a short break from the day's Information Search and Analysis to make himself a cup of coffee and a sandwich.

Ballistics had returned their report on the bullets fired at Ginsberg Memorial that morning. They had also supplied the shooter's identity information.

The images on his computer had stopped shifting. He checked it out, and discovered the facial recognition search he had started on David Fletcher had ended. He decided to finish his snack before looking at the results.

Assignments received during the last team meeting were queued on a list next to the keyboard. It was his intention to finish everything this afternoon. However, before resuming his research chore list, Felipe wanted to make a couple phone calls.

His first call was to his partner, Joshua Morgan.

"Hey. Morgan speaking."

"Hey, Josh, Fernando Rafael here."

"Oh, and how's your Latin self, doing?"

"No complaints. Just roughing it here in the air conditioning, thinking about you sweating your face off out there in the heat."

"You bum."

"Hey," Felipe said. "How you doing out there?"

"It's all good. I think I just got a break in the case. Saw a truck this morning inside Asami Motors' Service area."

"Yeah?"

"You might want to run it through our databases and see what we get."

"What is it?" Felipe picked up a pen, and started writing.

"MedSafe International Supply. Phone is 800-MED-SAFE. Website is *www.medsafeworld.com*. Their slogan is 'Anything medical. Anywhere. Anytime.'"

"Okay. I'm writing it down. Can you give it to me one more time?"

It was noon. Samantha Cruz was on her lunch hour. Today, she had decided not to eat at her desk, as she usually did. Lately, it seemed all her energy had been focused on Christine's case. And, for the past few minutes, she had been sharing with federal judge, Anne Ventura, a few of the facts she had been learning in the case.

"I love this stuff!" she told her boss.

"You thinking you want to change fields, Sam?" Anne asked her.

Samantha thought about it. "Not really, but you know. I love puzzles, and it's like I'm helping solve a real one. The stuff I'm learning is amazing. You know what I mean?"

The judge nodded and smiled approvingly. "I do know, baby," she said, in her best Southern Mama manner. "You just best be careful. You don't have the training Kit has, or the support. You just watch yerself."

Sam giggled. "I love it when you try to sound like my Grandma. You gettin' all urban and stuff."

Anne snickered and pointed to the files. "Just finish tomorrow's case load before you leave tonight, please."

"Yes'm," she replied. "But right now, I'm heading out for lunch. You want me to bring you something?"

"No, I have a dinner appointment later, so I'm going easy."

"You shouldn't skip meals, Judge," Samantha reprimanded. "It's not good for you."

"Oh, no. That's it!" Ventura retorted. "You got to go. Now. Lunch. Out of my office!" Sam found herself being shooed out the door.

The young clerk took her time getting out of the building. She had been sitting a lot lately, so a decision to take the stairs from the fifth floor, instead of the elevator, was an easy one. A few minutes, she was exiting the building.

She looked up and down the street to find her favorite vendor: "Frankie's Flippin' Favorite Foodtruck." It's owner, Franko Kovac, had emigrated to the United States from Croatia some fifteen years prior. After trying several entry level jobs, the last of which had been in fast food, "Frankie" had decided to strike out on his own.

"The food you Americans allow yourself to eat, just because you are in a hurry," he complained to Samantha one day. "You need healthy food. Foods that are not too much work to eat and still good for you."

Since then, Frankie had discovered his unique niche among foodies in Greenway's professional community. Each day, the menu served from his foodtruck varied. But Frankie had learned to consistently offer of his customers' favorites. His business was still growing, and people were begging for more.

"Hey, Doll!" he greeted Sam when it came her turn in line.

"Hey, Frankie!" she replied. "What's good today?"

"Oh, you know, man, it's all good," he informed her in his Eastern European accent. "It depends if I have what you are hungry for."

She laughed, reading the chalkboard. "I'll have the sausage, cabbage and rice special."

"What vegetable you choose?" he asked.

"I'd like the broccoli," she answered.

"You want salad with that?"

"Yes, please, with your Greek dressing."

"Green tea?"

"You know what I like," she told him.

"Keeps you coming back to see me," he answered, smiling.

"Hey, Frankie, I was wondering. Are all the foods you make Croatian?" she asked, curiously.

"Why you ask, Sweetie?" he wanted to know.

"I don't know," she replied. "You just make such wonderful combinations of food. Things I wouldn't have thought to put together."

"Well, some is Croatia," he agreed. "And some is in my head. So, thank you, Samantha. I'm so happy you like my cooking."

As she paid for her meal, Sam noticed a newsstand not far from where the vendor had parked his truck today. Thanking her friend, and finding a seat on the wood ledge of a tall tree planter, she first ate the small salad. Then, she opened the food box. The smell was heavenly, she decided. As she ate, she tried to decipher exactly which spices Frankie had used to create the wonderful experience she was having; two kinds of ground sausage, minced onions, peppers, garlic, had to be butter, mixed with a lime-and-parsley seasoned jasmine rice, and tiny pieces of cooked cabbage. Into this basic mix, he had stir-fried mini broccoli spears, her favorite vegetable. Quartered to the side of the Styrofoam box, were four quarters of grilled flatbread.

Sipping her Green tea, Sam then strolled by the newsstand. Browsing for new bridal magazines, she scanned over covers in the business periodical section. Momentarily, her eyes were drawn to the headline of one particular magazine. The cover photo portrayed a middle-aged, slightly graying, Chinese businessman. The headline read: *China's Second Wealthiest Shipping Baron takes American Bride.* The title never would have caught her attention before. But now...

Thumbing through the magazine, she found the cover story; a one-page write-up about Cheung Lui-Jing, and how he had found his "Lotus Blossom." Angelica, his new wife, had been so in love, she had left her home in America to marry him. They now were living in Hong Kong.

Staring at one of the pictures of the couple, Samantha felt another shock of surprise. Looking back at her from behind a camera somewhere in Hong Kong, was the face of Sandy Karduc, the second girl on the field office board.

"Hey, lady," the newsstand owner objected. "You gonna buy it or read it for free?"

"Sorry. I need five copies, please," Samantha told him, handing him her debit card. As soon as she had them in hand, she high-tailed it back to Judge Ventura's office to finish prepping the next day's case load.

Detective Peter Lynch had been involved in the interrogation process with the three men Chase had interviewed the day of the Ennis Lake raid.

The EMT's were both Americans. Both were well paid by auto-deposit every Friday. Neither of them were presently employed as medical personnel, although both had worked in that job description in the past. From what Pete could tell, their main duties in regard to human organ trafficking. Apparently, they were regularly assigned to assist the surgeon in his tasks, and to drive the ambulance.

Pete decided the ambulance had been used to keep up appearances and avoid suspicion in the public's perception. From what the detective could gather, the vehicle belonged to a medical supply company they all worked for; possibly a shell company owned by whoever was behind the case's crimes.

The surgeon, however, was much more helpful. His name was Randy Whitmore, MD. He had retired early at the age of fifty-five from medical practice, he said, but had retained his license just in case a family member might need help in the future.

He had moved three years ago to the Bahamas, with his wife of thirty years. They had purchased a nice home. Then, one day, a man had approached him on the beach. Would he like to make an easy, non-taxable two hundred thousand dollars a year? He would only have to work six months out of the year, and it was all perfectly legal. He had agreed.

The man had told him he would be working for a medical supply company to dissect human bodies for cryogenic research and transplantation.

Had he checked out all the details? Yes.

Had all the forms been supplied for his approval? Yes.

Did he believe the process to completely legal? Absolutely.

When Pete asked him to describe the surgeries he had performed, the surgeon balked, and asked Pete if he understood the process of organ transplantation.

"I think so," the detective told him.

"Let me explain a little about what these people do," Dr. Whitmore said. "You see, we are in the process of rescuing people from death, and some from a fate worse than death.

"We are provided with donated bodies. All of the families have generously and unselfishly agreed to allow us to use the body parts of their deceased loved one, to ease the suffering, and in some cases change the lives, of those who need those organ parts."

Becoming more intense, the surgeon began to use his hands as he spoke.

"You see, Detective, we now can cryogenically store human tissue for years. Tissue is vital in repairing the bodies of burn victims and other types of work where grafting is necessary. We also use veins and arteries. We can transplant bones. Recently, a little boy received the first double-hand transplant. The forearms and hands came from another little boy who had died in a car crash.

"We can do so much more now than we could do fifteen years ago. Did you know that every twelve minutes, a new name is added to a needed transplant list?"

"I didn't know that," Pete told him. "I thought the heart transplant was the most involved thing you guys do."

"Oh, no," said Dr. Whitmore excitedly. "There are markets for human transplants outside of our country, where the laws are not as strict. In Iran, families may sell a kidney from a living donor, to someone else needing one. These days, we can transplant kidneys, livers, lungs, eyes, and do so much more."

"What is the survival rate?" Pete asked, skeptically.

"It's getting better all the time," the surgeon replied. "There are drugs to fight the transplant rejection that was so dangerous years ago. And yes, it's always better to have a compatible donor, to ward off that possibility. But think about the hope we are giving people!"

"What would you say is the average age of harvested organs provided by the company you work for, Doctor?"

Dr. Whitmore considered. "Well, the best viable ages are anywhere between fifteen years of age and thirty-five years of age. Although, as in the case with the young boy who needed hand transplants, those cases must be individually matched."

"Do you know the name of the company you work for?" Pete asked.

"Not really," came the answer. "They pay me by direct deposit. It shows up in my statement as 'deposit-MSW800.'"

"Do you know the name of the man who recruited you?" the detected wanted to know.

"I do remember that name," Whitmore told him. "He said his name was Landon Morrow."

"Of course he did," Pete replied.

"What?" the surgeon inquired.

"Oh, nothing. Dr. Whitmore. Do you know how the people you work for disposes of unusable body parts, after the needed organs are harvested?"

"I would think there are laws governing that sort of thing, Detective," the surgeon replied. "And I assure you, our company is squeaky clean and above board in all respects. I know. I did my research."

"Thank you, Dr. Whitmore," Pete told him. "I'm going to have someone escort you back to your cell now."

After the surgeon left the interrogation room, Pete considered the answers the man had provided.

Where did the unusable body parts end up, he wondered?

How could he have possibly worked for a company, and not been aware of their purpose and activities?

For her part, Christine was spending the day interviewing young women rescued in the Ennis Lake raid. All morning, she had been considering the timing of ordering a second raid; this time on the house on East Biarritz in Springview. If the team could complete remaining interviews today, perhaps they could schedule the SWAT Team for tomorrow.

Before entering the Interrogation Room where the two kidnap victims from Mali waited, she made a cell phone call. Then, taking a deep breath, she dove into her day. Mentally, she made an adjustment to think in Arabic.

"Salaam!" she greeted them. "I am Christine Spada, and I work with the FBI. I need to ask you a few questions, to help us in solving this most unusual case."

"Peace to you, Agent Spada," the older one replied. "I remember us speaking the day you saved us from the house. I am Basyra, and my cousin's name is Houda."

Christine referred to her notes from the initial statements. "And you are ... how old?"

"I am thirteen, and my cousin is twelve. But we are women."

"By that, I take it to mean you have reached the years when you can bear children, because you have monthly bleeding."

Both girls nodded.

"Tell me about your families, please," Christine said.

Houda spoke up. "Our fathers are brothers. All of us left our homes in Algeria when the famine came. We all travelled together, and eventually came to Timbuktu in Mali." Her eyes welled up and she began to cry. At this point, Basyra took up the story.

"Houda's mother died when we reached Mali. So my mother became her mother, and all of us became like brothers and sisters."

"Did you have enough to eat in Mali?" Christine asked.

"There is war in many countries in Africa," Basyra answered. "There are armies operating with no government authority. But they kill just the same. Sometimes, they come in the night and steal away the boys to fight. They take girls to work in the gold mines and mercury mines. Many of us die in the mines, and in the fighting. At the end, we settled in the north of Mali. Then the famine reached us there. There was no food. And there are not many young men left in our country."

"So it is a very hard situation to live in," Christine observed.

"Yes, it is very hard," Houda rejoined. "Our fathers decided to make our brothers join the Islam army to keep them from being killed or stolen. All the people are afraid of that army."

"Does that army have a name?" the Agent asked.

"It is called a Jihad group. They have taken the name Al-Shabib," she answered.

"One day, a man came to our home," Basyra said. "We had no food. He told my father he would pay two hundred US dollars for each of us. My father told both of us that it was Allah's blessing. It was a sign that our god wanted us to live and not to die. My father took the money, so our family could eat.

"The man's name was Ali. He was from Mauretania. He was kind to us. He did not molest us. He did not hurt us. He fed us, and let us ride his camels for two days. Then, in a desert wadi, he sold us to another man who had a truck. The man had other women in the truck. He had bought those women as well. We still do not know the name of the man with the truck. But he paid Ali five hundred American dollars for each of us. The man with the truck put us on the big barge, and we came to America.

"First Houda was sick, and then I was sick. I think the water was not good. But when we came out in this country, the people at the house were good to us. They fed us. They gave us water, and shots, and medicine."

"Did the people in the house have a doctor who took care of you?" Christine wanted to know.

Houda smiled. "Yes. He is Dr. Whitmore. Do you know speaks Arabic? He has worked in Africa. He is very funny. He told the zombie leader we did not have to be dissected. He saved us. The zombie leader decided to sell us again."

She cocked her head sideways, and looked at the Agent.

"What does this word mean; this 'dissected?'"

"It is a medical term, Houda," Christine told her. "It means to cut something apart. Don't worry about it right now. It's not important now. We might have to talk about it later. For now, we just want you to be safe. Did they give you any papers?"

"No. No papers," Basyra answered, appearing confused.

Christine smiled at her. "Don't worry. Do you want to go home to your families?"

The girls looked at each other. Basyra answered for both of them. "There is nothing there for us. They sold us and sent us away. Please, can we stay here in this country? We are hard workers. We will learn to do anything required. Please help us."

Christine spoke with them for a few more moments, and then tucked the notes she had taken into the file-box. Nodding at a uniformed female officer, she told the girls they should wait for now with the other girls, until all the interviews were finished.

The next interview was with the two sisters from Haiti. She used her French for this communication. As they entered, she stood to greet them.

"Bonjour!" she greeted them. "I am Christine Spada, and I work with the FBI. I need to ask you a few questions, to help us in solving this most unusual case."

"Good day to you as well, Agent," the shorter one replied. "You are the same woman we spoke with the day we were taken from the lake house, yes? My name is Perkine."

"And I am Agnes," the taller one added.

Christine referred to her notes from the initial statements. "And you are … how old?"

Perkine answered first. "I am fifteen, and my sister is almost fourteen."

"Tell me about your families, please," Christine said.

"Our family is very poor, and we live in Port-au-Prince. We are the oldest of ten children. Our father; he works in the fields for a rich French man. Our mother is the maid in the rich man's house. In our country, our Father works hard, and is paid well. We are fortunate that our Mother has a job. She works hard and is paid well also. But there is not enough money to raise ten of us.

"A year ago, our father borrowed money from a man in Port-au-Prince to help us pay our bills. But the man became impatient and came to our father. He demanded all of the money sooner than he promised to wait."

Christine had heard similar accounts before. "What happened?"

Perkine shrugged. "My father paid him with us."

Christine assessed the girl's demeanor. She didn't seem hurt by the transaction. "Didn't that upset you? Being sold to pay a debt; like you were property?"

Perkine looked at her strangely. "Our culture is different from yours. We are not sons. We have no value, except to bear more sons, and keep a house. In my country, I have no right to have feelings like that. I am a woman. I do as I am told or I do not survive."

"I see," was all Christine to find to answer. Finally, she asked, "So, how did you come to travel in the boat and the shipping container?"

"The man my father gave us to in Port-au-Prince took us to Las Terrenas in the Dominican Republic. They put us in the big box," Agnes told her.

"Were there other girls like you in the box as well?" Christine asked.

The girls nodded. "Yes," answered Perkine, "about twenty of us. But some of them died, and some were taken away to go to other cities when they opened the box in the state of Georgia."

"How did they do that, exactly?" the Agent inquired. "I thought the box was loaded directly onto the train."

"It was, Agent," Perkine explained. "But some men stopped the train about two miles after we left the station. Those men came through and looked in each container. When they looked into ours, they took some of the girls and put them in two vans."

"Do you remember any writing on the vans or words; anything?"

Perkine closed her eyes. "It was written in English. I don't remember what it said. But there was a picture of a blue cross, and the world. And there was one of those listening things on it, like the doctor wears when he asks about your heart. The whole sign was red and blue with black letters."

"A stethoscope?" Christine clarified. "It works like this?" She sketched a little stethoscope for the girl.

"Yes, that is it exactly!"

The Agent continued her questions. "When you arrived at the house on Ennis Lake, you said you received medical care?"

"Yes, and food, and water," Agnes answered. "They gave us shots and medicine. The doctor was very nice."

"Do you remember his name?"

"Dr. Randy. He was funny. He said we both had good teeth, and would be good specimens for research."

"Oh," Christine answered. She smiled at the girls. "We will have to see about that, won't we? Did they give you papers?"

Both girls shook their heads.

"Do you want to go home to your families?" she asked.

The girls looked at each other. "We have talked together about this," Perkine answered. "We would love to go home if the situation was different. But we are women now. We do not want to be a burden on our family. Father and Mother are always so tired. There will be no money for a dowry for either of us. One of the girls with us in the big box told us that America is a place where girls can go to school for free. Is that true?"

Christine laughed softly. "Yes, it certainly is true. We want to help you. I will see what arrangements can be made. It might take me some time," Christine told them. That being said, she stood up and thanked both girls for their cooperation, and for the interview. As she did, she noticed Pete walking quickly towards the door to the Interrogation Room.

As a uniformed female officer accompanied the girls back to their waiting area, Pete stepped into the room.

"What's up, Pete?" she asked.

"Two things," he told her quietly. "First, the *authentic* Chinese interpreter is here. Secondly, we just got a call from Washington. Deputy Director Ben Edwards said to tell you there has been a double kidnapping of American citizens in Bruges, Belgium."

"When?"

"This morning. And you'll never guess who the victims are."

"I'm sure at this moment, I don't have the faintest clue."

Pete smiled at her. "Benjamin R. Asami, owner of Asami Motors, and Adrien R. Asami, his five year old son."

"They were taken together? At the same time?"

Pete nodded. "In broad daylight, from an outdoor café. His wife and daughter fled immediately to the American Embassy."

"Wow," Christine told him, as she tried to absorb the information. "This changes a lot of things, doesn't it?"

"I'm sure it will," he answered.

"Okay," she said. "Go ahead and finish up what you were working on. I just have a few more of these to do, and we can get out of here to debrief everyone at the field office. Can you let Francine, the uniformed officer in the waiting area, know to bring in the Chinese girl and the translator next?"

"You got it, boss," he replied, beginning to walk away.

"And Pete?" she called.

He turned around, anticipating.

"Have we done any questioning of the fake Annabelle? Her real name is Katika Knesevic. She fits into the case somehow, and might be privy to more information than we realize. Can you take care of that?"

"No problem," he told her. "I'll finish the set of interviews I working on, and then I'll interrogate her."

"And one more thing," she told him. "We need to organize a second raid for tomorrow. On the house on Biarritz in Springview?"

Pete smiled at her and nodded. "Wondered about that," he told her.

"And we've got to keep this one really quiet, just in case," she said. "I'm not even telling the Captain. I have a few doubts as to whether he might be complicit in all of this."

"Will do."

As Pete turned to leave, Christine went back to stand behind her seat in the Interrogation Room. She mindlessly flipped through the notes she had been taking during interviews. There were so many details.

She shook her head. She had to get her mind back in the game for now.

The door opened, and Chinese kidnap victim, Sung Li, entered with the actual Jennifer Zheng, her translator, right behind her.

Christine greeted them with a slight bow. "Thank you for coming. Please be seated."

The only thing different about Sung Li's story was she had *not* been sold by people she knew. Seven years ago, she had been an executive assistant to a wealthy vice president for an international company. The company was Chinese, with offices in France. She had been working in Marseilles, setting up facilities for a new branch of the company. Then, one night, meeting new clients, she went out for drinks. At the bar, someone had put a date-rape drug in her martini, along with a hallucinogen of some kind.

Three days later, she had awakened in the shipping container. She had no belongings, no identification, or money.

"I am a Chinese citizen," Sung Li told her. "I want to go home. Or back to my job in Marseilles. Can you help me?"

"I think we can work something out for you," she told the woman.

Christine was amazed. Sung Li's story was basically the same as the women before her. The hub house doctor, Dr. Randy Whitmore, had examined her and deemed her ready for sale.

"Did the doctor use those words?" she asked.

"I think so," Sung Li answered. "My English is very bad, but that was what I thought I understood the men in the masks to be talking about."

Then, Christine placed pictures of the men involved in the network, whom they had identified so far. She asked which man had promised the woman a passport and a job. After a quick study, Sung Li pointed to the photograph of the good-looking model type guy who had appeared in the videos.

"Do you know his name?" Christine asked.

"He told me to call him Garrett," came the reply. "And he spoke perfect Mandarin."

After a few more questions, Christine thanked Sung Li for sharing her story. She stood, in order to signal an end to the interview.

"Madam Agent," Sung Li said through her interpreter, "I believe I can help you in finding these people, and bring them to justice."

"How's that, Sung Li?" Christine asked.

"I have a photographic memory," the woman offered. "And I am artist. Would it permissible for me to draw pictures of things I remember, and write on them where I saw them? I'm not sure, but since you have no photographs, it might help you. What do you think?"

"I don't know if it would help us," Kit answered truthfully, "but I am certainly willing to give it a try. Thank you for thinking of it, and thank you for the offer." She looked at the uniformed officer. "Would you make sure Sung Li receives pencils and a sketch pad?"

The officer nodded. "Yes ma'am."

"Thank you," she told the woman. "You are very courageous."

"As are you, Agent Spada," the woman replied with a bow.

At the end of that interview, Christine decided to push the rest of the rescued women and the Miami runaway interviews to the next day. There was too much to get done before the early morning raid the next day.

Wrapping up for the day, Christine's mind began turning over recent events and partial discoveries n her mind. It was becoming clear why young women had been kidnapped. The oldest job occupation in the world.

There had always been money in sex and slavery.

But why kidnap young *men*?

The trafficking end of things didn't explain it all, and neither did the organ transplant idea.

There has to be something larger these people are protecting, Kit reasoned. *Why would they go to such lengths to kill a small boy, or anyone with information for that matter? Besides, they probably know we are on their tail.*

Now, we've caught up with them. Tomorrow will be a chance to get us one step ahead of them.

She picked up her cell phone.

"Hey Sam, its Kit."

"Good. How are you?"

"Not bad. I'm taking a break of debriefing the victims."

"Pretty much. Say, can I ask a favor?"

"We need another Search and Seizure."

"Just put, 'Investigation of human trafficking and Red Market activity.'"

"It's the house Pete mentioned in Springview. Address is: 4207 East Biarritz Avenue."

"No. Sorry, I don't have a name on this one either."

She giggled. "Wait. Use Landon Morrow."

"Can you get her to sign it, and bring it to the meeting tonight?

"Thanks. You're a doll."

"See you at seven. Spada out."

Chapter Eighteen

In the back of the transport truck, undercover agents Evan Davies and Patrick MacNaulty were in deep conversation with Yuri and Nicholas. Evan had asked them to explain as much as possible about their operation to him. It was necessary if he was to appear a part of their team.

So far, the transport had stopped at two of the wealthiest estates on the outskirts of Greenway, delivering three different boxes.

"How do we know where to go?" Evan asked.

"Gregor receives a text each morning with the code on the box, the address where it is to be delivered. The text also tells him the body part's expiration time. If we don't make the delivery before the expiration time, we don't get paid for that delivery."

"Is there a penalty for not making the delivery on time?" the detective inquired.

Nicholas shrugged. "Other than someone dying?"

"You know what I mean," Evan replied.

Nicholas chuckled. "We have never been late before. But Vitali said he checked the expiration dates on yesterday's deliveries in his text. All of them had forty-eight hours. We will have to work hard to deliver all of these today. It usually takes us one full day to deliver one box. We have two days' work to do in one day. So it will be busier than usual."

"It means we will drive through somewhere for food, and Gregor will drive like a demon on fire," Yuri told him with a smile. "I hope you don't have a weak stomach. It's hard to keep food down when he gets this way."

Gregor and Patrick laughed. "That's true," Patrick offered.

"What about long distance deliveries? The ones that require driving an hour or more?" Evan asked.

"Oh, our team does not fulfill those deliveries," Nicholas told him. "We only do deliveries to places inside the city and its suburbs. There are other couriers for long distances. Those workers can only deliver one or two Styrofoam boxes each day."

"Is it true we have been helping criminals?" Yuri asked.

Evan nodded. "I'm sorry, but yes, you have." He looked at all of them. "However, if you can prove you did not have knowledge of the inner workings of the organization, and were not part of the network, you might not be charged with a crime. If you cooperate with the investigation, I'm sure they will give you the opportunity to make things right."

"How is providing life-saving organs and tissues a crime?" Nicholas asked. "We are helping people live longer lives."

"It's a crime when the organs come from murder victims," Evan answered.

There was silence as the truth of what he was saying sank in.

"How many people have been killed?" Yuri asked.

"Too many to count," Evan answered. "We don't know if, or even how, we will be able to account for all of them, or discover exactly how long all of this has been happening. What can either of you tell me about the operations of the people inside the house?"

Yuri looked at him evenly. "I will tell you everything I know. We have always come in the early morning. A man in a zombie mask opens the door. Then, we wait for the garage door to open. We back up the truck, unplug the transport boxes from the garage wall. Then, we wheel them into the truck, where we plug them back in. We load up and pull out."

"Did anyone ever go inside to use the restroom, or to receive a message?" Evan asked.

"Only Gregor," Nicholas told him. "He is the leader. He might know more. He is the one who gets the texts, and answers them. The money is deposited into his accounts, and he pays all of us."

Yuri interjected. "If any of us would know about the people inside the house, it would be Gregor. He and Vitali have been doing this a lot longer than any of us have."

Evan fell silent. He would have to gain access to Gregor's phone at some point to find some answers. Or, perhaps he could convince the man to testify against his fellows. He looked at Patrick, who gave him a nod, a wink and a smile.

About that time, the truck came to a halt. Vitali turned around and looked at the four men seated in the back of the van.

"We need ten boxes at this location," he told them. He began reading off the code numbers. Yuri opened the storage box, and Nicholas sorted, pulling the needed boxes from the inside.

"Must be the Trauma Center again," Patrick murmured in English.

"Trauma Center?" Evan asked.

"Look. All of these boxes are small and flat. Must be tissue and skin for grafts," he replied.

"I thought all grafts were taken from the patient's own body," Evan said.

"Not anymore," the Irishman told him. "The market has evolved. Now, they look for young, unmarked, still-growing skin. They harvest it in small squares whenever possible."

The van fell silent while Gregor completed the delivery. As the truck pulled away from the curb, Vitali turned around to speak once more.

"We are driving through MacDonald's. What do you want to eat?"

Evan winced. He hated fast food.

When his turn came, he ordered a chicken sandwich. Vitali opened the metal gate to pass the food orders to each man. Then the delivery route continued.

Karen Stewart had just ended a long shift as the volunteer on duty at Ginsberg Memorial Hospital's Information Desk. She looked at her watch. Her friend, Krista, would be dropping the kids off in an hour. Band camp was ending today. There was just enough time to stop at the grocery store and pick up her husband, Nate's shirts at the cleaners. He was home tonight as well. Steaks on the grill would be a hit with everyone. Plus they were easy.

Pulling out her keys, she pushed the unlock symbol on her SUV's remote. Two beeps sounded. Getting in, she pushed the start button, and checked her mirrors as she backed out of the parking space.

Oh, great, she thought. Someone had parked sideways. She would have to make a three-point turn just to drive out of the parking lot. *Why couldn't people learn to be considerate?*

She sighed, shutting her eyes for just a moment, and leaned her head against the headrest. Outside, a car honked a horn.

"Okay, okay," she muttered. "Why is everyone always in such a hurry?"

Without warning, a hand came up from behind her on the window side, grabbing her hair. Hard. So hard it took her breath away. At the same time, another hand came around to the other side, shoving the cold, hard steel barrel of a pistol at her temple.

"You've made the people I work for very unhappy, Karen," a man hissed into her ear. "And you are going to help me make them happy with me again, or I am going to blow your brains out."

Shocked and instantly shaking, Karen was terrified. "Wh-who do you w-work for?" she asked.

"Oh, you sound just like the boy I'm supposed to dispose of," the man replied sarcastically. "Have you *always* stuttered? Or is it a new thing?"

The woman didn't answer. She was going through a mental search of all the boys she knew in her stepson's friend circle, and coming up empty.

"I d-don't know *anyone* who s-stutters," she stammered.

"Oh, yeah you do," came the angry answer, with a strong nudge of the pistol into her temple. "He's the kid Annabelle Carnes couldn't get in to see. You remember, don't you? You stonewalled her?"

As truth synced in her understanding, Karen looked into the rear view mirror, seeking to get a glimpse of the man's face. He was wearing a zombie mask.

"Please don't hurt me," she begged. "That wasn't my fault. It was my boss. She's the one you want."

"No, Karen, *you're* the one I want," he snarled. "And you're going to do as I tell you, or I will lay you out on the pavement right here. Now drive."

"Where am I going?" she asked tremulously.

280

"Stop asking questions. Just get us out of the parking lot, and turn right," he hissed. "Now!"

The field office meeting at Kit's townhouse that evening felt a little awkward at first. It was uncomfortable for the team to continue without Evan. Since it had been a long day, Kit asked each person to bring something to share, and she provided drinks.

To begin the meeting, Christine asked Samantha if she had any new discoveries that day. Samantha shared regarding the magazine article she had discovered during her lunch hour. She also distributed the copies of the periodical for the other members of the team. It was clear to everyone they had found the second girl, Sandy Karduc, now going by the name of Angelica Cheung.

She was living somewhere in Hong Kong.

"I thought we would find Erin Kasabian, or Erin's sister in the raid at Ennis Lake," Christine told the taskforce. "Instead, we discovered a little twelve year old, Allison Williams. Pete, you took her story. Is there much you can share?"

Pete shifted in his chair. "She's a really pretty little girl. The traffickers inserted a GPS tracker in her right shoulder, and inked the Chinese tattoo over the scar. They've done a pretty thorough job of hypnotic amnesia and re-programming. Her new name is Caressa Walters. We found a passport, birth certificate, Social Security card and Pedigree in that name. According to the documents, she is eighteen years old. There is also a document in the file signed by a Dr. Randy Whitmore. It certifies Allison is a virgin and has experienced Menarche, or her first period. It was all in a fold-over, weathered, leather portfolio with gold filigree markings. The markings look like a monogram of sorts. We have no idea where they were going to send her. She also identified Bereniece Fraire from the same raid as 'Miss Anastasia.' She said the older woman taught her how to walk, talk, and eat properly. She had been made to memorize questions and phrases for light conversation with people involved in business. She had been given verbal instruction in how to sexually please a man. She was also in the process of learning to speak in Arabic."

"Arabic?" Christine asked, curiously smiling. "How could you tell?"

"I did a few years with the Peace Corps. We worked in several locations over there, building bridges and such," he answered. "I used to speak it pretty well. Anyway, I think Allison was being prepared for shipment to the Middle East."

"Pete, I remember she said she had run away when her mother put her on an airplane in Miami. I assume she was flown here? Did she happen to remember where her grandmother lives?"

Pete shook his head. "She has not remembered anything more than the information she provided in her initial statement. But she did identify the different zombie masks from Fernando's briefing."

He looked at Christine. "He sent the images to my phone this morning. Allison said STAPLE HEAD brought her food to her, and talked to her while she ate. YELLOW EYED FANG-FACE sat in her room during the day, and was the one to teach her how to do her make-up. He also cut her hair and styled it. NO NOSE GUY was the one in charge of all the other zombies. OPEN GREEN CHEEKS ran video and security. BALD WONDER worked with him in the basement. ROTTEN GUMS GUY was their artist/forger. LASER-DEMON EYES did a lot of reading. She never saw UNDEAD BURNED GUY or SPLIT HEAD. But SPIKE NINJA did stuff like the laundry and the cleaning.

"If you don't mind, I'd like to ask the psychologist who is working with Caleb... Ainsworth, is it? I'd like to show these images to the boy, to see if he can confirm anything about the responsibilities each mask fulfilled."

Felipe spoke up. "I would say that Allison's observations confirm some of my own conclusions from watching the videos today. I THINK UNDEAD BURNED GUY and SPLIT HEAD do jobs having something to do with transportation or security, and that's why they don't show up all the time."

Pete continued. "Oh, Allison said they had a landscaping company come and take care of the grounds each week. The house had a pool, but she was only allowed to swim when no one else was in the back yard. And under guard. And that's another thing. All of the hub homes they have used to date have had high privacy fences around the entire back yard."

"Thank you, Pete," Christine told him with a smile. "You worked hard today. By the way, what did you do before the Peace Corps?"

Pete grinned. "I was in the Marines at eighteen. Did three tours in Iraq. When I got out, I went college on the GI Bill, and got my engineering degree. Then the Peace Corps. Went to the academy after the Peace Corps."

Felipe looked over at him. "You got a short attention span or something?"

"Wow, Detective, you must miss getting to fire your gun!" Samantha said, brushing his elbow with hers. "That explains why you look so old!"

In the midst of laughter, Pete chuckled.

"Yeah, yeah," he muttered. He looked around the room. "Somebody else want to take the hot seat?"

"I'll go," Chase volunteered. "Detective Lynch asked me to conduct the rest of the interviews with the rescued ladies today. There are two from Mexico, three from Nicaragua, and one from Columbia. All of them were unloaded from the shipping container at Ennis Lake. The stories have a common thread, it seems. Each girl was kidnapped, sold, or ran away to escape death. After the initial encounters, individual journeys were different.

"Each of these women are between the ages of twelve and twenty, and they were all loaded onto the same container in Las Terrenas, Dominican Republic. From there, the container made its way Georgia Port Authority. It appears the empty container was scheduled to be picked up later in the week."

"The records on the organization's computer inside the house indicate these ladies were all to be sold to the same vendor: an employment service in New York City. The name is Domestics International, Inc. They supply international domestic servants for those who can pay their fee. I checked out their website this afternoon, after all of the interviews were completed. For a deposit of two thousand dollars, Domestics International will guarantee a trustworthy domestic servant, of any nationality; the "hirer" providing the choice of gender. The website says the deposit is actually a finder's fee, and covers their costs only. An additional fee, based upon the skill levels of the domestic and the income level of the hirer, is assessed on a case by case basis. Apparently, the company contracts for domestics from all national backgrounds. This particular shipment was for Spanish speaking ladies only."

Christine looked at him in amazement. "Our rookie did well for himself today! Let's give him a hand! That was really well done."

The group clapped for Chase in encouragement.

"Okay," Christine said. "Josh?"

Josh had been eagerly waiting for his turn. He had sent the picture from his phone to Felipe earlier, and his former partner displayed the picture on the computer screen for all to see. Christine had seen the image, and knew what it meant for the team, but she had purposely left time for Josh to have a moment of victory.

"Agent Martin, please tell us what this is," Christine directed.

"I took this picture this afternoon at Asami Motors. This is one of their service bays. The sedan his Lurkers are using tonight was being driven into the first bay there in the picture. But the thing I noticed was the box truck being serviced in the adjacent bay. At first, I wasn't sure if it meant anything. But seeing the similarity in the 800 numbers, I think it's too coincidental that this vehicle is being serviced at Asami Motors, at the same time we are working on a case having something to do with medical supplies."

The group was quiet while each person assessed the projected image.

Josh continued. "I have a hunch this is the name of the medical supply company we have been searching for. The logo looks like the sign one of the girls from Haiti described earlier," Josh told them. "I didn't have time to do any research on the numbers or the website."

"But I did," Felipe spoke up. "Josh called me with the information. The website looks legitimate enough. They are a medical supply company, based in Europe, although the true location is not clear. MedSafe will only deal with licensed medical schools or laboratories, or facilities where transplants take place. In order to become a recognized customer, a company must go through their approval process. MedSafe also says they will provide a personal history with every product, along with a picture of the person who donated the organ.

"On the product page, there is a statement saying they guarantee all their products. The product list includes organs, tissues, veins, skin, eyes and ears. Additional products offered with no guarantee are fingers, toes and limbs. In small print on the last page of the website is this note: *'Please contact us directly regarding donated specimens for live genetic testing.'*

Samantha's mouth dropped open. "Are you serious right now? Really?"

Felipe dropped his character. "No, Samantha. I'm a stupid idiot. I totally made all of that up." He looked at her with a funny grin that was hard to read. "What is *wrong* with you?"

"What's *that* supposed to mean?"

"Well, I'm not the one getting all hot and bothered because they didn't understand the complexities of the case." He chuckled.

Samantha was a tad flustered by his sharp response. "Are you laughing at me?" She looked at Christine for support.

Felipe looked at Christine. "What? I'm just saying what we're all thinking!"

"Uh, no you *didn't!* Nuh-uh! That's it!" Samantha looked at him, and then began to talk rapidly in fluent Spanish.

Christine stopped short, looking at her new friend in disbelief. "Are you kidding me?" She looked at Pete. "She told me she didn't speak Spanish."

Pete drawled. "Apparently she lied."

Hearing their exchange, Samantha turned her head to look at Christine. "I *did* lie," she said in English. Then, flipping immediately back into Spanish, she continued in Spanish, lashing into Felipe in frustration.

Felipe watched Samantha in amusement. After sitting silently for a few moments, absorbing her ventilation, he spoke to her in Spanish.

"You done yet?"

She paused, and replied in Spanish. "What?"

"Are you done over reacting yet?"

"No. And I'm not over reacting. You laughed at me."

Felipe began chuckling once more, which spurred more reaction from Samantha Cruz.

Exasperated, she sputtered. "You just make me so mad. You, you … stupid, stupid … Man."

Felipe's eyes were shining. "You are beautiful when you are angry."

Samantha didn't know what to say. She involuntarily coughed, and took a deep breath. Those members of the task force who understood Spanish, began to laugh.

Samantha looked up and saw a still speechless Christine standing, watching with her hands on her hips. "Sorry Kit," she said in English, realizing the humor of the situation. Her face broke into a smile, as she glanced around the room.

"That means we weren't able to make our cover story stick," Kit told her.

"Oh, girl, please," Sam told her in English. "I knew from the day we met that 'Fernando' wasn't your man. You're a very bad liar."

"Yes, I am," Kit answered. "I've known that I'm not really good working undercover for that reason."

"That's true," Josh interjected. "That's another reason I still don't understand why you got this job and not me."

Ignoring Josh's complaint, Felipe looked at his former partner, and then around the circle. "Director Edwards wanted us to have a cover until we were sure about the security of the area, and the people Kit would be working with," Felipe told them. "Josh and I got here a good six weeks before she did, just to map out the lay of the land."

"Samantha, how did you know?" Kit asked.

"Remember when we went out to lunch your first day in the city? You told me at Wendy's you had just broken up with a guy named Josh. That would be this guy, right? It just didn't make sense to have 'Fernando' moving as your fiancé that weekend."

Kit was amazed. "Why didn't you say something?"

"Oh no, girl," Sam replied. "It was too much fun to watch you guys, and know the truth."

She looked at Felipe. "What is your real name, anyway?"

Felipe looked at her. "I am FBI Agent Felipe Ramirez, at your service, Senorita," he said, taking her hand and kissing the back of it, then maintaining his hold.

"Oh stop it now! Seriously!" Christine protested. "Before someone gets sick!" She looked around at the team. "He has to be called 'Fernando' outside this house until the case is solved, or until the Deputy Direction gives us further instructions."

Felipe looked at Christine, and then at Samantha, still holding Sam's hand. "Only if she agrees to go out with me," he said.

"You can't date team members, Ramirez," Christine told him.

"That's not a Bureau rule, Spada," he answered. "It's *your* rule. And just let me say this to that, since you and Josh were engaged for so long; 'hello, Kettle? I'm the Pot, and you're black!' Besides, she's not an agent ... yet."

Kit looked at him and put her hands up. "Okay, fine. I give," she said. "You want to tell us your input now?"

Felipe smiled at her. "Thanks, Kit," he replied. "I'd be glad to."

He looked around at the taskforce. "I heard Sam speaking in Spanish on her cell phone yesterday."

"You didn't tell me?" Kit asked.

"It's been a little busy, *Darling*," he responded.

The team responded with laughter.

Felipe spoke over the noise. "Okay. Okay. Okay, in all seriousness. When I ran the facial recognition on David Fletcher, his identity came back as matching the features of a Gregory Coonan, citizen of the United States. He has ties to the Irish Mob in Manhattan's Hell's Kitchen.

"When I ran facial recognition, this photo came up. It's a security photograph, shot in the Brussels' airport. He was accompanied by a young woman. We aren't sure if she was being delivered to a buyer, or if she is a co-worker. We do believe he has been marketing for MedSafe International overseas. His

287

involvement makes this case a little bigger than we originally thought.

"Now that we know who MedSafe is, we will begin working to find the decision makers behind the company. Specifically, we need to find the Board of Directors, a building, or something tangible.

"With that in mind, I gathered images of all the men we have encountered so far, who claim to be Landon Morrow. We are currently running facial recognition on each of them now, which may take a while. Like Josh, I'm working a hunch right now. I'm wondering if, just like the zombie masks, the name Landon Morrow might designate a certain task in the organization. Or, they might use the name as a default when those involved when they find themselves in compromising situations."

"Thanks Felipe," Kit said. "Man, it feels good to be able to call you by your right name again."

She looked at the group. "There are three more things, all of which are large ticket items. The first has to do with our Jane Doe. The doctors at Ginsberg Memorial did an MRI and then drained the blood from her brain. We will keep our fingers crossed, and pray. We hope she regains her memory. She was speaking in Spanish with one of the nurses' aids today, and seemed surprised when they drew it to her attention she was speaking a second language. She may require more surgery, but it doesn't appear there is any real brain damage; just bruising.

"Secondly, the owner of Asami Motors. We received a message from Washington, D.C. today that Mr. Asami and his son, Adrien, were kidnapped from an outdoor café in broad daylight in Bruges, Belgium. The kidnapping took place this morning."

"That means he's *not* the kingpin, doesn't it?" Samantha offered.

"That's exactly what it means," Josh told her. "I've been saying that same thing all along. The case is so much bigger than Asami."

"Great, Josh," Kit told him. "The second thing…. We have another raid on a hub house in the morning at seven-thirty. I will need all of you at the Precinct office, in Kevlar, with the SWAT Team at seven a.m.

"We still have a lot to cover on this case. I'm concerned we have not found any of the young men who are currently missing. Although, I did speak with a transplant surgeon today, and learned a lot about that field. The premium age for organs is between fifteen and thirty-five years of age. Which means, not all of our kidnap victims have ended up re-programmed and alive somewhere. Some may have been kidnapped just for the use of their body parts."

"I know it's late, and we all want to go home, Christine," Josh said. "But what about the body parts in the Eastgate bathtub? Why didn't *they* get used for transplant? Are they leftovers? Or rejected because they were defective?"

Christine looked at him. "We don't have an answer to that question. And it's an excellent question." She rubbed her hands together. "However, if we will each take a step back, and observe the progress we have made in such a short time, I think we will all realize things are beginning to gel, don't we? So, yeah. Let's call it a night and I'll see you in the morning."

Chase left as soon as the meeting was over.

Felipe and Samantha stayed in the field office, just talking.

Josh stopped on his way out of the door that night. "You know, Kit, I been thinking about us," he began.

"Yes, Joshua?" she replied, carefully.

"I think you were right," he said. "I was thinking about it today. I've been a real beast to you, and I know it now."

"Okay," she said slowly. "What was it, exactly, that I was right about? What part of our relationship are you talking about?"

"I just want to say that I agree with you. I don't think we belong together either," he replied. "Ben assigned me here because I asked him to. I was angry, because I thought you belonged with me. But now, I see things differently. I get what you meant when you left."

"Thank you for that Josh," she said, with genuine gratitude. "I appreciate that. I really do."

"You told me I'm not marriage material," he accused, defensively. "I remember you said that once. I wanted you to take

289

care of things, and be more, well, feminine.... No, more compliant, I guess. And I think I understand after working with you for these weeks how that just isn't something you can do. I just wanted you to know I think I could do a lot better too."

Christine drew in a deep breath. There it was. Ouch.

She felt like she had just been sucker punched. But why was she surprised? She had forgotten how quickly his passive aggressive side emerged with a jab. Why hadn't she seen it coming? He had been sullen all through the meeting.

Go figure.

"Well, thank you very much, Agent Morgan," she told him, with as much kindness as she could muster. "You've made my day. Now, I think if you've said your piece, I'll invite you to leave. Then, I'm going to shut out the light, go to bed, and hope for a better day tomorrow."

"I didn't mean it like that, Kit," Josh started to say, as he crossing the threshold to the outside. "You're twisting my words again. You know, you've got a real problem.... A man wants a woman who will make him look good; not be caught up in a career."

"Good night, Josh."

"Kit, you're gonna be sorry. I feel sorry for you. No man will put up with the way you are. There's no reasoning with a woman who can't give a little."

But Kit had closed the door. Again. In so many ways.

"I know, Josh. I got it. Really."

She leaned her back on the door and closed her eyes. "Somebody shoot me now," she whispered.

"That would not be a good idea." A man's voice startled her. She opened her eyes to see Pete leaning against the banister of the stairwell, finishing a chicken wing. She jumped in response.

"Sorry," he told her, licking his fingers. "I was just stealing one, last, tiny bite from the kitchen, and heading out. I didn't mean to disturb your conversation with Josh. Has he always been like that?"

"Like what?" she asked.

"Self-absorbed, shallow...arrogant? Is that the word?"

"Since the first day I met him," she answered quietly. "I kept thinking he would improve if I got to know him. That somehow, he would deepen as an individual, but he never has. At least he never has with *me*. It took me a long time to realize he wanted a Mama instead of a wife."

"How long were you guys together?"

"Five long, sad, wasted years," Christine sighed and opened the door once more. "I'm sorry you were exposed to that, Detective. Thanks again for all your hard work. Good night."

"Good night, Agent Spada. You deserve better."

"Thanks."

"You're welcome."

Before heading to bed that night, Christine plugged her cellphone in to charge overnight. Noticing there were two new messages waiting, she listened to them. Both were from Deputy Director Ben Edwards.

First message: "Kit Angel, its Ben. I do remember Eric Janzen. He and I go way back. At first, I didn't recognize the name, because your Dad and I always called him 'Rick the Red.' You're right. He was in the JAG Corps here. I was FBI, and your Dad was the Chief of Detectives. The three of us were like the Three Musketeers! If he is still the guy I remember from back then, he might be of help to you on this case. Let me know what you decide to do. Ben out."

Second message: "Kit Angel, its Ben. I need you to take a flight to D.C. as soon as you can. With Asami's kidnapping, there are some larger pieces falling into place here. I need to brief you personally. I'd rather not do it over the phone. And I have some footwork that I believe will go better if you do it, here in D.C. There's a lot at stake here. Call me when you get this, Kiddo. Ben out."

After she closed up the townhouse, and said 'goodnight' to Felipe, Kit climbed into bed. Then, she called Ben.

"Hello. Edwards speaking."

"Hi Ben, its Kit. Sorry it's so late."

"Hey kiddo, you sound tired."

"Long day today. Hey, I got your message. I can't take a flight until the day after tomorrow. Will that work?"

"It'll have to. Case starting to break?"

"Absolutely. And you should see Ramirez. He's gone over the edge for the part-time girl I hired. Announced it in front of the team and everything!"

"Ramirez did? That's unusual for him. Must be a strong attraction."

"I know, right?"

"But he's supposed to be *your* fiancé. What happened to the cover story?"

"Yeah, well, I guess you can only fool some of the people some of the time...."

"That's true. Just try to maintain the illusion outside the team. It's a pain, but until we get a few answers, I want to take precautions to make sure you're safe. How's Joshua doing?"

"It's okay, Ben. Thanks for taking care of me. And Josh is just being Josh. He's doing okay. He discovered the name of the medical company today. I'll have Felipe send you the links."

"That would be great. I'll book you a flight for day after tomorrow. Look for a driver with a sign at Dulles."

"Yes sir. How long will I be there?"

"Just a couple of days, unless we hit a glitch. There's a lot to go through here."

"Okay. See you then."

"Looking forward to it. And Kit? Pack something to dress up in. Ben out."

Before heading to bed, Christine called her mother. Maybe they could eat a meal together at the hotel or something while she was back in D.C. She knew it was later than her mother was normally up, but she didn't want to risk hurting their relationship by not telling her mom she was coming. Things were already strained with all the spooky God stuff the woman had gotten herself into.

Maybe someday soon she would be part of a case that would prove to her mother that the people she was surrounding herself with these days were off-the-wall.

Chapter Nineteen

The raid on 4207 East Biarritz Avenue went off without a hitch. It was evident the arrests the taskforce had been making, were taking a solid bite out of the structure of the organization. From what the team could tell, those working in the hub house were doing so on a skeleton crew. This time, there were no cryogenic boxes. There was no doctor or medical couriers. There was no transport team.

Nor were there foreign nationals awaiting forged papers and a buyer. Nor was a multiple murder waiting to be processed across the street.

Come to think of it, Pete reasoned, *the whole thing that morning felt kind of anti-climactic.* There were only seven guys, and two kidnapped victims. No chef, No "Anastasia," and only two computer geeks. He loved catching systematic crooks unawares. And these guys definitely had been caught napping. At least this time.

The two girls, kidnap victims, had been afraid at first. They hadn't known if they were safe with the SWAT Team, or if they should hide in their rooms. Someone had definitely messed with their minds.

There was a great bonus in the raid, however. They had caught the good-looking model guy from the videos. Having observed the man's actions on the small screen before the interrogation, Pete fully expected him to turn on his most charismatic smile, trying to weasel a way out.

"Good afternoon," Pete told him. "I'm Detective Lynch. I'm with the FBI, and I'd like to ask you a few questions for the record."

"Hi, Detective Lynch."

"What is your name?"

"I'm Garrett Jacobs."

"And how old are you?"

"I'm twenty-nine."

Pete put on his best poker face. It would not do for Garrett to realize they had been looking for him specifically.

"To encourage you to tell us the truth," Pete told him, "I've been instructed to inform you we know about the trafficking ring. We have been following you for some time. We have evidence of your personal involvement on video. So, this is your opportunity to come clean about your participation in the crimes being investigated. To speak with us voluntarily will go a long way in helping you receive a lighter sentence."

Garrett shrugged. "Everything I've told you so far is true."

Pete chuckled. "Thank you for that." He paused, looking at his notes. "What do you do for these people, exactly?"

Garrett looked at him. "You know they will kill me if I answer that, don't you?"

Pete nodded. "I do. However, do you realize they are going to think you gave us answers anyway? You've been detained as an indigenous terrorist. So I think they might try to kill you anyway."

Garrett stared down at the table. "I do marketing."

"Marketing?"

"Yeah. I'm the face the girls fall for. I send the texts and emails, and try to pull eligible girls away from their parents. I work to convince them that they are missing out on something – on a better life. It doesn't take much to convey the idea of greener grass waiting just outside their reach. It's my job to work on creating a desire for that better life inside of them. I dream a little, and then ask them if that isn't what they want too. I try to identify with them, so they ask me for advice."

"How old are these girls, usually?"

"Oh, anywhere from twelve to twenty-two."

"Does it work?"

Garrett shook his head with a half- smile. "Every time."

"Why do you do it?" Pete asked.

"Because I have to," Garrett replied. "At first, I thought I would be building a bank account. It's really easy money, and I make a lot of it fast. But, once you're in with these people, you can't get out."

"What do you mean?"

"They don't care. Really don't care. If someone, anyone, even their own mother was in the way, they'd kill them."

"Okay. Tell me about the girls," Pete instructed.

"What about them?"

"How do buyers find out about them?"

"They have been doing this a long time, and they're good at it," Garrett replied, still looking at the table, drumming his thumbs. "They use classifieds, web presence, word of mouth.... Everything."

"Have they ever had a girl sent back?"

"Not often."

"What happens to the girls who *are* sent back?" Pete wanted to know.

"They have other sales arms of the company," Garrett replied. "They piece them out."

Pete knew what the man's words meant, but wasn't ready to ask the question.

"Is the company related to 1-800-MY-BR DE?" he asked.

Garrett stopped drumming and looked up.

"You already know about that number?"

"Yes, we do."

"What else do you know?" Garrett asked.

"No," Pete replied. "That's not how this works. We are in this room to discover what *you* know, not the other way around. Do they only kidnap girls who are virgins?"

Garrett stared at the Detective. There was silence for a moment or two.

"Okay, if I spill what I know, can you protect me from them? They have eyes everywhere. And I need a guarantee you can rescue someone I care about, if they're still alive."

Pete smiled grimly. "I can't make any promises, Garrett, but we will do our best to keep you safe. If we can rescue your loved one, we will try to do so. Now, can I get an answer to my question? Do they only kidnap girls who are virgins?"

"No, not all of them. The Diamond-Class have to be. Those are the ones we try to wipe and reprogram."

"Wipe and reprogram?" Pete asked.

"Yeah, like a computer drive. I'm good at hypnosis. I've been messing around with it since I was a kid. I use a technique I call 'Synthesized Forgetfulness.'"

Pete added to his notes. "Where did you *learn* hypnosis?" he asked.

"I kind of taught myself. I watched a lot of YouTube videos when I was a kid. My Dad was hurting my sister, and she couldn't get away. I learned on her. I tried everything I could to help her forget what he was doing to her."

"What happened to her?"

"He got her pregnant, and she killed herself."

Garrett looked at Pete. His eyes were filled with pain. "No matter what I did, she couldn't deal with it."

Pete felt a pang of sympathy for the young man. "Sorry that happened," he said. "Maybe you helped her stay alive longer. You might have helped her more than you realize."

"Maybe," Garrett answered.

Pete redirected the interview. "Tell me about this 'Synthesized Forgetfulness.' Who teaches it? Where could I observe it being practiced?"

Garrett sighed. "I don't know of anyone else who does what I do. It's just a mixture of stuff I've picked up along the way. Stuff I tried with her, you know? And stuff I've discovered works along the way. It's kind of a mixture of relaxation, hypnosis and visualization techniques. The Parent Company wants me to help the girls forget their life, and hopefully their real name. When they leave the Creation Center, we want them to be fully trained and prepared for sale to a wealthy individual. It's my job and Miss Anastasia's job to make each girl a custom fit to their buyer."

"Wow. That's a tall order, isn't it? Who is the 'Parent Company?'"

"That's what the higher ups call us. The conglomerate that gives us orders."

"What's the Creation Center?"

"It's what they call each of the houses where all of the preparations take place," Garrett replied. "We were instructed to call the houses by that name, because we are creating a better woman. And, we are preparing her for a better life."

"What about the *parents* of these girls?" Pete asked. "Aren't you robbing them of their children? Aren't you *destroying* the life these girls have had... with a *family* and a *home*?"

Garrett guffawed. "Oh, that's rich!" he said sardonically. "Listen, every girl our organization has ever taken has been miserable when they were taken. We don't steal girls from homes where the family is intact. It's not possible to break that loyalty. Believe me, I've tried.

"No, the girls *we* take are from homes where the parents are divorced *and* oppositional; most of the time estranged. The process of wiping and reprogramming doesn't work unless a kid's trust has been broken. It's almost impossible for me to get inside the minds of girls who have loyalties to home and family. Our girls start out depressed, disillusioned, sometimes using, and searching for acceptance and approval."

"Isn't that almost every teen in America?" Pete countered.

"Maybe," Garrett answered, defensively. "But when the family is intact, they unite and help each other. They talk it through. They make sacrifices. The Parent Company learned those lessons by the failures in D.C., LA, and New York."

"Oh, I see," the detective responded.

"That kind of pulling together isn't what happens in the homes we hit. Every girl *I've* been involved in taking has been convinced she has no relationship with either one of her parents; that they care more about money, or job, or their own goals than they do about her."

"So now they hit a certain demographic on purpose."

"For sure. It's just a business."

Pete was silent for a moment.

"It's terrorism," Pete replied. "You murder American citizens. You blow up houses. It's a war.

Garrett looked at him, incredulous. "You're kidding, right?"

"Absolutely not," the detective answered.

For a moment, tense silence hung between them.

"It's just a business," Garrett repeated.

"Okay. It's just a business," Pete echoed. "So, how did you get started in this business?"

"I was a high school senior," Garrett began. "Some of what I tell the girls is true. I was at Helmstead High School in New York City. I was dating a girl in the middle school at the time... uh, at Corona Heights. She was fifteen, and I was eighteen. She was so great. We had so much fun.

"Both of us were from families that had fallen apart, so we both felt like we had finally found somebody, you know? It was like two broken pieces found each other, you know? I lived with my Dad, and she lived with her Mom. We fell in love. Real love. I would have done anything for her.

"It was the middle of her ninth grade year, and things got really bad for her. You know what I mean? Her Mom found out we were seeing each other, and the difference in our ages. The woman went *ballistic* about Melissa dating me. She started making accusations that weren't true. I think she was trying to scare her into breaking up with me."

"What kind of stuff did she accuse the girl of doing?" Pete asked, taking notes.

"Oh, drinking, smoking weed; stuff like that. Then, she started accusing her of sneaking out to meet me to have sex. She kept saying there was money missing. She hadn't done any of those things, but her mother didn't believe her. It didn't matter what she said."

"And had you guys done those things?" the detective probed.

"Not then," Garrett answered. "But we did later. You know how it goes: 'I might as well do it, because they think I'm doing it anyway.' One night, Melis' decided to run away. She came to my house, because she had nowhere else to go. My Dad took her in, and she lived with us. Then, we did end up having sex, and before the end of that school year, she got pregnant."

"What did you do then?"

"Well, I started looking for a job. I was going to graduate soon, and I wanted to be able to support her and the baby. I started going through newspapers. There was a classified. You know. Like, in the back of one of those free papers where people advertise stuff for sale? I think this one was called 'Peddler's Rag.' Anyway, the ad promised good pay, room and board with lots of opportunity for advancement, and a possibility of travel. I called the number, and went to the interview. They hired me. Turned out to be the Parent Company people."

"What did they have you do at first?" Pete asked.

"I started out as a courier," Garrett answered. "I drove from place to place, delivering envelopes and boxes. I think I must have been a medical transport courier. That was before they got so huge, you know? My room and board was provided at one of the Creation Centers. Eventually, they began to trust me more, and they made me part of an abduction team."

"What about your girlfriend? When did she become part of things?"

"Oh, it was a mess up. They targeted her. I didn't know we were assigned to take her, until we drove up in front of her house. I told them they had taken the wrong girl. That they made a mistake. That she was my wife, and was pregnant. For a while, I was afraid they were going to kill us both.

But, by that time, they had started using me to lure the girls. Melis joined me in the Creation Center in my room. The zombie leader dismantled a camera in one of the back bedrooms. At least they gave us our privacy. Then, later, they moved us from New York to the Greenway house on Parrot Circle. The zombie team leader there wasn't quite as understanding. I had to hide her, especially after the baby was born.

"We lived that way for almost five years. During that time, I kept being promoted. The big bosses trusted me. They put me in charge of determining what classification the eligible girls were to be placed in."

Pete interrupted him. "You mentioned that before; the Diamond-Class girl."

"Oh, that," Garrett answered, beginning a salesman's recitation.

"Diamond-Class is a girl who meets all the criteria for reprogramming, and is a virgin. Those are sold for two million dollars US, or better.

"Sapphire-Class is a girl who is not a virgin, but meets the criteria for reprogramming. Those are sold for a million dollars to men overseas who have a harem, a seraglio, or zenana.

"Ruby-Class is a girl who is not a virgin, does not meet the criteria for reprogramming, but is sexually motivated. These would be desirable for a brothel, or as a high-class call girl. Those are sold for two hundred thousand dollars apiece, depending upon her physical qualifications."

"What was your girlfriend's place in all of this?" Pete wanted to know.

"Whenever she went outside our room, they made her wear a zombie mask," the young man answered. "She did cooking and cleaning. But mostly, she took care of the baby. The longer we were there, the more responsibilities they gave me. It got so I never knew where I was going to sleep. I would be in New York one day, then back here, then Houston, then back here, then overseas...."

"And then what?" Pete asked.

"Well, I think our boy baby was almost five when they pulled me out of the house on Parrot Circle. They put me into the house on Mackaw, and told me she and the baby couldn't move with me. They threatened us. If I didn't continue to do what I had been hired to do, both Melis' and our son would die.

"They did let us talk on the phone after they moved me. There was no way for either of us to escape. They watched *everything.* When we were living on Parrot Circle together, when things were good, I had been afraid something would change in our situation at some point. So, we built a hiding place for her and the baby behind one of the closets. Later, when Melis' felt things were getting really dangerous, she would take the boy in there and hide.

Then, apparently, one of the big bosses came over from somewhere in Europe. She was serving him a meal, and he told her she would make a pretty corpse. We both knew that was a direct threat. They were planning to sell her, or piece her out. That's how they fund the *rest* of what they do."

"Do you know what *happened* to your girlfriend?" the detective queried.

"After a while, they stopped letting us use our cell phones. They stopped letting me call her. I couldn't go to see her or the baby. They told me she was shot in the head, and they pieced her out," Garrett said numbly. "I don't know what happened to the baby. They probably pieced him out too."

He shuddered, and his face grew sullen.

"How long ago did this happen, Garrett?" Pete asked compassionately.

"I was nineteen when the baby was born," he said. "I'm twenty-nine now. So ten years ago."

"I see," Pete said, writing quickly. Then, he looked up at the one way glass. "Excuse me, Garrett. I'll be right back."

Taking his pad with him, Pete left the Interrogation Room and made his way to the Crime Lab. Finding the first person he saw, he said, "I need a swab kit, please? I need to take some DNA from a suspect."

After receiving what he needed, Pete returned to Interrogation. He looked at Garrett. "I need to get a swab to test your DNA," he said.

"Okay," Garrett replied. "I'll tell you anything you need to know. Why do you need that?"

"It's just procedure," Pete told him. "We do this with almost everyone these days."

"Oh."

"I have one more question, Garrett, and then you can go back to your holding cell. But I do want to talk with you further as the investigation deepens."

"Okay. What is it?" The young man had had just about enough of the information-gathering this detective was doing.

"Just exactly who is Landon Morrow?"

Garrett looked at him. "Isn't that a pretty common name?" he asked. "Seems like I hear it everywhere."

Pete chuckled. "I know it keeps popping up in this investigation."

Garrett smiled. "Honestly, I have ideas. But I don't really know *who* he is."

While Pete was in Interrogation Room One, Christine was in Interrogation Room Two. She had asked to be the one to interview the two girls rescued from the house on East Biarritz. The first girl was fourteen. She had disappeared from a store in the Eastgate Mall five days weeks prior.

According to her account, she had been texting with Garrett for some time. They had made an appointment for him to meet her in a store in the mall. They had made plans to run away together.

When the time came, Garrett was there to meet her. But, he had unveiled a different plan. He had taken her to the house on East Biarritz, where she had encountered the zombies. They had given her immunizations, inserted a tracking chip into her right shoulder, and inked a Chinese figure over the scar.

Garrett had taken her through the initial Relaxation Classes, and had been successful in convincing her that her true Prince Charming would give her the life she really wanted. She had not, however, been yet provided with a new name.

"My name is Hannah. Hannah Millard."

"How old are you?"

"I think I'm fourteen. They tried to get me to believe I was older."

"Do you know where your parents are, Hannah?"

"My Dad was killed in Afghanistan. My Mom and I live in Monte Blanc."

Christine stopped writing. "Were you having trouble getting along with your Mom? Is that how you started texting Garrett?"

She nodded. "I did. My Mom is a control freak. She has a lot of rules. She says they are there to protect me, but I didn't believe her. Now I do."

Her eyes welled up with tears. "Can I go home soon? Can I call my Mom?"

"Yes, you can," Christine told her, "and we will provide you with that opportunity sooner than you think. We just need to get some paperwork done before we can let you go home."

"Okay," Hannah answered. "Thank you for rescuing me."

The second girl wasn't sure of her age. Her first answer was twenty-two, and then she faltered, thinking that was too old.

She couldn't remember her name. Her provided name was Charlotte Alice von Rothschild. She was told her mother had been a direct descendant of the Jewish Von Rothschild investment bankers of Austria. Her mother was deceased.

"Charlotte" told Christine her mother had fled from Austria to the United States to escape an abusive relationship with her father, during the pregnancy. He had become enraged when he discovered she was expecting a baby before their wedding, although the man had raped her.

The girl's story was very convincing. Even under scrutiny as strong as Christine's, she did not waver in her story.

She really believes she is telling the truth, Christine realized.

Sitting back, the agent assessed the girl objectively. The hair which had been short and brightly colored the day of her disappearance was now the natural color of her eyebrows. Matching extensions had been sewn in, providing her with almost waist-length hair, but cut into a geometric style. The girl in front of Christine was very polite and well-spoken; sure to be a positive addition to any environment. She seemed schooled in politics and carried a general air of bred sophistication. She had particular tastes, which Christine was certain had been instilled through hypnosis.

She even had a faint French accent!

"Charlotte's" skin, nails and makeup had been done that morning. When the raid on Biarritz had taken place, this girl had been in the middle of a photoshoot. Christine had to admit she did look twenty-two. Charlotte confided to Kit that she and Garrett had been scheduled to fly out of the country that same afternoon. The photos were to be mailed to the couple as a wedding present from the Parent Company; owners of Creation Centers Worldwide, Inc.

On the kitchen table in the Biarritz house that morning, the SWAT Team had discovered two antiqued, leather, fold-over portfolios. Both were embossed with a sort of monogram, in gold filigree, although each one was different. Searching inside the second portfolio, Christine found a pedigree matching the one the girl had just verbally recited. Also in the leather pouch were the same type of papers as those intercepted by the FBI from other "Creation Centers" in regard to other girls they had rescued.

After the interviews she had conducted over the past week, Christine discovered she was now able to look at the packets through new eyes. She understood their meaning.

Looking at the "Menarche and Virginal Certification" paper, Christine noticed a small number in the right bottom corner of the page, just under the signatures and notarization.

"Charlotte," she said, "do you know what this number means?" She turned the page upside down, and placed it in front of the girl.

"Oh, that," the girl answered. "During my time in the Creation Center, my Prince Charming requested I be outfitted with a tracking chip. He values me, and doesn't want to lose me. That is the number of the chip. So, if I am ever lost to him, or to the kind people at Creation Center, they will be able to find me again, and take me to a safe place. They inserted it the first day I entered the Center."

"Did they tell you the name of your Prince Charming?" the agent wanted to know.

"No, it is a surprise. But, they did tell me that he lives in Monaco, and is very rich. He has lost two wives before me, so he might be grumpy sometimes. They showed me how to comfort him, and what to do so he will love me. Garrett even showed me how to do some of the relaxation techniques he used with me."

"What does the tattoo on your shoulder mean?" Christine asked.

"It means 'prosperity and blessing' in Chinese. My benefactors wanted to mark me, so that prosperity and blessing to follow my life wherever I go. It is a unique symbol, given only to me."

Sure it is, Christine thought silently. *The same symbol has been in the same place on every girl we've rescued so far.*

She maintained her silence.

Kit looked at the doctor's signature on the page, and noted it was *not* Randy Whitmore.

"Charlotte, who is Dr. Amy Rutger?" she asked.

"Oh, she's a surgeon who works for them," Charlotte replied. "I know she helps with the Creation Centers, but she is also responsible to supervise some of the medical deliveries. She travels a lot. The Creation Centers help a lot of people all over the world."

"Are you sure they *help* people?" the agent queried. "And how many Creation Centers are there?"

Charlotte looked distantly, somewhere just left of the agent's head. "Someday, if I had a dream job, I would want to work for them. They are wonderful people. They help people from everywhere. They have centers all over the world."

"Do you know how they started?"

"Not really," the girl answered. "But I heard a lot of languages while I was there. It made me want to be better at the phrases Miss Anastasia was teaching me."

"Did you know any of the languages they spoke?"

"No. They said something about picking a woman up from the airport one day. She was from Croatia. Maybe one of the languages was Croatian."

Christine evaluated her. "These people are not wonderful, Charlotte. They are murderers and kidnappers. They are very dangerous people."

The girl looked at her blankly. "I'm sure you believe what you are saying is true, but you have never been inside a Creation Center, to know what it's like. You might be right. And it's true: I'm not sure Charlotte is my real name. But if they are killers, like you say, why didn't they kill me? They didn't hurt me. They helped me."

Christine took her hand, and asked kindly, "Did they ever handcuff you?"

Charlotte grabbed the girl's hand with both of her own. "Yes, they did. But they did it for my *protection.* I don't think *you* understand. These are *good people.* They *helped* me."

Christine looked at her evenly. "Okay," she said. "So, help me understand, then. *How* did they help you?"

Charlotte just stared at her. "It's impossible to put into words! You just have to believe me!"

"Don't you realize they stole you in the middle of the night? They stole your life; stole your name, your identity, and even your mind?"

Charlotte shrugged. "Whatever they did, they did to give me a better life."

Christine sighed. "Whatever. Who is Miss Anastasia, Charlotte?" Christine wanted to know.

"Oh, she is a very special lady. She has trained hundreds of women, getting them ready to please their husbands. My Prince was chosen especially for me, and I was prepared just for him. Miss Anastasia helped me by teaching me how to walk, how to speak properly, what manners are needed in various situations, especially with nobility and heads of state."

Charlotte lowered her voice to continue. "She even taught me how to please him in bed."

"Oh, she must be a very smart woman," Christine commented, encouraging her to continue her rhetoric.

"Oh, she *is*," Charlotte told her. "She taught me some phrases to say in his language; in French. I have been learning to speak his language. They used a conversational computer program. And Miss Anastasia started speaking French with me all the time after I had been there about two weeks. After *three* weeks, I wasn't allowed to speak to her in anything except French.... I didn't do very well at first, but she helped me when there were words I didn't know."

Christine wondered just how deeply the re-programming had affected the girl's true identity. Was the core personality *still buried* under there? And if she had been deeply altered so quickly, would confronting her with truth cause a fragmentation? She wasn't sure. But she decided to give it a try.

Carefully, she picked up the Certification paper, and placed it back inside the portfolio. Then, she reached into the file folder to her right, and pulled out another piece of paper. Quietly, she placed it in front of Charlotte, and then turned it over.

"Please tell me what you see," she said.

Charlotte stared at the page for a long time. She was looking at a Missing Persons poster. In its center was her own picture, although her hair had been short, with streaks of fire engine red at the time. The caption read, "Have you seen me?" The hotline number was listed under the words.

The girl began to read out loud.

> "Kidnapped from her bedroom in the middle of the night, authorities are looking for any information leading to the recovery of this girl, Erin Kasabian, as well as the capture and arrest of the abductors. If you have seen this girl, please call our hotline."

She looked up at Christine. "It says here the girl in the picture's name is Erin Kasabian. Is this me? Is that my real name?"

"You mean you think you *aren't* a Rothschild?"

"I don't know for sure," came the answer with a sigh. "I just don't *know!* I feel so confused. I have forgotten so many things. When I *try* to remember, my head starts to hurt. I am looking forward to my new life in Monaco, but I do wish I could remember what happened behind me; my life as a child, or even six months ago. My benefactors have told me stories about my life, but they are things I don't really remember. Sometimes I feel like I'm watching another person live my life."

She looked at Christine, her eyes filling with tears. "Can you help me?"

"That is my job," the Agent answered. "I'm trying to help you. The best way I know to help you is by telling you the truth. What would you like me to call you; Erin or Charlotte?"

"Did you know Erin?" the girl asked.

The next day was Saturday. Christine was determined to take some personal time before her afternoon flight to Washington,

D.C.'s Dulles International Airport. So, she put aside any plans she might have had for sleeping in.

Samantha arrived at the townhouse at seven fifteen that morning. She was dressed in solid black exercise gear, complete with jewelry and makeup.

"Where you goin' this morning? You still going to Zumba with me?" Kit couldn't help but giggle. "You will sweat that off in half a minute. But I gotchu. I know what you doin.'"

"Felipe *asked* me to come a little early," Sam replied with uncharacteristic shyness.

Christine matched her tone and accent, in fun. "Oh, Felipe *asked* you to come a little early... Girl, this is *my* home. Did *I* ast you? No, but I'm glad you're here. Come on in."

"Are we still on for Zumba?" Sam asked.

"Yes, we are. I just need to get my shoes on and grab and a hair tie." She looked her friend up and down. "Maybe I should change while I'm in the bedroom. What do you think?"

Felipe stuck his head out into the hallway. "Is that Samantha?"

She looked back at Christine, and kiddingly she pushed past her. "I'm so glad he wasn't really engaged to you," she said softly. "I thought he was fine the minute I saw him."

Christine giggled and pushed her down the hallway. "Oh, go say 'hello!'"

"Right here, Felipe," Sam answered back, moving towards the sound of his voice, down the hall.

Christine went back to her room to find her sneakers, and a ponytail holder. She could hear muffled laughs and conversation coming from the hallway. Then there was a shut door, and silence for a few minutes. Then the door opened once more, and conversation continued.

Emerging once again from her room, Christine noted Felipe had dressed hurriedly. His buttons were not matched.

"Oh, look what you did, Felipe!" Samantha was saying. "Your buttons are mismatched!" She began to speak in Spanish. As she spoke, she began to unbutton and reposition his shirt properly.

Felipe said nothing. He just stood, watching with a goofy smile on his face, as Sam's fingers reworked the buttons on his chest.

Christine picked up a pillow from the couch and threw it at him. "You jerk, Ramirez! Stop it! You did that on purpose!"

Felipe put his hands out to his sides. "Wha---?"

Samantha stopped, and glanced from Felipe to Christine, not knowing what to think. Felipe grabbed her hands, and murmured something in Spanish.

"Oh, cut that out," Christine told them. "I'm going to Zumba. Doesn't the class start soon?"

"Sorry, Kit. Coming." Sam pulled away, her eyes fixed on Felipe. "It was idea, Felipe. I'm driving. We gotta go."

Christine waited, but Samantha just stood in place, staring at Felipe. Finally, Kit took her by the shoulders and turned her around. Pushing Samantha out the door in front of herself, she spoke over her shoulder.

"Ramirez, I'm happy for both of you, but you gotta stop. I think I threw up a little in my mouth just now. You know I speak Spanish, and I can hear you, too. You're disgusting."

"What?" Felipe responded. "I didn't do anything. We were just talking!"

Walking out to the car, Christine made a call to Eric Janzen. When he didn't answer, she left a message on his cell phone.

"Hi, Jannie, this is Kit Spada," she said. "I would love to get together with you and take some time to catch up. I also would like to talk with you about joining with our team to solve the case we are currently working on. Would you call me as soon as you possibly can, please? I think you have the number, since we've spoken several times. But just in case, the number I'm calling from is my cell. Oh, and Ben Edwards said to tell you 'hello.'"

"Sorry, girl," Samantha told her when she was done with the call. "Felipe is just such a great guy. I've never met anyone like him, and it's not fake. You know what I mean?"

Kit nodded. "I do," she admonished. "Please, just help me keep my focus on this case."

"Yes, ma'am," came the answer. "Hey, can I take you to my favorite foodtruck after Zumba, to make it up to you?"

Christine looked at her. "Absolutely!" she declared. "In fact, you want to skip class and go now?"

Sam smacked her arm. "No, we need the workout."

"True. But yes, let's go after."

"Fabulous!" Samantha laughed. "This will be a good time."

It was around ten-thirty when the two young women headed downtown to find Frankie's Flippin' Favorite Foodtruck. Parking in a space near Franko's normal haunt, they exited Samantha's car. Kit fed the meter quarters, while Sam looked for the vendor.

"That's funny," she said. "He's usually right here."

A lady sitting on the bench inside a nearby bus stop. "Who you lookin' for?" she asked.

"Frankie," Sam told her. "Do you know where his truck is today?"

"He was here early this morning. Dude made me breakfast," the lady told her. "But then he left 'bout nine or so. Said something 'bout Greenway Park."

"Thanks," Sam told her. "Thanks so much."

"No sweat," the woman replied. "Have a happy."

Sam looked at Kit. "We have to go three blocks over to Greenway Park. You want to walk or drive?"

"Are you kidding me," Kit replied. "Zumba kicks my butt. Let's drive."

Getting into her car, Sam looked at her friend in kidding disapproval. "Girl, we've got to get you in shape."

"Oh, shut up," Kit replied.

Three blocks over, they found Frankie's foodtruck, parked near the playground at Greenway Park. The side window was closed, and the vehicle looked abandoned.

"Here's his truck," Sam told Kit, "but it's all closed up."

"Maybe he's taking a walk before the lunch rush," Kit offered.

"Could be, but that's not like him. He never leaves this truck. I'll be right back." Samantha pulled her car alongside the foodtruck.

She opened her car's driver's door and exited. Realizing what her friend was about to do, Christine was spurred into action. She opened her door, exited, and moved in behind Sam.

Together, they walked around the truck.

On the second trip around, Christine noticed marks of red on the outside of the large vendor window. Had she not been looking for them, they would have blended in with the paint job. Looking more closely, she realized the marks were bloodied fingerprints created from pulling down the metal slide.

"Knock on the door, Samantha," she ordered, pulling her weapon. "Something's wrong."

Concerned for Frankie, Sam began pounding on the passenger side door of the foodtruck. She continued to beat the truck with her fist until suddenly the door opened.

Looking down, she saw Franko Kovac, huddled into a ball, holding his head.

"Baby girl, don't make so much noise!" he complained.

She knelt down. "Frankie! What happened to you?" she asked.

"It's nothing," he answered. "Just a few idiots who wanted my cash. Come in, quickly, before someone sees you."

He semi-walked, semi-crawled to the bench where he slept most nights. He lay down, resuming what must have been his prior position.

Samantha had switched into caretaker's gear. "How did it happen?" she demanded, reaching for a damp rag. "Kit, look at this!"

Christine had already been observing the man. She had assessed him as being eastern European, honest and hard-working. But he was terribly afraid of something or someone, and he was lying about the incident.

"Who did this to you?" the agent asked. "These are not the wounds someone has from being robbed."

Frankie looked up, as though seeing Christine for the first time. He noticed her gun, and put both hands up. "Hey man, I told you," he protested. "I don't know anything."

"No, Frankie!" Sam comforted him softly. "It's okay. It's not like that. Honest."

"Frankie," Christine said gently, putting her weapon away, "my name is Christine Spada. I'm a friend of Samantha's. I work in Law Enforcement. Who did this to you?"

Frankie looked at Samantha for confirmation. "It's true," Sam told him. "In fact, she's with the FBI."

"Can she help me?" he wanted to know.

"I don't know, but you should ask her," Sam replied.

"We go somewhere safer than here?" he begged. "Someone, anyone can hear me in truck."

"Where do you want to go?" Samantha asked.

Frankie shrugged and looked at Christine. "My sister, she is evil person. I left Croatia to get away from her. Somehow, she find me. I have no address. Just green card and post office box. Is horrible situation. America is not far enough away from her."

"Give me a minute," Christine told him. She exited the truck to grab her radio from Sam's car. Finding it, she immediately made a call.

"Christine Spada, FBI. We need an EMT and a tow truck to Greenway Park immediately. We have a man down."

Ten minutes later, an EMT team from Mercy Hospital was on the scene. After they stabilized Franko, Samantha helped him pack a few belongings and toiletries. She then loaded the vendor into her car.

"I no want hospital," he declared. "I safe with you. I feel fine."

"But you might have a concussion," Samantha told him.

"If I fall down, you take me to hospital then," he insisted.

"Take him to the precinct," Christine told her. "Call Pete, and ask him to help Franko look through the mugshots. I'll wait for the tow truck, and have it taken to the field office."

She looked at Franko. "We will help you, Frankie. My team will help you while I am away. They will keep you safe."

"Thank you." He murmured. "I appreciate this. What is your name again?"

"Just call me Christine," she answered, w th a smile. "We will help you to find a safe place."

Later that day, Felipe drove Christine to Greenway International Airport. She was due in Washington for a dinner meeting with Deputy Director Ben Edwards, and part of the D.C. support team at six that evening. She was anticipating a tight schedule.

During the thirty minute drive, the two agents fell into a discussion about Felipe's relationship with Samantha.

"Seriously, Kit," Felipe was saying, "If things are this dangerous, I can wait to see where this goes with her after this case is over. I don't want to do anything to jeopardize what we are doing here."

"It's really fine, Ramirez," Kit told him. "I've known you a long time, and I know you are a dedicated agent. I think you can handle it without becoming distracted. And from what I can tell of Sam, she would be great for you. Strangely, I trust her. And you know that's a lot coming from me. Especially, in such a short time.

"After all, she's a clerk for a federal judge. Anne Ventura is a seasoned official, and is a close friend of Director Edwards. Just for Sam to get where she is, she's been through almost as many background checks and security authorizations as each person on the team. And think about it. How much of that stuff did *you* have to endure just so you could work this job?"

"Does she have a security clearance?" Felipe asked.

"I don't think so," Kit answered. "That's a good thought, though. Since she's in on this case, so I'll talk to Ben about clearing her for whatever he thinks is necessary. He already knows she's my admin."

"You think she needs a weapon?" he asked. "I'm concerned for her."

Christine smiled. "I'm sure you are."

313

"No kidding, Kit," he said. "It's different this time. I've never met anyone like her before. We're on the same wave length. It's like we speak the same language."

"Literally," she answered with a laugh.

"That's not what I mean," he chuckled.

"I knew what you meant, Felipe. I was teasing," she told him.

"I get it," he said. "I just don't want to mess this up. It's too good."

"I meant what I said before. I'm happy for you guys," Christine said. "My only concern is that I want us all to follow Ben's directive. The fiancé cover was his idea, and I'm not sure if we are supposed to continue to maintain it, since all the surveillance devices have been taken care of. I'll ask. And yes, I'll see about a weapon. She does need some training."

He chuckled. "I can do that."

"I'm sure you can," she replied, letting the matter drop for the time being. She paused.

"There must be something bigger going on with this case. I keep feeling Ben's called me in for more than just an update. He said there was something he couldn't say over the phone. I guess we will know soon enough."

"I've had that thought myself," Felipe told her. "I feel like the team is beginning to gel rather well. Pete and Evan are both really good detectives, and they're good guys as well. You chose well."

"The last Captain of Police recommended them on his way out three months ago," Christine said. "The new Police Captain came in the week after he left for Barbados. So the new guy handed me their recommendations. Both of them have pretty impressive histories, and service records. They both interviewed well, and have been good about taking orders and follow-through.

"And, there's a bonus with each of them. They both have bilingual skills, which we know we've all found necessary in this job."

"That's true," Felipe told her. "How did the old Captain afford life in Barbados?"

"I don't know the answer to that question yet," she answered, looking out the window. "I hope he wasn't paid off, or worse, that he isn't in Barbados and was executed. That would mean these people somehow knew about our involvement in Greenway beforehand. That would make our efforts thwarted at every turn. If that is what is going on, it means we will get just enough evidence to keep us hooked in the investigation, but never find enough to convict."

"Yeah," Felipe answered, steering the car to the airport exit.

"Can I ask you to do a couple of things for me while I'm gone this weekend? I hope to be back by Monday or Tuesday. I won't know my return flight date until Ben lets me know what he is expecting us to do."

"Sure," he answered. "What do you need?"

"We need to bring in Omar Kasabian for questioning. He left out a lot of information in his first interrogation. There is no way he can be a manager in Benjamin Asami's business organization, and not know what's going on over there. Especially with his older daughter having been kidnapped prior to Erin. You'd think a father would mention that, wouldn't you?"

"And he hid Erin's phone from us," Felipe reminded her.

"Yeah, he did," she answered. "Please pick him up."

"And," she continued, "now that Asami's been kidnapped, we need to investigate the operations of the entire structure at Asami Motors. It needs to be a surprise, so they don't hide the books or other evidence. This is our window. Oh, and find out if his wife and daughter are still in Belgium, please."

"Anything else?"

"Come to think of it, yes. It's troubling me we still have so many missing persons in the middle of this. We need to find out where they are; their bodies, or their remains, or where they have been placed after sale. Closure is going to be hard to achieve on this one, but the families need it.

"Erin, or Charlotte von Rothschild, told me her tracking device is numbered. I found the number on the 'Menarche and Virginal Certification' page in her portfolio. It's in the lower right hand corner. And she said her Prince Charming was in Monaco, had been married twice before, and was very rich. From what she told me, it sounds like they were preparing her for a man with an anger problem. Oh, and they were teaching her French with the immersion method."

"You want me to see what I can dig up?"

Christine nodded.

"Oh, Kit?" Felipe added.

"Yes?"

"Pete wanted to be sure you knew before you left for D.C. Garrett Jacob's DNA came back as positive in a paternity test for Caleb Jacobs."

Christine was stunned. "Wow."

Felipe nodded. "He wanted to know what you wanted him to do about that."

"Nothing, just yet," she answered. "Garrett's probably headed to prison sometime in the near future. It would be a shame to allow them to attach, and then have to pull a father-figure away. Doesn't seem fair to the boy."

"Sorry I interrupted," he told her. "Anything else?"

She stopped and tried to reconnect her thoughts. "Yeah, let's see. Oh, and if Pete isn't busy, ask him to go back over the Eastgate murders. There are pieces we don't have, like why the body parts were different temperatures. Like why did they use a hotel room, and not a more sterile facility? Why the edges of the body pieces were so roughly cut and shredded, instead of cut cleanly with a scalpel? Have Pete see if Dr. Whitmore was recognized by any of the hotel staff. Stuff like that.

"And I'd like to find out who Dr. Amy Rutger is, and where she came from. I'm sure Pete will have some questions of his own to follow through on. If he gets a minute, we need to do a quick background check on the new Police Captain. If the Department has a mole, the people we are trying to catch could just as easily inserted an imposter into that position, as they could a patrol officer or detective's position."

"Will do," Felipe responded as he pulled the car up to the curb. "I'll be looking forward to texting you some of these answers in the next couple of days."

"Thanks, 'Fernando', my love," she told him, reaching over to give him a hug.

"Mi Amor." He kissed her lightly, and popped the trunk. "You need help?"

"No, I got this," she replied. Getting out, Christine lifted her bag and briefcase from the trunk's depths and closed it again. "See you soon, Honey," she told him.

"Te amo!" Felipe smiled and waved as he drove away.

Kit turned and walked into the airport, pulling her luggage behind her. As she did, she felt her cell phone vibrate in her suit jacket pocket.

"Hello. Spada speaking."

"Hey, Kit. It's Eric Janzen."

"Hey Jannie! How are you?"

"I'm good. Thanks for your message. I had just about given up on hearing from you."

"Well, you know how it is," she replied. "Now that I'm federal, I had to do a background check on you."

"On me?" he asked. "Really? Why? Don't you trust me?"

"You were JAG Corps. You know it's not that simple anymore. I'm just supposed to make sure all my associations meet with Bureau approval."

Eric paused. "I do get it," he said. "Well, did I come up as trustworthy?"

Christine laughed. "That would be an affirmative. And Deputy Director Ben Edwards says to tell you hello."

"How is the old dog these days?"

"You'll have to ask him yourself, sometime," she answered. "Hey, I have a question for you."

"Yeah?"

"I'm on my way to D.C. for a few days, to identify some issues on the case we're working on. When I get back, I'd like to ask for your help in regard to the Eastgate Precinct."

"What do you need, Kit?"

She paused. "Well, I need some background on a few of the people you work with in that precinct. It seems like some of the detectives over there might have been hooked into an international trafficking ring."

Eric was silent.

"Jannie, you still there?" she asked.

"Yeah," he said slowly. "That just seems so out of the loop for this precinct. Are you sure, Kit?"

She smiled grimly to herself. "Pretty sure," she answered, thinking of Detective Alexander Boyd, now locked up for committing multiple murders.

"Okay, Kit," came the reply. "You know I'm here to help in any way I can. Just call me."

"You can count on it, Jannie," she said. "Thank you. Spada out."

In a well-apportioned, finely furnished suite of rooms, a middle-aged man sat at an oak dining table. He was oblivious to the luxury of his surroundings. His head was bowed, held in both of his hands.

The time for weeping had passed. Now, he felt as though there was just an empty hole where his stomach used to be.

How would he explain all of this to his wife, he wondered?

Their son was gone; stolen from their lives in broad daylight. Gone.

For all he knew, his own life was over as well. Apparently, he had missed the cues that others in the organization had clearly noticed. The responsibility for the presence of federal authorities in Greenway was being placed, partially at his feet. Those who held the reins of The Parent Company had sent Punishers to pull him back into line.

And punish him they had.

They had taken his boy.

The life of a man's firstborn son was quite a price to pay, he considered.

Benjamin Asami had thought his only responsibility had been to provide vehicles, and repairs on those vehicles for these people. He wished he had been able to refuse them at the beginning. But that was before he knew.

It had taken a long time for the truth to sink in. But by then, it had been too late. Now, he had been involved so long, he was too afraid to ask any questions at all. He had tried to maintain an automatic response of compliance in anything he was told to do.

But the Punishers' team leader had said he had failed to meet The Parent Company's expectations. How, he wondered? What had he left undone?

He knew there had been a problem with Omar Kasabian's girls. But that hadn't been his fault. That had been Garrett's doing.

This is probably about that fiasco, he realized. *Sounded like Omar; to take a son to replace two daughters.*

In fact, reflecting about it now, he thought he remembered seeing Omar's face in the limo just before they had put the bag over his head. It now appeared the man was more than just a car salesman. He had been planted in the dealership long before Asami had been approached.

He had been too trusting, he realized.

In frustration, he hit the table with his fists. It was impossible to tell these Company people from every-day, run-of-the-mill "normals!"

They should tell a person!

It was creepy to always feel as though someone with control over his life was watching!

And just how was he supposed to recognize them?

Worse; how was he supposed to read their minds?

Chapter Twenty

It was the wee hours of the early morning in the City of Greenway. In the main lobby of Ginsberg Memorial Hospital, everything was quiet. The regular volunteer for the downstairs Information Desk had gone missing.

But not many were aware of her disappearance.

Yet.

The night before, while a gun was held to her head, Karen Stewart had called her husband. She informed him she had been asked to stay on at the hospital overnight. She explained she would be helping in the surgical waiting areas, due to an unexpected, extra surgical load. Noticeably shaken, she had spoken with him for less than five minutes. But in that time short time, she had managed to send him a signal that something was terribly amiss.

Karen's husband, Anthony, was the son of an Italian mother and a British father. In addition to learning his native English, Anthony's mother had insisted he learn to speak in Italian as a child; determined to raise her son with bilingual abilities.

"Trust me," she told him. "You will thank me someday. Knowing two languages will open doors for you. Mark my words, you will be surprised how many. It may even save your life someday. Besides, I want you to be able to communicate with my mother, your Nonna."

When Anthony and Karen married, it became natural for Anthony to teach his new wife the ancient language as well. Teaching her Italian had proved invaluable. When the children were smaller, the two of them had lapsed into Italian, when it was necessary to discuss adult matters.

So, in the midst of a life-threatening situation, it naturally occurred to Karen to insert some Italian into the phone conversation with her husband.

"Ciao! Anthony," she began. She couldn't ever remember calling him by his name, or beginning a conversation with the common Italian greeting. Just using his name would alert him, she reasoned.

"Hey!" he answered. "Where are you?"

"Oh," she said. "The hospital has a few unexpected, emergency surgeries happening. They are short-handed, and asked me to stay through the night tonight. They want me to help in the surgical waiting areas. Mr. Rapire was very demanding."

There was a pause. Slowly, Anthony spoke in response.

"Okay," he said slowly. "What do you want me to feed the kids for dinner? I got your text about going for groceries. Do you want me to just give them the Malvivente pasta?"

"Oh, that would be great," she answered. "I'm sorry. I know this is unexpected. Please hug Matthew, and tell him I still think he's a little schioppo."

Anthony laughed. "No, you are, Babe."

"I love you."

"Me too. See you when you get home. I got this."

When she ended the call, Karen hoped with everything in her being the gunman holding her hostage didn't speak Italian.

"What were those foreign words you added to your conversation with him?" he asked suspiciously. "If you warned him, I promise, I will kill you."

Karen looked at him, using all of her inner fortitude to appear calm.

"My husband is Italian," she told him. "We always add a little of his language to our conversations. If I hadn't used Italian, he would definitely have thought something was wrong. In fact, we speak in Italian sometimes to keep our kids from knowing what we are talking about."

"All right," the man told her gruffly. "Good enough. Now, you're going to get me onto the Crazies' Floor, or you won't ever see him again."

In the Stewart home, Anthony Stewart had ended the call and immediately dialed the police.

"Hi, I need to speak with someone about something happening with my wife. I think she's been kidnapped."

322

The officer answering the telephone immediately routed the call to the Westwood Village Precinct, fourth floor; temporary office for the FBI. The phone on Peter Lynch's desk rang.

"Good morning, Detective Lynch speaking."

"I need help. I think my wife has been kidnapped."

Pete was instantly alerted. "Sir, what is your name, please?"

"My name is Anthony Stewart. My wife's name is Karen."

"Oh," Pete remembered, "isn't she a volunteer at Ginsberg Memorial Hospital?"

"You know her?" Anthony asked, surprised.

"I was the FBI detective who worked with her when we captured the intruder there," Pete told him.

"Oh, good," Karen's husband answered, relieved. "Her shift ended about two hours ago. She texted me then, and said she was stopping by the grocery store to get food for dinner. Then, she was supposed to pick up the kids at Krista's house."

"Krista, I take it is a carpool friend," Pete interjected.

"Yeah, they trade driving days with us. Anyway," he continued, "she just called me from the hospital. She told me that Mr. Rapire had asked her to stay and work another shift, helping with overflow on the surgical waiting areas."

"Who is Mr. Rapire?" Pete asked, confused. Having been involved with the administration of Ginsberg Memorial during the present case, he didn't recognize the name.

"That's what I'm talking about," Anthony told him. "We speak Italian and English at our house. When Karen and I want to talk about stuff without the kids getting it, we speak Italian."

"That's awesome," Pete told him.

"'Rapire,' in Italian means 'kidnap' or 'abduct.' And there is no one by that name at Ginsberg." He paused.

"All right, is that it?" Pete asked.

"No. I asked her what she wanted me to feed the boys since she didn't get groceries. I wanted to be sure I was understanding what she was saying to me. I got the feeling someone was with her, listening, you know, and she was scared. I asked her if I should use the 'malvivente' pasta, and she said that would be great. 'Malvivente' means 'criminal.'"

"Okay," Pete answered.

"Then, when she hung up, she told me to tell our son, Matthew that he is her little 'schioppo.' In English, the word schioppo, means 'gun.'"

"I'm sorry that's happened to you, Mr. Stewart," Pete told him. "Do you know her license plate? And please tell me what kind of car she drives."

"It's a white, 2013, Ford Explorer, Limited Edition. License plate is XY-3477."

"When did her shift end?" Pete asked.

"At four this afternoon," Anthony told him. "Is there anything you can do?"

"I'm going to drop everything and work on it right now, Mr. Stewart," the detective answered. "Give me your phone number, and let me call you right back."

Anthony spent the next couple of minutes giving Pete his cell phone numbers, in addition to the family's address and email contact information. Pete recommended he leave the house and take the children to a safe location. It was possible the kidnapper was going to show up at the Stewart home. The last thing any of them wanted, he told the distraught husband, was a larger hostage situation.

Following Pete's directive, Anthony packed bags for himself and the children. He had driven a little over seventy miles to his parents' home. Upon arrival, he had called Pete's cell phone. Additionally, the husband had called his employer and requested a Family Emergency Medical Leave.

As soon as they ended the call, Pete called Howard Pulmyer, Hospital Administrator, to make the Ginsberg Memorial staff aware of the probability of Karen Stewart being forced to approach the twentieth floor at gunpoint. He suggested several scenarios the staff could follow to thwart the gunman's plan, delaying to provide law enforcement some sort of advantage, preserving Karen's life.

His third call was to Felipe. Seeing this new development, they would need to pick a confidential team to set up an ambush on the twentieth floor. They needed the team immediately. Pete wasn't sure about asking the SWAT Team, nor was he sure whether he should trust the new Police Captain. He didn't want to use this situation to flush out a mole. Not when an innocent woman's life was at stake.

Felipe suggested Pete call three people he knew, who were seasoned officers, from other precincts. They should be men or women Pete himself trusted. He should minimally explain the situation, and then ask those people to meet himself and Felipe on the eighteenth floor of the hospital. Only those who could meet at those elevators in thirty minutes, in Kevlar, fully armed with backup ammunition, should be involved.

While Pete made his calls, Felipe contacted the Ginsberg Hospital administration once more. He requested they provide a trustworthy staff person to meet the team on the eighteenth floor of the hospital, at the elevators, in thirty minutes. Could the staff person also bring an elevator key to the nineteenth and twentieth floors? They had no idea when the killer might show up, but they did know they needed to get into position before the killer arrived with Karen Stewart.

From the moment the operation began, hospital administrators had seen to it that volunteers assigned to the front desk were replaced by a hospital security officer, who dressed in scrubs and wore a stethoscope for effect.

Thirty minutes later; three and one-half hours after Karen's abduction, the rescue team met on the eighteenth floor. There were ten altogether; seven men, and three women. Each one had come to help on their own time, in response to Pete's call for help.

"Here's the plan," Pete told them. "We don't know when this guy will show up. He might show up in the middle of the night tonight, or sometime in the morning. The point is we know he's coming. However, we do know his target; a little boy who is presently hiding in a room on the twentieth floor. He is being moved as we speak, as are the adults who were injured in the last attack."

"These people are witnesses in what I believe will prove to be a high profile, national case. We are working with the FBI on this. These men are Agent Felipe Ramirez, and Agent Joshua Morgan, and they are taking point on this."

Felipe began to speak. "We need to set two of you downstairs in the waiting area by the doors. Drink coffee, read magazines, whatever you have to do to stay awake. The killer could show in an hour. He could show sometime tomorrow. Please do your best to stay alert."

Josh pulled a stack of printed photos out of his flak-jacket. As he did so, he spoke. "Each of you, please take one of these. These are pictures of Karen Stewart, the woman who the killer is holding hostage. She was abducted three hours ago. We expect the gunman to use her to get to the twentieth floor. If you see her, even if she is alone, make no approach. Instead, text Pete's cell phone. He will be the first man in the line of sight by the stairwell."

"Now," Felipe told them, "we will be putting the elevators out of commission very soon now. They will be open and inactive on the nineteenth floor. Hospital Administration will be posting signs that the elevators are down for cable maintenance and repair. This will force the killer to take the stairs. When we know he and Karen are past the eighteenth floor, three of you will move in, coming slowly and at a distance, up the stairwell behind them.

When they arrive on the twentieth floor, Pete will be waiting the nurse's station, posing as member of the hospital staff. We are sure they will ask which room the intended victim is in. And we will go from there."

"Are there any questions?" Pete asked.

Everyone in the circle shook their heads. "Let's do this," one of the detectives from the SouthPark Precinct said.

"Okay then, let's go." Pete assigned individual tasks, and walked each person through their task. Then each one scattered to their assignment and waited.

That had been eight hours ago. At each quarter-hour, Josh had ordered a radio check-in from each station posted. The initial concept was to keep everyone awake; invested in the stratagem Pete and Felipe had chosen.

At this point, however, the routine was crowding in on frustrating.

The two detectives in the lobby had read every magazine on display. They had even watched one of the children's videos with a little girl who was waiting for her grandmother to come back downstairs from visiting someone.

Detective Grace Mimms and Detective John Elsworth were from the Eastgate Precinct. They had done undercover work several times as a married couple, so the assignment was nothing new.

It was a little after three-thirty in the morning when Grace caught sight of Karen Stewart. At first, the woman came into the lobby alone. She walked straight to the Information Desk. Surprised to see a person seated at the desk at that time of the night, she spoke.

"Hi, Jerry. Why are *you* sitting here? I thought we were supposed to leave this desk empty after midnight."

The security guard smiled at her. "Hey, Karen. The police are ready for him. Don't be afraid. You okay?"

Karen nodded silently.

Jerry glanced sideways. "Where's the guy?"

Karen posed as though she was making small talk. "He's on his way in. He has a gun, and some kind of explosive device in his pocket. I'm supposed to be getting a key to the Mental Health and Recovery floors, please," she said.

Seeing a shadow approaching through the revolving glass door, Jerry shifted his demeanor. He shook his head. "I'm sorry, ma'am, the elevators are down for cable maintenance and repair. You'll have to take the stairs."

As Jerry was finishing his statement, a man wearing an unseasonably warm jacket walked up behind Karen. Standing just behind her, he began rubbing her arms.

"Are you okay, Baby?" he said. He had a heavy accent.

"Yes, I'm fine," she answered. "The man says the elevators are shut down for cable maintenance and repair."

The man looked at Jerry. "Then how will we get up to the twentieth floor to see our nephew?"

Jerry smiled at him. "I apologize, sir. They are asking all of us to use the stairs for most of the next week. I'd let you use the surgical elevators, but they've told us they are for doctors' emergency use only." He patted his stomach. "I guess I'll be losing a little weight whether I want to or not."

327

"So, which way to the stairs?" the man wanted to know.

Jerry pointed to the stairwell door across the lobby. "Right over there," he said. "Is there anything else I can help you with?"

"No," the man replied, smiling brightly, and pushing Karen towards the stairwell. "You've been very helpful."

Jerry and the two detectives in the lobby observed silently as the door's hydraulics pulled the entry to the stairwell closed.

"They're on the way up," John Elsworth warned over the radio. "I repeat, they're on the way up."

In the lobby, John texted Pete's phone: "Coming your way."

As the gunman and hostage entered the stairwell, Karen saw a nurse coming down from the floor above. She looked at her abductor, concerned.

"Act natural," he sneered. "So, you will stay alive."

"Hey Karen," the nurse said offhandedly. "They put you on two days in a row?"

"Yeah," she answered. "It's good though. Just helping this guy get to the right floor."

"Gotcha. Have yourself a nice day," the nurse said, exiting just below them on the lobby floor.

As soon as she entered the lobby, she pulled a police radio from her pocket. "Stairwell's clear. All floors notified. They are on the way up."

On the lobby floor, the "nurse," Detective Angie Meadows, moved with Grace Mimms and John Elsworth to pass through the public barricade on the lobby elevator. Upon entering, they inserted and turned a key, and pushed the button for the twentieth floor.

Jerry remained behind to make sure the lobby stayed clear. He moved to the revolving glass doors and posted a sign: "This entrance closed. Please use the emergency room. We apologize for any inconvenience."

He then secured the entire entrance area, using the roll yellow caution tape Pete had provided him.

On the seventh floor, Detective Janet Eschovar sat in the snack area provided for the hospital staff. Dressed in scrubs, she appeared to be a nurse taking a short reprieve from her duties. The café wall provided the entrance to the oversized stairwell. As with everything else in the building with see-through visibility, the entrance to the seventh floor from the stairwell was constructed of bulletproof acrylic panels. The wall directly across from the snack area was covered in a mural of a countryside by the sea, complete with indirect lighting. The clear acrylic walls, and sliding door were set back from the stairs, providing a sort of shelf outside the acrylic, which was fenced off, to provide a seating area for several tables. Flower boxes and silk trees completed the illusion. Smooth jazz music played at an ambient volume, piped in from somewhere downstairs.

Having spent eight hours in the small room, Detective Eschovar decided it would be her favorite place to come if she worked here. It was a great place for anyone who needed a minute to regroup or have a private conversation. Or just eat. Totally better than the cafeteria.

Detective Meadows' radio warning had alerted her. She stood, and moved to the vending machines, creating the appearance she was purchasing a sandwich. In her peripheral vision, she saw movement. Waiting until the individuals passed, she looked up the stairwell through the glass walls to be sure.

"Seventh floor clear," she radioed. Taking a bottle of water from the fridge, she put it in her scrubs pocket. Then, she headed to the surgical elevators, where she pushed the button for the twentieth floor.

Passing the eighth floor entry, in the stairwell, the gunman spoke into Karen's ear. For the first time, she thought she placed his accent. Where was he from, she wondered, wracking her brain?

"That eating place is nice spot," he told her. "Maybe I bring you back there to kill you when this is over."

Having gained a little confidence from Jerry's encouraging words downstairs, Karen responded. "You won't have to kill me if you keep pushing me like this. I've got to take a break and breathe a little. I'm not used to taking the stairs."

The man let go of her, and watched her sit down on the stairs. "Okay, sit," he said. "I think I sit down too. Luka not used to stairs too."

The two of them sat in silence, breathing deeply, gaining breath for several minutes.

"Why are you doing this?" Karen asked him.

The man looked at her. "Why you want to know? You think you delay us?"

"Hey, I've been with you all night, man," she said. "You didn't rape me, but you could have. You didn't hit me, but you could have. You seem like a nice guy, except for a little anger problem."

The gunman chuckled. "My majka; my mother, used to say same thing. I have anger problem."

"She is gone now?" Karen asked.

"Da," he answered. "My sister, she kill her."

"Your sister killed your mother? That must have been difficult for you."

"Da," came the response. "But now sister kill me too if I do not get results. You will help me get results."

"It sounds like your sister is the one with the anger problem, Luka," Karen told him.

Hearing this comment, the man burst into spontaneous laughter. "Da! Da! This is true!" He laughed, until Karen saw him wipe a tear from his eyes. "You are funny woman, Karen. You make me laugh. If situation different, we be friends. I know it."

"You really don't have to do this, Luka," Karen told him. "You can make a different choice."

There was silence in the stairwell.

Then, Luke put his hands to his knees to push himself to a standing position. "No, no, I must do," he told her, sighing. Brandishing his weapon once more, he motioned for Karen to stand up.

"We finish job," he told her. "Let's go."

In silence, the two continued. Periodically, Luka would chuckle to himself, and mutter something in his own language.

"What are you saying," she asked.

"*Anger* problem," he replied, with another laugh. "You think *I* have anger problem. Zrinka has *anger* problem. *I* am *pussycat*."

330

Karen looked at his face, and realized his brief, vulnerable moment had long passed. He tightened his grip, propelling her upward.

In room 2002, Agents Joshua Morgan and Detective George Hendricks had positioned themselves in beds formerly occupied by Officer Rick Anderson and Dr. Jim Ainsworth.

In room 2003, a child-sized manikin from the Pediatric Nurse's Training Wing had been placed under blankets in the bed formerly occupied by seven-year-old Caleb Jacobs. An unattached IV appeared to be providing the youngster with antibiotics and fluids.

Behind the room's dividing curtain, a powered speaker provided continuous sound effects of a ventilator, heart monitor, and movement alarm. Sitting on the bed were Agent Felipe Ramirez and Detective Alicia Montenegro, armed and waiting.

On the eighteenth floor, Detectives Carl Jamison and Don Landers glimpsed the top of Luka's head as he made his way past the small, safety-glass window. Giving the gunman time to get to the nineteenth floor entry from the stairwell, the two officers quietly exited their floor. They began their own climb behind him. That way, if Luka doubled back for any reason, he would be caught in a trap.

On the nineteenth floor, Luka reached out to open the door to enter. He discovered the door was locked.

"Is locked!" he said to Karen in frustration.

"Isn't the boy you want on the *twentieth* floor anyway?" she offered. "Sometimes they lock these doors during the day to keep the more disturbed patients from leaving the floor. But the twentieth floor is always unlocked."

"You are sure?" Luka clarified.

"I'm not really in a position to lie to you right now," she replied sardonically.

Luka chuckled once more. "Da, this is true statement," he observed. "You funny woman. We go one more... up to twenty."

331

Luka forced Karen to open the door to the twentieth floor, and walk straight ahead to the nurses' station. Appearing oblivious to their presence, Detective Peter Lynch sat at a computer typing in what appeared to be patient information.

"Excuse me," Karen said.

Pete did not look up. He acted as though he hadn't heard her.

"Excuse me," Karen repeated. This time, Luka pressed in behind her.

"Oh, I'm sorry," Pete replied, looking up. "I was in the middle of a chart. How can I help you?"

"Too many stairs," Luka said, trying to make conversation, averting any suspicion.

"Oh, man," Pete told him. "I'm not looking forward to this next week, I can tell you. Anytime I have to go somewhere in the building, I have to climb the stairs. I hope they get the elevators fixed sooner than next week. When I was in college, I blew out one of my knees, and...."

"We don't care about knee," Luka told him. "We want to see nephew."

"Oh, I'm sorry. That's just me talking." Pete rambled. "What do you need?"

"He is the little seven year old boy?" Karen offered. "The one who stutters? His name is Caleb Jacobs."

"Oh, you guys are his *family?*" the detective gushed. "This is great! He hasn't had any visitors at all!"

He stood up. "Would you like me to show you to his room?"

"No," Luka growled. "We are fine. No show. Just tell room number. We find. Now. *Please.*"

"Absolutely fine. No problem." Pete seemed flustered. "Let me see here....." he fumbled through some papers, and appeared to find the room number.

"He is in room 2003. He is sharing it with a very sick lady, so please try to keep things quiet."

"Da. We will," Luka answered. "Thank you."

Positioning Karen in front of himself, Luka propelled her down the hallway towards room 2003.

As the unlikely couple passed the open door to room 2002, Josh noticed Luka's gun poking into Karen's kidney area. Just before they entered 2003, Josh watched Luka pause before opening the door. What was he was doing something in preparation?

Slowly, as Karen and Luka entered room 2003, Josh Morgan and George Hendricks exited room 2002, moving in to block the door. In a few moments, they would enter, but not yet.

Inside the room, Luka pushed Karen aside. He lifted his pistol, which now had a silencer attached. Lifting it up, he aimed at the child's form in the bed and fired five shots in rapid succession: head, heart, stomach, and each arm.

Then, he looked at Karen, aiming his gun at her. "Unplug the breathing machine!" he ordered.

"What? Why?" Karen asked, surprised.

"The woman is on breathing machine. Just do what I say. Unplug her. She is threat to us." Luka was insistent. When Karen still hesitated, he fired a shot into the wall behind her. "Do it now! GO!"

"Fine! Okay!" she cried, her heart pounding with fear. She hurriedly moved around the curtain, and leaned in carefully, expecting to see Sarah McMillan. Instead, Felipe locked eyes with her and motioned for her to be quiet and duck down behind the hospital bed. After waiting for her to comply, he reached up and turned off the powered speaker.

As soon as the sound stopped, the door to room 2003 flew open. Startled, Luka emptied the rest of his gun's magazine through the curtain, hoping to do away with both Karen Stewart and Sarah McMillan completely.

Simultaneously, Josh, George and Pete stormed through the door. They tackled Luka, kicking his gun out of reach, then securing his hands behind his back with a tie wrap.

At that point, Felipe pulled back the curtain to reveal the officers' presence, and the absence of Sarah. He also pulled away the covers from what would have been Caleb's bed to reveal the training manikin.

"Karen, you okay?" Pete asked.

The shaky hospital volunteer stood to her feet, and wiped her face with her hands.

"Yes, I am, thanks to you guys," she said. "How did you know?"

"Your conversation with your hubby last night had Italian code words, right?"

"Yeah, but I wasn't sure he picked up on them. He was so nonchalant," she answered.

"Oh, no," Pete told her. "He got it. He called us as soon as you guys hung up, and told me all about it. The team was set up here within three hours after that phone call."

"Been here all night, too," Josh added. "Just in case this guy dragged you in here sooner."

"Thank you all," Karen murmured, looking around the room.

"Get him outta here," Pete told the uniforms just arriving in response to someone's 911 call over hearing gunshots inside a hospital. Take him to Ennis County, to Sheriff Jackson's facility. I'll let them know you are coming. And don't discuss any of these details with anyone, even other Law Enforcement."

"Yes, sir," both officers nodded, taking Luka into custody.

As soon as they were gone, Pete dialed Sheriff Jackson's cell.

"Hi. This is Pete Lynch. We are sending another detainee your way. Name's Luka....."

"Can you please put him in a private, walled, isolated cell with no electronic devices available to him?...."

"Yes."

"He's a terrorist."

"Thanks. Lynch out."

Chapter Twenty-One

The phone rang three times.

"Hello."

"Hello, may I speak with Darlene Kasabian, please? This is the Detective Peter Lynch with the FBI."

"Yes," the maid replied. "Please hold for a moment, sir. I will go and get her."

"No problem."

Pete waited for a few moments.

"Hello," a cultured voice answered. "Evette Kasabian speaking."

"Ms. Kasabian, this is Detective Peter Lynch with the FBI."

"Oh," she interrupted, eagerly. "Are you calling about my girls?"

"Well, yes, in a way," Pete replied. "We have Erin here at the Westwood Village Precinct. She was rescued from a facility earlier this week. She is presently debriefing her experiences with our agents. We will be glad to allow you to see her soon."

"And Elizabeth?"

"Is that your older daughter?"

"Yes, I haven't heard from her in over a year. I feel like a horrible parent. It's just that she would run away and be gone for months. Every time we called the police. No one could find her, not even the private detective we kept hiring. So, this time, it didn't even occur to me that someone might have taken her. In fact, I didn't realize something could have happened to her until a few days ago. Her boyfriend called me, and said he had been questioned by the FBI. She never arrived at his home."

"That is what he told us as well, ma'am." Pete paused. "I'm calling for several reasons. First, to reconfirm to you that your younger daughter, Erin, has been recovered. However, she has experienced some re-programming and hypnotically-induced changes in her behaviors. She also looks completely different from the Erin you are used to seeing. Part of the reason for this call, is to help you to be prepared rather than shocked when you see her in a few days.

"Okay," Mrs. Kasabian replied slowly. "What else?"

"Secondly, I called to see if you had been in contact with either your daughter, Elizabeth, or your ex-husband, Omar."

There was a quiet wait, as Evette gathered her thoughts.

"Is Omar is missing now?" she asked.

"It appears so, ma'am. We can't seem to find him. He has not been to work at Asami Motors for over a week now. They have made the assumption he is taking sick leave. His car is in the driveway at his home, but he is not there either. We did have a car there, watching for him to come home. It is important we speak with him. But he hasn't been home for more than a week now."

"Is his passport missing?" she inquired.

"Excuse me?"

"Well, when he travels outside the country for business, he always takes just his passport. He uses a car service, and pays for everything with his credit card, or with traveler's checks. I know my ex-husband, Detective. If he had any inkling you were making him a suspect, he would run. There are many places his family could hide him."

"I see," Pete replied, making a note or two. "Did he tell you he was planning to leave the country?"

"No," she answered. "But it wouldn't surprise me. He still has other business ventures in his home country with his family. He never involved me much. There are many things I don't know, even though I was married to him. But then, his attitude is part of the reason we divorced."

Pete was intrigued. "Ms. Kasabian, is Omar a good father?"

An involuntary snicker was heard from the other end of the line. "He was a good *provider* when we were married," she answered. "But he has always put his own need for money before any relationship. Recently, I have even wondered if he might have sold the girls himself, and pocketed the money. He never spent any of his money to help me with the children, even when we were married."

336

"Is it possible he might have been part of the disappearance of either girl?" the detected asked.

"I don't trust him," she answered candidly, "and that isn't just a bitter woman talking. He was always very secretive with me. I was concerned about sending Erin to see him, but I thought it was just my own paranoia. I always assumed that every man would be careful about his own daughter's safety. But then, none of the children are really his."

"Oh?" Pete inquired, surprised. "When did he become their step-father?

"Their father died before Erin was born. I married Omar when Erin was a toddler," she answered. "Edward was the only one who recognized him for what he is, I think."

"Edward is your son?"

"Yes. He lives up in Brookville, with his fiancée."

Pete was writing. "Ms. Kasabian, are you aware of any signs Omar might have been involved in Erin's kidnapping? I mean, besides your own suspicions, Ma'am?"

"After she disappeared, Omar did confide in me he found Erin's phone. When I asked for it, since I pay the bill, he refused, and asked me for her passcode. I lied to him. I said I didn't know it. I suggested he give it to you people to help in the investigation. He refused, and told me he was going to hold onto it for protection."

"Protection? From who?"

"I honestly don't know," she answered, sighing. "That was when I began to think he might have been involved."

"Why didn't you call us?"

Evette Kasabian paused for a moment. Then she answered carefully, her volume instinctively lowering. Pete could hear her palpable fear coming through the phone.

"Are you kidding? Do you have any idea how scary his family is? I didn't want to be an obituary notice in some newspaper!"

"I see," he replied quietly.

"But," she spoke again, brightening. "I am fully willing to help you. Would you like to look inside his house again?"

"Do you have a key?" Pete replied.

"I sure do," Evette answered, "and you are welcome to it. I'm the only owner of that house."

"Mrs. Kasabian, could you meet me there, say, in an hour?"

"Sure. See you there, Detective."

It had been a busy day. The events of the morning, added to the hours of alert waiting the night before, had taken a toll on Agent Felipe Ramirez's energy levels. He rubbed his eyes again. Glasses had replaced his contacts as soon as he had arrived back in the field office. Gym shorts and a T-shirt had replaced his dress clothes.

Waiting for yet another online result, he finished his second energy drink of the morning, and crumpled the can. Beside him, on a coaster, was a large espresso. The lists requiring research were becoming longer and longer.

He gazed through his glasses at the computer screen.

The serial number from Erin Kasabian's tracking chip had been entered into several databases. He was hoping the search would lead him to the chip's purchasers, or it's producers. Even better, to more of the missing young women.

After perusing the evidence gather to date, Felipe began utilizing banking and financial broker sites through the FBI network. He located three older bachelors living in Monaco, each of whom earned annual income in the millions of euros. As soon as the search was finished, he would ascertain the likeliest candidate to discuss with Interpol as having been a buyer.

He picked up his cell and called Samantha. After four rings, her answering message played.

"Hi. It's Sam. Leave a message, and I'll get back to you."

"Hey, Chiquita, Christine needs a Search and Seizure ASAP. Call me, please."

Noticing the computer search had stopped, Felipe ate the last spoonful of his yogurt and threw the empty container into the trash. He sat down once more at the desk. Sipping on his espresso, he searched through the websites listed as having the GPS tracking chip he was looking for available. There were only two companies selling implantable chips using serial numbers as part of their tracking system. Both of these companies sold their product globally. However, the company from which Erin's chip had originated was the one drawing Felipe's interest; Global Individual Tracking Technologies, International, or GITTI.

The company did have offices in the United States. He entered their information into the FBI network database. What else did they sell? Who owned GITTI? Where were they headquartered? Where did they make most of their sales?

Detective Evan Davies and MI6 Agent Patrick MacNaulty waited silently inside the refrigerated box truck. Evan was thankful for the vehicle's chilled air, in light of the hot, humid, Southern weather. He and Patrick had both begun wearing lightweight jackets during delivery hours.

Strapped to the inside walls of the delivery truck were the two powered, cryogenic, stainless steel storage boxes. Evan considered. Two days prior Gregor had received a text, instructing him to pick up a load of long, Styrofoam boxes. When they arrived, there had been twenty-five to be loaded.

"What's in those?" Evan asked.

"Cadavers," Patrick told him. "They use them for medical conferences, medical schools, autopsy training, and so on."

"Did this group do this same stuff on the other side of the pond?" Evan asked.

"Oh, yes," MacNaulty responded. "They are doing exactly the same thing in America they have been doing in Europe. Two years ago, a student from a Medical School in Paris, France, alerted Interpol. She was participating in a Surgical Practice Class, and recognized one of the corpses the class was working on. It turned out to be a mate of hers who had gone missing a year before."

"How old was she?" Evan asked.

"The medical student?"

"No, the victim."

"The victim was a young *man*," Patrick told him. "He was twenty-six years old. He left behind a wife and small son."

"So, on your end, this case started with illegal medicals," Evan reasoned aloud. "Here, in our country, it started with kidnapped teenage girls."

Patrick looked at him evenly, an edge of anger slightly visible. "The problem with these people is that they have their hands in just about everything. One of the suspects MI6 is investigating with Scotland Yard, is a member of the House of Lords. So, if that's the case in the British Isles, I'm sure they have infiltrated even parts of your own government on some level."

Evan responded grimly. "A wise man once told me, 'Corruption knows no boundaries.' This must be the kind of situation he was referring to."

"Aye, mate," Patrick agreed. "Just as there are ties in New York City to the Old Irish Criminal Underground. I believe you call it 'Hell's Kitchen.'"

Evan smiled. "Guess that means we will be working together for some time to come, aye?"

"Aya," Patrick replied, using the old Irish dialect.

"So," Evan suggested, "do you think we should take pictures of the faces in these boxes before we deliver them?"

"Aya again," MacNaulty replied with a smile. He pulled out his cell phone and texted Gregor.

We need to stop to purchase shipping tape.

As they waited for the back doors to open, and shipping tape to be provided, Evan and Patrick set to work opening each of the cadaver boxes by removing the sealing tape. As each lid was lifted, Patrick held the lid above the box, as Evan snapped a quick picture of each face. After each picture was taken, Patrick lowered the lid once more. The two men then slid the photographed but unsealed cadavers to the far side of the truck.

They had worked through more than half of the containers when Nicholas opened the back door of the truck. He handed Evan two shopping bags with several rolls of clear shipping tape and a tape gun.

"Hey, Nic," Evan asked, "where's Vitali today?"

"He is feeling under the dog today," Nicholas replied.

"You mean under the *weather*?" Evan asked.

"No, *sick under* the dog," Nicholas clarified.

"Oh, the phrase in our slang is: 'sick *as* a dog,'" Evan responded. "The second slang phrase is 'under the *weather*.'"

"English is too difficult," Nicholas told him. "From now on, speak only Russkie to me. You are here in nice cold, and I am in cab with air conditioning no working... *and* you make me work with Gregor. I shut door now."

Laughing, Evan turned around. "How many boxes are left?"

"I am in cold," Patrick replied with a Russian accent. "You make me stay with dead people." He paused, then reverted to his British accent with a chuckle. "Probably eight more."

Together, they finished taking pictures. Then, sensing time was an issue, they each worked on sealing each box once more with shipping tape.

"Photos are a good idea. We should do this from now on," Evan told Patrick. "I'm glad I purchased this burner phone. When it's full, I'll find a way to drop it in the mail to my boss, Agent Spada."

The flight to Washington, DC, arrived earlier in the capital than posted. Christine Spada stood in the baggage claim area of Dulles International Airport, waiting for her luggage. A tall man in black dress pants and dress shirt approached her. In his hand, he held a sign reading "SPADA."

"Excuse me," he said. "Are you Agent Christine Spada?"

"That's me," she replied.

"Your car's waiting just outside the door, ma'am," he told her.

"Super," came the answer. "I'm just waiting for my luggage to be unloaded. If you want to wait in the car, I'll be right with you."

"No, that's fine," he answered. "I'll wait with you, if you don't mind. Director Edwards was very clear. You are to be protected at all times."

Just then, her cell phone rang. "Excuse me," she said. Stepping away, she answered. "Hello?"

"Agent Spada? This is Dr. Torres from Ginsberg Memorial. I am the neuro-surgeon working on your Jane Doe."

"Yes sir. How can I help you?"

"Oh," he replied. "I'm just calling to let you know that we have relieved more pressure from Jane's skull. I was able to cauterize the bleeders in her frontal lobes. As of the last twelve hours, the swelling has begun to go down, and her fever has broken."

"What does all that mean?" Kit asked.

"Well, based on her recovery rate so far, I think she might regain some of her memory. So, in a few days, it's possible she will know her name, and remember something."

"Oh that's great!" she exclaimed. "I should be back in Greenway before the end of next week. I will call you, so we can see her together."

"Sounds like a plan," the physician responded. "I'll wait to hear from you."

As she closed the call, Kit turned around, and almost walked into the young agent Ben had sent to pick her up.

"I'm sorry, I couldn't help but overhear your conversation, he told her. "My phone does the same thing. Blasted earpiece is too loud. You know, Director Edwards is right about you. He said you are a great agent because you are sincerely concerned about the people involved in every case you are assigned."

Christine was intrigued. "That's very kind of him to say," she murmured. "And, what's your name?"

"Oh, I'm sorry," he answered. "I'm Jamey Donaldson. I just transferred in from Chicago. I was assigned there, to the same case your team is working on in Greenway. Edwards had me re-assigned here to the D.C. office for the duration."

"It's good to meet you," Christine replied. "I guess we'll be working together while I'm here."

"That's true," Jamey answered. He pointed to the motorized luggage round. "Here come your bags. Ben asked me to take you to your mother's house to stay while you are in town."

"Oh." Christine flinched just a little, before she caught herself. She glanced at Jamey.

"You don't *want* to stay there?" he asked, observing her.

"Oh, it's not that," she replied. "It's fine. My mom has just changed a lot since I left home. Sometimes it feels like I don't really know her. I've been gone so long."

"I think that's why the Director wanted to put you together. He's been talking to her quite a bit lately."

Christine assessed him. What was he telling her? What did he know? And why was he watching her so closely?

In the kitchen of Omar Kasabian's home, Detective Peter Lynch and Evette Kasabian were in the midst of conversation.

"I did call his work place, and ask to speak with him," Evette was saying. "Sometimes, Omar will get busy, because Mr. Asami asks for his undivided attention. He only takes my calls when that happens."

"Did he take your call?"

She shook her head. "They told me what they told you. He is out sick."

"Wow," Pete replied. "So, how often does he travel out of the country for Asami? And is it usually a covert thing?" Pete asked.

"During our marriage, it was about once a month or so," she answered. "I think he was purchasing foreign cars, and arranging shipment back to the dealership. At least, that is what he told me. But he never explained why he couldn't talk to me about it."

"Is there any way to discover where he might be right now?" Pete asked. "I have some questions I need to ask him about your daughters."

"Do you really believe he was involved?" Evette inquired.

Pete nodded. "It's looking that way. We have your older daughter's DNA from a few things her boyfriend had held onto. As soon as Erin has completed her debriefing, we will be glad to reunite you."

"You said Omar was their stepfather?"

Evette nodded. "He had many unreasonable expectations for me as a single mom," she told Pete. "Somehow, I was supposed to just add him to the long list of things I was already doing."

"Meaning, you continued to work, and raise the children. Did he help you at all?"

She shook her head. "Not really," she answered. "In fact, I continued to pay all the same bills I had been paying. When we married, I added his cell phone and car payment to my responsibilities. After we were married, he held on to the money he earned, and spent it as he wanted to. I took care of everything else."

"You said your name is on the deed for this house?" Pete asked.

"Yes, it is, "Evette said. "During the years we were married, Omar was physically abusive to me, even though I was supporting him. I just wanted to avoid conflict, you know? So when I had endured enough, I bought another home and left him. You see, when Omar gets angry, there's no telling what he will do, so I just kept paying for this house, and let him continue living here. My new home is where Erin lives most of the time."

"Well, let me look through this house, and see what if what evidence I can find. Where would he leave something with DNA evidence?" Pete asked. "Like a toothbrush, or something with his skin or body fluids on it."

"Oh! Sure! I'll help you look!" Evette told him. She opened a drawer in the kitchen. "Omar usually keeps his passport and money belt in here." Finding the drawer empty, she closed it, and open every drawer. All of them were empty, except for basic kitchen tools.

"Look! He's been cleaning things out," she noted. "Let me look for his laptop and iPad."

While Evette checked the kitchen and laundry areas, Pete made his way down the hall to search the bedrooms. A few moments later, they both were headed back to the living room.

"He cleaned it out!" Evette declared. "He left the dishes and the pots and pans; that kind of thing. The garage is empty."

"So are the bedrooms," Pete told her. "No clothes in the master. Only empty furniture in the other bedrooms. And it's been cleaned well. I'm not sure there is any DNA to f nd here."

"I might have something of his at my house," Evette offered. "You want me to look?"

"Please," Pete answered. "And I'll need to send the Crime Lab over here."

"No problem, Detective," she said.

Pete looked around, assessing the empty house. "No, he's long gone. And it doesn't look like he's coming back anytime soon."

In Ben Edwards' office, Christine and Jamey were working through files of missing persons. They had worked back through two decades of cold cases so far. Director Edwards had pulled and re-assigned a third agent named Molly to help as well. At the moment, she was searching through computer personnel files, searching for older women with diplomatic immunity, whether married to, or somehow otherwise connected with foreign ambassadors.

"Well, I think all of these will give us a good beginning place," Christine said, patting the stack of files. "We've gone back almost twenty years here."

Jamey looked up at the stack of files. "That's a pretty short stack, Christine," he told her. "Are you sure there weren't more that could be connected to this case?"

Christine shrugged. "I don't think so. I already had several in the file-box of evidence I've been amassing over the past three or four months."

She began thumbing through the files, seeking to place them in chronological order. As she did so, Jamey opened them, looking for evidence to tie the missing person's disappearance to the case at hand.

"Do you see anything that could be a common thread, tying all of these together?" he asked her.

Christine continued to work, not looking up. "I think anyone aged twenty-five to thirty-five could be an at-risk for a medical abduction. Any young woman aged twelve to twenty could be a sexual trafficking victim. Any child could be a 'pieced out' victim."

"Pieced out?" Jamey echoed.

"Oh, sorry. Yeah, 'pieced out,'" Christine answered. "It's a phrase one of the kidnappers used. It means the dead body was cut apart and turned into transplantable parts."

Jamey shuddered. "We didn't get that far in Chicago. We just figured it was a trafficking ring."

"It is a trafficking ring," she told him, "but now, it appears there is a second direction to their activities."

Without warning, she was reminded of the dream her mother's friend, Joanna, had experienced. The two black trees and their shadows were prevalent. What had she said were under them? A picture of Eastern Europe under one, and a graveyard under the other...

Just then, Molly stuck her head in the door. "Christine? Can I show you what I've found so far?"

"Sure," came the answer.

Molly walked into the room, and stood next to her. She lifted up a printout, which she had slipped into a clipboard.

"Okay, here we go," she said, pointing to the first page. "I first ran a comprehensive search of all female staff with diplomatic status, who were or are presently assigned to Washington DC, from any nation, or with the United Nations. I ran the search back for the past twenty-five years. There are two printouts here. First one, the names are in chronological order. Second one, they are in alphabetical order, depending on your need when you look them up. "

She flipped past the first few pages before continuing. "After I did that, I removed all of the female diplomatic core who died in the printed station or another station overseas after leaving the post here in D.C."

She flipped to the last few pages. "Then, I filtered out those who are still alive and/or married."

She pulled out the last page, and handed it to Christine. "We are left with eight women, each of whom is well-versed in international etiquette and diplomacy, and cultural traditions. Each one is multi-lingual. Also, each of these women would have qualified to teach and prepare young women as a 'Miss Anastasia.'"

Christine took the page and checked over the list. "This is really good work, Molly," she said. "We already have Dame Margaret Kearnan. And I took a statement from Lady Bereniece Fraire when we raided the last hub house in Greenway."

Molly handed her a highlighter, which she used on two o the eight names on the list.

Christine looked at Molly. "Can you do a complete search of each of the six women still on the list? Bank accounts especially. Look for regular deposits of the same amount. Also, double check their addresses against the hub houses we have already closed down."

"You mean Creation Centers?" Molly asked. "I mean, isn't that what the one girl called them?"

Christine nodded. "That's true. It's a little scary, you know? It's like they totally erased her personality, and her normal brain function. It was like talking to a robot."

"Sounds a little like a Stepford wife," Molly commented.

"I agree," Kit told her. "How long will it take?"

"Not long, I would think," Molly replied, walking away with the clipboard.

"Oh, and Molly?" Christine called after her. "Call me Kit."

"I think I found something," Jamey said to Christine as Molly was leaving.

"What you got?" the agent asked.

"Look here," he told her. "I think this was the first case."

He opened a file, which was the first in the stack, and began placing the pages out on an empty table. "This one pre-dates any of the hub, I mean Creation Centers. It was a case here in the city, which eventually became an FBI investigation. But it was never solved."

Christine moved over to the table. "What were the dates on it, Jamey?" she asked.

He looked through the file. "Uh, March 10th, 1999. Says here that Chief of Detectives Anthony Spada and his partner, Detective Derek Hansen, worked with Agent Ben Edwards to solve the case.

The girl's name was Andrea Lockwood, and she was fifteen years old. She was taken from her bedroom in the middle of the night, and disappeared. Here is her picture."

Jamey pulled the photograph of the missing girl from the file, and placed it on the table. Suddenly, staring at the eyes of the kidnap victim in the picture, Christine was completely overwhelmed. She sank numbly into a chair, and picked up the photograph to double-check. She looked more intently to get better look.

Of course it was.

It would be silly to think anything else.

She was silent for a moment or two.

"Oh," she said quietly. "Oh. Oh my."

"What is it Christine?" Jamey asked, concerned.

Shocked to the core, she looked up at him. "My Dad was Anthony Spada. He called this girl 'Little Andrea Lockwood.' This is the case he was working on when he was murdered."

"When was he murdered, Christine?"

Numbly she answered, as though it was an automatic response. "July 25, 1999."

Jamey picked up his cell phone. "Director Edwards, sir? We have made some discoveries you should know about. Could you come to your office, please?"

Back in Westwood Village, Pete and Felipe were building another Search and Seizure team. They would be visiting the Asami Motors Dealership the next day.

On Sunday afternoon, the team arrived, much to the surprise of the salesmen and managers on duty.

"Who is in charge here, please?" Agent Ramirez asked the woman behind the reception desk.

"At the moment, that would be our sales manager," she replied.

"We are here to fulfill this warrant," he told her. "Please ask him to come up front."

When the sales manager arrived, Pete gave him a copy of the Search and Seizure order. He then instructed the team to confiscate all files and records, especially those from Benjamin Asami's office. Leasing and sales records were also to be confiscated.

"Can you tell us anything about Mr. Asami's present whereabouts?" Felipe asked the sales manager.

The man looked at him blankly. "We were told he had been kidnapped somewhere overseas; that his wife and daughter were in Belgium. I haven't heard anything more than that." He looked at the receptionist. "Have you heard any news?"

"I haven't heard anything either," she answered. "But I only work weekends."

She picked up the phone. "Let me call the service manager, and the weekday receptionist. Either one of them would know more than we do."

While she was making phone calls, Felipe worked to help uniformed police officers in loading boxes of files into the van. Pete looked through the car lot, for cars with dealer plates, seeking to match the numbers with those Josh had recorded. Specifically, they were searching for the vehicles used by the trafficking ring in the past few months. Each time he found a car with permanent plates, he snapped a picture.

Upon completing calls, the receptionist signaled to Felipe. "Apparently, Mrs. Asami called yesterday from Belgium," she informed him. "The service manager said she and Annette, their daughter, are returning stateside today. She said she will be in the office for Mr. Asami in two days, and to hold all important matters until then."

"Has she come into the dealership to work for him before?" Felipe wanted to know.

"Not to my knowledge," the receptionist answered. "Should be interesting."

"Yeah," the agent replied. "Say, when she called, did she happen to say if she saw who took them?"

The receptionist looked at him in disbelief. "I thought you guys would be all up on this. You don't know either?"

349

"We do have some theories, ma'am. We can always use more information. I just wondered what Mrs. Asami had mentioned. And oh," Felipe continued, as though it were an after-thought. "Why isn't their son coming home as well?"

The receptionist's eyes grew wide. "You don't know?" she asked. "He was kidnapped when they took Mr. Asami. He's such a cute little kid too. I hope he's all right."

"Me too, ma'am," Felipe replied. "Me too."

"It's so good to have you home!" Catherine Spada exclaimed. "Even if it is just for a few days!"

Christine walked into her mother's embrace, and responded with a reserved tap on the older woman's back.

Catherine pulled her daughter back and looked her in the eyes. "You're burping me again," she observed. "You okay, Kitten?" she asked.

"I'm fine, Mom," Christine answered. "The case I'm working on is just really on my mind right now."

"You need some rest, and some good food," came the reply. "Maybe later we could go and get our nails done together. You want some coffee?"

Christine glanced at Jamey. "I'm not sure, Mom. Agent Donaldson here picked me up, and I'm supposed to go to the office with him."

Not to be deterred, Catherine looked to Jamey for help. Apparently missing Kit's signals, Jamey spoke. "I'd love some coffee, Mrs. Spada," he said.

"Oh, please, son, call me Cathy. Mrs. Spada was my mother-in-law."

Jamey chuckled. "Okay, then."

"I'm just going to put my luggage in a bedroom," Christine told them. Looking at her mother, she asked, "Where do you want me?"

In route to the kitchen, Cathy spoke over her shoulder. "Oh, your room is just like it was when you left for college. Except, it might be a little cleaner now and more organized. You know how it is when a woman lives by herself. She has to find things to do."

"Yeah. Thanks, Mom." Christine made her way down the hall to her childhood bedroom. Inwardly, she was beginning to feel somewhat emotionally shaken. Could she handle staying here? She had not anticipated experiencing this subconscious knee-jerk response.

Even the smells are the same, she noted. *Mom's been baking again. Were they the little Russian Teacakes, or her Chocolate Chippers?*

Christine had never been able to decide which one was her favorite. She found her mouth was watering in anticipation.

As they talked over coffee, Christine found herself asking questions.

"Mom, can I ask you a question?"

"Sure. Anything. You know that."

"What do you remember about the Andrea Lockwood case?"

Catherine moved from her stance by the kitchen sink. She dried her hands on a towel, and came to sit at the table.

"I haven't heard that name in years," she said. "Why?"

"Oh, her name came up as being connected with the case we are currently working on." Christine tried to speak nonchalantly.

Catherine Spada touched her daughter's arm. "That is the case my Tony was working on when he was killed. Her disappearance was disturbing to your father."

"I remember," Kit said. "He sent us away."

Her mother nodded grimly. "Yes, he did. And they killed him for it. Someone he trusted executed him, mob style."

Kit held her mother's hand. "I remember."

Catherine lapsed into thought. "He called me, and said he was meeting someone about the case, and then he was going to get a bite with one of his colleagues. He tried to protect me as much as possible. If the people he was looking for thought I knew, it would have put me in danger."

"Did he say where the meeting was?"

Catherine took a sip of her coffee. "Somewhere in DuPont Circle."

"I miss him, Mom." Christine spoke factually, almost without feeling.

"I do too," her mother replied. "Every day."

Christine paused. "I miss you too. Sometimes I feel like I've lost you. Why did you have to get so involved in the God thing? Why religion?"

Her mother smiled. "Not religion, Kitten. I dealt with a lot of fear when your father was murdered. But then, I found peace. The Holy Spirit comforts me all the time. It's not just a God 'thing,' Kitten. It's a relationship. He talks to me."

Christine sputtered. "God *speaks* to you? You do realize that's a symptom of schizophrenia, right? You're not going crazy on me, are you?"

Her mother laughed. "There is a reality to the spiritual realm, Kit. You can't tell me Joanna's dream wasn't right on the mark."

"Whatever, Mom," she answered. "Answer me this. How is it that the same God who let Dad be murdered, now wants to keep me safe? If He is the same God you talk about, and He can do anything; He could have prevented Dad's murder. So why didn't He?"

There was a sticky silence in the room for a moment.

Finally, Catherine Spada sighed. "Well, I don't know the answer to that question, Kitten. All I know is that my God doesn't kill. Jesus gives life. He gives *good* things. It will really help me, and yourself if you would just try not to blame Him for things He didn't do."

Almost an hour later, Kit and Jamey departed the Spada home. Both agents carried small Tupperware containers of both Russian Teacakes *and* Chocolate Chippers prepared by Cathy Spada. Each container was specifically marked for their co-workers in the D.C. office.

"Kit, please call me when you are on your way home, so we can eat together this evening," Catherine requested as Christine departed.

"I'll try, Mom," came the non-committal answer. "I just never know when that will be."

"I can call Ben Edwards and request a time if you like," her mother offered.

"No, please don't do that," Kit told her. "Please. Just let me do my job."

"You sound just like your father," her mother replied. "Give me a hug before you leave, now. Family traditions shouldn't ever die."

Chapter Twenty-Two

It was Monday morning before Detective Peter Lynch was able to get with Agent Joshua Martin, to delve back into investigating the Eastgate murders.

Somehow, the two sides of this case were tied together, Pete realized. He just couldn't see how, or where. It was becoming evident that ultimately, at the top of the flow chart, there was someone much bigger and more powerful than Benjamin Asami orchestrating the crimes.

Felipe's notepad was open on the table, with the notes of Christine's investigation directives prior to boarding the plane for Washington. Reading them over, Pete decided to create a sort of investigation map to help him answer the questions she had raised.

Christine's question #1. Why were the body parts in the hotel bathtub different temperatures?

Well, Pete considered, different temperatures would indicate different sources. Had some of the body parts been frozen, while some had been room temperature? Obviously, some had been cut apart in the hotel room. Had that been the source of the blood spatter? Where had the warmer parts come from?

He looked back at the Medical Examiner's report. All the pieces from one body appeared to have been previously frozen, or held in a cryogenic state. That had been the leg and arms and spine of Edward Glascow. Apparently, Mr. Glascow had disappeared in July of 1999. What was the day?

Here it was. Edward Glascow had been reported missing on July 26, 1999. What had his profession been? Who had he worked for? Why this guy?

Searching through the files, Pete found a few answers he wasn't expecting. He jotted down some notes.

Now, where had the warm body parts come from? Those would belong to more recent victims. The other three sets of body parts belonged to Andrew Thomasson, a twenty-five-year old stock broker, Jeremy Zarduc, a thirty-two year old automobile technician, and Vladimir Gocszinski, a twenty-nine year old wedding photographer.

No connections in their professions. And they were all different in their ages.

Hadn't one of the girls on the field office board been named Zarduc? He searched for the file. Yes, Sandy Zarduc. Here she was. Had come from a large family. She had been the youngest child. After her parents' divorce, she had lived alone with her mother. According to the file, her oldest brother, Jeremy, had disappeared about the same time she had been abducted. Perhaps the young man had seen what happened, and tried to rescue his sister? It was the best theory he had so far.

He searched for connections between others whose body parts had been in the Eastgate bathtub. Where had they all come from? He began to check Gocszinki's professional record. The man had fallen off the record books two years before his disappearance.

Had he been a photographer for these people, in one of the hub houses? He looked for and found the fingerprints discovered on the camera equipment at the house on East Biarritz. He ran a search to see if they were a match for Gocszinski. It appeared they were. Okay. So, yes, the guy *had* been a zombie at one point.

He moved on.

Who was Thomasson? Had his been a simple abduction? Or had he become involved and then become a problem to be disposed of like Gocszinski? And if he had been disposed of, how had a stock broker become involved with this group in the first place?

He looked into Thomasson's professional file. The man had worked at an investment firm downtown. Pete called the firm. Who were Andrew's clients, and what recent trades had the young man made just prior to his death? The office manager took Pete's questions, and provided emailed answers while they spoke on the phone.

Looking through the list of Andrew's clients, Pete made a few additional interesting discoveries. He added more notes to those he had previously jotted down.

Christine's question #2. Why would they use a hotel room, and not a more sterile facility?

Good question, Christine, Pete mused.

It seemed as though everything else about this case had been closeted; organized; methodical. Even down to the creating and printing of false pedigrees; the recruiting of widows from international diplomatic corps; the training of languages; the wiping, reprogramming and hypnosis of young women's minds.

Thinking it through, he realized. If the rest of this case had been as highly systematized and meticulous, then the use of a hotel room communicated the opposite.

Haste, panic; a lack of planning.

What had happened to cause these normally detailed criminals to react, rather than move according to plan?

What could have sparked such a reaction? And how had it all been missed by the housekeeping and management staff at the Best Western Hotel? Why that hotel? Had money changed hands? Had the criminals used the same location before?

Pondering, he decided to visit the hotel once more.

First, he re-examined the guest room where the bathtub discovery had been made. Walking through the Crime Lab's scenario in his mind, he double-checked the details as he understood them. Everything made sense so far, he decided.

Then, making his way to the hotel's office, he made arrangements to meet with the manager on duty at a local restaurant for coffee.

Arriving early, Pete decided to record the conversation. He set up his digital recorder, positioning it just behind the salt and pepper shakers, hidden by the bud vase filled with the flowers on the table.

The manager of the Best Western arrived almost half an hour late. He was shorter in stature than most American men, Pete noted. Was he Pakistani, or Indian, or perhaps from the Middle East? The agent stood as the man approached, extending his right hand.

"Thank you for coming, sir. My name is Detective Peter Lynch. I am working with the FBI."

"Hello," the man said, looking around. "My name is Ganesh Singh. I am manager at the Best Western. You are alone?"

"Yes, I am alone," Pete replied. "Mr. Singh, I just wanted a chance to speak with you about the unfortunate discovery the police made in your establishment a few weeks ago."

"Yes," Singh replied, sitting down on the booth. "That was truly unfortunate. Are you closer to solving the mystery?"

Pete assessed him. "I have hopes, but I really don't know," he replied, cautiously. "I was looking over the case, and I have discovered we still have some questions. I was hoping you might be willing to help me learn the answers."

"I will be glad to help you if I am able," the manager answered. "My family owns the hotel. I am an owner and the general manager. These murders were a tragedy which we are afraid will now mark our establishment for failure. The law of Karma has been broken, and the energy of the place is now filled with anger and death. I have seen our reservations go down since the discovery of the body pieces was on the television news."

"We are truly sorry for that negative publicity," Pete offered. "And I can tell you we will be glad to help in any way we are able. Can I ask you some questions?"

"Certainly."

"Do you trust everyone on your staff? Is it possible that money changed hands with someone who works for you, without your knowledge or your family's knowledge?"

The man faltered. "I don't know, truthfully. I thought everyone was trustworthy, but now I seem to be suspicious of all of them. We have never had a problem like this before."

Pete made a note. "I was told the security camera in that part of the hotel doesn't receive a signal. Did you disable the camera?"

Ganesh was honestly surprised. "I didn't know it wasn't working until someone called from your department. We have since investigated it, and replaced the camera. It is working now. It does appear that someone had tampered with the machine. But I don't know how long ago it happened."

Pete made another note. "Do you still have that camera? Do you think we could have it?"

"Certainly," Singh answered. "Please understand we have nothing to hide. I believe the old camera is still in the maintenance room."

"Thank you for your help, sir," he said.

"My sister, Kamini, is the over-night manager," he offered. "I think she might possibly have more information for you than I do." Before Pete realized what he was doing, Singh pulled out his cell phone, and made a call.

In perfect Hindi, he spoke on the telephone. Pete could hear a woman's voice coming through the earpiece, also speaking in Hindi. When the conversation ended, Ganesh smiled and closed his phone.

"Detective," he said. "On the day of the bathtub discovery, my sister says she was puzzled by several men who came into the hotel around two in the morning that day. Two of them were the men who had checked into the room the night before. They were pushing three steel boxes on wheels.

"She says she was working the desk that night. The men told her the boxes were full of medical supplies. She was sleepy, so she just went back to sleep. She said she forgot to tell me before."

Pete looked at him in surprise. "Are you sure?" he asked. "Stainless steel boxes on wheels? Did she say how big the boxes were?"

Ganesh answered. "She said like a four-foot cube. She said she had to leave the desk to help them find the service elevator, because the boxes were too bulky for the one in the lobby."

"I wasn't aware there was a service elevator," Pete told him.

"Oh, yes," Ganesh replied. "When someone needs to decorate for a wedding, or cater for a conference, we ask them to use that elevator."

"Is that elevator included in the security footage we already have?" the detective wanted to know.

359

Ganesh thought for just a moment. "Come to think of it, there is a small camera *in* that elevator. It is monitored in the kitchen, rather than in the security office. Would you like that video footage as well?"

Pete nodded. "Yes, sir, if you still have it," he replied. "That could give us the break we need on this case."

"It is less than sixty days ago, so we should still have it," the hotel owner told him. "My sister oversees the kitchen. I will ask her."

"Can I make an arrangement to speak with her?" Pete asked.

Ganesh was apologetic. "It is highly improper in our culture for our women to speak with a stranger who is a man," Ganesh answered.

"Even to a policeman?" Pete pressed.

"I will gladly convey her words to you," Singh answered. "If she wishes to come back in a better life, she must not dishonor herself."

"Can you call her back, please?" Pete asked.

Ganesh nodded, and complied dutifully. Again, he spoke in Hindi. He looked at Pete, "Kamini says 'what is your question?'"

"Is the service elevator footage still available? And secondly; Does she think she would be able to remember the men's faces if she saw them in a line-up, or a picture?"

Ganesh spoke, listened, and nodded to Pete. "Yes to both."

"Would she be willing to identify the men we have in custody, to help us find the criminals?"

Ganesh spoke, listened, and nodded to Pete again. He then spoke in Hindi once more. He looked at Pete. "She will come now," he said. He went back to speaking in Hindi, apparently telling his sister where to meet them.

"Thank you," Pete told him.

Ganesh shrugged. "My sister will be here in ten minutes."

They spoke for a few minutes until Kamini arrived. She greeted her brother, put her veil in place, and then nodded toward Detective Lynch. "I am glad to do whatever I can to help," she said to Ginesh, for Pete's benefit.

"What do we need to do?" Ginesh asked.

360

"I will meet you both at the Westwood Village Police Precinct," Pete told him. "Come to the fourth floor."

"We will see you there."

When he arrived back at the precinct, Pete was relieved to find Chase Stanford in the office. As the newest member of the taskforce, the young man received all kinds of assignments from his teammates. Today was no exception.

Had he run out of investigative tasks? Pete gave him one. Call every medical facility in the Greenway area that might have a sterile facility large enough for a surgery to take place. No, it didn't need to be a hospital, or a medical center. They were looking for facilities which were presently closed, or recently remodeled during the same week of the Eastgate bathtub discovery.

It had occurred to the detective that perhaps an unexpected repair or remodel might have caused a sudden relocation for the highly organized criminal network. It was worth checking out.

Pete then made his way to the County Correctional Facility to make arrangements for a line-up of those male detainees who had been involved in the case thus far.

As he waited in the observation room with Kamini and Ganesh, Detective Lynch ran over Christine Spada's third question in his mind.

Christine's question #3. Why were the edges of body pieces roughly cut and shredded, instead of cut cleanly with a scalpel?

Rough edges of separation also communicated haste. Or perhaps new workers. Or maybe just the loss of the criminals' usual surgical facility.

When he had spoken with the Crime Lab, the medical officer seemed to think the separation tool had been a chainsaw. But no one in the hotel had *heard* a chainsaw that night...

What else could leave a rough cut edge like that, and not make the noise of a chainsaw? He called the Crime Lab once more, finally speaking with a forensics officer named Cammie Jackson. She had been the one to suggest the idea of a chainsaw, she revealed.

But, when Pete mentioned to her the problem of noise in the hotel, she lapsed into deep thought.

"Okay, Detective Lynch," Cammie said. "If that isn't the implement used, I'll have to do some experimenting."

"When I interviewed the manager, he told me the hotel had been full that evening," Pete told her. "There were no complaints of noise or irregular behavior that night or even the night before. In fact, no one had a clue anything out of the ordinary had taken place, until the maid, Rosa, went in to clean the next day."

"Okay, Pete," Cammie replied. "Give me a couple of days to see which tool generated the patterns we noticed on the photos. Are the body parts still in the morgue?"

"Yes, ma'am, they are," Pete answered. "And oh, by the way, could you please check on the status of Cameron Boyd and his wife's autopsies?"

"Okay, Detective, I'll do some research and get back with you."

While Pete was on the telephone, hotel owner, Ganesh Singh, and his sister Kamini, arrived on Westwood Village's fourth floor, and were made comfortable in the observation room. As soon as Pete had ended his call with Cammie, he joined them.

Ganesh greeting him with a handshake. "Hello, Detective Lynch," he offered. "This is my sister Kamini."

"It's nice to meet you," Pete said. "Thank you for coming in to help us."

Kamini looked down at the ground, and did not reply. Her face below her eyes was veiled once more.

"She will speak to me, and I will speak for her," Ganesh informed him. "Also, she stopped at the hotel and made a copy of the service elevator security video."

Surprised, Pete responded. "Thank you! I will let you both know if we need anything else."

Then he turned his attention completely to the Hindu woman.

"Kamini," he explained, "we will be bringing out two different groups of men from the holding cells in the jail next door. The men will stand in line and face this window right here. The glass on their side looks like a mirror, so they will not be able to see you at all. The light in here will be off, and the lights in that room will be on.

"When all of the men are in position in that room, I will ask you to tell me which of them in the line you recognize. Use the numbers they hold up to identify them. Then, I will ask you to tell me where you saw them, and what they were doing."

"I can do this," Kamini said to her brother.

"Yes, you can," Pete replied.

In all, there were twelve men who had been detained so far in connection with the case they were working on. This meant there would be two groups of six shown in the line-up. As the third man in the first group entered the room, Kamini's involuntarily gasped, and put her right hand to her lips.

"You see something?" Pete asked.

She looked at her brother. "Number 3 was pushing one of the boxes that night."

She kept watching. When all of the first group was in place, Pete asked her to study their faces. Had she seen any of them besides Number 3?

Kamini looked carefully. "I am not sure, Ganesh, but I think Number 5 was there also. He had on a different hat. Could he take off his hat?"

Pete spoke into the microphone. "Number 5, please take off your hat."

Number 5 complied.

As he did, Kamini responded immediately. "Number 5 was there too," she said affirmatively.

"Are 3 and 5 the only ones you recognize from this group?" he asked. "Are you sure? Look carefully, please."

Kamini nodded. Ganesh replied. "Yes, she is sure."

Pete spoke into the microphone once more. "Okay, 3 and 5 remain. Second group please."

As the second group filed in, Kamini studied each face closely. She was silent for some time.

Pete watched her. What was she thinking, he wondered?

Finally, she looked at her brother. "Ganesh?" she said. "I think all of these men, except 8 and 10 were there that night."

"All of them?" Pete asked. "Are you sure?"

"I am absolutely sure," Kamini said to her brother.

Pete spoke into the microphone. "Return these men to their cells, please."

Looking down at the numbered list of detainees, the detective circled the numbers 3, 5, 7, 9, 11, and 12. As he did so, he circled those Kamini had identified, reviewing their descriptions:

3. Dr. Randall Whitmore, one of the two surgeons known to have been involved in the brokering of transplant organs, and in the trafficking scheme.

5. Garrett Jacobs, the front man. The charmer who then worked to wipe and reprogram.

7. Gerard Albertson, who had originally given his name as Landon Morrow at the house on East Biarritz. He was wanted by Scotland Yard for a long list of crimes, not the least of which was kidnapping.

9. Lieutenant Alexander Boyd, a presently suspended detective with the Westwood Precinct, who apparently had worked as muscle and informant for the criminals. He had murdered the entire Marshall family; father, mother, son and daughter. The murders of Boyd's brother, Cameron, and his wife were still being processed. The two children of that family were still unaccounted for.

11. Jim Phillips, a private courier of transplant organs. So far, his identity checked out, as did his story of being hired as a free-lance employee of BetterLife Pharmaceuticals, a medical supply company operating out of Boston, Massachusetts. To date, his background checks showed no priors, at least stateside. They were waiting on replies from Interpol.

12. Austin Caine, another private courier of transplant organs. Caine's stateside identity also checked out. However, Caine was working as a free-lance employee of NewBeginnings Medical, a supply company based in Seattle, Washington. He also had no priors, and was being held until they received replies from Interpol.

Pete found it interesting that the Chinese girl, Sung Li, had also identified Randall Whitmore and Gerard Albertson as being the men who had promised her a passport and a job in America. Apparently both men were world travelers.

And, interestingly enough, in pursuing the answers to Christine's third question, Pete realized that Ganesh and Kamini had answered the fourth. Yes, someone on the hotel staff recognized Dr. Randall Whitmore. Now for the fifth question.

Christine's question #5. Who was Dr. Amy Rutger? Where had she come from?

Sitting down at his desk, Pete dialed Felipe.

"Hello. Ramirez speaking."

"Hey, Fer -- I mean, Felipe. It's Lynch."

"Hey, Pete. What's going on?"

"I've been working on investigating the questions Christine mentioned to you, and I'm down to Amy Rutger."

"Yeah, the second surgeon."

"Have you done any preliminary work on that yet?"

"I did do a search. Let me get the notes. Here. She graduated from Duke, did her residency at Boston General, where she also finished a fellowship in thoracic medicine. She transferred to Johns Hopkins Teaching Hospital as an instructor in 1993. She became Chief of Surgery at Johns Hopkins in 1998. She retired at sixty in 2010. According to her Facebook page, she moved to Kenya, to work with a medical charity named "Health for Kenya" that same year."

"When did she begin to surface in relationship to The Parent Company?"

Felipe paused. "It's not clear. Since she was overseas beginning in 2010, she could have been involved in some way since then. I did send a request for her employment record with Health for Kenya, and we are waiting for their reply."

"Is there anything else about her we should know?" Pete asked.

"Well, I'm doing a search for family members and close associates now. So far, no aliases have surfaced. I'm also looking at the Health for Kenya organization, to see who runs it."

"You've done all that needs to be done, Felipe," Pete told him.

"We'll see," came the answer. "This case has more twists than a corkscrew. Just when I think I've figured something out, I am led to another bend in the road, leading elsewhere."

"It just keeps getting bigger, doesn't it?" Pete asked.

In the opposite corner of the Westwood Village Precinct, Chase had just finished calling every medical facility listed in the City of Greenway and surrounding communities. After hanging up the phone, he made wrote a note on a spreadsheet he was creating.

He looked across at Josh Martin. "Hey Josh," he said. "What are you doing here?"

"I just dropped by to pick up my mail. I have some bills due that I need to pay," Josh answered. "Do you know where they put my incoming paperwork?"

"Oh," Chase replied. "It's over there." He pointed to a basket on top of a filing cabinet with Josh's name on it.

The agent walked over to the file cabinet and brought the basket down to rifle through his mail. He began discarding junk mail, and pulling pertinent envelopes together.

"Hey Josh?" Chase asked. "I'm supposed to find medical and surgical facilities the trafficking ring might have used, or might still be using."

Preoccupied, Josh answered. "Okay."

Chase looked at him. "What other types of businesses have surgery rooms, or sterile places these people could use?"

"Like an operating room?" Josh asked.

"Yeah," Chase replied. "Exactly like that."

Josh stopped rifling and returned Chase's gaze. "Oral surgeons; where they take out wisdom teeth... Um.... Veterinarians do surgeries... And maybe some doctors' offices; you know, maybe one that has more than one doctor?"

"Those are good. Got any more?"

"What about industrial kitchens?" Josh asked. "They have stainless steel kitchens, so cleaning up could be made sterile."

"Thanks, Josh," Chase told him. "If you think of something else, call me?"

"Glad to," Josh answered, holding several envelopes between his teeth.

Chase sighed. He wasn't even near a finish line. And after speaking with Josh, there wasn't even a hint of one in sight.

Resigned, he began a new spreadsheet.

Chapter Twenty-Three

It was around three in the afternoon when the telephone rang on the fourth floor of the Westwood Village Precinct. Chase answered the call.

"Good afternoon, Officer Stanford speaking."

"Sir, I need to speak with someone from the FBI." It was a woman's voice.

"Yes, ma'am," Chase replied. "How can I help you?"

"I think my daughter is missing."

Chase snapped his fingers to get Josh and Pete's attention. He pointed to the phone he was holding too his ear. He put his hand over the mouthpiece, and whispered loudly.

"Another girl's missing. It's her mother."

"Can I have your name, please?"

"Maria Estavez," the woman replied. "My daughter's name is Camilla Estavez."

"How long has she been gone?" Chase asked.

"I really don't know," Maria answered, beginning to cry. "She left July 30 to go to her father's house in Argentina to visit for a few weeks. I was working out of town, from July 15 to today. My mother stayed at our home, and took Camilla to the airport to catch her plane on July 30.

"Then, because I wasn't home until today, Mama also went to pick her up at the airport yesterday. But Camilla wasn't on her plane. When she wasn't there, my mother waited until the government phone was working in the village where he is, and called my husband in Argentina. Carlos told her Camilla never arrived July 30."

"So she has been missing since July 30?"

"Yes, I think so."

"How old is Camilla, ma'am?"

"She is fourteen."

"Do you believe your husband is telling the truth?" Chase asked. "I mean, is it possible he is lying to you, and he just didn't send her home?"

She paused. "I don't think so. He is an engineer, and is working for the government there, building roads and bridges right now. Our marriage is good. Since it is difficult for him to find work here, he works there. We just need the money. Camilla is his joy."

"To tell you the rest; I called Delta Airlines. They also confirmed what he said. The airline has no record of her boarding the departing flight here in Greenway. She checked in at the front desk, but never arrived at the gate. Her luggage was checked, and travelled to Argentina, but was never picked up at El Plumerillo Airport."

"Was she supposed to call you when she arrived? Or send you an email?"

"Carlos is working in an area where there are almost no cell phone towers, or internet. He is staying in a small hut in a border village in the mountains."

"Mrs. Estavez," Chase responded. "Can you hold for a moment? I want to give you to a more experienced agent."

He looked at Josh. "Can you take this?" he asked.

Josh shook his head. "I have to get back to Asami Motors. I've already been here longer than I should be." He looked at Pete as he stood up to leave, mail in hand.

"Sure." Pete nodded, and picked up the phone. "Hello? Mrs. Estavez? This is Detective Peter Lynch."

For the next half hour, Pete took down information regarding the missing girl. He also made an appointment to meet the mother at her home to search for evidence.

On his way to the Estavez home, Pete considered the case. Fourteen year old Camilla's abduction was different from those they had encountered so far in this investigation. Had others been kidnapped in this way, he wondered? He would make sure to get a photo ID and something to provide DNA for the investigation, just in case.

Then, still driving, Pete called the Greenway Airport Administrative Offices. He alerted the security office to the abduction which had taken place almost five weeks prior. He also requested a copy of all surveillance videos in the passenger and TSA areas of the International Concourses and Gates from July 30 be sent to the Westwood Precinct FBI office.

Close to five that afternoon, Joshua Martin made two phone calls. The first was to Felipe.

"Hey, Felipe. This is Josh."

"You'll never believe who I just saw."

"Yeah. Lina Asami is back in the country. She just walked into the Dealership. And she has *both* of her kids with her; Annette *and* Adrien."

"I know. That's what I thought too. No one let us know it had been resolved."

"Yes, the boy *was* kidnapped. Maybe they let him go."

"That's true. Maybe she paid a ransom."

"No, I don't see Benjamin Asami anywhere."

"Okay. I'll pick up a burner phone, and call him, and see what happens."

"Martin out."

Psychologist, Dr. Jim Ainsworth, and social worker, Sarah McMillan, were sharing a quiet cup of coffee in a family conference room. The Behavioral Health Center on the twentieth floor of Ginsberg Memorial Hospital was very quiet this time of night. No group sessions or workshops took place after six at night.

All residents were in their rooms.

All medical personnel were centered at the floor's nurses' station, or in the small kitchen and snack area attached to it.

As of late, Dr. Jim had been using the family conference room as his place to conduct therapy sessions for those who had been traumatized by the shooting. He was still in recovery himself; unable to leave the hospital.

Tonight, Ainsworth's focus was Sarah. She had been having recurring nightmares the past three nights; reliving the day of her shooting. In every dream, she saw the shooter's face, and a knife came down, but rather than cut her in the face, it cut her in the neck, severing her jugular. Then a machine gun opened fire, shredding the shower curtain. Every time the dream presented itself, she woke up in a full sweat.

Sarah's surgical wounds had been healing quickly. She had been nightmare free immediately following the shooting. But, on the day her stitches were removed, she took a long awaited warm shower. That evening, the nightmares had begun. Panic attacks and struggles with temporary paranoia had started the same day.

Ainsworth had provided Sarah with some self-regulating exercises to help her in dealing with the sudden and unexpected daggers of fear within her own mind. But now, how could she stop the recurring dreams?

"Thank you, Dr. Jim," she told him. "Hopefully I'll feel a little more equipped the next time this happens."

"There's nothing wrong with taking a little medication to help you sleep," he told her. "Especially right now, when your defenses are down, and your weaknesses are so prevalent in your thinking."

"I will consider meds," she told him. "Can I ask you a question?"

"Sure."

"You finished the Psychological Evaluation on Caleb Jacobs, right?" she asked.

Ainsworth nodded. "Yes. And I did an academic placement assessment as well."

"What were your findings?" Sarah asked.

Jim smiled. "According to Detective Lynch's notes from speaking with Caleb's father, Garrett Jacobs, the boy is around ten years old."

"Ten?" she replied. "That explains a lot for me. I *knew* he was older than seven."

"He is actually an old soul, if you ask me," the psychologist confessed. "Some of his observations indicate a greater emotional development than most boys his age."

"I've noticed that as well," Sarah agreed.

"Honestly, I expected him to have Obsessive Compulsive Disorder, or, at the very least, some type of Generalized Anxiety Disorder. I thought he probably had developed ticks, some kind of schizophrenia or fragmentation due to his environmental influences, and lack of bonding.

"He does have abandonment issues, but no sociopathic tendencies, which is surprising. Due to Caleb's bonding development delays, there is some difficulty with emotional labelling, but that is to be expected. His trust issues run deep. When he gets past his issues of trust, he does typically respond with empathy, which is unusual. However, his personal sense of destiny and purpose is very low. I believe we have a limited window of time to help him develop strong personal values and people skills. We have a lot of work to do."

"Speaking of his trust issues," Sarah said, "I have one thing I would like to take care of before he goes through his surgeries. His recovery will be long and difficult, and I think he needs a few positive memories to hold onto during his recuperations."

"What do you have in mind?" Dr. Jim asked.

"He has asked me several times about going to the zoo," she answered. "I told him I would take him. I was planning to do it the same week the shooting took place, so it was delayed."

Jim tapped his chin with the pen he was holding, thinking. "Let me work on something," he told her. "When is the surgery scheduled?"

"They are waiting on a pediatric surgeon from Texas to arrive. The examining orthopedic was concerned due to what he called "severe angulation" in both femur bones, and both arms. Caleb also has severe scoliosis, because he has had to compensate so drastically when he sits down. For that reason, they want to try spinal surgery as well at some point. But they are going to repair the damage he has experienced in his limbs first."

"I see," Ainsworth replied. "That means we have a deadline. I wonder if the Make-A-Wish Foundation would be able to help."

"That's a good idea!" Sarah responded. "I will begin making calls tomorrow."

"And I'll work toward a few things on my end," Dr. Jim told her.

The sparkling, white buildings comprising the Sanitarium's grounds gleamed brightly in the late afternoon sun. The deep, blue, Therapy Pool was shaded by tall palm trees bordering the property. Lush, green, manicured, Exercise Areas were congregated with wheelchair-bound, and recovering ambulatory patients. Each resident had been assigned an individual, medical staffer.

Presently, each twosome was preparing to enter the Refectory for the evening meal. Live classical music could be heard, emanating from the large dining facility. Formally-clad serving staff could be seen through the large windows, scurrying to light candles on the tables, prepping each table for the Patient Supper Hour.

The staff at Avenir-Sain Centre de Restauration *(Healthy Future Restoration Center)* were all well-educated. To be bi-lingual was a prerequisite, with English being one of the languages spoken. In addition, each staffer also held medical credentials as a registered nurse, a licensed physician, or, was a medical student.

In this area of Switzerland, most everyone spoke French.

The Therapy Pool was filled with patients involved in a Rehabilitative Stretching Class. In the midst of a quick conference with their instructor, the Sanitarium's Director observed the progress of those in the water.

"All of them seem to be moving forward today," the instructor offered.

"Yah, I see," the Director replied. "I need your help with a new patient when you finish here, please."

"Oh? A man or a woman?"

"A man. He signed himself in."

"Is he in the Lower Level?"

"Yes, in the Research Lab."

"I will be there as soon as we finish here, Dr. Hern."

Dr. Inga Hern turned to walk back to the Sanitarium's main building. "Thank you," she spoke back over her shoulder.

The instructor watched her go. "Wonder what you'll have me working on today?" he murmured.

Dr. Inga Hern had been the Director of Avenir-Sain for the past ten years. She was the great-granddaughter of Dr. August Hern, infamous Nazi doctor of Auschwitz. Inga loved her great-grandfather dearly, and sincerely believed he had been sorely misjudged by the world.

Why, he had made the most of a difficult situation, hadn't he? He had collected thousands of human heads during the war, enabling him to conduct important "anthropological and anatomical studies."

As a child, little Inga had considered her great-grandfather a brilliant man. Since his death, she had tried to learn as much about him as possible. It had become her firm belief he had furthered medicine in his day. Why, under Adolf Hitler's direct orders, he had discovered a method for distilling cyanide from the pesticides of his day. He had then developed cyanide pills and gas for use with Jewish prisoners in the death chambers of Auschwitz, and other Nazi death camps.

Besides, she reasoned, didn't multiple nations and espionage agencies use those same pills and gas today?

This week, she had discovered she was more like her great-grandfather than she had ever thought possible. A week before, body parts of more than eighty Jews had been found in a Strasbourg laboratory. The body parts had been used by her great-grandfather for experimentation in the forties.

Why couldn't the world see?

He had added so much knowledge of the human body to the international practice of medicine as a result of his studies. As a direct descendant, she had even formally requested several jars of the specimens in Strasbourg be donated to the Sanatorium. As of yet, she had received no reply.

August Hern had been a great man, she reasoned. An SS captain, and chairman of the Reich University in Strasbourg, he had saved test-tubes containing a stomach and intestines belonging to an unnamed victim. He had been studying the effects of the gas chambers on the human frame when he died.

No wonder German medicine was globally superior, she considered.

Emerging from the elevator on the Lower Level, Dr. Inga Hern ran her ID badge through the scanner. As soon as the scanner cleared her, a small window opened automatically. A female computer voice spoke: "Welcome, Dr. Hern. Retinal scan, please."

Inga took the required position. When the computer was satisfied, double doors into the Research Lab opened, allowing her entrance through the glass walls.

Walking through the doors, she made her way to the back wall, where a cell's locked, steel door waited. Sliding open the feeding window in the steel door, she viewed her patient.

Quiet as a lamb.

She drew a large ring of keys from her lab coat. Unlocking the door, she entered.

The man lay on a twin cot against the far wall. His right wrist was handcuffed to the metal headboard. Pulling out the chair from a table against the near wall, she sat down, and pulled out a small pad of paper.

"We have almost completed your intake examination," she said. "I just have a few more questions."

The man on the bed groaned. "Why are you doing this?" he asked, his voice hoarse and raspy.

"You came to us, remember?" Inga answered, with a shrug. "You signed your own admission papers. To provide money to your family no doubt. Such is the reason for most of our residents."

"I didn't sign willingly," the man protested. "You know this, Inga. Let me go."

"Now, now, Benjamin, don't back out on me now," Dr. Hern cooed. "We already have the tests prepared for you."

Asami shuddered. He had heard of MedSafe's "donated specimens for live genetic testing." But he had never given thought to what happened to those people.

"Wh-what are you going to do to me?" he asked.

"We aren't planning to do anything with you that hasn't been tried before," she answered with a faint smile. "And, if you survive, we will allow you to leave, and still pay your family."

A knock was heard on the steel door.

"Come in," Inga answered nonchalantly.

The instructor from the Therapy Pool stuck his head inside the room. "Is this where you need me to be, Director Hern?" he asked.

"Oh, Coonan," she replied. "Come on in. I'd like you to meet our newest volunteer for the Program."

She motioned to the instructor. "Gregory Coonan, this is Mr. Benjamin Asami. Mr. Asami is a former associate of The Parent Company, and now he is no longer one of us. Mr. Asami, this is Gregory Coonan, from New York City in your country. You might know him better as David Fletcher. He used to be your chauffeur.

"Mr. Coonan is a Life Management Expert, and he is on loan to me from the Irish Mob. He has been an associate with the Parent Company for more than ten years. Now, I know he might be a little scary at first, but please believe me when I tell you he is a really nice guy."

Asami opened his eyes, and stared at the man. "Hello, David," he said. "I didn't know you worked with these people."

Coonan laughed. "It's Greg, Ben. But we'll be spending lots of time together. We will renew our acquaintance."

Inga pulled out the handcuff keys from her pocket, and moved towards the headboard. As she moved to reposition the handcuffs so she could open them, she gave orders to Coonan.

"Gregory, dear, would you please go and get the yellow plastic case of syringes we prepared yesterday from the refrigerator?"

"Yes ma'am," he replied, moving out of the room.

"Now, Benjamin," she began. "In order for our research to be recognized as accurate, it is vital we certify you are in excellent physical condition when we begin our testing. Can you sit up, please?"

Coonan re-entered the room. She continued speaking as she examined the patient.

"Your eyes look good. Your ears are clear." She put a stethoscope on his back. "Please take several deep breaths for me."

Asami complied.

"You are all right," she told him.

"But I don't feel good," the patient protested.

"You're just trying to delay things."

"No, really…. My throat is really sore."

She patted his arm. "Benjamin, you are in the peak of health. You will be just fine. Now, we are going to begin giving you a protocol of injections. I'm going to let you in on what we are doing in our testing, because I need your full cooperation in the process. As we move forward, you will need to communicate with me. Tell me what changes happen in your thinking, and in how you feel. That way, we will know if we are being successful in the process."

"What are you trying to do? Is this a new form of torture?" Asami asked.

Inga laughed lightly. "Oh, nothing like that," she cooed. "Right now, our company is trying to learn how to match animal and human DNA. Or, at least discover those animal species which are compatible with human DNA. So far, we've been successful in some regards. However, we still have a long way to go if we are to meet our goals and those of The Parent Company."

"Wh-what are those goals?" Asami asked.

She smiled coquettishly. "Why, to build a Master Race, of course. You have worked with us so long, and still you are unaware of our purposes? No wonder you failed The Parent Company."

She looked at Gregory. "Hold him, Gregory," she ordered.

Coonan complied, coming behind Asami to take the man into a wrestling hold. It wouldn't have mattered, however. From lack of food and water, Asami was too weak to resist.

Inga Hern took up the first syringe, and jabbed it into the man's arm. It apparently burned going in, because Asami whimpered profusely. Consecutively, Inga emptied five syringes. Then, she handed him a lollipop.

"I'm sorry," she said. "The only flavor I have at the moment is cherry. I hope that is all right with you. We will be back in two hours with some food and another series of injections."

Asami looked at her, rubbing his left wrist where the handcuff had dug in. "Could you leave me some water, please, Dr. Hern?" he asked.

She kept her focus on Benjamin. "Gregory, would you get Mr. Asami some water, please?"

Coonan left the room once more. When he returned with water, Inga left. Gregory sat down on the chair where Inga had been.

"How are you feeling, Mr. Asami?" he asked, in the same tone he had used when working as the family's limo driver.

Back in Greenway, Felipe had set the network computer to begin a search for all background information for the present Greenway Police Captain, Allen Edwards.

As the field office main computer searched, Felipe moved on to the team's next project, utilizing a laptop. For several days now, he had been working to set up a telephone surveillance system utilizing burner phones, and recording equipment. The phone numbers from which the calls came would be untraceable, bouncing from one continent to another throughout the duration of the call.

Josh and Pete had joined him in this endeavor. Josh would be making the calls, and Pete would be monitoring the connections. Felipe would monitor the computer feeds.

"Ready?" Felipe asked them both.

The two men nodded.

"Here we go." Felipe dialed the first number. "1-800-MY-BRIDE."

Josh took the telephone. He mentally prepared his acquired accent. The phone rang three times. Felipe began to trace the call, seeking to pinpoint the actual location of the number.

"Good evening, 800-MY-BRIDE," a woman's voice answered. "How may I direct your call?"

"Yes, I was calling regarding the classified ad I found in the back of one of my periodicals," Josh stated, sounding like a European high-brow.

"Yes?"

"I am interested in finding a wife," Josh explained. "Is there another number I should call, or could you direct me to someone who could help me?"

"Oh, yes sir," came the reply. "Hold just one moment, and I'll connect you."

"Thank you," Josh answered.

As the line went to a holding pattern, Vivaldi played through the speaker. Then, a man's voice came to the phone.

"Good evening. This is Landon Morrow. How may I serve you?"

"Hello," Josh said. "I am calling about a classified ad I read in the back of one of my periodicals."

"Which advertisement did you read?" the man asked.

"It said I could find a wife through your company."

The man chuckled. "Oh, yes. You most definitely *can* find a wife through our organization. We will make every effort to find the perfect woman just for you. It is our hope to procure a girl who fits with your very soul."

"That sounds very positive," Josh said.

"Let me gather some information from you, if I may," the man claiming to be Landon Morrow requested.

"Absolutely."

"What is your name?"

Josh picked up the profile Felipe had spent weeks creating. It was a good thing he had printed it out for him, Josh realized.

"I am Lord Sigmund Hummel, Earl of Denmark and Chief Counselor to the King," he read.

"What type of wife are you looking for?" Landon asked.

"I'm not sure what you mean by that," Josh replied. "Could you explain?"

"All right, I understand this process may be new to you. Let me take you through the checklist."

"Thank you."

Morrow paused. "How old are you?"

"Forty-two."

"How old would you like your bride to be, assuming we can find someone in your category?"

"I'm middle aged, but I have never been married, and would still like to have children before I am too old. A woman my own age will not be willing to have babies, I don't think."

"So, you'd like a younger woman. Say, in her twenties?"

"That sounds like a good idea," Josh said.

"I assume you would like her to have a solid pedigree, with no criminal record, and be well-versed in social graces," Landon suggested.

"Is it still possible to find such a woman?" Josh asked.

"There are additional fees for specialized requests," came the reply.

"Oh, I see. What are your fees, by the way?"

"The basic bride can be procured for one million."

"Euros, I assume?"

"Yes, by wire transfer only. That is our policy."

"I understand," Josh told him. "That would not be a problem."

"Specialized requests are additional to the basic fee," Landon continued. "And we will need half down as a deposit, to secure your place. Women of this caliber are difficult to find. So, we put all of our resources together to concentrate on your need alone until we find her."

"I see," Josh replied. "That sounds reasonable enough."

"Now," said Landon. "I am going to read off a list of questions regarding your preferences. Please answer each question as concisely as you can."

"All right."

"Are you ready, Mr. Hummel?"

"Yes, sir."

"Eyes?"

"Blue."

"Height?"

"Around 5' or a little taller."

"We already did age. Hair?"

"Blonde."

"Nationality?"

"European, if possible."

"Languages?"

"Some Danish would be nice. But I do speak English."

"Sexual history?"

"I would prefer as little as possible."

"Yes, sir. Would you prefer a virgin?"

"Is that a choice I can make?"

"It is a little more difficult, but it can be managed."

"I see," Josh replied. "I assume there would be an extra fee for a virgin?"

"Another million."

There was a pause in the conversation.

"Mr. Hummel? Are you still there?"

"Uh, yes. I'm here. It just sounds too good to be true."

"No, sir," Morrow responded. "We are just that good. I can name some of our satisfied clients, if you wish. And, I encourage you to make telephone calls to our referrals. We guarantee your happiness for at least one year. And we promise the woman will be arrive ready, anticipating your romantic life with her."

"I think I'm definitely interested in utilizing your services to find a bride." Josh told him.

"Excellent! You won't regret it! May I get a valid email address, where I can send you the information for the deposit's wire transfer, and our references?"

"And how much is the deposit?"

"Just five hundred thousand today. The rest is due upon delivery."

"Delivery?"

"Yes," Landon told him. We hand deliver each bride, accompanied by a bodyguard. The bodyguard stays with her, to keep her safe in her new environment, until one week after your wedding."

"That is absolutely agreeable," Josh replied. "If I receive positive information from your references, and I am still inclined to do business with you, what will I need to do to fully begin the process?"

"You will need to provide us a wedding date, at least four months away. That allows us time to search for your perfect woman and prepare her just for you. During that time, we will also do a background criminal check on you. We want each of our brides to be placed in suitable environments. If we must procure a bride for a man, say, of a criminal nature, there are additional fees involved."

"I totally understand," Josh told him. "My email is *earlsigmundhummel@danske.gov*. I will be looking forward to hearing from you."

"Thank you, Mr. Hummel. I am excited we will be able to do business together. Good-bye."

"Good-bye."

As soon as the call terminated, Pete let out a whoop.

"We're in!" he cried.

"Well, not quite yet," Felipe told him. "By now, they are googling Mr. Hummel, and discovering the photos we planted on the Danish Royals' website. The royal family has been very cooperative in helping us, since rescuing women involved in trafficking is one of the queen's many philanthropic endeavors. They added our words and photos to their website, and even added a short biography of Earl Sigmund Hummel to the site, with pictures.

"Are we taking this one all the way to a sting?" Josh asked.

"I hope so," Felipe replied. "Well done! Okay, you guys ready for the second call?"

Josh and Pete traded equipment. "Just in case they record and search for matching voice prints on calls," Felipe had told them.

"Sure," said Pete, "picking up the phone once more.

Felipe dialed the number: 1-800-MED-SAFE. The phone rang twice, and Felipe began the trace.

"Good evening. This is MedSafe International. How can I serve you?" This time a man's voice had answered.

"Yes," Pete began. "I am interested in obtaining several cadavers for a medical conference our hospital is conducting in a few weeks."

"Hold please while I connect you to that department."

A woman's voice spoke. "MedSafe Educational. This is Emily. How may I help you?"

"Hi, Emily," Pete replied. "I am interested in obtaining several cadavers for a medical conference we are having in a few weeks."

"Oh, yes, sir," Emily answered. "Is this for a demonstration of surgical skills, or for a practice environment?"

"What is the difference?"

The woman giggled. "Well, in a *demonstration* setting, you only need one cadaver, because everyone in the room except the teacher will be *watching* the procedure and taking notes. In a *practice* environment, there should be enough cadavers for each surgical student to have their *own cadaver* for a complete learning experience.

"If that isn't possible, or the cost exceeds your budget, we have dealt with educational settings who provide one cadaver for two participants in the past. Those participants then work on one cadaver as a team. Smaller schools and conferences might have teams of three or four learning from one cadaver. We don't recommend teams greater than four, simply because the entire purpose is about hands-on learning, and the students need to actually try the procedures they are taught."

"I see," Pete replied. "How much is one cadaver?"

"Twelve hundred euros."

"I see." Pete paused as though he was taking notes. "Now, there are some other items I need as well for the same medical conference. Do you provide discounts of any kind for bulk orders?"

"I'm sorry, sir. Our prices are already lower than most, and we are an internationally providing company."

"Where do your cadavers come from?"

"Oh," Emily replied. "We are different from most cadaver providing companies, in that we are completely invested in the lives of the families who donate to our organization. Just so you know,

384

we are a completely donation-based organization. Every cadaver comes with the story of the person whose body is being donated. Also accompanying the cadaver is the person's complete medical history, and an account of how they died."

"That's very complete," Pete told her. "What is the cost for body parts, such as a leg, or an arm, for surgical training in regard to tissue transplants, veins and arteries?"

"We recommend each student be provided with their own human limb for learning. Have you considered our soft plastic models?"

"We already have those," Pete told her. "These students are advanced, and already licensed. We are simply honing their surgical skills. The class is: "How to Complete an Arterial Transplant."

"Well, human limbs also come with the same paperwork we supply with each cadaver. There are no scars or tattoos on any of our limb products. Legs are four hundred apiece. Arms are three hundred apiece. Do you want to place an order?"

"I do," Pete replied. "However, I need to go back to the board now, and defend my budget request."

Emily laughed. "We hear that all the time," she told him. "I'm so glad I was able to help you. Do you have any other questions?"

"No," he told her. "I think I have all the information I need for the moment. Thank you."

"No, sir. Thank you. Have a great day."

"You too."

When the calls were completed, the three men looked at each other in amazement.

"Don't *they* sound legit?" Josh said mockingly.

"Well," Felipe said. "That was informative. I wonder who provides most of their donations."

Chapter Twenty-Four

"Well, there's my girl!"

The booming, baritone voice of Deputy Director Ben Edwards carried across the entire department floor. He stood at his office door, watching Christine exit the elevator with Agent Jamey Donaldson. As she made her way through the maze of desks, friends she had worked with in D.C. stood, or walked over to say "hi." For that reason, it took more than twice as long to travel to Deputy Director Edwards' office. When she did finally arrive, she gave him a good hug.

"Good afternoon, Ben," she greeted him. "It's good to be here again."

"It's good to have you back home," he told her. "Did you have a good visit with your mom?"

Christine nodded faintly. "Yes, I did." She looked at him. "I have to ask. Why did you have me stay with her this visit?"

The Director looked around the floor. "Come on into the office," he invited. "We have a lot to talk about."

Ben indicated two empty chairs in front of his desk. "Sit down, guys," he said.

"Jamey, I called you in, because I want you to help Christine with this investigation from this point onward. Felipe Ramirez has been keeping me up to date with the taskforce's investigation to this point, but I know there are details you will be able to recall. Facts that will help her team in putting the pieces together to wrap this case up, and take us to the next level."

He leaned up against his desk, his arms folded. "Kit, to answer your question; I had you stay with your mother, because I think she knows some things about this case, but doesn't realize it. They are locked away in her grief over your father's murder."

He paused. "You do realize this case against The Parent Company began here in D.C., don't you?"

Christine looked at him carefully. "No, sir, I didn't know that. Is that why you assigned it to me?"

Ben shook his head. "No. We had no idea these were the same people your father was closing in on sixteen years ago. And there weren't enough similarities in the D.C. case and the missing girls in Los Angeles when we opened the present investigation ten years ago. But now, seeing the connections, I wonder if I should pull you off, for your own safety."

Christine's thoughts went to her deceased father.

"Little Andrea Lockwood," Kit murmured.

"She was fifteen, and the case hit him hard," Ben told her. "It was like he was looking for his own child."

"I remember," she replied. "The week before my birthday, he was gone every night. In the mornings, before I left for school, he would talk to me about her. He warned me to be careful, and not to respond if someone I didn't know tried to talk to me."

"Do you remember him pulling you from school the week *after* your fifteenth birthday party?" Ben asked.

"Yes, I do," she answered. "But he and Mom told me it was an extra special birthday present. It was a treat to stay at my grandmother's home in Virginia Beach. I remember going for a walk on the beach every day. And then, Mom came to get me."

"When did she tell you?"

Christine looked down at the floor. "She told me on the drive home," she murmured. "We cried together. Mom started changing after that. Sometimes it's like I don't even know her."

"Do you remember what she told you?"

Kit considered for a moment, and then answered carefully, trying to make sure she had the facts straight.

"She said Dad he had been working on a case having to do with a missing girl. He had been trying to find some very dangerous people. I asked her if they were the same people who had stolen Little Andrea Lockwood, and she started to cry. We had to pull the car over to the side of the highway. We sat there awhile. Just quiet, you know?

"Then she said Dad had been found in an alley off of Dupont Circle, somewhere around the Jamaican Embassy. He had been shot twice in the head, and once through the heart. After she told me, she held me and let me cry."

"Did she tell you *how* he died?"

Christine reached for a tissue, and blew her nose, and dabbed tears away. "Not then. I think I researched it during the time I was assigned to the police force here on patrol."

Ben leaned forward, and took her hand. "Christine, did your mother ever tell you the *real* reasons why your Dad pulled you from classes the week after your birthday?"

Surprised, Kit shook her head. "No. Was there more to it than I was told?"

Ben stood up to walk around his desk and sit in his executive chair. "Yes, Angel, there were. The Parent Company threatened to kill you *and* your mother if Tony didn't back off the case. He called me, and I joined him, with Derek, his partner, in the investigation. He also asked Eric Janzen, whom you said is now beginning to help your team in Greenway.

"We all worked together on the case until your Dad's death.

"The week he was found dead, this organization – they now are calling themselves 'the Parent Company -- just seemed to drop off the face of the earth. The hub house, or what they now apparently call a 'Creation Center', was blown up the day after his death. I don't remember how many died. Biggest load of C4 I've seen; before or since."

"Then, when they surfaced in Los Angeles five years later, none of us realized they were the same people. So we didn't put it together until your team sent one of the first reports on this case last week. The Parent Company seems to be very skilled at covering their tracks.

"By the time we realized what was happening, they had exploded into the monstrosity we are dealing with now."

Kit looked at him. "I don't remember Daddy's partner. His name was Derek?" she asked. "Is he still on the force for D.C.?"

"He is," Ben answered. "He's a Captain now, and heads up part of District 3."

Christine shuddered. "That's a rough area," she commented.

Ben nodded. "Yeah, it is. And it's in an area of the city where a lot of international crime seems to take place. But Derek's been on the force in the city for so long, he seems to know just about everyone. His experience gives him a heads-up; a foot in the door with people."

"Happy for him," she said.

"I'd like you to meet him," Ben told her.

"Absolutely," Kit answered. "Whatever will help."

"So, here's what I need from you this weekend," her mentor continued. "I need you to talk about your father's death with your mom, and make note of anything she might mention we don't already know. At the moment, the Parent Company has mushroomed somehow, into a huge conglomerate. They have a lot of fingers, in a lot of pots. That means we have a lot of unraveling to do. In the end, everything hopefully will lead us back to one person, or one group of people who are in responsible for all of this. The trafficking and the medical supplies are obviously connected. I do think they are different arms of the same conglomerate.

"I don't mind if you and your people continue to investigate the medical supply side, since I know Detective Davies is still undercover. We eventually will solve that side of things. But right now, I want us to work on giving the parents of missing girls some closure. We need to focus on closing down this systematized system of abducting young women in our cities.

"Which brings me back to the Andrea Lockwood case. While you are staying at your mother's, try to see what she remembers your father talking about; things he might have said about the case off-handedly. See what she remembers about discoveries he might have mentioned, or if your father mentioned anything he was afraid of during that time.

"I've been talking with her a lot more lately. She's more fragile than you realize. So, try not to get into conflict with her. We're coming up on your birthday, and also...."

"The anniversary of Dad's murder," Christine finished, with a murmur.

"There are a few more things I need to fill you in on," Ben continued. "But I think that's all we need to cover for today."

"Okay," Kit answered. "By the way, Pete Lynch wanted me to ask a favor of you, before I forget."

"What is it?" Ben asked.

"He is concerned that our new Police Captain at Westwood Village might be a covert member of The Parent Company. He wanted to know if you could run a background check for us."

Ben smiled. "Are you worried about the man?"

"I don't enough about Westwood Precinct to be worried," Christine told him. "Pete's been on the force for a long time, and I trust his instincts. He keeps telling me the Captain doesn't fit with the men; that he seems a little off; like he has his own agenda. Especially when we ask for his input on this case."

"I see," Edwards replied. "Sure. I'll look into it. Pete sounds like he'll make a good agent."

"I like him," Christine confessed. "He's a little rough around the edges, but he's a great guy."

Felipe carried his breakfast and coffee into the field office. He had decided to go through emails before beginning his research projects for the day.

The first email in the queue was from Background and Identity. The subject line read "Dr. Amy Rutger."

Felipe opened the report, and read it.

Then he picked up his phone. It rang three times.

"Spada here."

"Christine, its Felipe."

"Hey fiancé of mine!" she kidded him. "What's up?"

"The identity history search came back on Dr. Amy Rutger, and it's pretty eye-opening."

"What does it say?" she asked.

"Well," he continued, "she married in 1993, during her time at Johns Hopkins. When she married, she kept her maiden name, for whatever reason. She married a Dr. Gordan Asami, Chief of Staff at Mercy Medical Center, also based in Baltimore. The couple had one child, a son; Benjamin Rutger Asami, who presently lives and works in Greenway."

Christine was silent for a moment.

"Kit? You there?"

"Yeah," she answered slowly. "So were both of his parents involved with The Parent Company? Or just her? Did Benjamin hook her into it, or did she hook her son?"

"I know. What came first, the chicken or the egg? There's no telling," he answered. "I can do some checking if you like..... And oh, Asami's wife, Lina, is back in Greenway, with *both* children, but without her husband. Apparently, she came back with a coffin, and is planning a memorial service."

"Something's up there," Christine answered. "Are we sure Asami is dead?"

"Josh has been doing surveillance over there this week," Felipe told her. "How's the trip going?"

"It's going well," she responded. "Director Edwards is sending me home with another agent. His name is Jamey Donaldson."

"I know him!" Felipe exclaimed. "He was in the Chicago field office, right?"

"Yes, that's him. Seems like a good guy."

"He's really good, Kit," he told her. "He's had a lot of field training too. And he's good at languages."

"Sounds like he might be a fit," she commented.

"I think so. Say, do you know yet why Ben wanted you to come up there in person?"

"I'm getting an idea," Kit answered. "I'll have to wait 'til I get back there to talk about it."

"Got it. Hope your day is great."

"You too. Thanks. He's got me staying with my mother. Spada out."

In Interrogation Room One, Pete sat with Franko Kovac, working through the binders of mugshots on file. Nothing so far.

"Mr. Kovac," Pete asked. "Can you tell me what happened this morning?"

"They came after the breakfast rush," Franko told him. "They said my sister had been arrested, and it was my fault. I have no idea what they are talking about. They say because I park truck in front of Federal Judicial Building, I have become spy for American government. I am not even yet a citizen."

"I understand," Pete replied. "What is your sister's name?"

"She is Katika. Katika Knesevic," Franko answered. "When we live in Croatia, she was big, important person. She work for ... how you say..... Military Security and Intelligence Agency. She was good person then. She get in trouble in 2005, because they see her kill man with hands for no reason. She did work for government to redeem herself. She is good with gun, and with computer.

"She try to kill me many times. I finally run to America. She became spy, and now works for ... for opak... no, how you say in English ... evil.... Dah, now, she is evil."

Listening to Franko, Pete's mind had been fueled into overdrive. The background check on the fake Annabelle Carnes had come back as Katika Knesevic.

Was this a coincidence, he wondered, *or had the last raid, on the house on Biarritz, caused a chain reaction in the organization they were trying to shut down? And if that was so, how had the fake Annabelle sparked an attack on this man from inside the Correctional Center?*

"Excuse me," Pete told him. "Let me do a little checking, and I'll be right back. "Can you wait, please?"

"Dah," the man nodded. "I wait. No problem."

On the fourth floor of the Westwood Village Police Precinct, Chase and Felipe were working through the completed spreadsheets Chase had built over the past few days. Overall, there were more than one hundred locations in Greenway with built-in facilities where surgery of some type could be completed. During his investigation, Chase had called many more than one hundred.

The spreadsheets reported stats only for surgical facilities which had been undergone remodeling during the month of the Eastgate murders. Chase had created a separate, comprehensive list of all the locations he had called, the date, and the person he had spoken with. Felipe was now helping him to narrow the list of possibilities down, using search factors.

"We need to remove all the buildings you have on those sheets that don't have an entrance ramp, and elevator from the list," Felipe told him.

"Okay." Chase moved his hand down the spreadsheet columns indicating entrance and exit information. He paused and looked up. "Here's one that has an entrance ramp, but it's all one floor. What do you think?"

"Are there surgery doors the steel boxes would fit through?"

"I hadn't thought about that," Chase murmured. He looked through the lists on all three spreadsheets, crossing out all localities not fitting the needed requirements.

While he and Felipe worked on that project, Peter Lynch was reviewing the security tapes from the hotel's service elevator. Just as Kamini had stated, the men she had pointed out in the line-up a few days prior could be seen in the video feed.

Pete called to Felipe. "Hey, Ramirez, look at this," he called.

Felipe made his way to Pete's desk. "What is it?"

"Look at this," Pete told him. "There are *four* of those steel boxes going *into* the hotel. But they don't take them all out at the same time. Why do they do that?"

"You think they were filled with body parts going in?" Felipe asked. "Remember there were only a few that were still cold the next day."

Pete tapped his desk, thinking. "Do you remember any markings on the outside of the boxes we took from the house at Ennis Lake? Where are the pictures from that raid?"

"I think the Crime Lab still has them," Felipe answered. "What are you thinking?"

Pete mused aloud. "I wonder if the boxes were all hooked up for cryogenics before they came into the hotel. What if there was a deadline of some kind that forced The Parent Company to come up with a way to dismember bodies and pull transplant parts out? What if the two steel boxes of transplant parts we intercepted in Ennis Lake, had come from the *hotel* and were awaiting the couriers? Remember, when we stumbled onto the hub house there? The boxes were a bonus."

"Well, yeah," Felipe told him. "They *were* a bonus."

Then it dawned on him what Pete was saying. "Oh, I see. You think the hotel was a last minute thing. Okay. If that's true, why *that* hotel? What's close to that area of the city?"

Chase spoke, still working on the spreadsheets. "Maybe the medical facility they used was close by, and it just made more sense to them."

Felipe looked at the younger man. "That's brilliant, man! Are there any potentials on your lists close to that hotel?"

"I don't know the downtown area very well yet," Chase answered. "What are the streets listed?"

"It's in the Eastgate area," Pete replied, counting with his fingers as he began naming the city's connecting streets. "The main ones would be Balata, Cut-shot, Divot, Eagle, Follow-through, Grand-Slam, Hosel, and George Franklin Grant Boulevard. The cross roads are numbered. The Precinct goes from East Main through Fortieth."

"Give me a couple minutes," the rookie replied. "I've got three spreadsheets to go through.

"While you're doing that, I'll run down to the Crime Lab for the pictures of those steel boxes."

As Pete left, Felipe copied the faces of the six men on the security video, loading them onto a flash drive. Then, he moved to the computer at Christine's desk, and pulled up the videos from the Chicago houses, as well as the ones in Greenway and Ennis Lake.

"What are you looking for?" Chase asked.

"I going to run facial recognition on the eyes of the six men Kamini identified, and see if they match any of the eyes on the Zombie tapes," Felipe answered. As he was speaking, he began running the downloaded images through the program.

In the Washington, D.C. offices of the FBI, Deputy Director Ben Edwards was holding a meeting. Derek Hansen, who served as a Police Captain for District 3 of the capital city, had been invited to meet Christine Spada. Fifteen years prior, Derek had been investigative partner to Anthony Spada, Christine's father, on the D.C. police force. It was Ben Edwards' intention to renew acquaintances, and hopefully discover connections between clues in the present Parent Company case.

"It's good to finally see you again, Christine," Hansen was saying. "For a while after your Dad's death, I stayed in contact with Cathy, your mother. But then, time just got between us. I'm sure you understand how people can drift apart."

"Absolutely," Christine answered. "I have to admit, I'm not good about staying in contact with her either. My job just seems to take over sometimes."

Ben interjected. "Kit, do you *remember* Detective Hansen?"

Christine appraised Derek for a moment. "I can't say that I do. But it's been sixteen years, and I was a self-absorbed teenager at the time."

Hansen smiled at her. "Try to picture me with a full beard and glasses," he said. "Tony and I worked undercover much of the time. I was always the nerd....'"

"And Tony was always the muscle," Kit murmured, finishing his sentence. She studied him a little more closely, experiencing a glimmer of recognition. Ben handed Hansen his eyeglasses, which Hansen put on.

"Okay, and the hair wasn't gray," she noted slowly. "It was dark brown. So was the beard and your mustache." She paused. "You came to my fifteenth birthday party too, didn't you?"

"Yes, I was there," the detective responded.

"With your wife, or your girlfriend?" she asked. "Grace something."

"Mimms," he replied. "We were engaged for a long time, but then suddenly, she called it. I think she left the department not too long after you moved away."

Ben was intrigued. "Where did she go?"

"I'm not sure," Derek told him. "I'm sure she's still in police work, though. Another guy left the department about the same time, and I always wondered if they had been secretly hooking up when I had been away on assignment."

"What was his name?" Christine asked.

"John Elsworth." Hansen said the name without emotion or effect.

"That must have been some birthday party," Ben remarked, gazing at Christine. "Kit told me she remembers Rick the Red being there as well?"

"That's right!" Derek exclaimed. "Janzen *was* there as well." He glanced at Kit. "What did you used to call him?"

"Uncle Jannie."

"That's right. He worked in the city, but he was with the military; the JAG Corps, if I remember correctly," Hansen said. He looked at Ben. "Where is he now?"

Christine caught Ben's warning glance. "It's hard to say," she said.

"Well!" Ben said, rubbing his hands together. "Let's all sit down at the round table in the corner, shall we?"

When they were seated, he opened the first file folder of three, stacked on the table. "I'd like us to work together, and review the files having to do with the Andrea Lockwood disappearance."

Hansen looked surprised. "You mean the case Tony and I were working on when he died? We never found any leads at all," he told them. He looked at the three file folders on the table. "Are those the cold cases that got my partner killed?"

Ben nodded.

"I've been back through those files time and time again, Ben. I don't want to be rude, but it's a waste of time."

"I know, I know," Ben answered, in a fatherly manner. "But humor me. Please. You and I both know that Tony was like a brother to both of us. I'd really like to help Kit understand what happened, now that she works in the field, and all. I know she is here looking for some answers, and I for one, wouldn't mind doing as much as I can to help her clear up one old cold case file. So, let's help her, shall we?"

Derek Hansen shot Christine a dirty look, and sighed. "I guess," he answered. "How long is this going to take? I've got a date tonight."

Christine laughed lightly. "I promise we won't keep you too long, Detective," she soothed empathetically.

"I have three files here," Ben Edwards redirected, opening the first in the stack, and pulling out its contents. "We have Andrea Lockwood's kidnap file. We have the hub house explosion, and its evidentiary file. And we have the German Ambassador and his wife who also disappeared about the same time as the hub house bomb."

"That reminds me," Christine told him, "I'm having Jamey do a search regarding something we are discovering now that ties in with the German Ambassador's disappearance."

"He mentioned that to me this morning," Ben replied. "Remind me. And, I do need to speak with you about that when we are finished here."

Christine nodded.

"Now, let's start with the first file," Ben Edwards directed. "Derek, take a look at these, if you would, and tell me what you remember."

Back in Westwood Village, Pete was reviewing the hotel's security video from the service elevator a fifth time. Watching carefully, he analyzed the four steel boxes as the six men in question maneuvered them down the hallway.

He watched the entire collection twice before he saw what he had been hoping to see. The image on the first box was only visible for two frames, when a hand slightly shifted in position. Rewinding and replaying in freeze-frame, he enlarged the area to gain a clearer view. Coming into focus were two Chinese characters.

Right clicking the image, Pete copied the characters into a translation file.

The two images came back as "for transplant" in English.

After his initial discovery, Pete found the same characters on a second box. After looking for more hand positions to shift, he noticed different markings on each of the two remaining boxes.

Following the same freeze-frame procedure, Pete translated the markings on the second and third boxes. The character on the second box translated "arteries and bone marrow." The character on the third box translated "hypothesis testing."

Looking through the pictures of the steel boxes he had borrowed from the Crime Lab, he realized the boxes they had taken from the house on Ennis Lake were both marked with the Chinese characters reading "for transplant."

"That's weird," Pete said to himself. "So, apparently there had to have been *four* boxes. Where are the other two?"

Sitting back in his chair, he considered what practical steps might have been followed by the six men that night.

He picked up the phone, and dialed the Crime Lab. He asked for Larry Taylor, the department manager.

"Taylor here."

"Hey, Larry, it's Pete Lynch."

"Hey, Pete. What's going on?"

"I need a favor, if you can. Can you look at the Eastgate body parts, and look for something for me? I'm in the middle of trying to solve a puzzle."

"Sure. What are you looking for?"

"Is there anything about any of the Eastgate body parts that would render them unfit for transplant or research?"

Larry paused, thinking about what Pete was saying to him.

"You mean like genetic research?"

"I think so," Pete replied. "I'm not a medic, so I'm not sure what those words mean in your field of expertise."

"I'll look at that right away."

"And Larry?"

"Yeah?"

"I have one more question."

"Okay."

"What hypotheses would someone work on with a dead human body?"

"What?"

"You know, like a fifth-grade science project. Test a hypothesis and prove it?"

"That's quite a question," Larry responded. "I'll have to give that some thought."

"Thanks, man."

"I'll call you later. Taylor out."

Pete went back to reviewing the security video. About two hours after the four boxes had been taken up in the service elevator, one man came down with the first box. It was marked "for transplant."

So, this was one of the boxes at Ennis Lake.

An hour after that video footage, both the "bone marrow and arteries" box, and the "hypothesis testing" box came down the elevator.

So, what had been the original purpose for the body parts left in the bathtub, he wondered?

He checked the remaining amount of unviewed video. The problem of how the stainless steel boxes got into the hotel had been solved. But now, the Chinese characters stamped on the boxes had provided him with a new problem. Instead of three boxes, there were supposed to be four. And, supposedly, the as-of-yet undiscovered box would have a Chinese character stamped on it as well.

What else could someone do with a dismembered human body, he wondered?

Chapter Twenty-Five

It was Tuesday morning at the Greenway Children's Zoo. By special arrangement with the Make-A-Wish Foundation, its President and Chief Executive Officer had contacted the Greenway Children's Zoo's Conservationist Board. Would they be willing to close the zoo for a private exhibition until three in the afternoon, when other children were let out of school?

Ten-year old Caleb Jacobs was more than excited than any other time he could remember! Today, he was going to get to go to the zoo!

At nine-thirty in the morning, Dr. Jim Ainsworth, Sarah McMillan, Louisa Richards; Detectives Peter Lynch, Felipe Ramirez, Joshua Morgan; and ten uniformed officers departed from the hospital and headed to the zoo.

Sarah McMillan was in a wheelchair as well. Fellow social worker, Louisa Richards had come along to push her chair and keep her company. Caleb was also in his own wheelchair, being pushed by Dr. Jim Ainsworth.

As they passed through the main entrance to the zoo, two uniformed zoo workers came to join the group.

"Hello," a young woman said, crouching down to speak with Caleb. "My name is Jody, and I work here at Greenway Children's Zoo. If you have any questions about the animals, I'll be glad to answer them. And, when it comes to the zoo, I'll explain anything you want to know."

A young man shook Jim Ainsworth's hand. "You must be Dr. Ainsworth," he said. "My name is Kevin, and I'm one of the curators here. Jody and I will be your guides for the Zoo Tour. We have some really great things for Caleb this morning. We have delayed our feeding schedule just for him. And, we have a raptors exhibit prepared we know you will all enjoy."

"Thank you, Kevin," Ainsworth replied quietly. "I really appreciate your team preparing this experience for Caleb. As you can see, by his bone deformities, he has a long way to go in the healing process, to even reach just a sense of normal. He will be receiving corrective surgeries next week. So we really appreciate you all making this encounter possible."

Greenway Children's Zoo was the foremost children's zoo in the nation. With an interactive petting and feeding area, pony riding trails, and a six million gallon salt-water aquarium, the zoo was known all over the world as a hands-on animal rehabilitation and recovery center.

Sarah had been to the Greenway Children's Zoo many times, usually with children rescued from difficult home situations. But today had a different feel, she realized.

"What would you like to see first, Caleb?" she asked.

The boy looked at her with bright eyes. "I w-want t-to s-see it all, p-p-please," he said, with a big smile.

Everyone within earshot laughed.

Jody patted the boy's shoulder. "Caleb, the Greenway Children's Zoo is built in a big circle. So, if we start here, and just follow the path, we will see all of the exhibits in just a few hours."

"Wh-what all is th-there?" the boy wanted to know. Suddenly distracted, he pointed. "Wh-what's that?"

Jody looked in the direction he had indicated. "Oh, that's a male peacock. He is trying to impress the female peacock with his bright feathers. Isn't he beautiful?"

She looked at Caleb, who was fascinated, and couldn't take his eyes from the bird. "Wh-why isn't he in a c-cage?" he asked.

"Oh, we let the birds like peacocks, quail, ducks, swans, geese and chickens just roam around freely. They love to be where people are, and we want it to be fun for everyone."

Jody lowered her voice to a whisper. "Sometimes, Caleb, even the little Humbolt penguins get out, and waddle around. They are so cute. Every once in a while, one will waddle right up to me, and peck my leg until I give him something to eat."

Caleb giggled. "I th-thought all p-penguins lived in th-the ice," he said.

"Oh no," Kevin told him with a chuckle. "The Humbolt penguins live in Africa, where it is hot much of the time."

"W-wow," Caleb responded. He looked at Jody and at Sarah, whose wheelchair was next to him. "Wh-where d-do we s-start?"

Jody patted the boy's arm, and stood up. She pointed just ahead. "See those tall palm trees, Caleb? Just on the other side of them, we will go to our first stop. It's the Primate Habitat."

"P-P-Primates?" Caleb asked.

"The chimpanzees, the orangutans, the gorillas, the lemurs; every specie of monkey we've been able to obtain," she told him. "Have you ever seen a big primate up close?"

His eyes wide, he looked up at her. "N-no. J-just on t-t-tv."

"Would you like to see them up close? Or touch one?"

Caleb nodded his head vigorously. "Y-yes, p-p-please!"

"Okay, then. First, we are going to go into the parts of each exhibit that everyone else sees when they come to the Children's Zoo. But then, we have something very special planned just for you. In every habitat we visit today, you will get to go behind the enclosures, and help feed the animals. Would you like that?"

"Yes!" The boy's answer was emphatic. "Th-the b-big hippos t-too?"

"And the *tigers*," she replied, rubbing his head.

Kevin spoke up. "And Caleb, thanks to Make-A-Wish Foundation, when we stop for lunch, we have a special show prepared for you. Our Raptor Center will be letting you see the golden eagle, and the owls, and the falcons. In fact, if you are brave enough, you will be allowed to put on a leather falconer's glove and hold a hooded Peregrine. Are you feeling well enough to meet that challenge today?"

"Th-th-the b-b-b-birds th-the kn-kn-knights used? Are y-you k-k-kidding?" Caleb was filled with excitement and anticipation for what the day held in store. "L-let's g-go!"

Everyone in his circle burst into laughter. It was going to be a good day.

Molly had been working for several hours.

It was time to find the original "Miss Anastasia."

Beside her was a printout of her computer research; a list of women who had held potential to be recruited by The Parent Company. At the moment, Molly was running down those leads; confirming which women had been actually recruited to work as "Miss Anastasia."

But Christine was on a different track.

Agent Spada was spending her day interviewing the Heads of Staff in international embassies based in Washington, D.C. Ben had made appointments for her, and for Jamey, to complete within the next few days. There were one hundred and seventy-six foreign missions in D.C. Ben had made arrangements with each one he felt might pertain to the case. He had also insisted she be driven around the city by another agent, posing as a chauffeur, but serving as a bodyguard.

"I know you're capable," he had soothed. "But just trust me on this. When you do find the responsible parties, you will need backup. And Logan Vernick is one of my best."

Ben was right, she realized. Still, the independent streak in her still would have liked to do this thing alone. All of this meant things would take longer than anticipated. It also meant today would be a longer day than expected.

She took a sip of her Starbucks and sighed.

And, she contemplated, this also meant staying with her mother long enough to experience another conflict. Oh, well... Some things in life just could not be avoided.

Putting her head back on the seat, Christine observed the agent Ben had assigned to drive her around between embassies. Logan Vernick. He was nice enough, and Ben trusted him.

She considered the case, and how the present implications might tie things together. He thought patterns began to take a path of their own.

She hoped the evidence would not take them into countering international espionage agents. If profit monies involved in *any* of the abductions had been funneled through an embassy, prosecution would be frustratingly impossible.

Every diplomat working with an international embassy had been provided with diplomatic immunity. From her time on the force in the capital city, she knew that although most of the ambassadors were honest and hard-working, some were not. Several small businesses in the city had gone bankrupt in the past ten years, due to shoplifting and refusal to pay credit debt. It had been a problem during her tenure, and had become even worse in the present days.

No, if an embassy *were* involved, the most the FBI would be able to do, would be to request parties involved be expelled from the country, then hopefully prosecuted in their own country.

Could that be the reason it had been so difficult to find the kingpin, she wondered?

It had been a shock that her father's murder now appeared to be connected with the present case. His body had been found in the Dupont Circle area. For that reason, Ben suggested she begin investigations in that part of the city.

She glanced at her watch. It was eleven in the morning. So far, she had spoken with Heads of Staff in six of the embassies around Dupont Circle; Jamaica, Namibia, Morocco, Eritrea, El Salvador, and Mozambique. So far, obtaining a history of the women attached to each embassy had not been a problem. Files had been kept, copied, and willingly provided at her request. There had been no attempt to redirect her, or secrecy regarding the history of embassy staff.

Honestly, she was hoping for a little difficulty to surface soon, providing a clue. Hopefully, the day wouldn't be a complete waste of time. At least they were narrowing their focus.

After Logan pulled into the parking area for the Argentinian Embassy, Christine prepared to exit the car. She grabbed her laptop bag and opened the car door.

"Be careful in there," her new bodyguard urged.

"Thanks, Logan," she replied. "I will be."

In the Westwood Village Precinct, Chase Stanford noted the printer had begun an automatic printout. Checking its purposes, he noted information was spooling regarding the new precinct police captain. It wasn't ready yet. He would leave it alone.

After all, it was Felipe's assignment.

Besides, he had finished surveying the spreadsheets he had constructed of medical facilities in the Greenway area. Looking through the lists, Chase transferred the information for those eligible facilities which had been closed during the week before, and the week of the Eastgate murders.

There were only eight, he realized. Each one on the list had doors to allow four-foot dimensional cubes, to be wheeled through. Ramps had been installed, or elevators. Surgical areas, or stainless steel kitchens with sinks for cleanup, and drains in the floor were present in all of them.

The young officer then decided to put the potential dismemberment sites in order of distance from the Best Western where the discovery had been made.

Only five were within a ten-mile radius of the bathtub.

In the Greenway Children's Zoo, Dr. Jim Ainsworth's wish-fulfilling team had stopped to eat lunch together. As they walked into the picnic area, Pete Lynch heard his cell phone ring. He looked to see who was calling. It was Larry from the Crime Lab.

"Hey Larry. Pete here."

"Hi Pete. I've got the answers you asked for about the Eastgate murders."

"Yeah," Pete replied. "Go ahead and tell me, but then I'm going to ask you to call me back and leave it on a message. I'm not where I can write anything down right now, and I need to be able to reference the information later."

"How about if I email you a packet with all of it?"

"That would be perfect. Thanks," Pete told him. "So, what did you find out?"

He could hear Larry shuffling papers on the other end of the line. "Okay. Your first question. You asked if there was anything wrong with the body parts found in the bathtub, preventing them from being used in transplants."

"I remember."

"And yes," Larry told him. "The legs have tattoos or scars, which render the skin tissue inoperative for transplant. The arms have pins, or damage. The tissues in all of the body parts have been bruised, or otherwise rendered unworkable."

Pete paused. "So, what you're telling me is that all of those body parts were probably rejected by the surgeon who dismantled the bodies."

"That's exactly what I'm saying," Larry replied. "Your second question. You wanted to know if any of the body parts could be used to prove a hypothesis, or for research."

"I did ask you that," Pete recalled.

"Okay," Larry answered. "These particular parts are not usable for research of any kind, due to their condition. However, the method in which the bodies were dismembered indicates that they could be conducting research of some kind. Just because of how the cuts have been made."

"Okay," Pete replied. "Thanks. What kind of research could happen? Could you include that in your packet of information?"

"No problem."

"Oh, and say, can you connect me with Cammie? She was doing some investigative work for me as well."

"Sure," Larry told him. "Hold on a minute."

Pete waited until Cammie came on the line.

"Hi, Pete," she said. "I have some news for you."

"Were the cuts made by a chainsaw?" he asked.

"No," she answered. "Not possible. The cuts from a Dremel 4000 cutting tool would cause the same type of uneven edges as we found in these body parts. Those tools come with a myriad of attachments, and they are compact and portable. Anyone could have carried one or two of them into the hotel room, and out again, without much noise taking place."

"You mean like the little drill things?"

"Exactly," she replied. "Or even something like they use in the Asian nail shops."

"Thanks so much, Cammie," Pete told her. "You've helped me more than you know."

"Talk to you later, Pete," she said.

"Yeah, Lynch out."

Silent, and oblivious to the luncheon taking place some thirty feet away, Pete considered the information he had just received.

If the body parts in the bathtub were deemed unfit for transplant, or research, or testing of some kind..... Why were they left in a bathtub for the police to find? Why hadn't they been removed?

Unless.....

Unless they had been discovered before they were supposed to be removed.

Focused, he called the Best Western hotel. Ganesh answered the telephone. No, he told him. Rosa had worked a normal day, and had arrived at the room in question about the same time she did every day. Nothing was unusual about the situation from a staff standpoint. Thanking Ganesh for his help, Pete hung up.

He would have to check it out further later. Right now, a young boy needed his attention, as well as his protection for the rest of the afternoon.

Besides, he reasoned, the Raptor Center's one-of-a-kind presentation was already in full swing. Fully realizing he was truly a kid at heart, the detective didn't want to miss it.

In the lobby of the Washington, D.C., Argentinian Embassy, Christine waited for the Head of Staff to join her, keeping their appointment.

She was studying the molded plasterwork around the ceiling, as well as the paintings by indigenous artists. She was unaware of the woman descending the stairs, until she stood next to her.

"Ola, Senorita Spada," she said softly, in greeting.

Startled, Christine jumped, and then looked at the woman, laughing. Her expression sparked an amused smile from the Argentinian diplomat.

"Excuse me," she said. "I was just gazing at this beautiful craftsmanship."

"Si, it is beautiful, yes?" the woman replied. "I am Emelia Cuellar, the ambassador's head of staff in Washington, D.C." She extended her hand in greeting.

"Oh," Christine responded lightly, responding in kind, "he has other heads of staff?"

Emelia smiled. "Si," she said. "We have consulates in several cities in your country. He has offices and staff in each one. However, as I serve in the capital of your country, I oversee all the hiring and firing for those who serve him and the country Argentina on American soil."

She motioned towards two closed French doors just off the lobby. "Would you like some Argentine tea, or coffee?"

"I would love some, thank you," Christine replied. "I feel so ignorant at this moment. I had no idea your country had more than one consulate. Where does the ambassador have other offices?"

Emelia led her into a formal sitting room, furnished with Eucalyptus tables and leather couches.

"Please be seated," she said. "Coffee or tea?"

"Coffee, please," Christine responded.

"Excuse me." Emelia rang a bell, and a maid appeared. Emelia ordered coffee and pastries on a tray in flawless Castilian.

Christine decided not to disclose her knowledge of Spanish, in order to gain a clearer understanding of the inner workings of the embassy.

"I am sorry, Senorita," Emelia told her. "You asked me a question. Ambassador Santos has offices in each of our consulates. They are located in California, Florida, Georgia, Illinois, Washington and New York City."

Kit had pulled out a pad, and was making notes. "Where does he spend most of his time?" she asked.

"He tries to divide his time evenly between all of them," Emelia answered. "Although he ends up here in Washington about six months out of the year, because of his political responsibilities. He also has assistants who help him in each of the other offices."

Christine smiled. "That is amazing," she said. "Can you tell me about your staff? Does everyone come to you already trained in diplomatic affairs?"

"Oh, no," Emelia laughed gently. "Most of our staff are hired in Argentina, and brought here untrained. We have two diplomatic attachés who are responsible for training in deportment and cultural behavior."

"May I ask who these attachés are? They must be extremely knowledgeable."

Emelia looked at her, assessing her. "Miss Spada, I can assure you, our diplomatic staff are fully vested and investigated before we allow them to join us on American soil. Do I have reason to be concerned? Are you investigating something of foul play involving our ambassador?"

"Oh, no, I'm sorry," Christine responded. "I am actually trying to find older women who might have held the same post in years past. Argentina is not the only embassy I am visiting with these questions. We are trying to solve a case which has stretched across several states here. The people I am looking for are terrorists."

Emelia put her hand to her heart. "O, Dios mio!" she exclaimed. "How can I help you? We will give you any assistance you need."

"Thank you," Christine replied, with a bright smile. "I just have a couple more questions."

"Would you like me to call our two cultural instructors, and arrange a meeting for you?"

"Perhaps in the near future," came the answer. "But it is really a simple matter. I think you can give me all the help I need at the moment. I really don't want to disrupt the embassy's schedule."

"If it will help, I can offer you the records of our cultural attaches before the two we have now," Emelia offered.

"Oh, that would be wonderful," Christine gushed. "How kind of you to offer."

"Yes," the staffer replied. "Let me go and get you a file of those personnel, and of anyone else I think might be of interest to you. I might be gone for a short stretch of time."

"I understand," Christine told her. "I will wait here, and enjoy my coffee."

While Emelia was gone, Christine thought about the progress of the case so far. The Parent Company had operated in Los Angeles, Chicago, New York City, and in Greenway. Was it a coincidence Argentina held consulates in each of the same cities?

Wouldn't it be an interesting development if Argentina turned out to be the embassy where all the pieces came together? It would also be telling, if Emelia's provided list of embassy staffers omitted names existing on Felipe's researched list. If that were so, she would have to ask Ben how to proceed.

Strange, she considered. *Would Argentina's involvement dictate a change in the direction of their investigations?*

Truthfully, Christine realized she had expected any international involvement to have originated with political liaisons with Croatia. Suddenly, there was much more investigating to do.

Christine pulled her cell phone from her bag, and dialed Felipe.

"Ramirez here."

"Hey, Felipe, it's Kit."

"Hey, Kit," he replied. "How goes your investigation?"

"So much to tell you," she answered. "How about there?"

"Well, Franko identified his sister, and the other man... Luka, as paid assassins for The Parent Company," Felipe told her. "Both are from Croatia. We are going to use Franko as an interpreter for Luka, and run a bogus session, just to see if they might already know each other. We need to make sure all of this isn't just some big smoke screen."

"That's great," she replied. "Good idea. What about the other name Luka mentioned.... Zrinka, I think?"

"Still working on that," came the answer. "Hey, you called me. You need anything special?"

"Oh, yeah," she answered. "I wondered how the background search on our Police Captain turned out."

"Nothing of note to report," Felipe told her. "He is just an average guy with an average background, who worked his way up the ranks to Captain."

"Really?" she asked. "That surprises me. I thought for sure something more sinister was going on. Would you do me a favor?"

"Sure," he replied.

"Run a facial recognition search on him, and see if this is a bogus identity that someone created. If he has a real name, we should be able to find it."

"Will do."

"Things going well with Samantha?" she asked.

"Yes," came the answer. "Better than I could have asked for. She's still a little shaken up over the Franko thing."

"I would be too, in her shoes," Christine said. "Take care of her Ramirez."

"My pleasure," he answered.

"Oh, and Edwards gave her a security clearance at your level," Christine told him.

"That's great!" he exclaimed. "So now we can talk about the case with permission."

"That's an affirmative," she laughed. "Okay. Gotta go."

"See you later."

"Thanks, Felipe. Spada out."

The screaming from other cells had awakened him.

His body clock told him that some time had passed, but Benjamin Asami wasn't sure just how much time. His thoughts had been tormented the past few days. Now, in his bare cement-block cell, sleep eluded him.

He rubbed his arm.

The drugs they were injecting into his body were beginning to have an effect on his mind…. and his body. He hadn't been brave enough to ask his questions yet.

What was he being punished for?

What were their plans for him?

Inga had divulged on the first day that he would be allowed to leave when their experimenting was completed. He was still holding out hope.

Were they testing a new drug?

Were they preparing him for a genetic experiment?

He remembered a rumor he had heard through The Parent Company grapevine several years prior. They had succeeded in mixing frog DNA with a tomato. The process was called "adding a genetically modified organism to edible plant matter." The goal of the process had been to provide buyers with "perfect tomatoes." Someone unknown person had "borrowed" the research and marketed it on a wider scale.

"It was never our intention to feed those genetically modified organisms to the public," one of the big bosses had told Benjamin. "We guard our secrets."

But now, thinking back, Asami realized that was probably the exact thing they had done.

After all, he remembered bitterly, *"perfection sells."*

And The Parent Company was good at faking perfection.

Now, it was common practice for grocery stores to stock vegetables altered with "genetically modified organisms."

And wasn't faking perfection the standard operating procedure behind the trafficking in human lives they did? Or the selling of body parts for profit?

Always. There was someone, somewhere, who wanted perfection. And was willing to pay for it.

Considering The Parent Company's other ventures, he shuddered. Why had he had joined with these people? He had been privy to their secrets.

He had been …. Well ….. *involved.*

How had he become so callous about the stealing of human lives? Yes, he had enjoyed the money, and the luxuries they had provided.

But now……

His own life had being stolen away.

And worse….. where was his son? Had they "pieced out" his boy for those who could pay?

413

He rubbed his arm again.

And his leg had begun hurting in the last few hours.

They came every two hours around the clock. There had been no hypnosis, or re-programming performed on him. He was sure the goal for his captivity was genetic testing.

What were they injecting into his body?

He looked at his leg, where the pain had begun. An open sore had erupted since yesterday on the back of his thigh. It was circular, and black.

Had they given him cancer, Benjamin wondered? He knew it was possible to trigger the carcinoma cells already dormant in every human body.

He sat down on the desk chair and pulled on his leg to investigate what was happening. Something strange was emerging from the wound. It was hard. And it hurt.

Had they shot him, and he hadn't noticed it?

Had they given him a hallucinogenic? Was he imagining all of this?

The pain was sharp, as though like something a pin was sticking into him. Only it was from the inside, not the outside.

What was it, he wondered?

His arm began to react to the angle he was using to reach the wound. It felt strange, as if something was crawling under his skin. He looked at his forearm and witnessed a ripple moving under the surface. He felt another sharp pain in his forearm.

It was like..... like.....

He remembered working in the rose garden with his mother as a boy. That day, a thorn had pricked his hand, causing it to bleed.

This felt like that.

But it was happening from the *inside.*

Spurred by his need to understand, Asami stretched his skin, seeking to put his fingers into the leg wound. He wanted to extract the hard piece of matter; to pull it out; to see it more clearly.

Just as he finalized the required contortion, and his hand drew close to the offending piece of hard matter, the door to his cell banged open.

"Benjamin Rutger Asami! I wouldn't do that if I were you," Inga Hern said in a raised tone. "You could have that mess on your fingers and growing on your hands if you touch it."

Asami looked at her, stunned.

"What did you *do* to me?" he asked hoarsely.

She smiled. "We need to know how to combat the disease growing inside of you," she answered.

"Genetic testing?" he queried.

"Something like that," she told him. "We have injected a series of aggressive plant and reptile derivatives into your body. These derivatives have the possibility of changing your appearance. It is our hope that we will at some point develop a human mutation able to survive the cold winters of Siberia, and still adapt to a desert terrain, without a need for water. We would even like to give individuals the possibility of making their own oxygen at some point. It is my considered opinion that the earth's habitat will demand such mutations in the future, given the problems of global warming and pollution.

"For your instruction, please listen. You will develop these root eruptions all over your body, and the texture of your skin should begin to change. More reptilian, I think. It might take some getting used to. At that point, we will begin to experiment with antidotes we are in the process of developing."

"What have you done to me?" he demanded.

She shrugged, unconcerned with his responses. "It is of no consequence, Benjamin. What matters is the project. Your life is a means to take us closer to the solution we require. Even if all you provide is another failure we can cross off the list.

"So be encouraged. You will be remembered. You are finally going to be worth something. You are going to be a great asset to the Cause."

"But I don't want to die yet," he told her. "Can't you just tell me what I did wrong, and let me fix it? Whatever it was, it was unintentional. Can't you put me back like I was?"

She assessed him, coolly. "I know, dear man," she cooed. "The pain; the struggle seems unbearable right now. It is going to become harder, so be prepared. If I give you something to ease it,

415

the results of our tests will be tampered with. And no, there is no way to put you back like you were. Even if I could, I would then be ordered to shoot you. You have just outlived your usefulness to them. So they gave you to me. You, Benjamin dear, no longer have a reason to exist."

She shrugged, as though she had just read a shopping list, checking her nails.

Asami was stunned into silence. So this was a personification of Evil. He shuddered, although the room had no chill.

Suddenly, he had nothing left.

He stood, and walked to his bed, where he slumped over. Something was pounding in his head. Agonized, he watched Dr. Inga Hern wave to him as she left his cell.

"We will be back in one hour with your food, Benjamin," she called over her shoulder. "Do try to work up an appetite."

Chapter Twenty-Six

Mid-afternoon, Detective Evan Davies emerged onto the fourth floor of the Westgate Village Precinct.

"Hey, Chase!" he greeted the younger man. "Where is everybody?"

"The left this morning for the Greenway Children's Zoo. They'll be gone all day," Chase answered. "Caleb Jacobs is going in for his surgeries in a few days, and Dr. Ainsworth arranged a custom visit with the Make-A-Wish Foundation."

"That's great!" Evan replied.

"How'd your undercover go?" the younger man asked.

"Assignment went well; without a hitch," Evan smiled. I'll just spend some time typing out my documentation on that assignment."

"Sounds good," Chase replied. "I'm going for coffee. You want some?"

"Sure," Evan told him.

After delivering the coffee, Chase went back to perusing his spreadsheets, ensuring he hadn't missed anything.

About ten minutes later, the phone rang. Evan answered.

"Good afternoon, Detective Davies speaking."

"Good afternoon, Detective. Is Peter Lynch there?"

"No," Evan replied. "He's out on assignment today. Can I help you?"

"Yes, this is Cammie from the Crime Lab. I have a match on some DNA he asked me to run down for him."

"Okay," Evan answered. "I can take the message."

"I will email it to him as well," Cammie said. "I just wanted him to know that the little fourteen year old girl with no memory; the one Agent Spada is calling Jane Doe; she is a familial match for Maria Estavez. Maria was the mother who came in some time ago, saying her daughter had been kidnapped from the airport. So, it's likely that the Jane Doe is the missing child."

417

"Oh, that's great," Evan told her. "I'll write Pete a note. I've been out of the office, undercover, so I have no idea what the contact information would be. I know he'll be thrilled. I'll have him call you as soon as he gets back."

"Thanks," Cammie said. "Good news always helps in one of these."

"You know it," Evan answered, before hanging up. "Sounds like there's a reunion in the offing."

"It's what we like to see!"

In the Greenway Children's Zoo, Caleb had been fascinated the entire day with the activities planned for his benefit. He had held a baby lemur. He had hand-fed a teenaged gorilla. He had held a bottle to feed a baby zebra, and petted a giraffe. He had been followed by a Humboldt penguin, and thrown feed to swans and peacocks. He had held fish to feed sea lions, otters, and dolphins. He had thrown chunks of meat to polar bears. He had counted the sharks and sea anemones in the aquarium. He had even had his picture taken with an Australian wallaby.

His favorite part of the day had been spent spraying water on a baby elephant and its mother, in the midst of the keepers bathing the animals.

Sarah McMillan noted how wonderful it was to hear the boy laugh aloud for a second time. The first time, had been at his "birthday" party.

It was close to the end of the day now. As Make-A-Wish Foundation's finale in granting Caleb's wish, the boy was invited to join zookeepers in the central food preparation area for Large African Cats on the north end of the zoo's Savannah Enclosure. The large acreage was home to lions, cheetahs, cougars, and the like, in as natural an environment as Greenway's Zoological Society could provide.

Dr. Jim Ainsworth had begun to experience weariness in standing and walking just after the Raptor Center's Demonstration.

As a result, the psychologist asked if one of the agents could trade places in pushing Caleb through the zoo. Noticing how drained and pale he looked, Louisa requested a wheelchair. She then insisted Dr. Jim take the seat, and recruited Josh Martin to push the chair for a while. As a result, Peter Lynch took over for Ainsworth, powering Caleb's wheelchair, accompanying the boy through the rest of the exhibits.

At the moment, Pete was standing near Caleb's wheelchair in the one room most of the zoo's visitors wished they could gain permission to enter. This was the "kitchen," where vitamins and proteins were mixed together; where chunks of raw meat were injected with needed medications.

Caleb was captivated by the actions of the Children's Zoo's Animal Care Specialists as they prepared food for the African Lion enclosure.

Francine, the zookeeper on duty that particular day, began explaining to Caleb what was happening.

"Hi, Caleb," she said. "We are getting ready to feed the lions now. We have to make sure they get exactly what they need so they grow up to be healthy. Especially the babies. In the wild, African lions only live to be around fourteen or fifteen years old. But the ones we take care of in zoos usually live to be much, much older; almost twenty years. I think the reason large zoo cats longer is because we feed them healthy food, and they don't have to fight with other lions for their territory."

She opened a cabinet and pulled out three huge bowls, which she placed on the large counter. She opened another cabinet and pulled out a package of large syringes, which she placed next to the bowls. Then, she walked over to a double-doored, built-in freezer, and opened one side.

"You see, Caleb," she continued, "big animals like lions, tigers, and jaguars, are what we call 'carnivores.' That means they like to eat meat."

"Th-then I'm a c-c-carni-v-v-vore t-t-too!" Caleb declared.

Francine laughed. "Yes, you are!" she exclaimed. "That's right! And so am I! I don't know about you, but I love cheeseburgers!"

"M-m-me t-too!" the boy replied.

Francine pulled two large packages, wrapped in brown paper, out of the freezer, and added them to the countertop. She began unwrapping them, revealing several 3-4 pound chunks of meat in each package. She threw away the wrappings.

From a refrigerator on the far side of the room, she pulled a tray filled with vials and bottles, and added it to her collection.

As she filled the syringes with various vitamins and medications, she kept a steady flow of conversation going, keeping Caleb entertained. When she was finished filling the syringes, she injected their contents into the meats.

"C-can w-we f-f-feed th-them n-now?" Caleb asked.

"Almost," Francine told him. "I have one more step to do."

She walked to the corner, and opened the top of a steel box, pulling out a roll of meat, similar to a loaf of bologna.

"This seems to be their favorite food these days," she told Caleb. It's like sandwich meat, but it has a little more flavor."

"What is it?" Pete asked her.

"I'm not sure," Francine answered. "The Greenway Meat Packers Union donates these meat rolls to us. From what I understand, they are made from cuts of meat they can't really sell under the USDA ratings. So, they make the cuts into these sausage rolls for the animals. We inject a little extra protein into the meat, and the larger carnivores seem to really enjoy it."

"Do the Meat Packers donate anything else?" Pete wanted to know.

"They do," she told him, "but not to this enclosure. They provide several 50lb bags of fertilizer a couple times a year as well."

"Dung?"

"No, bone meal. It has the most nutrients for the soil. The staff here uses it in all of the flowerbeds and landscaped areas."

"I see." Pete glanced at Caleb, to see if the boy was still listening. He hadn't meant to ask a question and interrupt the flow of the boy's adventure. But he fell silent, noticing a change in the boy's demeanor.

Caleb's eyes were wide, and filled with fear. He had pulled his thumb into his mouth, and brought his legs up to his chin. Alarmed, Pete knelt down in front of the boy.

"What is it, Caleb? Are you okay?" he asked.

Caleb didn't answer, but stared straight ahead.

"What's wrong?" Francine wanted to know. "Did the syringes upset you?"

Pete motioned to her. "Look at me, Caleb," he said. "Buddy, look right in my eyes."

The boy complied.

"No one is going to hurt you here. You are with me, and you are safe. I promise." Pete spoke calmly and gently. He took the boy's free hand. "Tell me what's bothering you, please."

The boy pulled his thumb out of his mouth. "Th-the z-zom-b-bies are h-here," he said, tears beginning to fill his eyes.

"Where?" Pete looked around the food preparation room. "There's no one in here except Miss Francine. Did you *see* a zombie outside?"

Caleb shook his head to indicate no, holding his thumb in his mouth once more.

"What is it?" Pete was dumbfounded.

In response, the boy silently lifted a shaking hand, and pointed to the corner of the room.

At first, any connection with the case didn't register with the detective. Perhaps the boy had seen a shadow that scared him, or some clown was playing an ill-timed joke. Pete glanced around the room, looking for a person wearing a zombie mask. But then, as his thinking began to settle, slowing down, he followed Caleb's finger. His eyes came to rest on the stainless steel box from which Francine had taken the meat roll.

"The box?" he asked. "Is this one of those boxes?"

The boy nodded. "It's a B-Body B-Box."

"A Body Box," Pete echoed. "Are you sure?"

He nodded once more.

Pete walked over to the corner. He noted the box was plugged in. He looked for a symbol on one side. He found one. He pulled out his phone and took a picture of the box, and the symbol found on it.

For a few moments, all was silent as Pete looked through the symbols he had emailed to himself from the Ennis Lake video images. A few moments later, he found the same symbol on his phone.

"This is the symbol we were missing," he said out loud, excitedly. "This was the fourth box! The Chinese symbol on it means 'recycle.'"

The detective looked at Francine. "Madam Zookeeper," he began. "I'm sorry, but on behalf of the FBI, I need to take this box, and the remaining meat rolls it contains. Actually, I think you have helped us find the missing link in a case we are working on at the moment."

Francine smiled. "Are you making an evolutionary joke, Detective?"

Surprised, Pete answered. "No, honestly. I've been looking for a stainless steel box just like this. It's part of the case we are working on."

"Oh, I see," she said.

Pete walked over to Caleb. "Did you know it would be here? Have you been to the zoo before?"

Caleb shook his head.

"But you asked to go, didn't you?" Pete asked. "How did you know?"

The boy nodded. "I d-didn't kn-know. Th-the Z-zombies t-talked ab-bout the z-zoo, and th-the l-l-lions," he said. "S-so I t-tried to f-find the s-silver b-boxes on the T-TV. I w-watched th-them on T-TV, b-but I n-never s-saw a b-box, or a z-zoo."

Listening, Pete realized the boy had been looking for answers to explain the questions he had been pondering about his life while living on Parrot Circle.

Pete took a deep breath, and decided to try to communicate on Caleb's level. He hoped he would have the right words to help the boy discover some of the answers he needed.

"Caleb, I think the zombies brought the box here and left it," he said. "I think they bring it here full, and come and get it when its

422

empty. They must exchange an empty one with another one that's full of more meat rolls."

He looked at Francine. "Would that be accurate?" he asked.

"That's exactly what happens, Caleb," she answered, speaking to the boy. "Don't worry. The zombies aren't here."

"R-really?" the boy asked, relaxing just a little.

"Really," she answered. "If a zombie did come here, we wouldn't even let it come inside the gate."

Caleb looked up at her. "R-r-eally?" he asked.

"You bet, Champ," she told him, rubbing the top of his head.

Pete looked at Caleb. "Can you stay right here? I need to get Felipe. I'll be right back."

Francine came to stand with the boy, while Pete was out of the room. She hugged him. "It'll be okay, Caleb. Don't worry," she told him.

Pete and Felipe returned in a few moments, and removed the box from the room. Felipe radioed to the precinct.

"This is Agent Ramirez, FBI. We need a police van to the Greenway Children's Zoo to pick up evidence."

"Caleb, I'm going to make sure you get an award of some kind!" Pete told him. "Did you know you might have just found the final piece of evidence we need? This closes the circle on our case! I could have missed the whole thing, were it not for you!"

"R-Really?"

"Really," Pete told him. "And, since I have to wait for the van with Felipe, you will have to wait with us. Is that okay?"

"R-Really?"

"Yes, sir. Absolutely!" came the reply. "And, since we have to wait, I think we should let you feed the big cats now."

"What a great idea," Francine said. She began gathering the bowls of prepared food, and led them all to the openings into the African Cats habitat.

Pete pulled out his pad, and made a note. *"Greenway Meat Packers Union. Bone meal fertilizer. Other outsources?"*

The next day was a busy one for the Westwood Village Precinct office. Pete began reviewing the service elevator footage one last time, to identify which of the men being held were responsible for which Body Boxes. He would then invite them to explain what their duties had been the night of the Eastgate Bathtub incident.

He had sent the meat rolls and stainless steel box to the Crime Lab for processing. He was interested to know if the meat rolls were animal and human matter combined, or if they were all human remains. He was hoping there were still fingerprints somewhere on the surface of the stainless steel.

He was confident the Crime Lab would do a complete forensic examination.

It was good to have Evan back, he considered, although the poor guy was still working on his documentation from undercover work. If no emergencies took place, Pete was planning to help his partner get back up to speed with the rest of the team over lunch.

Across the room, seated at Christine's desk, Felipe was also working. Upon his arrival that morning, the agent had reviewed Chase's work, in distilling all of the spreadsheets down to one page.

"Great work," he told the younger officer. "Very good. Let me do a quick check on the printouts here, and then let's go together to do some investigative work."

Picking up the automatic printout, he perused it. "Wow," he commented. "I'll have to call Christine on this."

"What is it?" Chase asked.

"Well, we did an initial background check on the Police Captain. It came back as normal as apple pie. So, just to be sure, Agent Spada asked me to run a facial recognition search on the man as well."

"What does it say? Is it bad news for us?" the officer wanted to know.

Felipe shook his head. "I don't know, actually. It came back as 'Access Denied. Security Clearance Level not met.'"

"What does that mean?" Chase asked.

"It means whoever this guy really is, he is way above my national security clearance. Either he's a government plant, or this case is bigger than we thought. Or both."

"Oh," Chase replied. "What do *you* think it means?"

"I don't know what to think."

"Do you still want to head out to check the medical facilities in Eastgate?" Chase asked.

Putting the printout down, Felipe smiled. "Yes, let's go. I can call Christine from the car."

Armed with the Chase's one-page, distilled list of medical facilities, as well as a list of site discovery questions, the two men headed for the elevator.

Joshua Morgan was heading out to begin a little investigative work of his own. Having worked through the plan with Ben Edwards and Christine the night before, he would be the point man in the next phase of investigation regarding The Parent Company.

The investigation would begin at the Asami Motors Dealerships.

Dressed in a dark gray, tailor-made, Italian suit, Armani shirt and silk tie, Josh looked like a million. He had searched for some time to find the perfect dress shoes, and had finally settled on calves' leather, black slip-ons.

He was headed to the dealership, where he would apply for a part-time job. The idea was to appear as though he didn't need a part-time job. His cover had been prepared beforehand, by the Bureau in Washington.

This would be a long-term undercover assignment. And it would be dangerous. Without question.

The idea was to stimulate the curiosity of the dealership. In fact, as an ultimate goal, Josh hoped to draw the attention of the newly widowed Lina Asami. Ben felt it was time the Bureau delved a little deeper. They were in need of more answers. Infiltrating the organization was the only way they could obtain the information needed.

Just as Josh was heading out, the elevator opened. A young Chinese woman exited, almost bumping into him.

"Oh, I'm sorry," she offered immediately.

"No, ma'am, I apologize," he replied. "I shouldn't have been in such a hurry." Silently, he assessed her red silk sheath dress, and her black pumps. Long, black, straight hair. Lipstick matching her dress. Almost no makeup.

Simple, he determined, *but elegant. Exotic. Beautiful.*

"Forgive me?" he asked, intentionally charming.

She blushed and smiled. "Oh, no. I'm sorry. I am looking for Agent Christine Spada?" she said.

"I'm sorry," he answered. "Agent Spada is out on assignment. Can I help you?"

"I am Sung Li," she told him. "I was rescued from the shipping container at the house by the lake. I think it was Ennis Lake?"

"Yes, I remember," Josh said. "You look like you are feeling better."

"I am, thank you," she said.

"Oh, I'm sorry," he realized, extending his hand. "My name is Joshua Martin. I'm also an agent here. I was heading out to begin an assignment."

She shyly shook his hand. "Can I give these to you, then?" she asked, offering the sketch pad she had been holding under her arm. "I asked Agent Christine if I could help her by making sketches of the things I saw in my imprisonment. I can leave them with you, and she can call me when she has time. I left my information on the first page of the sketch pad."

"Oh, yes!" Josh answered. "That's great! I will put them right here on her desk."

He took the sketch pad from Sung Li, and walked to Christine's desk. He left the sketches in the stack of mail waiting for her return. He then returned to the elevator where he pushed the button. The door opened immediately. Josh bent his elbow, and extended his arm.

"Miss Sung Li," he offered. "May I escort you to your car? Or perhaps I could take you to breakfast?"

"You are very kind," she answered, slipping her arm through his. "Come to think of it, I am very hungry for breakfast. That would be amazing."

Ben Edwards was on the telephone when Christine arrived at his Washington, D.C. office that morning. Seated at his desk, in mid-conversation, he motioned for her to come in and have a seat.

"I understand," he was saying.

"Yes. We need to and I will."

"Oh, I know you think that's funny. Those aren't the facts, though. You'll just have to trust me on this."

"No. No. It's not."

"I will. Sure.

"Let me call you back in a little while."

"Okay. Edwards out."

Ben closed his cell phone, and turned his desk chair around.

"Thanks for your patience, Kit," he said. "How's your day going?"

"Pretty well, actually," she answered. "I'm here to see if you think it would be good for me to meet alone with my Dad's old partner, Derek Hansen."

Ben assessed her with a smile. "Feeling a need for a break from embassy interviews, are we?"

Christine nodded. "I'm tired, that's true. But, I think I'm getting a handle on things. Everyone I had appointments with yesterday was very helpful. I did discover the Argentina Embassy has consulates in every city where The Parent Company has operated hub houses."

"Did they provide you with a list of personnel who might have been approached to become a 'Miss Anastasia?' he asked.

"Their Chief of Staff was very helpful," Christine replied. "Unlike the other offices I visited, Emelia Cuellar does all of the interviewing, hiring and firing for all of the staff in all of Argentina's consulates. And every staff member is a citizen of Argentina."

"Hmm," Ben responded. "And the embassy is in DuPont Circle. How far is it from where Tony was found?"

"Less than three hundred feet," she told him. "The DuPont Café, where Dad had dinner that night, is also in walking distance. I wondered if someone had stayed at the inn near there. It's the DuPont Circle Inn now, but before 2009, it went by another name. I think back then it was the Jury's Washington Hotel. Do we have a record of who the owners were back then?"

"We should have," Ben told her. "If I'm not mistaken, it belonged to the Jury family. They still own many properties in the Hospitality Industry in our area."

"Do you think they might still have records for 1999 and 2000 for that hotel?" she wondered.

"It never hurts to ask," he told her. "Some people hold on to things like that for years, and some clean closets every year. Let me get you an address. It would be a good question to ask someone in that family. If they do still have those records, we might discover something about their clientele."

"Thank you, Ben," Christine responded. "Now we know The Parent Company was responsible for Dad's murder, I think it would help Mom and me, if we could learn who was involved, and why. I think it would help her especially to have closure."

"I agree," Ben answered. "I'll be right back."

Several minutes passed before Kit received the address in the Washington, D.C. area where the Jury family lived. Knowing she intended to visit the former owners as soon as possible, Ben made a telephone call, requesting an immediate appointment for her. Did the family have guest records prior to selling the hotel in 2009? Of course, they told him. Many well-respected diplomats had signed the register over the years. All the records were paper, and were in storage, however. Would that be a problem? Ben assured them their openness was appreciated. An agent would arrive at their home within the hour.

Christine was excited to have Ben's permission to actually investigate some of the questions surrounding her father's murder.

Checking the address, she noted it was actually located north of the city, in Takoma Park, Maryland. It was only twenty five minutes from DuPont Circle; in a quiet, tucked away suburb, close to Embassy Row. Apparently, the family had lived in the same house for many years.

Walking out to the car, she responded to a text from Samantha. Was she coming home for the weekend? She didn't really know yet. The original plan had been to return on Monday or Tuesday. But here it was - Thursday.

It was definitely time for a conference call.

She looked for the Bureau's car. Logan had pulled it up in front for her. He was so kind. Still concentrating on her text to Samantha, she got into the back seat.

"Hey, Logan," she said absently. "Thanks for bringing the car around."

"You're welcome Agent Spada," a man's voice responded. Didn't sound like Logan, she realized.

"You okay?" she asked.

When there was no answer, she looked up to investigate. Instead of Logan's smile, she was surprised to see a masked man's eyes watching her in the rearview mirror. She looked to the back doors of the car, both of which opened at the same time. Another masked man got in, sitting beside her on the left. A masked woman got in, sitting beside her on the right.

Suddenly, she felt the pin-stick of a syrnge in her arm.

A black bag was placed over her head.

The car's tires squealed as they pulled away from the curb. That was the last thing she remembered before everything faded to black.

Chapter Twenty-Seven

Christine opened her eyes in complete darkness. She had no idea where she was, or how long she had been unconscious. She reached for her service revolver. It was still there, in her shoulder holster. She reached for her secondary firearm. It was still in the garter holster on her thigh.

Who had abducted her?

What did they want?

She tried to sit up, and realized she had not been tied down, or handcuffed. Extending her hands in front of herself, she felt along the walls, until she came to a door. Finding the handle, she found the door unlocked.

Strange.

Cautiously, she opened the door into a dimly lit hallway.

Suddenly, two shadowy forms appeared in front of her. From what she could tell, they both were masked, dressed in all-black. Taking a defensive stance, she assessed her situation. Then, from nowhere, a third figure pounced on her from behind. Forcibly, she was dragged into a room across the hall. A single chair was the only furnishing in the room, which was lit by a lone, hanging lightbulb.

Weakly, she tried to resist, but whatever had been injected into her neck had greatly diminished her ability to focus, or to fight back. Within minutes, a leather strap held her to the back of the chair, her arms held by straps to the armrests. Her legs were attached to the chair's legs.

Without warning, she was struck across the face.

"If you don't stop this, we will kill you." Whoever was threatening was using a voice modulator. It was impossible to detect the actual voice of the speaker. Then, a second modulated voice spoke, accompanying another head punch from the other side.

"You are endangering everyone you love."

"The Company knows where you live." Another blow.

"We know your secrets." Yet another.

Then, suddenly, shots rang out in deafening closeness. Christine wondered whether the breaths she was taking in were to be her last. Trying very hard, she leaned the chair to one side, and fell over. Being closer to the floor made her a more difficult target to hit.

As the side of the chair hit the floor, she also hit her head. The pounding pain in her head intensified as a result. It felt as though something had broken inside. But, she could feel her conscious mind slipping away once more.

"Here, I come, Dad," she murmured. "It will be good to see you again."

Josh Martin stood inside Asami Motors Used Imports Dealership office. He perused the parking lot, looking through the large plate glass wall, which served as the front of the building. With his hands in his pockets, he surveyed the car lot for potential buyers.

His undercover identity had been well established by the Bureau. His new name was John Fitzpatrick. He was presented as the son of a wealthy Irish businessman, dishonorably discharged from the army, convicted of assault with a deadly weapon, and recently released from federal prison. According to records the dealership had checked online, Fitzpatrick's family was reputed to have ties to the New York mob.

His approved employment by the new CEO of Asami motors made a large splash in the typically conservative management of the dealership.

"Give the man a chance," Lina Asami told the personnel department. "He might be very sincerely seeking to rebuild his life."

Initially, the sales manager had hired him on a two-week, probationary status. But now, having been a salesman for Asami for that two weeks, Josh was even surprised at his success in the job. He had never considered himself a salesman.

However, so far, it seemed he could have made a good living in this new field. He had sold four, luxurious, pre-owned sports-cars since his first day: a 2010 Jaguar, a 2014 Porsche, a 2009 Corvette, and a 2013 Mercedes S-Class Hybrid. His commissions in the two-week period totaled close to five thousand dollars.

Responses among his co-workers were a mixed bag. One thing was for sure. The general manager of the Asami Conglomerate had taken notice. Josh had been called into the man's office for a meeting.

Actually, it was more of a second interview.

Would Fitzpatrick be interested in working more closely with Mrs. Asami? Since the abduction and murder of her husband, and the kidnapping of her son, the new CEO was feeling extremely vulnerable. Now, she found herself in dire need of a bodyguard. Could he shoot? Did he know how to fight? What were his actual skills? If he would be willing to make a job change, the man would relay Mr. Fitzpatrick's response to Mrs. Asami. When she was ready, she would contact him. If he wasn't interested, his refusal would not become an issue. They would simply move on, and interview someone else for the position.

He had told the manager he would think about it, and get back to him in the next couple of days.

Josh smiled. Of course he would take the job. This was the break the Bureau was looking for. He hoped to be able to work his way into the infrastructure of the dealership's organization. From there, he would eventually be able to uncover the controlling members of The Parent Company.

Grabbing his suit jacket, he walked out onto the dealership parking lot. A young woman, a red-head, was looking at the one and only Ferrari on the lot. Someone had to move it soon. Every employee in the dealership's branches had given one dollar a week towards a jackpot. Additionally, there was a running bet to see who would win the monies by being the first one to sell the sports-car.

An hour later, he closed the sale of the Ferrari in the general sales office. Not only had he won the jackpot, but he had a date for dinner that evening as well.

This was turning out to be a pretty good day.

Samantha was in the middle of her lunch hour. She was once again standing outside Frankie's Flippin' Favorite Foods foodtruck. Today's choices included Franko's Burek: a delectable pastry, filled with heavy cheese. Although Frankie sometimes shaped cheese and apple Burek, his lunchtime offerings today included a meat version. Fried rabbit was also on the menu, along with two types of Croatian homemade candies.

"This is really good, Frankie!" Sam told him, biting into some fried rabbit. "It tastes a lot like chicken."

"In my country, rabbits are cheaper than chicken," he told her. "I hope this plan works. I will serve these foods until Friday. Does your friend really think making Croatian foods like this will draw out the people they are looking for?"

Sam smiled. "You know what they say, 'sincere love can be seen when a person talks about their favorite food.' Sooner or later, those who are involved with The Parent Company from your country will be drawn by the authentic cuisine you are serving."

"But I still also make the pizza," Franko answered.

"Yes, you do," Samantha laughed. "And I love it! Can I get another soda, please?"

"Sure," Frankie chuckled, tossing her a can. "It's on the house, or the truck."

A woman who had joined the line behind Samantha spoke up in an eastern European accent.

"Hey, You! American woman in front! Someone else wants to eat here, too! I only have the thirty minute lunch time."

Samantha smiled at Frankie. "I think I'll sit down to eat. Looks like we will be having dinner *and* a show."

For the rest of the afternoon, with full consent of her boss, Federal Judge Anne Ventura, Samantha took pictures of Frankie's customers with her camera. She continued to enjoy all the tastes of Croatian cuisine Frankie's foodtruck had to offer. Free of charge.

While Samantha was snapping photos, Chase and Felipe were working through the list of medical facilities the younger officer had distilled down from his spreadsheets. Accompanying the two officers, were several members of the Crime Lab. In each location, the foursome provided a court order, requesting permission to examine the newly remodeled areas of the facility. Once inside, Crime Lab members looked for evidence of blood spatter and human remains that might have been left behind.

Six of the eight locations showed no evidence of the Parent Company's involvement prior to remodeling. The seventh, an Emergency Veterinary Clinic, had re-opened two days prior. Two of the clinic's rooms consistently used for surgery had been completely modernized.

But the Vet Clinic's third surgery room proved to be a treasure trove of evidence. Human blood and matter were discovered in cracks between the floor tiles, as were human blood splatter remnants on the walls.

Felipe and Chase promptly arrested the entire staff, and called in warrants for those employees not present, including relief vets and maintenance crews. Chase then called for back-up and transportation of suspects.

The afternoon would become very busy indeed. Spurred on by curiosity, the team began to intensify their search for whoever had connected the Emergency Veterinary Clinic with the Eastgate Murders.

Whoever it was; the person had connections with the Best Western hotel, the Greenway Meat Packers Union, and the Emergency Veterinary Clinic.

Delivery personnel?

Maintenance workers?

Anyone and everyone who might have had access to all three facilities would be questioned over the next few days. Special scrutiny would be applied to the surgical vets who had worked in the Clinic. Had they been the ones to dismember human remains?

Or had it only been Randy Whitmore, and the men on the hotel elevator's security videos?

On the twentieth floor of Ginsberg Memorial Hospital, Caleb Jacobs was in the midst of psychological and emotional preparations for surgery. Three pediatric, orthopedic surgeons had volunteered to work together as a team, donating their time and skill. Ginsberg's Board had donated facilities and medications. By the end of the next week, Caleb would have straightened arms and legs. His spine would be strengthened with plates, pins and screws, correcting the scoliosis that had already begun to crowd his internal organs, threatening his life.

Dr. Jim Ainsworth was doing an excellent job of preparing the boy for what he would experience, not only immediately before and after surgery, but during his recovery period as well.

In fact, the psychologist was doing such a good job, Caleb was beginning to look forward to his life after healing from his multiple operations. He knew he would be able to walk without pain, without a limp, without feeling deformed. He was actually beginning to believe Dr. Jim's words that he would soon be to stand up straight, with no need to hunch over. No longer would he find it necessary to make circles with his shoulder blades in order to stop the continual pain that travelled from his spine into his head.

In the Swiss Alps, the kitchen staff of Avenir-Sain Centre de Restauration were preparing a healthy luncheon for the residents. The tables were set with fine china, and classical music could be heard, piped through the campus-wide speaker system.

Today was Family Day. Today, the grounds were open for visitation with friends and family members. This evening, a live concert and comedy show would be presented in the auditorium for all to enjoy. The afternoon's programme was filled with optional activities and electives. One such available activity, although not well attended, was a tour of the Sanitarium's grounds and research facilities.

One of the smaller, yet more secure of the campus buildings had been the first to be constructed. Known simply as "Le Infermerie" *(The Infirmary)*, it was the location where residents whose lives were close to an end were provided with dignity and care in preparation for the end of life. Rooms for visiting family members were attached to each hospice room, and as with the all housings on the Sanitarium campus, luxurious accommodation abounded.

Presently, there were no residents or visitors residing in Le Infermerie; which made the physician's mission easier to fulfill.

She had given herself the assignment. She had fought through her mental arguments and fears. She had decided.

Her involvement would end today.

It could only happen on this day, and she only had thirty minutes to complete her task. After thirty minutes, the computer controlling the campus security cameras would resume filming, having archived the prior week's events. Such a respite from hacker-proof security only took place once every two months.

Impending snowstorm or not, today was the day.

With her white lab coat covering her clothing, she strode purposefully down the hallway to the stairwell. Casting furtive glances all the while, she eased through the door, knowing she would be finding her way down to the lower levels in complete darkness.

Pushing a button on the side of her watch, she checked the time. Twenty-seven minutes. She took off her shoes, and leaned against the rail on the far wall. It only took minutes to feel her way down two levels, to the genetic testing cell block.

If it had been anyone else, she wouldn't have bothered. But there were limits to a woman's loyalties, she reasoned. They could not do this. She had served them too long, and too well.

She could destroy them with what she knew.

Opening the door to the cell block floor, she pulled a key from her pocket, and opened the large, metal service door which served as a cautionary barrier to any unauthorized personnel. When the security cameras were resetting, all technologies were also reset. So, for this thirty minutes, the door could be opened with a key, rather than a numeric code and retinal scan.

She hurried to the refrigeration lab, where she gathered a collected of syringes and vials. She moved to the cabinet, where she took a prescription bottle from each row of categorized pills. She dropped the items into the small backpack she carried over her arm. Then, she grabbed a gurney and two sheets.

She checked the time. Nineteen minutes.

Taking a deep breath, she left the lab and made her way to the cell block. She had memorized the number of the particular cell where he was being held. The information had cost her dearly.

It would be worth it.

She pushed the gurney down the hallway, and found the cell door. Fifteen minutes.

Taking out another key, she opened the door and walked into the cell of Benjamin Rutger Asami. She rushed to his side, assessing his vitals.

"Benjamin?" she called. "Can you hear me?"

The man groaned. "What do you want now?"

"Benjamin, I've come to get you out of here," she said. "We only have minutes. Can you stand?"

Shaky, he tried to lift his head.

"They have given me drugs," he moaned, slurring his speech.

"We have to go! Sit up!" she whispered urgently.

Faltering, Benjamin sat up, with great effort. The woman put her arm around him, under his arms, and helped him onto the gurney.

438

"Lay down, now," she instructed. "I am going to give you a shot, and then cover you. Lie still and quiet. Do you understand?"

Benjamin looked at her. "No problem," he said.

Pulling a large syringe and vial from her lab coat pocket, the woman loaded the syringe and injected Asami quickly. She covered him with both sheets, and placed the syringe back into her backpack with the others.

She checked the time. Nine minutes.

Pushing her cargo in front of her, she closed the cell and locked it. She then made her way to the elevator, now running on emergency batteries. She pushed the button to take them up to the ground floor.

"It could get dangerous now," she told herself.

Five minutes.

She pushed the gurney out the Infirmary door to the nearby helipad. A guard approached her.

"Dr. Rutger?" he asked. "What are you doing here?"

Inwardly shaking, she sighed nonchalantly. "Oh, we had a test go the wrong way in the genetic lab. I have been asked to take care of disposal."

The guard frowned. "Don't we usually burn those?" he asked.

"We do," she told him, waving her latex covered hands where he wouldn't miss them. "However, this one is infectious. And, although the man is dead already, The Company was afraid it might cause a plague. So, I am instructed to take his body to the Crematorium by helicopter."

"Oh, I understand," the guard said. "Just so I do my job, may I check your credentials, please?"

"Certainly, Andre," she replied. "And remember, I was never here."

"Secrecy insures success!" he replied with a smile, quoting a Company motto.

"Secrecy insures success," she replied, looking him in the eyes. "I will see you later, okay?"

Andre smiled and saluted, his right arm held straight out and upward. "Yes, Madame Rutger," he answered.

"Andre," she said softly, "if you don't touch the body, you will be safe. I could use your help to load the stretcher onto the heliocopter."

She handed Andre and the pilot individual pairs of surgical gloves. "Just to keep you healthy, gentlemen," she cooed. "I will not allow either of you to come down with a plague, or even a nasty virus. Never on my watch."

Both men laughed and put the gloves on. "Thank you," they said.

"Be careful not to touch the sheets over the body. This infection causes even dead bodies to move due to nerve involvement. It would never do to scare either of you. The first time it happened to me, I almost jumped out of my skin!"

"Yah, we will be careful," the guard answered. "Anything for you, Madame."

She smiled coolly, and watched as the pilot and guard lifted the gurney's stretcher-top into the helicopter's side compartment.

The helicopter lifted from the pad. Leaning back against the headrest, Amy sighed. By tonight, she and her son would be safe on the Rutger Family Estate in Czechoslovakia.

Back in Greenway, Pete was sitting across the table from Luka Knesevic. Soon entering Interrogation Room One would be his sister-in-law, Katika Knesevic, and two other Croatians with ties to The Parent Company. Pete had also invited Katika's brother, Franko Kovac.

"Is the Parent Company based in Croatia?" Pete asked.

The people gathered in the room waited for the translation.

"Oh, no. Not at all!" Katika answered. "I work out of my own country. I have team there. It seems no one knows where they operate from. They are in many places all at once."

"Can you give us the names of the people involved?"

There was silence in response to the question.

"Can any of you give me an answer?" Pete urged.

The people around the table, looked at each other, hesitant. Finally, one of the Croatians who had joined them from Frankie's foodtruck spoke up.

"I am Trevor. The Parent Company uses women to make their purposes bigger. Kzinka is the boss, and she is very ruthless."

"No, she is not the boss," Luka told them all. "Kzinka is manager. Parvati is boss."

Pete picked up his pen and began writing. "Parvati who?" he asked.

Luka looked at him evenly. "Parvati Kearney," he answered. "He lives like king in Croatia in castle. He is owner, and how-you-say mind-master of Parent Company."

"You mean master-mind?" Pete smiled at him.

"Dah," Luka replied, frustrated. "He is owner."

"Or part owner, anyway," Pete told him. "Are there others who have been involved with Parvati, who could be based in other countries and also be owners?"

Luka shrugged. "Is possible. Kzinka travels many days, many places."

"Katika knows," Trevor volunteered. "She can tell you many things."

Katika's eyes widened. "They will kill me. You know this is true. Parvati has eyes everywhere."

The second woman, who had volunteered to come in for the meeting at Frankie's foodtruck, who had been silent to this point, timidly raised her hand. "May I speak, please?" she asked.

Pete motioned to her. "Yes ma'am," he told her. "Please do."

"I am Karolina Kearney," she offered. "Parvati is my second cousin. He is ten years older than me. My mother is his cousin. My grandfather is his oldest brother. My parents came here just before I was born, to get away from the criminal activities he is involved in.

"Parvati was here in America when I was baby. He killed my father just after we arrived, because my father said 'no' to him. My mother and I came to Greenway because it was so far away from New York City. We thought we would be safer in the south of your country."

Karolina looked around the table. "I want to say he has many associates who are rich like him from killing and stealing. I want to help put him under the ground forever."

Pete looked at her, assessing her. Was it stamina or anger she carried?

Christine opened her eyes slowly, and then shut them once more. Even greatly dimmed light in the room hurt her eyes. She groaned. Her head seemed to be pounding in rhythm to beeps coming from somewhere nearby. She tried to change her position, but felt hampered by tubes coming out of her nose.

She raised her hand to feel what exactly was connected to her.

"Kitten?" a man's voice spoke softly. "Just lay still, please. You're in Intensive Care. You're going to be okay."

"Who?" she whispered hoarsely. "What happened?"

The man's hand grasped hers and gently patted her arm. "You were shot, little one."

Christine's mind was scrambled. No one had called her "little one," since her teenage years. Who was this person? She was certain it wasn't anyone on her team.

"Uncle Jannie?" she asked. "Is that you?"

"In the flesh," he answered with a chuckle. "You nailed it on the first guess."

"What are you *doing* here?" she asked, trying to lift her head.

Janzen's huge hand came down gently on her forehead. "Not so fast, Kitten. You are under strict instructions not to move just yet," he told her. "You want to know why I'm here? I'll tell you.

"When I heard Mimms and Elswood had 'volunteered' to 'help' your team apprehend the second hit-man, I decided it was time to stop waiting for you to call me. I invited myself into the case.

"I started following them. I had always suspected them of being involved in your father's death, but we never had any hard evidence. I've had some leads over the past sixteen years, but nothing I could get my hands around.

"So, when I called Ben, I let him know what I suspected. I told him that both Mimms and Elswood had failed to show for duty at Eastgate Precinct since the day you left for D.C. It was then Ben mentioned they had both involved in the Ginsberg hospital sting. He told me to get here and shadow you."

"But he assigned me a bodyguard," she whispered. "Why the overkill?"

"Both Mimms and Elswood were present at your fifteenth birthday party. I remember Tony, your father, confiding in me that The Parent Company had offered Derek Hansen and those two pay-offs. They wanted them to look the other way as they set up their network here in the capital. I didn't get it then, but now, looking back I realized your Dad's partner, Derek, as well as Mimms and Elswood, had agreed to take the money.

"I'm just guessing, but it's my theory the three of them must have propositioned your dad the night of your birthday party. They wanted to hook him into it. He told me he was expecting that to happen at some point. The Parent Company had already contacted him, threatening to hurt you and your Mom. He must have given them a flat 'no,' and then sent you and your Mom out of town."

Christine opened her eyes and looked into the eyes of her father's best friend.

"Thank you," she mouthed. She pushed the button to raise her bed to more of a sitting position. "I can't stand this stuff."

She grabbed the tubes which went from her nose down into her stomach. With a strong pull, she pulled them out. As she did so, Jannie began to chuckle.

"You are just like your old man, Kiddo," he told her. "Tony never tolerated those things either."

Just then, a voice was heard from the door. "Christine? Oh good, you're awake!" Catherine Spada scurried to her daughter's bedside.

"Hi, Mom," Christine whispered weakly. "Have I been here long?"

"Since yesterday," her mother answered.

443

Catherine looked at Jannie. "Eric?" she asked, looking at his face. "Are you Eric Janzen?"

"That has been my name for a long time, lovely lady," Jannie replied. "It's been a long time since I saw you last. Ben Edwards asked me to shadow our little Kitten here."

Christine pushed the tilt buttons on her hospital bed, raising it a little more. Her mother bent down to hug her.

"He saved my life, Mom," she said.

Catherine's hand went to her chest. "Oh, dear God!" she cried. "What happened?"

Kit looked at her mother with a smile. "I think we finally know what really happened to Dad."

Catherine sat down on the bed next to her daughter. She looked at Jannie. "How? Tell me what you know," she said.

Listening to her mother and Jannie talk through the discoveries they had made over the past few days, Christine relaxed, and put her head back on the pillow. As they compared notes, they caught up after sixteen years of distance, Christine Spada finally relaxed, and found herself dozing once more.

In Greenway's Westwood Village Precinct, fourteen year-old Camilla Estavez was being reunited with her mother, Maria. For the past few days, she had been experiencing a gradual return of memories.

Simultaneously, on the same floor, Allison Williams was sitting with her grandmother, also experiencing a reunion. Here and there, in various spaces on the floor, comparative family reunions were taking place between parents and their daughters.

During these heart-warming moments, Detective Peter Lynch was sitting in a jail cell with Garrett Jacobs. The Assistant Attorney General had just ended a conference call including both men. The government had extended an offer to Garrett. In exchange for information and cooperation in searching out and closing down persons and/or parties involved in the structure of The Parent Company, Garrett would receive a reduced sentence.

"Thank you for the opportunity to get my life back," Garrett told the detective.

"Hey, man, you're welcome," Pete replied. He paused, watching the younger man, assessing him. Garrett was aware of his gaze.

"What?" he asked. "Is there something else I need to do?"

Pete paused. Silently, he prayed his words would find a welcome audience.

"Garrett, I have something to tell you," the detective began. "Remember how you told us about your girlfriend, Melissa Anderson?"

"Yeah," Garrett answered.

"And you told us about the baby boy you guys had?"

Garrett nodded. "Yeah."

"Well," Pete told him, "I have some news for you."

"Okay. Did you find out what happened to them?"

Pete smiled. "We did. Apparently, Melissa and your son, Caleb, were kept in the house on Parrot Circle. That's what you said you thought had happened, right?"

Garrett nodded once more.

"According to what we have been able to discover," Pete continued, "Melissa sort of committed suicide, because she was going to be placed into the Trafficking System."

"Who told you that?" Garrett asked. "The Company told me she was shot in the head."

"She was," Pete responded. "But there is a lot more to the story."

"Like what?"

Pete locked eyes with him. "I need you to listen very carefully, and not say anything until I am finished. What would you say if I told you that you have a son and he is still alive?"

Garrett looked at him, stunned. "My boy is still alive?" he asked. His eyes misted. "That would be too good to be true."

Pete nodded. "Well, he is. He was discovered at the Parrot Circle house. He is getting ready to have surgery tomorrow."

"Surgery? Why?" Garrett asked.

"He was badly abused after the Parrot Circle house stopped being used. I think the deformities caused by the abuse might have actually changed his life. The Company couldn't piece him out, and those who stayed in the house didn't have the heart to kill him. He's a smart kid. He learned to stay out of the way.

"In the simplest of terms, his bone structures need correcting. Without the surgeries, he won't be able to grow any taller than he is right now. I really wasn't sure what was going to happen. But the social workers who found him on Parrot Circle are two amazing women.

"As a result of their efforts, three surgeons, Ginsberg Memorial and the Make-A-Wish Foundation all partnered together, to provide surgery and aftercare for Caleb. He's going to be just fine."

"Oh." Garrett replied, looking down at his hands. "I wish that hadn't happened to him."

"It was out of your control, Garrett," Pete told him. "The best you can do is try to build a relationship with him from this point forward."

"Thanks for that," Garrett replied.

Pete redirected the conversation. "I took the liberty of doing a paternity test, and I have the results right here. We have confirmed that you are Caleb's father."

There was silence in the room. Then Garrett spoke softly.

"Wow," he said. Do you think I would be allowed to see him?" he asked.

Pete smiled. "I was hoping you'd ask me that. I'd love to take you to see him."

"When can we do that?" the young man asked.

"I thought we should see him before his surgery," Pete told him. "Like say…. Tonight. But before we go, I have to make a few requests, per our Director."

"Name it," Garrett told him.

"Okay," Pete instructed. "You cannot tell him you are his father. Not until this case is completely closed. We will allow you to have contact with him however. Our psychologist, Dr. Ainsworth, has indicated we have to do everything we can to prevent Caleb experiencing more trauma in his life. Any additional trauma could totally halt his development, and injure his ability to recover from the trauma he has already experienced. Dr. Ainsworth told our team that if he is to adjust and develop in a healthy manner to adulthood, he will need guidance, training and counsel for a long time.

"If Caleb were to be taken into a negative situation, or shocked into a fearful state, he could experience a fragmentation, or worse, a split from which it would be difficult to help him regain sanity. So, for now, you are just a friend of mine, and you wanted to meet him."

Garrett nodded slowly. "I get it," he said. "I can do that."

"All right then," Pete answered. "If I allow you to be free of your cuffs, will you promise not to run?"

"If I run, I lose my son, right?"

"That would be true," came the reply. "And, if you run, when we find you there would no chance of a plea deal. You would go away for a long, long time, and miss his most important years."

"So why would I run?"

Pete smiled. "That's why I need your promise. We are recording this, after all."

"I promise not to run. I promise not to tell him I am his father. I promise to only act as though I am your friend. I promise to give you all the information I possibly can." He paused. "Is there anything else you need?"

Pete chuckled. "I think that about covers it," he said. "Let's go."

When they exited the elevator on the twentieth floor to Ginsberg Memorial's Behavioral Health floor, Pete led Garrett to Caleb's room.

"Hey, Caleb," Pete greeted the boy. "I hear you're going to have surgery tomorrow."

"Y-y-yes!" Caleb exclaimed. "I'm g-g-going to g-get straight arms!"

"That's what I hear," the detective replied. "Congratulations! Say, I brought a friend with me tonight. Is that okay? They would like to meet you."

"S-sure. D-d-do I kn-know th-them?" the boy asked.

"I don't know," Pete answered. "You can let me know if you think you do. How's that?" He motioned for Garrett to enter the room.

Caleb nodded. His curiosity was peaked. All his observation skills were on high alert. He held his breath, watching the door, waiting for the appearance of Detective Pete's friend.

Was this another good surprise?

Garrett took his time entering the hospital room. He peeked around the door jamb, looking for Caleb's face. When he saw the boy's face, he smiled.

"Hi Caleb," he said. "I'm Garrett, Pete's friend."

"Hi, G-Garrett," the boy answered. "D-do I kn-know y-you?"

"I don't know. Do you?" the man answered.

"M-my D-Dad's name was G-Garrett," Caleb said, looking at Pete. He looked at Garrett, gazing into his eyes.

"Are y-y-you m-my D-Dad?" he asked.

Garrett looked at Pete for instructions. How should he answer? What was the right answer now?

Before he could answer, Caleb spoke once more.

"Y-you *are* m-my D-Daddy!" he said. "Y-you b-built th-the s-safe place in the c-c-closet!"

Garrett looked at him, assessing him with a small smile.

Caleb looked at Pete. "Th-the z-zombies d-d-didn't make him w-wear a m-mask! B-But th-then they t-t-took him away."

Garrett glanced at Pete once more.

Pete shrugged and smiled. "Go ahead, Garrett. He knows. He recognized you. No trauma in that, I don't think."

Garrett sat down on the bed, and held out his hand. "It's so good to see you again,"" he said, his eyes filling with tears. "They told me you were dead."

"Oh, D-D-Daddy!" Caleb cried, throwing himself into his father's arms. "I'm s-s-sorry! M-mommy m-made m-me sh-sh-shoot her!"

Stunned, Garrett looked at Pete. Instinctively, he hugged the boy tight, and began stroking his son's hair. "It's all right now, Caleb. We both have done things we aren't proud of. It's going to be okay."

Hearing those words, Caleb burst into a harder form of weeping. So much so, that Sarah McMillan came hurriedly into the room from across the hall.

"Caleb!" she called. "What's wrong? Are you scared?"

Then, she caught sight of a weeping Garrett, holding his long lost, ten year-old son. She looked to Pete for an explanation.

"Dad," Pete informed her quietly. "Long, long story."

Sarah smiled, tears rising in her own eyes. Pete ushered her out into the hallway. "Let's give them a little private time," he whispered.

Chapter Twenty-Eight

It was mid-afternoon when the group of Croatian informants rejoined in Interrogation Room One. As they entered, one and two at a time, from a lunch break, Detective Evan Davies was waiting at the table. With him, were members of the Ennis Lake Medical Transport team: Nicholas, Gregor, Vitali, and Yuri. Also seated at the table was Patrick McNaulty, MI6.

Evan greeted each of the Croatian informants in Italian as they entered. Since Italian was more widely spoken on the Croatian coast, and Parvati's castle was located near the coast, it was his hope to discover if anyone had been close to the kingpin and his leadership circle. He also wanted to observe physical cues and responses between the parties as they sat together in the room.

It would make sense some of them might have known each other before arriving at the Westwood Village Precinct.

"Bonjorno! *(Hello!),*" greeted the detective. "Com'era il tuo pranzo? *(How was your lunch?)*"

Several of the group entered, responding with glances of confused, uncomprehending silence. Who was this new, apparently official, detective? Why was he in their shared debriefing room? And why was he speaking in Italian instead of English?

For his own part, Patrick McNaulty was keeping his focus centered on each new arrival, and his or her subsequent reactions to Evan's words.

"Molto bene! *(Very good!).*" Patrick's head tilted, as he realized he was hearing the perfect accent. Sharpening his observation skills, he was surprised to discover he recognized two faces within the Croatian group. Karolina Kearney and Trevor Johannssen? How and when had they become part of the group in Greenway? Or, were they here to hide from Parvati Kearney? Or worse, was it possible they were both here on Parvati's orders?

451

After thinking his observations through for a few moments, he wrote a short note to Evan, indicating they needed a private conversation to compare notes.

Glancing at the note, Evan asked a question.

"Karolina?" he asked. "Is Parvati the one in charge?"

She returned his gaze, her eyes wide with fear. "I cannot say," she stammered.

"Cannot or will not?" he parried.

Nervously, she looked down at her hands. "I don't know," she replied quietly.

"What is it, Karolina?" Katika asked her in Croatian.

Karolina replied carefully. "I came here to be safe from them. You still kill for them, so don't ask me again. You know what is wrong with me."

Luka spoke up, defending his sister-in-law, also speaking in Croatian. "She is arrested now, the same as you," he said. "The same as me. If we don't cooperate, we will suffer."

"Better an American prison, than a Croatian one," Katika told them. "I would like to keep my eyes, and my arms, and all of my body just as it is, thank you. We all know what they do to people who go against their plans."

"Then I suggest you accept our help," Patrick interjected in fluent Croatian. "When this is all over, we will help you to be safe. Help us stop them."

The three of them looked at him, shocked into silence. It was Katika who spoke first. "You have to be kidding," she said derisively. "Do you have any idea who you are dealing with?"

"That is what we are asking you to tell us," Patrick answered.

Luka began to speak in English once more. "Okay, okay, okay," he said. "I will tell you everything I know. I have wondered how long I could continue to do their dirty business."

He looked at his sister-in-law, Katina. "Aren't you tired? Don't you want a new life? Wouldn't it be a good idea to take their offer of starting over?"

There was silence. Luka looked over the entire group from his country.

"We will not get better offer than this," he said. "We want many times to be free from Parent Company." The last two words were spit out with vehemence. "I say we all agree to help these people. Let us all get out this business. Why are we afraid? We have all known that if we stayed with them we would end up in grave. What is the difference? Now we do the right thing, and have opportunity to walk away."

There were a few moments of strained silence, and then, one by one, individuals spoke up.

"I have texts to make delivery of transplant parts," Gregor said, finally. "If you help me, I walk away."

Yuri nodded. "Me too."

"I will help you," Franko said. "I don't know anything, but I'd be glad to work for you."

"I want to see end of Company," Trevor offered. "I am willing."

Nicholas laughed. "I am in trap," he said. "I need to get out. I want to do good work."

"They have taken everything," Katina said. "I am always looking over my shoulder. I am tired of killing for them."

Vitali sighed. "I am weary of the lying and the money. They make promises, but I am empty inside myself."

"I am tired too," Karolina said. "I look many years for way out. But they tell me they will cut me into pieces and sell me like bits of bakery bread."

She looked at Patrick and Evan. "How do we go forward? What do we do?"

"We will train you," Evan answered. "And then we will put you each back in a place to bring down the Company."

Timidly, Karolina put up her hand. "I have one more thing to tell," she said. "You say before you need to know if Parvati is big boss?"

"Yes, I did say that," Patrick answered.

"Parvati is distraction. He is money handler, and how-you-say... communication broker?"

"What does that mean?" Patrick inquired.

"He is tracing phones, making passports, creating documents. He is international lawyer," she told them. "The people who are bosses live in other countries. Three other. They like to deal with Croatia people because our country have no embassy here, and no how-you-say ... send back to country for trial?"

"Extradition," Evan told her.

"Ex. Tra. Dee. Shun." She echoed. "Dah. That is it. They like country who has embassy here, so there is how-you-say .... Immunization?"

"You mean diplomatic immunity?" Evan asked.

"Dah," she answered. She looked at her comrades. "He is very smart man."

She continued. "Such immunization is not good," Karolina answered. "They can do almost anything and have no trouble with police. It is same all over. There are people like that here too."

"The person in charge is group of people. One of them is here now."

"This week?" In Greenway?" Evan asked.

Karolina nodded. "Is woman. Lives here, and she has much power. Sometimes she is in charge, and sometimes Zrinka is in charge. The man who leads is in Belgium. I never meet him yet."

"Who is the man?" Patrick wanted to know.

"I don't know his name," she answered. "But I can describe."

"I'll put you with an artist after this meeting," Patrick told her.

"But the woman. The woman who lives in Greenway is from Ireland. She lives with husband and children in city here. She is very rich; very dark, very mysterious woman. She has much evil in her heart. She is big person in Parent Company, but she is how-you-say-...underneath... uh... behind what is seen. She is assassin sometimes."

Evan sighed. "Do you know her name?"

Karolina thumped her thumb against her opposite palm. "It stays here, yes?" she sighed, not really waiting for an answer. She glanced at Katina for support.

Katina nodded.

"She is Parvati Kearney. But I do not know her American name."

It was three weeks before Christine was cleared to return to work, flying home to the Greenway field office. The first place she went on her first day back at work was the office of the Westwood Village Police Captain to request an update on the case.

On approach, she noticed the door to the Captain's office was ajar. Through the frosted glass, she could tell that someone was sitting across from the Captain's desk.

Perhaps he was in a meeting, she reasoned. She decided just to stick her head inside to say "hello," so the Captain would know she had resumed her normal duties.

"Hi, Captain," she said, leaning in. "Just wanted to tell you I'm back as of today."

"Christine!" he replied. "It's so good to see you! All recovered, I hope?"

"Yes, sir," she answered. As she turned to go, the other man spoke up.

"Well, don't greet *me*, Kit," he said jokingly.

Startled, she took a better look at the man seated in the chair, just outside her peripheral vision to the right.

"Ben?" she queried. "What are you doing here?"

"Every once in a while, a father has to make time for his kids, don't you think?" he laughed.

"Thank you, but I thought we said goodbye yesterday in D.C." Christine replied, confused.

"I mean Allen. My son."

"Allen?" she echoed.

"Yes, Allen Edwards. He's been posing as the Police Captain for the last 90 ninety days." Ben raised his arm to indicate the man behind the desk. "Best CIA man I know. He's my son."

"Wait a minute," she replied, piecing a few things together. "You mean, you let me think he was working for the other side? You let my team spend time checking up on him? Why didn't you tell me?"

By now, she had stepped into the office fully, and taken the other chair near where Ben was sitting.

Ben laughed. "And miss all the fun?" he said.

At that point Christine slapped his arm. "I should hit you or something," she declared.

The older man rubbed his arm with a chuckle, and looked at Captain Edwards. "I think you just did. Ow."

Allen interjected. "You responded perfectly, Agent Spada. I really thought you were going to recognize me. After all, I was in your house all the time when we were kids."

She looked at him more closely. "I do remember you. Are you still going by 'Al?'"

He chuckled. "I'm Al, or 'Patch' to my friends, but the Agency likes to use our full names, just like the Bureau."

"So, you're CIA," she concluded.

"Yes," he told her. "We've been tracking this ring all over the globe for some time, and I have to say, your team was impressive. Cohesive, with solid follow-through. Because of your people, we have peeled back a layer we were having a hard time decoding. We were hoping all of this lead us to the source people. Now, we have a better concept of who they are, where they come from and how they operate. The Bureau and the CIA is in your debt."

Christine blushed. This was high praise indeed. "I'm so proud of all of them," she responded. "Can I relay that message?"

"I'd like you to," Allen replied. "We also have an offer we would like to put on the table."

"Oh?" Christine asked.

"We would like to pull your entire team into the next steps of this investigation. Your man, Joshua Martin, is already undercover at the Asami estate. He has been hired as Mrs. Asami's bodyguard. The story is that she has become afraid for her life and those of her children since her husband's murder."

"Oh," Christine said. "Asami is dead?"

"That's the story we have been told. While I'm sure he is headed that way, my guess is that The Parent Company has him held

456

captive somewhere. We have had difficulty discovering what kind of deal the kidnappers made with Mrs. Asami, regarding her son. She came home with a coffin, and both of her children intact."

"I see," Christine listened thoughtfully. "If anyone can charm their way through, Josh would be the right man for the job."

Ben spoke up. "Say Kit," he asked, "your team has given me the details on the case they have covered, and I know we've kept you in the loop for the most part. But we didn't get a chance to talk about the whole international involvement thing. The day you were attacked, you had spent time in the Argentine Embassy. Do you think they are a definite connection to this case?"

"I'm not sure yet," she answered. "I think we have hit a couple of speed bumps."

"I'm all ears," he told her.

"Well, for starters, it's obvious some sort of government based assistance is happening, giving them a sort of camouflage. After speaking with Emilia Cuellar, the Argentine Chief of Staff, I'm beginning to think someone who works for the Argentinian Embassy might be involved. That would create a problem of diplomatic immunity for us, wouldn't it?"

"Not necessarily," Ben answered. "When it comes to dealing with terrorists, we have a little lee-way in some areas."

"That's good news," Christine responded. "I'm also discovering what you said to be true; the case is a lot larger than we first anticipated."

"Tell me about that, Kit," Ben asked.

"Well, for one thing, these people call themselves 'The Parent Company.' They reprogram the girls they take. They choose girls who are unhappy with their lives, and dis-associated from their parents. So, their process has a head start to begin with. You add hypnosis and their alienation techniques, and it's difficult to break through, even after they are rescued.

"The girls consistently call the hub-houses, 'Creation Centers.' They refer to the kidnappers as 'benefactors.' They know they are being purchased, and still refer to their buyer as 'Prince Charming.' I'm telling you, it was like talking to a Stepford Wife.

"It's scary, Ben. They have polished their system. Tasks inside the Creation Centers are determined by the design of the zombie mask worn by the workers in each center. I know we want to shut them down completely, but they are so thorough, we will have to come up with a creative plan. I hope their system is the same in every country where they operate.

"These people have their fingers in everything from trafficking human lives to medical supplies to transplanting body parts. Pete called me last night to tell me about the discovery they made yesterday. Short story is they treat human bodies like beef. Parts unusable for transplant are removed from the bones and mixed into a meat roll, and fed to large zoo animals. Bones are ground into fertilizer. The facilities they use would also be part of their organization.

"I'm sure you know they have base offices all over the globe, not to mention the 800 numbers and classifieds."

"You're right," Ben told her. "And we will need to be creative to close this group down completely. I have been on the phone the past couple of days with agencies in several other countries. We are setting up an initiative to finish them, but we will have to go through creative avenues. And, I received word from one of our agents in Switzerland, that Benjamin Asami is still alive. I suspect he is being used for some sort of genetic testing in a facility there."

"All of this means we will all be getting into deeper water when the piece we are working on right now is over. We began with the trafficking end of their operation, which I believe is their main resourcing arm. If we can limit their maneuvers here in the States, then we can significantly reduce their organization. How are you faring with that end of the investigation?"

"Well," she told him, "now that we have an idea of how the Creation Centers work, Felipe has discovered we have better results when we use programs that recognize physical qualities, like facial recognition software, or fingerprinting, or DNA. The have the means to create alternative identities. And they are good at it. It wouldn't surprise me at all if someone who worked for Witness Protection were at the helm of that division of their activities."

458

Ben chuckled. "Your team has broken this case wide open. You have put together what they do and how they do it. What remain are the arrests, and the pinpointing of the kidnapped victims. Thanks to Felipe, the office here began following the serial numbers of the GPS tracking chips purchased by lot numbers. We have located more than thirty young women, each of whom was sold as a virgin bride."

"What will happen to them?" Christine asked.

"The ones under legal age will be returned to their families," he told her. "Those who are now over eighteen, will be reunited with their families. They will be allowed to choose which country they would like to live in. All of them will be provided with counseling and recovery care, where it is desired."

"So, what are you wanting us to cover now?" she asked, sensing the current case was coming to a close.

"All of the individuals arrested to this point need to go through the system. We will be taking depositions and recording eyewitness testimony for some time. I think it would be a good idea to have you do some interviews to see who might be of use to you as we move forward with this case."

"You want me to do that?" she asked.

"Why not you?" Ben queried.

"I just thought you probably would want someone more experienced," she offered.

"I think you're ready to lead a field team," he told her. "And if we don't put you into new situations, how will you ever gain that needed experience? I do want to eventually have you lead the field office here in Greenway," he answered.

She laughed. "Okay. Okay. Thanks for thinking I can handle taking this further. All I can say is that I will do my best."

"No sweat, kiddo." Ben told her. "You've earned it. I have to finish making arrangements with a couple foreign governments, and then we will proceed with Phase Two."

Epilogue

Inside the shooting range at FBI Bureau Headquarters in Washington, D.C., Samantha Cruz was completing her training as an FBI Agent. If she passed this run through of the course, she would receive her certificate, and become eligible for field training.

It had been a long twenty weeks. She was ready to return to her home in Greenway. Graduation would be taking place on Friday.

She had been in touch with Agent Felipe Ramirez during her training. He had emerged in her life as a good man; someone to be trusted. It was obvious he had romantic ideas about her future.

At the moment, she was unsure.

But only time would tell.

Judge Anne Ventura continued to be a mentoring figure in her life. The judge had been saddened to lose her as a clerk, but was happy to learn Sam was continuing to the next step in her life; heading into a field where her law degree would serve her well.

"I always wondered how you would do as a lawyer," the judge had told her. "You like adventure too much. This seems like a perfect fit for you. However, I would suggest you finish what you began there, and take the Bar Exam. You never know when you might need to represent someone."

Samantha had taken her advice to heart. In the midst of her training, she had been studying for the Bar Exam as well. When she wasn't asleep. It was her plan to take the Bar as soon as she returned home.

Special Investigator Christine Spada had been promoted to Field Chief, and the Bureau would be completing the new field office building in Greenway in a couple of months. Chase Stanford, Evan Davies and Peter Lynch were also completing the Bureau's twenty-week training course this week.

During the training season, Kit had returned to Washington, D.C. as well. She had stayed in her mother's home during that time. She had had the opportunity to witness Catherine Spada's blushing responses to being courted by Eric Janzen, her "Uncle Jannie," and deceased father's best friend.

They were cute together, she considered. And staying in her old room had been good for her. She felt as though many pieces of her life long buried and repressed were beginning to surface; coming now into focus.

Pete Lynch had been kind to her. She had come to a realization somewhere in the process of The Parent Company: Phase One. He was a good man, seeking to overcome a difficult and rocky life's beginning. He had eased up from his coarse humor and biting sarcasm. She felt as though she was getting to know him finally. He was developing into a good friend.

Sarah McMillan had been awarded temporary custody of Caleb Jacobs, who was now just a few weeks away from completing his physical therapy. The boy had gained six inches in height, new strength in his arms, and the ability to walk without a limp. Sarah had maintained his counseling with Dr. Jim Ainsworth, in addition to placing him with Behavioral Therapists and a Speech Therapist.

She had also hired a tutor to help him with the gaps in his academic learning.

Garrett Jacobs had been immediately reinserted into The Parent Company. After making a plea deal, he had entered into a fist fight with Evan Davies. After each hit, he would look in the mirror, and ask for more.

"It has to look real to them if you want them to believe me," he coached Evan. "Come on! Make it real!"

Utilizing a mask and a black SUV with unidentifiable plates, Evan had dropped Garrett off, bruised and bloodied, at Asami Motors, and sped away. He made sure to stay in the sight of the security cameras.

For his part, Joshua Martin was deep undercover. He was now living at the Asami Estate just outside of Greenway. Christine knew he was hard at work, preparing the ground for the next segment of the case.

She was having difficulty being patient for those steps to begin. The sting involving the Danish royal family was still in play, almost ready for its run. Erin Kasabian and several of the Croatian informants had been in training and preparation here in D.C. as well.

It was surprising how many of those injured by The Parent Company had stepped forward, volunteering to help bring the organization down. For example, Maria Estavez and her daughter, Camilla, had undergone a few weeks of field training, and then applied for work in the Argentine Embassy. The Bureau had supplied them with credentials and a cover story.

And Christine's new friendship with Emelia Cuellar, the embassy's Chief of Staff had unexpectedly blossomed. Christine had introduced the two to Emelia, explaining they had been abandoned by Maria's husband, and desperately needed to earn income. Would Emelia consider hiring Maria, and giving them a place to stay, since they were from Argentina? Emelia had agreed, and had immediately put Maria to work in the Washington, D.C. Embassy.

Maria's training as a florist, and in clerical work, in addition to her bilingual skills, made her valuable as a staff member in Emelia's eyes. The woman's new position was to oversee and organize all floral arrangements, centerpieces and guest preparations in the embassy.

Christine could feel things revving up once more. Phase Two was about to begin. It was going to be exciting.

She could hardly wait.

Christine Spada's crime solving adventures are continued in "Zombie Sightings."

If you would like to read more of Debbye Graafsma's books, or her counseling curriculum, or music, they are available at lulu.com, and amazon.com.

A Note from the Author

The problem of child and teenage abduction and human trafficking is a real problem in our day. Although the situations and individuals named in this work are fictitious, the problem in our world is real.

If you would like to obtain an Identification Kit for your child, grandchild, or for a class of children, the real FBI has partnered with a group known as "The National Child Identification Program," since 2002. The organization was begun by the American Football Coaches Association in 1997.

You can find them online at: *www.childidprogram.com*.

When you request a kit, they will send you:

- All you need to take inkless fingerprints;
- Cards for detailing your child's physical descriptions—including a body map for pointing out scars, birthmarks, and other identifying features;
- A place to keep current photos; and
- More recently, an easy-to-use swab to take and store a small DNA sample.

www.ingramcontent.com/pod-product-compliance
Lightning Source LLC
Chambersburg PA
CBHW020922020726
47495CB00002B/299